"Simply put, the finest crime suspense series I've come across in the last twenty years . . . your basic can't-put-'em-down thrill rides."
—Stephen King

China Lake

"Do me a favor, okay? Lay your hands on . . . *China Lake*. [It] had me at page one. Miss Gardiner makes it all work. . . . Amazingly entertaining."   —Stephen King

"[An] exciting mix. Great stuff."—*Independent on Sunday*

"With a colorful cast of richly delineated characters, a protagonist with whom the readers will easily identify—all big hearted, quick tongued, and hair-trigger tempered . . . a fast-paced ride through some of the more dubious nooks and crannies of the American dream."
—*The Guardian* (UK)

"Fast and hard-edged. Buy it, read it."   —*Hull Daily Mail*

"A cracker, with memorable characters, memorable lines, and a plot that races along to an explosive ending. A great summer read."   —*Huddersfield Daily Examiner*

"Very well written, racy, and witty."   —Tangled Web

"From beginning to end, *China Lake* is a book no reader of thrillers will be able to put down. Great characters, dynamic plot, nail-biting action—Meg Gardiner gives us everything."   —Elizabeth George

Mission Canyon

"Fiction at its finest . . . many nail-biting moments and hand-wringing twists."
—*The Evening Telegraph* (Peterborough, UK)

"A harrowing (and all-too-timely) story of corporate greed and evildoing in quirky Southern California."
—Jeffery Deaver

continued . . .

Crosscut

"Full of classic Gardiner one-liners . . . but mostly there's a serious freezerload of scare-you-silly chills."

—Stephen King

"A tense and exciting thriller where almost anything seems possible. A conspiracy theorist's must-have."

—*Independent on Sunday*

"Easily one of the best thrillers I've read this year. I could barely wait to get to the next page. If you start this book, be prepared to be unable to put it down. Meg Gardiner has written a cracker."

—Caroline Carver

"This book rips. It makes *Silence of the Lambs* look like Mary had a little one—it never lets up."

—Adrienne Dines, author of *The Jigsaw Maker*

Jericho Point

"Meg Gardiner dishes out the gripping plot in tense helpings. Short, punchy chapters keep the pace flowing, and you'll find it impossible to find a resting point."

—*Evening Times* (Glasgow)

"[Gardiner's] depictions of the criminal elements of the Hollywood fringe and the local drugs culture is a tightly observed slice of realism. This is a relentless, claustrophobic examination of mistaken identity and the terror of being accused of a crime for which you are not responsible."

—*Sherlock*

"Fast-paced, witty, and brutal."

—*The Independent* (London)

"**If you read Sue Grafton, Lee Child, Janet Evanovich, Michael Connelly, or Nelson DeMille, you're going to think Meg Gardiner is a gift from heaven for thriller/mystery readers.**" —**Stephen King**

"Meg Gardiner is a welcome addition to the ranks of American thriller writers." —*The Daily Telegraph* (UK)

"Meg Gardiner has rekindled my interest in thrillers." —*The Independent* (London)

"Meg Gardiner is a class act at the top of her game." —*My Weekly*

"Meg Gardiner has a powerful style—fast-paced, immediate, and imaginative." —*Sherlock*

"Meg Gardiner goes from strength to strength." —OneWord Radio

"Meg Gardiner is brilliant at making the over-the-top seem utterly convincing." —*The Guardian* (UK)

"Meg Gardiner hard-boils her American crime with the best of them. . . . If you like Sue Grafton and Janet Evanovich, you ought to have discovered Gardiner by now." —*The Evening Telegraph* (Peterborough, UK)

"Meg Gardiner takes us to places we hope we'll never have to go in reality." —Caroline Carver

Also by Meg Gardiner

China Lake
Mission Canyon
Jericho Point
Crosscut

The Dirty Secrets Club

KILL CHAIN

AN EVAN DELANEY NOVEL

Meg Gardiner

Delafield Public Library
Delafield, WI 53018
262-646-6230
www.delafieldlibrary.org

AN OBSIDIAN MYSTERY

OBSIDIAN
Published by New American Library, a division of
Penguin Group (USA) Inc., 375 Hudson Street,
New York, New York 10014, USA
Penguin Group (Canada), 90 Eglinton Avenue East, Suite 700, Toronto,
Ontario M4P 2Y3, Canada (a division of Pearson Penguin Canada Inc.)
Penguin Books Ltd., 80 Strand, London WC2R 0RL, England
Penguin Ireland, 25 St. Stephen's Green, Dublin 2,
Ireland (a division of Penguin Books Ltd.)
Penguin Group (Australia), 250 Camberwell Road, Camberwell, Victoria 3124,
Australia (a division of Pearson Australia Group Pty. Ltd.)
Penguin Books India Pvt. Ltd., 11 Community Centre, Panchsheel Park,
New Delhi - 110 017, India
Penguin Group (NZ), 67 Apollo Drive, Rosedale, North Shore 0632,
New Zealand (a division of Pearson New Zealand Ltd.)
Penguin Books (South Africa) (Pty.) Ltd., 24 Sturdee Avenue,
Rosebank, Johannesburg 2196, South Africa

Penguin Books Ltd., Registered Offices:
80 Strand, London WC2R 0RL, England

Published by Obsidian, an imprint of New American Library, a division of Penguin Group (USA) Inc. This is an authorized reprint of an edition published by Hodder & Stoughton. For information address: Hodder & Stoughton Ltd, 338 Euston Road, London NW1 3BH

First Obsidian Printing, October 2008
10   9   8   7   6   5   4   3   2   1

Copyright © Meg Gardiner, 2006
All rights reserved

OBSIDIAN and logo are trademarks of Penguin Group (USA) Inc.

Printed in the United States of America

Without limiting the rights under copyright reserved above, no part of this publication may be reproduced, stored in or introduced into a retrieval system, or transmitted, in any form, or by any means (electronic, mechanical, photocopying, recording, or otherwise), without the prior written permission of both the copyright owner and the above publisher of this book.

PUBLISHER'S NOTE
This is a work of fiction. Names, characters, places, and incidents either are the product of the author's imagination or are used fictitiously, and any resemblance to actual persons, living or dead, business establishments, events, or locales is entirely coincidental.
   The publisher does not have any control over and does not assume any responsibility for author or third-party Web sites or their content.

If you purchased this book without a cover you should be aware that this book is stolen property. It was reported as "unsold and destroyed" to the publisher and neither the author nor the publisher has received any payment for this "stripped book."

The scanning, uploading, and distribution of this book via the Internet or via any other means without the permission of the publisher is illegal and punishable by law. Please purchase only authorized electronic editions, and do not participate in or encourage electronic piracy of copyrighted materials. Your support of the author's rights is appreciated.

3 0646 00159 3023

For Paul
Again, and always

ACKNOWLEDGMENTS

For their help with this novel, my sincerest thanks go to Ann Aubrey, Adrienne Dines, Mary Albanese, Suzanne Davidovac, Kelly Gerrard, Tammye Huf, Jennifer Spears, HeeJung Wescoat, Ali Gunn, Paul Shreve, Kate Shreve (proofreader extraordinaire), Nancy Fraser, and, as always, my invaluable editor at Hodder & Stoughton, Sue Fletcher.

1

Don't ever pray for insight. You're liable to get it.

Picking up the pieces, holding on to people I love, I've been able to sew the story together. It's not the story I grew up with; it's a narrative that's stitched together like emergency surgery on a catastrophic wound. Life is repaired but the damage lingers. The scar tissue is numb and deep. The family who fought to protect you stands exposed more brutally than if by an X-ray.

Don't believe it. I love you, kid. Lies and all.

I wasn't there that night, when he saw them coming. But now I know.

Sunday

The rain beat down. Branches scraped his shoulders as he rushed past. He threw an arm in front of his face to shield himself, breathing hard. In the dark, he was losing his bearings. The road was somewhere up ahead.

His pursuers were behind him.

Phil Delaney ran, fighting to see, eyes swollen from the beating. His right knee wouldn't hold much longer. He had snapped the kneecap back into place after they dislocated it. When they walked outside for a smoke, he slung his foot between two beams of wood in the barn and hauled backward, like yanking on a tangled piece of string to snap the knots loose. It had worked when his high school coach did it to him on the football field all those years ago in Shawnee. It worked as fast tonight, and when the bones popped he fought down a shout and escaped through a gap in the slats of the barn.

Now he was covering ground, but his leg felt like a couple of straws held together with rubber bands. His adrenaline was draining away. Beneath it the pain was coming like a roar.

Behind him in the brush, he heard the dog.

Over rocks and roots, the trail climbed toward Highway 1. The dog wasn't trained to track and probably couldn't keep his scent in the wet. It probably heard him, but the only way to be quiet would be to slow down, and hell if he would sacrifice speed to gain a negligible advantage in stealth. The dog was indisputably trained to attack. The bloody bite on his arm testified to that.

Want me to call him off? Then tell us what we want to know, cocksucker.

Phil looked back. Beams from their flashlights jinked as they ran.

Of everything he had steeled himself for, this was the last thing he had expected. A dozen years since he'd been in-country. Ten since he had left the navy. In all that time there had been no repercussions, not even a hint. And then, halfway through a spring afternoon, as he drove along a remote California highway, they ambushed him.

Why now?

Finding him wouldn't have been the hard part—over the past year, anybody watching television could have caught his face on CNN, STAR News Asia, or BBC World. Though the people behind him weren't foreigners. They spoke with the flat American voices of trailer-park punks.

No, these thugs were Yanks. And the one with the ratty black ponytail and goatee, the one wearing the biker boots—Phil had met his kind too many times in port-town taverns. Southern Comfort and a bar fight, guaranteed. Spoiling to dish it out, as long as he was fighting somebody smaller, weaker, or being held down by three other punks.

But why now? How had they put it all together after twelve years? The op had been dirty, a disaster, but the extraction had been clean. And the only other person involved would never have betrayed him. Not Jax.

But these people knew about the connection. Worse, they had managed to track him and pinpoint his exact location on this road today. They'd cut him off, dragged him out of the car, and, as he buckled under their fists and boots, he knew the plain truth. Someone had sold him out.

Headlights swept overhead. Even out here in the back of beyond, a vehicle came past every five or ten minutes. He could keep ahead of these bastards that long. He clawed his way up the slope.

Who had known he was in Santa Barbara? The family, his son and daughter and ex-wife. His legal team, Jesse and Lavonne. And Jax.

Except that Jax wasn't here. She had never been here. The message he received asking him to meet her had been a lure.

His foot caught a rock and pain boomed up his leg. Gasping, he lunged up the trail. Goddammit. He was strong but he was fifty-nine years old, and hell if he was anywhere near the shape he'd been in as a young man. One more wrong step and the knee could blow, and then nothing save growing a pair of wings would get him out of here.

The dog barked, closer. They had tracked him and found him, but he wasn't the ultimate target. He had to send a warning.

The clouds parted and moonlight frosted the landscape. The brush thinned and—oh, glory, he saw the road. Breathing heavily, he ducked behind a tree trunk. He couldn't break cover until he heard a car coming.

He knew what they wanted from him. They wanted what Jax had hidden. They wanted power, and they wanted destruction. Riverbend. They thought he could give it to them. And if they couldn't get it from him, he knew who they would target next. They'd go after his children and his grandson.

He had to keep his family clear. No matter what, none of them could be touched by any of this. He had spent his entire adult life making sure of that. He couldn't falter now.

Down the hill, close, a voice cried out, "This way!"

It was the woman, the wraith with bad teeth. She had the ravenous eyes of an addict who wanted to finish him so she could get to her next hit of methamphetamine. Maybe that was why she'd kicked him in the face.

He took out his phone, cupping one hand over the display so the light wouldn't give away his position. He would never get hold of Jax or her husband. He had seconds at most. Hands shaking with fatigue, he scrolled through the names stored in his phone until he found one he hoped he could trust. Who could take action tonight.

Hell, he didn't have a cell number, just the home phone. He dialed.

A bout of noise broke from the bushes behind him. The number began ringing. Answer, man. Answer.

The dog crashed through the brush into the clear. It pulled up, staring at him, mean, panting, butt-ugly. He held still. He couldn't show fear.

The phone clicked through to voice mail. Dammit. The dog lowered its head, growling. He was going to have to run, but not before he left a message. Ten seconds, that was all he was going to get.

"It's Phil," he began. "I'm in trouble, so you have to do this for me."

The dog inched forward, teeth bared in the moonlight. More noise rattled through the brush. Flashlights zigged and caught him in the eyes.

He spoke rapid-fire into the phone, laying it out. "Do it tonight. Tomorrow will be too late. And—"

The dog advanced. Still, stay rock still.

"You have to keep my daughter out of this. Evan cannot

know. Keep her clear. Do you hear me, Jesse? If you don't, my family becomes part of the kill chain."

The two punks burst through the brush. Phil broke for the road.

His knee held, and he erupted into the clear just as headlights swept around the curve. His heart soared. He raised his hands, waving at the driver to stop. The car braked to a halt, headlights gleaming.

Phil ran toward it. The door opened and the dome light came on, a man and a woman inside. He saw fur, diamonds, anticipation. He stopped. The woman showed her teeth, smiling in recognition. The driver got out. Young, eager, with a cocky smile. In his hand he held a gun.

"Hello, old man," he said.

Phil held his ground, drawing on his last reserves of strength, getting ready.

2

Branches clawed at me. Sodden from the rain, they wept as I careered past. The brush was dense, the mud slick. A hundred feet down the ocean bellowed, pitching itself against the rocks.

"Evan, stop."

I heard the alarm in Lilia Rodriguez's voice but kept going, digging my heels into the grade to brake my descent. Morning sunlight bled through the clouds, gilding the broken saplings and gouges in the hillside that signified the fall line.

"It isn't safe. Wait," Lily called.

Above on Highway 1, flares smoked and sputtered, electric pink. Lily's colleagues from the sheriff's department were directing a wrecking truck with a winch and two hundred feet of cable, and the Santa Barbara County search and rescue team was planning its next move. When I ran down the slope they had yelled at me, too.

My foot tangled with a root and I tripped to my hands and knees. Rocks scraped my palms and tore through my jeans. I bumped down the slope, scrabbling for purchase, and slid face-first into a manzanita bush. I bungled to a stop. Behind me, Lily yelled, "Aw, jeez." I sat up, heart galloping, and saw the car.

The back end was undamaged, taillights intact and

metallic blue paint shining. It was canted skyward at a seventy-five-degree angle, wheels and undercarriage exposed. The grille had wrapped around a boulder in a vile high-speed embrace.

Lily pushed through the bushes, out of breath, and stopped short. At the sight of the wreck, her tough-girl expression slipped.

Clawing to my feet, I edged down the grade toward the open driver's door. "Dad."

There was no answer. He wasn't inside. I knew that; Lily had told me that when she came to my front door. The driver's door was buried a foot deep in the mud. It had dug a scar down the hill during the car's descent. Bracing my hands against it, I leaned in. The windshield was shattered, air bag deployed, the engine block jammed halfway through the front seat. A cup of 7-Eleven coffee was splashed across the dashboard.

I spun around, looking up the hillside. "Phil Delaney. Dad."

Lily picked her way toward me. She was wearing jeans and a sheriff's department jacket and a gun holstered on her hip, pixie haircut flipping in the wind. From beneath her professional stoicism the compassionate, wary kid peeped through.

"Evan, this is dangerous. Come back up top."

I held on to the doorframe, peering at the heavy brush on the hill. The snake of panic wound around my chest, binding me, closing my throat.

"He has to be here, Lily. Someplace."

"Search and rescue's calling a chopper out to scan the hillside. As long as the rain holds off—"

"He could be unconscious, or too weak to signal us." Tears rose in my voice. "We can't just walk away."

But I felt the tilt of the earth beneath my feet and heard the pounding of the ocean below, the greedy Pacific that fills the depths and hoards too many who fall into its grasp.

"Come on," Lily said.

*   *   *

When Lily and I crested the lip of the hill onto the highway, the wind bit us. It was a chill April morning. The
mountains, soaked from a winter of heavy rains, were florid
green. Silver clouds hung ragged along their peaks. A fire
truck and sheriff's vehicles clogged the roadside, lights
spinning. In the center of the highway, a California Highway Patrol officer directed traffic around the scene.

Parked behind the sheriff's cars was a black pickup
truck. Standing next to it, talking to a uniformed deputy,
was Jesse Blackburn. His eyes caught mine and all my defenses collapsed. I ran and threw my arms around him.

"Ev, I'm so sorry," he said.

I pressed my face against his chest. Feeling him work to
keep his balance, I tightened my grip. He steadied himself
on his crutches and put an arm around my back.

"How did you find out?" I said.

"Brian tracked me down at the rehab center."

Bless my damned brother. How fast Jesse had driven to
get here didn't bear thinking about.

"You should have called the switchboard. I was there the
whole night," he said.

"I didn't want to interrupt."

"Delaney." He pulled me hard against him. "Interrupt."

I shook my head. Glad as I was to have him here, I hated
to think that he had torn himself away from a situation
where he was badly needed.

The deputy cleared his throat. "Ma'am?"

When I looked up he touched the brim of his hat. "Ben
Gilbert. That's a treacherous hillside. You need to stay up
here on the road."

"Then call out the cavalry and find my father. Otherwise
I'm going to do it myself."

Jesse pulled me tighter, hoping to forestall a full-blown
outburst from me, and nodded to Gilbert. "When will the
SAR helo get here?"

"Fifteen, twenty minutes." Gilbert looked at him more closely. "You have a background with the coast guard?"

"Open-water rescue. Used to be with the county."

Gilbert tried not to stare too overtly at the crutches. Lily, though saying nothing, looked openly quizzical. I doubted she had ever seen Jesse standing up.

Gilbert jammed his hands into his coat pockets. His voice was crisp. "We're trying to get a time line here. Your father left Santa Barbara yesterday afternoon, that right?"

"Around one," I said.

Which would have put him here—forty miles north of my house, along this isolated strip of wild country—near two p.m. Acid threaded across my skin. The car had hung wrecked in the chaparral for almost a day without anyone knowing. Without my knowing.

I peered down the road. "Can you tell where it went off the highway? Where do the skid marks start?"

Gilbert's face crimped. He rubbed his index finger along the side of his nose. "There were no skid marks."

He looked down the highway at my Mustang. Two black stripes trailed behind it, the skid marks I'd laid when I came ripping around the bend. I saw no others.

"There have to be," I said.

"Ms. Delaney, I've been a cop fifteen years. When a car tears through the brush and buries itself in boulders two hundred feet downslope, that indicates a violent event occurred on the roadway. Braking before such a hard crash leaves black skid marks that are visible even after days of heavy rain. And we got nothing here."

"What, are you saying that he didn't brake?"

Gilbert looked regretful, as though he were about to hand me something bitter. "No. Least, not long as he was on the highway."

"You think he just ran off the road?"

"Wet pavement, high speed, it can happen."

"He's not a reckless driver."

I kept staring at the road, my mind forming nightmarish glimpses of what it had been like hitting the curve that fast.

"What if he swerved to avoid something? An animal, or even another car."

Lily put up her hands. "Don't get ahead of yourself."

"If he was swerving, and the tires caught the edge of the shoulder, and . . ."

Gilbert shook his head. "Sharp swerve on this curve, we'd still expect to find tread on the road."

Jesse said, "But you don't know, do you?"

"That's right. We don't."

"Yes, we do," I said. "We know he's out here someplace, and we have to find him."

Gilbert's expression was smooth, his eyes the green of the mountainside. "Ms. Delaney, how did your father seem when he left your place?"

"He seemed eager to get to San Jose. He had a business meeting planned."

Even as I said it, I heard the overstress in my voice. Dad hadn't been eager. He'd been edgy, which now seemed ominous.

"Was there anything on his mind that could have distracted him? Anything bothering him?"

"No," I said.

"You sure?"

In the wind, my fingers felt numb but my face grew hot. Gilbert, I realized, knew who I was. He had heard my family's name in the news, understood about my father, knew what had happened to me.

"Ma'am, no disrespect. But we are speaking about Phil Delaney, correct?"

Lily shot him a glance.

Jesse let go of me. "Deputy, you're about to make a guess that's way offtrack. Don't."

"I'm just covering all the angles. At this stage we can't exclude any possibilities," Gilbert said.

I felt myself coiling. "You're suggesting he drove off the road deliberately?"

"I'm saying we had a man here who was under a lot of pressure."

Lily made a face, muttering under her breath, "Gilbert ..."

Jesse's voice went frosty. "Man, stick to the present tense."

My blood pressure was rising. "You think he committed suicide?"

I stepped toward Gilbert, but Jesse put a hand on my arm, holding me back. The deputy softened his tone.

"I don't mean to make a difficult situation even tougher, but at this stage we can't rule anything out."

But though he tried to sound soothing, he was sizing me up as if I were a freak in the circus tent.

"Anything else you want to know?" I said.

His gaze lingered on me. "You did it, didn't you? You're the one who pulled the trigger."

I gave his stare right back. "Yes."

He eyed me some more and jammed his hands back in his pockets. "Would you happen to have a photo of your father? To show the search and rescue team?"

"Yeah."

I took a snapshot from my wallet. It had been taken at the breakwater in Santa Barbara, and showed Dad with his arm around my shoulder, the ocean sapphire behind us. He looked good: weatherworn, with his frosty hair poking out from under a U.S. Navy baseball cap, dark eyes reflecting his restless need to take on the world. Except for my long legs I don't look much like him, with my tomboy figure and caramel hair. What he gave me wasn't his looks but a taste for Tennessee whiskey and mournful country songs. Jesse had been behind the camera, and Dad was regarding him with a look so cool as to be a challenge. I was smiling but seemed slightly irked. I could have done without their jousting—Jesse's wisecracks, Dad's one-upmanship. Back then, I didn't know how lucky I was. The photo was taken before violence invaded our lives, before I shot the psycho who was trying to kill me, before Dad sacrificed his reputation on a pyre in atonement.

I handed the snapshot to Gilbert. "Keep it as long as you need to."

From below on the hillside the SAR team called up to the crew of the wrecker, asking them to lower the winch cable. Gilbert excused himself.

Lily frowned. "Sorry about that."

"State of play," I said. "Not your fault."

The wrecking crew began extending the winch.

"They'll be careful when they move the car, won't they? I mean, if Dad's . . ."

Jesse said, "He's not under the car."

I knew he was right. Dad hadn't been thrown out and trapped under the vehicle. The fact that the driver's door had knifed a long track into the mud spoke otherwise. The door had sprung open long before impact.

Jesse put a hand against the small of my back. "You look chilled to the bone. Let's get out of the wind."

We climbed into his pickup. He turned on the engine and set the heater on high. For a few moments I stared at the wrecker.

"Dad did not kill himself."

"Hell, no. Die without a fight? He's too mean."

I grabbed his hand, knowing he meant that as a compliment. He rubbed his hands over mine, trying to warm me, and gazed at the diamond solitaire on my finger. It had been some months since he'd put it there.

"You didn't tell Gilbert about your dad's mood when he left," he said.

"No. He'd use it as ammunition."

He gazed out the window. "What do you think happened to him?"

Dread balled in my throat. Dad's strange good-bye rose in my head, a warning.

"I don't know." The wind gusted, rocking the truck. I

swallowed the urge to cry. "How bad were things with Buddy?"

"Don't worry about that right now."

But he was worried himself—the circles under his blue eyes told me so. As did the fact that he had spent the whole night at the spinal injury unit, his cell phone turned off. His face, handsome and worn with sleeplessness, looked troubled. I squeezed his hand and he shook his head.

"The kid's right on the rim," he said.

Buddy Stoker was nineteen years old, and, three months past the motorcycle wreck that had paralyzed him, his morale ranged from despondent to terminal. He was one of the SCI patients Jesse worked with as a peer counselor at the rehab center.

"I've thrown him a line, and I'm hounding him to hang on. I don't know if he will."

Hanging on, Jesse knew, could be hell. When a BMW rammed his own bike, he went from all-American to paraplegic in half a second. A year of hospitals and rehab brought him to the shattering reality that his legs would never work right again. Fucking Fact of Life Number One, he called it. Some things you cannot change. But these days he told the newbies it was nonetheless possible to get back up and keep going, that you could navigate the world without walking it.

"His folks are with him; don't worry," he said. "And this is where I need to be right now."

"Thank you."

The wind shook the truck. Outside, the wrecking crew worked the winch. The cable went taut as they started to haul the car up the hill. I blinked at the sight, my throat constricting.

I thought, Dad, what the hell happened out here?

Whistle-blowing is like prophecy: Tell the truth and people never thank you. They stone you for it. So you'd better be tough.

My father was a rusty nail. But for months he'd been reeling under a hail of rocks.

Phil Delaney, for decades an insider—ramrod-straight naval captain, weapons designer, graduate of the Naval War College, sometime naval intelligence agent, and chartered member of the old boys' network—had become an outsider. He blew the whistle on a dirty government operation, one that had caused people to die. People I grew up with. And for that he was made to pay.

The government had yanked his security clearance. His consulting business had dried up. He was being shunned by the military and intelligence worlds to which he had dedicated his life. The men in the shadows wanted him made an example of. An ambitious U.S. Attorney was eager to oblige, and had spent months investigating him in hopes of obtaining an indictment. My father had become a pariah.

He had done it for honor. For duty. For the dead.

He had done it for me.

I thought back: Less than twenty-four hours ago, he had been standing beside me under a soaring blue sky, watching a bunch of kids take their marks at Los Baños del Mar pool. Flags snapped on masts along the beachfront. Around the pool, noise was rising, spectators hooting and stomping. Near the starting blocks, sunlit and serious, Jesse gathered the kids on the team he coached, psyching them up. Dad watched with a smile that gradually faded to wistfulness, until he turned away and gazed out at the ocean. I wondered if he was thinking about Jesse's sure touch with kids, and me with my empty arms. When his cell phone rang, he strode for the exit.

I found him outside, staring at the marina as if expecting enemy fire to erupt from the fishing fleet. His white hair bristled in the sun.

"I have to leave," he said.

I frowned. "Now?"

"This isn't a diversionary tactic. It's business."

Business? Right. "What's going on?"

"I'll call you tomorrow. Meantime, hold out against the forces of darkness. You have the moral high ground."

"I drove off that talk radio guy with a rake, not principle."

In the months since Dad blew the whistle I had consistently rejected interview requests from the media. That only egged them on, because I'm a freelance journalist myself when I'm not cadging work with law firms, writing appellate briefs, revising my new novel, and generally doing what Dad thought of as avoiding a grown-up career. Newspapers, tabloid television, and moonbat bloggers had been contacting me with questions, outrage, and, in the case of one conspiracy nut, the request to let me be artificially inseminated with his pure, libertarian, non-CIA-contaminated sperm.

When a spook blows the whistle, all the ghosties come out to play.

Dad put his arm around my shoulder. "Don't worry; your old man's fine. I knew the score going in. Jesse and Lavonne told me flat out: Don't do it unless you're willing to start over. You pull the fire alarm like I did, you never work in the industry again."

Lavonne Marks, Jesse's boss, was counseling Dad on strategies to keep him from being indicted. He gave me a sidelong glance.

"I'm not feeling sorry for myself. And don't you either, Kit. Not on your life."

"I wouldn't dare."

From my experience of men in pain, pity corrodes you both. Support works better. And occasionally a kick in the butt.

Which, annoyed that he was leaving so abruptly, I delivered. "If you're meeting with Jax Rivera, tell her it's time to stop yanking my chain. You and I have a deal, remember? You talk about the work you did with her; I listen."

For a second he held my gaze, as though considering whether, finally, to give up the unexhumed ghosts that filled his past.

"I love you, Kit. You're a better daughter than I deserve. Always know that." He kissed my forehead. "I don't know when I'll see you again."

Something in his casual tone sounded ill-omened. "Dad?"

He touched my face. "You can't believe everything you hear. Remember that, if everything else fails."

It felt as if a fist had grabbed my stomach. "I should have known something was going to go wrong. I should have pressed him harder, or gone with him."

"Don't think that way," Jesse said. "The guilt train stops right here. Park it and get off."

I pinched the bridge of my nose, refusing to cry. I would cry when Dad climbed out of the SAR helicopter, bold as brass, saluting the pilot and thanking him for the lift. Jesse put his hand on the back of my neck.

"The visit was good, till the end. He's warming to you," I said.

He gauged my face and said, "Yeah. But he doesn't trust me yet."

"He will. When he knows you as well as I do."

Outside, the wrecker winched the car up to the road. Jesse and I got out of the pickup. The fist squeezed my stomach.

The car was a gruesome carcass. The hood was crumpled and the driver's door swung like a broken wing. Carefully the crew of the wrecker hauled it onto the flatbed and began strapping it down.

Gilbert came over. "The Highway Patrol's Accident Investigation Unit will take the lead on reconstructing what happened here. They'll want to talk to you, but you don't need to hang around waiting for them."

I nodded absently, remembering Dad loading his things into the car and hugging me good-bye.

The chassis whined as the wrecking crew cinched it down. I walked to the wrecker and stood on tiptoe to peer at the car. I could only glimpse the driver's seat. I boosted myself up onto the flatbed and opened the back door.

"His computer case is gone," I said.

The driver of the wrecker said, "What are you doing?"

I turned to Jesse. "I saw him put his computer case on the floor behind the driver's seat."

Gilbert approached. "Ms. Delaney, what are you doing?"

Scooting along the edge of the car, I popped the trunk. As it yawned open, my stomach sank. There was Dad's carry-on suitcase.

Gilbert's mouth pinched. "The computer must have been thrown out in the crash."

"He put it flat on the floor in the back. And the car didn't roll, didn't flip. If anything, the impact should have wedged it tighter under the driver's seat. But it's gone."

The wrecking crew shot me dirty looks. I didn't care. Edging my way around the side of the car, I climbed into the backseat. My chest tightened as I thought of Dad being in the car when it went over. But now I was feeling something else, an urgency, a prickle of distrust. As if things unseen and malevolent had been at work here, beyond a wet road and the force of gravity.

The smashed windshield sagged in its frame. On the mangled steering column, the keys hung in the ignition. I smelled mud and gasoline and coffee. The coffee cup was still jammed in the cup holder.

The coffee cup. I grabbed it and climbed out.

Jesse approached the side of the flatbed. "What is it?"

"He didn't kill himself. Nobody stops for hot coffee on their way to commit suicide." I held up the cup. "And they certainly don't buy the extra-large mug so they can get free refills."

Traffic nudged along the road, past pink flares and a Highway Patrolman waving cars around a wrecker. The white Mercury edged its way toward the scene.

Boyd Davies slouched in his seat, one hand slung over

the top of the steering wheel, toothpick between his lips. He wore shades and a baseball cap, his black hair pulled into a ponytail. He wasn't worried about the goatee. Nobody was going to recognize him.

In the passenger seat, the woman who called herself Bliss kept scratching at her arm. She was skinny as a cigarette and had short piss-blond hair. She was like a thing you heard out in the tall grass, a skittering sound on the air, dry and pitiless as a lizard. She was pulling scabs off with the scratching. Crank bugs, Boyd thought. She got high last night and was crashing hard, thought beetles were crawling under her skin. Meth, no question. He was keeping notes for his report.

"That's it," she said.

They'd found the car and hauled it up the hill. It lay crushed on the back of the wrecker. Uniforms were crawling all over the place, fire and CHP and sheriffs. A woman had climbed up on the wrecker, was crouched down talking to a deputy and a plainclothes and a guy looked like he'd busted his knee, leaning on crutches. The woman was gesturing to the deputy, showing him a coffee cup.

"Who's she?" Bliss said.

He glanced at her, and at the rest of the scene—a pickup truck, and a Mustang that had laid rubber when it squealed to a stop.

"Investigator," he said. "Else, maybe family."

"They're looking for him," she said.

Let them look. He cruised past the wrecker, getting a good eyeful of the woman, the emotion on her face. Family, yeah. Now, wasn't that interesting.

"I think what we have here is an actual lead," he said.

She turned to the backseat. Christian was asleep, shades crooked, hair draped over his face.

"Leave him be," Boyd said. "Get on the phone. We take this to the top."

3

I was thirty-three when I found out my dad was a spook. The revelation came at a bad time.

Philip Delaney left Oklahoma to spend his life in the blue-water navy. He ended up in the desert, an expert in missile guidance and explosives technology at the Naval Air Warfare Center in China Lake, California. That's where I grew up: in a world of pilots and researchers who worked under the sun to perfect the machinery of death. It was a happy childhood.

Dad's job was to protect me, my brother, my mother, and our country, to eliminate those who would make war on us, and to keep our fighter pilots alive in the skies. He was a warrior, and my hero.

But the reality was completely different. My father set up a shield, beneath which he lived another life entirely. He worked for naval intelligence. He had such a knack for clandestine work that he hid the truth even from my mom. Maybe, in the end, that contributed to their divorce.

And I finally learned the truth because a classified project went disastrously wrong at China Lake and led to the deaths of my high school classmates. It nearly killed my mother. It caused me to take a life, and cost me the chance to start a family. Faced with such wreckage, Dad could no longer live with the lies and denials. He went public with the truth.

Since then, through months lost in regret and shock, I

had become determined to know the reality of my father's past. And he had promised to talk with me, but secrecy was a habit deeply ingrained in Phil Delaney.

"Opposition research."

That was how he described it to me, walking on Stearns Wharf one day, tilting back his hat and watching the sun shatter on the water. To destroy the enemy, weapons researchers needed to know what the enemy was up to. His job had been to find out who the bad guys were and what toys they had. He sussed out their technology.

In those days Latin America and Southeast Asia foamed with dictatorships, coups, drug wealth, machete massacres, cartels, and blood feuds. Hearing him talk about such places, I felt my heart sink. Technology was clean and precise. Foreign jungles were chaotic and bloody. *Remember the times,* he said. *Remember the stakes. The Cold War. Communists. Drug warlords. Terrorists. And we didn't have police powers in Venezuela or Burma. We couldn't just march into the jungle with a search warrant and get the information we needed.*

I understand, I said. *I'm not a kid.*

He stared at the water. *No. You're a tough girl, Kit, but even with all you've been through lately, you don't understand.*

And now I feared that I never would.

Ten thirty: nothing. No sign of Dad, despite the search and rescue helo, despite my inarticulate prayers. Just CHP investigators poring over the scene with cameras and measuring equipment, and clouds threatening rain, and my stubborn refusal to leave, until Jesse pointed down the highway at the TV news van heading our way. I peeled out in the Mustang.

By the time I got back to Santa Barbara the clouds had broken up. The city unrolled like a Mediterranean carpet, mountains looming green against the sky, red tile roofs spooling through palm trees all the way to the spangled sea. I dropped the car at my place and hopped into Jesse's truck.

"Sure you don't want to skip this?" he said.

"Positive." I didn't want quiet, or time to think. I wanted to do something. Anything. "Sure you don't?"

He looked dog-tired. He hadn't been home since before the swim meet yesterday.

"First things first," he said.

We needed to find his boss, Lavonne Marks, and bring her up to speed. We drove to the Belchiesa Resort, across Cabrillo Boulevard from the beach, where the California Bar Association was holding its spring conference on trial advocacy.

"You know we're bound to run into Gray," Jesse said.

"If he can stop preening for the cameras."

Nicholas Gray, the U.S. Attorney who was circling my father like a vulture, was giving the keynote address at the conference. Earlier in the weekend he had managed to interrupt Dad's meeting with Lavonne and Jesse in a restaurant at the resort's conference center. Give him a chance of publicity and he became omnipresent.

Jesse left his crutches in the truck. The conference center was extensive, and walking more than a hundred yards didn't work. He got the wheelchair out of the backseat. I slammed the door of the truck and we headed into the lobby, passing a poster for the keynote address.

"Screw Gray. Let him try to make hay out of this," I said.

A tendril of wind brushed my arms as the doors shut. Jesse's gaze lengthened. "Shields up. You're about to get your wish."

Looking over my shoulder, I saw the men in dark suits walking toward us.

The tall one was Nicholas Gray, Assistant United States Attorney for the Central District of California. Gawky and purposeful, he swept along ahead of two underlings in matching blue pinstripes. They looked overdressed for Santa Barbara, where half the population wears flip-flops and Sex Wax T-shirts. To their own weddings.

"Just the people I was looking for," Gray said.

One of the suits, a young guy, popped the top on a soft drink can and handed it to him. "Diet cola, sir." He nodded at Jesse. "J-man."

"How you doing, Drew?" Jesse said.

Gray took the soda without a glance. "Ms. Delaney, we heard about the car wreck. I'm sorry."

"Thank you," I said.

He eyed Jesse. "Here to attend my speech?"

"For the margaritas. What's up?"

Gray managed to smile with just his long white teeth, no eyes. "If you'll excuse us, I need to speak to Ms. Delaney about her father."

Bald and buzzardy, Gray had a firm voice and a sympathetic expression. His mien was assiduous and concerned. And I was having none of it. Nicholas Gray was a scalptaker. The West Coast's chief federal prosecutor, he was determined to indict my father under the Espionage Act.

Jesse didn't move. "Ev?"

I nodded to Gray. "Talk."

He nodded, a *very well* gesture. "I've spoken with the county sheriffs. Their deputy thinks the crash was deliberate." He took a sip of his soda. "I have to agree. But I don't think your father committed suicide."

I took a mental step back. "Are you suggesting foul play? Did somebody run my dad off the road?"

He didn't actually snap his fingers, merely lifted an eyebrow at his soda bearer. "Farelli?"

Drew Farelli had a sheen of perspiration on his forehead, and cheeks that spoke of a love for his mom's cannoli. He was jingling coins in his pocket.

"I talked to the deputy—Gilbert's his name. There's no evidence your father's car was hit by another vehicle."

"What's going on?" My head was throbbing. "Have the sheriffs found him?"

Gray ran a hand across his shiny skull. "I can see the strain is taking a toll on you. Would you like to sit down?"

"No. Have they?"

"They haven't."

If I didn't count to ten, I was going to bite him.

Jesse eyed Gray with a calm like a shard of ice. "Nicholas, what's going on?"

Gray gestured to the second suit. "This is Special Agent Ceplak, from the Bureau."

A Fibbie. My heart dropped even farther into confusion and failing hope.

Ceplak said, "Ms. Delaney, it's no secret that your father is a person of interest to us. He's been recalcitrant for months, jumping fences to stay ahead of the U.S. Attorney's investigation."

"And?"

"I think he's done it one final time. He isn't out there on that hillside. He wasn't in the car when it left the road." He glanced at Farelli. "What did the deputy tell you?"

"Driver's door was open from the top of the fall line. Suitcase was in the trunk, but no computer case." He jingled his coins like he had the DTs. "And from the damage pattern to the brush on the hillside, it seems the car was moving only a few miles an hour when it left the road."

"What?" I said.

Ceplak nodded. "And they've found tire tracks in the mud. Also a footprint. The car went over at a few miles per hour, then gained speed. What happened is, your father got out, took his computer, and pushed the vehicle over the edge."

"That's crazy."

"Trying to make it look like a back-road suicide. Remote site, nobody around—it could have worked, but he made a mistake. He took the computer. That gives the game away."

"Game?"

Jesse put a hand on my arm, trying to stop me from rising to the bait. But it wasn't his father they were slandering.

Gray crossed his arms. "He didn't want to stick around.

Is that because he knew we're getting close to evidence that will lead to an indictment?"

Drew Farelli jingled the coins in his pocket. Gray maintained his facade of earnest righteousness, glancing from Jesse to me.

"Your father was with the two of you immediately before he disappeared. What did he tell you before he left town?" he said.

"Where do you get off—"

"Has he contacted you since the crash?"

I forced myself not to take a step back. "God, the search and rescue team is still out on the hillside trying to find him—"

"Let's call a spade a spade," Gray said. "Your father disclosed classified information. Granted, his legal team helped him skirt the edges of the law. But that's what he did."

Don't spit. Just don't.

"He endangered national security. He can claim he did it for some nebulous greater good, but that won't exonerate him."

Farelli said, "We're going to get his phone records. If you've been in contact with him, we'll find out. If it turns out you knew about it beforehand, you could be considered an accessory in his flight to avoid prosecution."

"Flight? For chrissake, he hasn't fled."

Gray said, "Your reluctance to cooperate is disappointing, though understandable. But if his legal team is involved, that's an entirely different matter."

Jesse looked away, mouth skewing. "Are you just going to kick dirt at us, or do you have an actual point?"

Gray paused for a moment, as though marking Jesse's name on a mental shit list. "If Ms. Delaney cooperates fully in our investigation, things will go more smoothly for her father."

"Cooperate? You mean betray my dad. Forget it."

"You needn't speak in such dramatic terms."

"But that's what you mean—you want me to pin something on him he didn't even do. No. He hasn't gone anywhere."

Gray's pate shone under the lights. "Who does your father know in Colombia?"

"South America? I have no idea."

"How about Thailand?"

"What are you talking about?"

"Why would he have reason to go to the U.K. twice within the past nine months?"

Bam, I felt as though he'd hit me with a skillet. Dad had been out of the country?

Farelli said, "And then he came to Santa Barbara. He talked to you, and conferred with his attorneys, and then poof, he vanished."

Gray pursed his lips. "If it's within your power, contact your father and convince him to surrender. This can still be handled quietly, but only for the next few hours." He glanced at Ceplak. "After that, I imagine the FBI will announce the likelihood that his disappearance is a hoax."

"I imagine we will," Ceplak said.

"From there, it's out of my hands. But I foresee the media taking an interest in the story. Former intelligence officer with contacts in some awfully seedy neighborhoods fakes his disappearance ahead of indictment.... Nothing I can do about the way they'll play it."

"Oh, don't even—"

"Ev." Jesse held my arm.

Gray crumpled the soda can and tossed it in a trash can. "Let me hear from you."

4

I stormed out of the conference center, pushing open the door. "Bully."

The day was sunny and breezy. "User. Publicity hound." I stalked toward the pickup truck. "Leak the story to the *Los Angeles Times* and let them bury Dad's reputation for good. That's Gray's plan. Keep himself on the front pages and at the top of the news hour."

I grabbed the door handle but the truck was locked. "Hoax, my ass. He cares nothing about Dad. The car went over a cliff and he insists it's a hoax?"

I yanked again on the door. "Inquisitor. Spiteful, grand-standing . . ." Wouldn't open. Turning, I saw that Jesse was still inside the conference center, speaking to Drew Farelli. I was talking to myself.

I leaned against the truck. Clouds riffled past the sun. Across Cabrillo Boulevard a picket line of palm trees guarded the gleaming ocean.

Dad's car had been pushed over the edge.

And I didn't believe for one second that my father had done it. Somebody else had, and then they'd done some-thing to my father. Heat swept through me, fear and thrill all together.

Dad was alive.

Jesse finished talking to Farelli and wheeled over to the truck. "Drew's toeing Gray's line. I got nowhere."

"He's Gray's cocker spaniel."

"He's a decent guy, just anxious to please. Always was, even in law school." He unlocked the truck. "You thinking the same thing I am about your dad?"

"He's been abducted."

His face was grave. "You'll never get the FBI to pursue that avenue."

"No." I opened my door. "I have to take another road."

I got in but he held still, hands on his push-rims as though keeping the brakes on. "You going to contact her?"

I nodded. Grimly, he held my gaze.

Colombia. Thailand. Intelligence officer with contacts in seedy neighborhoods.

If those were the questions, there was one answer: Jakarta Rivera.

Jesse drove me downtown without comment, face cool behind his shades, and dropped me at the bank. Inside, I followed a teller into the vault and gave her the key to my safe-deposit box. My palms were tingling.

Jax Rivera was a recurring apparition in my life, a specter who had seemingly manifested out of malign chance. A former CIA agent, she was glamorous, conniving, and violent. She now ran a small business with her British husband, killing people for money. They seemed a happy couple. And they liked me. Talk about unwelcome attention.

When we first met, they offered me a job ghostwriting their memoirs. I laughed and walked away, calling their story a lie. But though the offer was spurious, their story was not; they had come to Santa Barbara on a job. Then Jax left me a thick manila envelope containing dossiers she and Tim North had assembled over the years: notebooks, photographs, memos that named names, places, dates, deaths. I barely leafed through them before getting a big hairy chill, shoving them back in the envelope, and taping it up.

If Dad's disappearance had anything to do with his work

for naval intelligence, the one person who might be able to provide me with a clue, or help, was Jax. Because, I had recently discovered, they knew each other.

I didn't have her home phone, didn't know where she lived, didn't even know whether Jakarta Rivera was her real name. All I had was that fat manila envelope containing the dossiers, locked in my safe-deposit box.

When I slid it from that box, it felt heavier than I recalled. I thanked the teller and walked the six blocks to Sanchez Marks feeling as though I were carrying a sack of cobras.

For years I had wondered why Jax and Tim chose me as their dead drop. To help write their memoirs? A pretext. Because Jax was a fan of my fiction? I wanted to believe it, but couldn't—Jax had an affinity for lies, guns, and Prada, and she didn't strike me as a science fiction fan. To provide a safe harbor for stolen secrets they kept as self-protection or blackmail? Now you're talking.

Because Jax had worked with my father? That was what I wanted Dad to tell me about, and what, despite his promise, he refused to divulge.

Maybe Jax would. Maybe today. I neared the courthouse and turned the corner, heading toward the Spanish-style building that housed the law firm. At the entrance, sunlight bounced off the windows. Inside, a man was crossing the foyer toward the door. When he saw me he stopped dead.

My heart would have dropped, but it was already flat on the floor. He stared at me, mouth pinched white. Traffic slurred past on the street.

Finally I opened the door. "How are you, P.J.?"

He was lean and had put muscle on his shoulders. His brown hair was shorn, his blue eyes distant. He looked so much like Jesse that it stole my breath. I hadn't seen him since he got out of jail.

He pushed past me through the door, turning sideways to avoid any chance of touching me. "My brother isn't here."

"Yes, he is."

"You're wrong."

He stalked away, pulling his motorcycle keys from his jeans pocket. I held the door, cheeks burning, thinking, *Say something. Now, before this gets worse.* He reached the corner of the building, and his gaze caught on something out of sight in the parking lot. Abruptly he rushed around the corner, calling, "What are you doing?"

Behind the noise of traffic, I heard voices arguing. I hurried after P.J. When I rounded the corner my pulse quickened.

In the parking lot Jesse stood in the open doorway of the truck. A Volvo had screeched to a stop behind it and the driver had climbed out, a big man, gray and unshaven. He was two feet from Jesse's face, waving a sheaf of papers at him.

"What were you doing, bringing Buddy out here at two a.m.? The cops thought you were escapees from a home."

I stopped near P.J., my eyes wide. Jesse saw us and shook his head.

"And the cops left, because we were minding our own business. Mr. Stoker, last night Buddy was drowning. I got him out of the rehab center so he could breathe."

It was Big Bud Stoker, father of the injured kid Jesse counseled at the rehab center. He looked like a wrecking ball on the downswing.

"And took him out to practice wheelchair tricks—like that'll help? I don't want him learning to hop curbs in a wheelchair. I want him to walk again."

"I know you do."

Jesse had undoubtedly pulled himself to his feet so he could impose himself on the situation physically. But though the crutches gave him his height, they took away his balance and ability to maneuver. And Stoker looked ready to punch him in the mouth.

"I know what you think," Stoker said. "Buddy should accept this. Bullshit."

"He has to deal with what's happened. I'm sorry, but that's the brutal truth."

"I knew this was your doing. Buddy told us to quit trying to cure him." Stoker poked him in the chest with the papers. "You think a cure is fantasy? How do you know?"

"Don't do that."

"What's your problem? You so bitter about getting hurt, you want others to give up too, so you can have company?"

"Back off. I talked to Buddy about pulling himself up from the void because I've been there," he said. "Man, I know ten ways to let go, and a few ways to hang on. Give up? No way. I told him to stay strong and dig in."

Stoker spread his arms. "Can you even remember being in Buddy's shoes? Wanting this so much?"

"Of course I can."

"Then tell me that's changed. Look me in the eyes and tell me everything's beautiful, you're just great. Tell me you don't want to walk again."

Jesse's voice sharpened. "I lost my legs, not my mind. Of course I do."

"Then don't you dare tell Buddy to accept this blow. Not until you go to the end of the line yourself." He waved the sheaf of papers. "Here's what Buddy's giving up on. Take a look at what he could have. What you could have, if you'd just take the chance." He tossed the papers at Jesse. "Tell me that's not worth the fight."

The papers swirled to the ground. Stoker stalked back to his car, got in, and squealed out of the parking lot. Jesse stared at the pages flicking on the asphalt, his jaw tight.

P.J. picked them up. He dusted them off, held them out, saw that Jesse didn't have a hand free. I reached to take them, but P.J. tossed them onto the front seat of the truck and turned to his brother.

"That sucked," he said. "And it isn't even lunchtime."

"It's okay. I love the smell of napalm in the morning. What are you doing here?"

"Never mind, I'll come back later." P.J. looked at him sideways. "The cops showed up?"

"It was a misunderstanding. No harm, no foul," Jesse said.

"Sure. Just another Blackburn getting nailed. Who turned you in?"

He glanced at me, quick as a slap, and walked off before Jesse could grab him.

"No, it's absolutely not okay. P.J. was beyond rude," Jesse said.

"It'll take time; I know that."

He paced me along the flagstone path to my door. "He needs to grow up. I'll talk to him."

His voice was solid, but a twinge of pain crossed his face. He was walking a tightrope between me and his brother.

"Let it go," I said, knowing that neither of us could do so. What could I say to P.J.? "Sorry you confessed to me, and I told the cops the truth?" He had set out to commit identity theft and ended up an accessory in a college girl's death. If he couldn't admit that his own actions sent him to jail, if he still thought I was the source of his problems, his world was going to spin off-kilter for good. And yet I felt like garbage.

My little house sat chilly behind its trellis of star jasmine, shivering under the live oaks at the back of the property. I unlocked the door with a headache pounding beneath my skull. The kitchen smelled of scorched coffee and huevos rancheros. I tossed the manila envelope containing Jax Rivera's dossiers on my desk, sat down, and rubbed my temples.

Jesse checked his watch. It was early afternoon, and he had a three-o'clock colloquium at the trial advocacy conference.

"You need to go home and change, don't you?" I said. He was wearing a Blazers Swimming shirt, hadn't shaved, hadn't been home since before Dad left yesterday.

Delafield Public Library

"I have clothes here." He rolled his shoulders. "Mind if I hit the shower?"

"Go ahead." He spun toward the bedroom door. I snagged his arm. "About Stoker."

His face was halfway between pensive and driven. "Later." He headed off, nodding at the envelope. "Dig the spiders out of there, then shred that thing."

When I opened the flap, my nose filled with the musk of old papers. It was close to two years since Jax had delivered the envelope and vanished. I pulled out the contents: notebooks, photos, reports time-stamped with the notation *D.O.*—Directorate of Operations. Photocopied memos from Vauxhall Cross, where Tim North once worked for British intelligence. A hand-drawn map. Tim's sharp pen strokes, listing his contacts in an Asian operation.

Until now, this was as far as I'd gone. The first time I opened the envelope, I gaped in distress at all this information and couldn't rip my eyes from it. Jesse had torn the papers from my hands, stuffed them in the envelope, and said, "Send it back."

"I can't. There's no return address."

"Then get some lighter fluid and matches. Torch it."

And, alarmed, I nearly had. But I decided that doing so would be equally dangerous, because someday Jax and Tim might come asking for this stuff. And I never knew whose side they were on, including mine. Jax once told me that she'd drugged a lover and shot him in the head for betraying her. I considered that an admonition.

Feeling rattled, needing a gut check, I pulled up an old computer screen grab—the single photo I had of Jakarta Rivera and Tim North.

Jax was a sinewy black woman in her forties. Her gaze was as sharp as a two-way mirror: She could see out, but you never saw in. She was wearing Caterpillar boots and fifty thousand bucks' worth of diamonds. Behind her, Tim stood half-shadowed, cool and grim and as hard as the barrel of an M-16.

I found her note: *Read up, and let us know your price. Come on, you know you want to.*

I hadn't wanted to write their memoirs. I hadn't contacted them. But now I found the phone number she had written down, a voice mail with a Los Angeles area code. There was no message, just the tone. I cleared my throat.

"It's Evan. Get in touch. Dad's missing."

When I hung up, I stared for a moment at Jax's image on the computer screen. A knock at the door made me jump.

Through the French doors I saw Thea Vincent bumping her little fist against the glass. She smiled, bouncing on her toes.

When I opened the door she hurtled in and hugged my legs. "You left your door open before."

She was the color of molasses and built like a brick. I picked her up. Nikki came in behind her, face sober.

"You took off like a shot earlier. Was that gal with you the sheriff's detective who . . ." She put a hand on my shoulder. "What's wrong?"

I told her about Dad and she put a hand to her mouth. She'd known my father for more than sixteen years, since the day she and I moved into our dorm room as college freshmen. Tears rose in her eyes. Normally she was feisty and prone to tell people off, but these days, swelling with her new pregnancy, she was tender.

"But the U.S. Attorney thinks he's alive?" she said.

"And on the run."

"That's baloney. But alive is good."

Thea smiled at me. I took her little hand in mine. Nikki gave me a poignant look and quickly banished it.

"You planning to do something about the situation?" she said.

"Yes."

She raised an eyebrow and, when I acknowledged that, took a breath.

"Tell Jax hello for me. And watch yourself."

*   *   *

When they left I felt the old ache. Beautiful as Thea was, and happy as I was for Nikki and Carl, seeing the Vincents still revived the pain of my miscarriage.

My pregnancy had been wild luck, like catching lightning with my bare hands. SCI screws up a lot of things, having kids among them. Even months later, loss, desire, and fear that Jesse and I might never again get so lucky rang through me like a gong.

On the coffee table I found the sheaf of papers that Big Bud Stoker had thrown at Jesse. It was an application to join a clinical trial at UCLA Medical Center. It was crumpled and dusty, but Jesse had smoothed it out.

I went into the bedroom, locked Jax's dossiers in my fire safe, kicked off my shoes, and pulled off my heavy sweater, feeling antsy and at sea. And puzzled about the man in my life.

Never once in the years since he'd been run down, through all his grief and struggle, had I heard him say aloud: Yes, I want to walk again. Until today.

When I knocked on the bathroom door, he said, "Yeah."

The air inside was steamy. In the shower, water beat down on his head and shoulders. I stopped in the doorway.

I'd recently had the bathroom remodeled. The gleaming new fixtures included a huge walk-in shower with a bench seat and a grab bar, for a twenty-nine-year-old who had been a world-class athlete, whose freedom of movement had been stolen from him, and who needed to look at his feet to know whether they were on the floor. He ran his face under the shower spray and shook the water off.

I'd been aware for some time that he had turned a corner. The hit-and-run, the miserable attack that had split open his world, no longer held emotional sway over him. The flashbacks were gone. He had relinquished his anger. The things that kept him so busy—working, coaching, peer counseling—he did not to stave off despair, but because he cared. He had freed himself from the nightmare.

I shut the door, steam swirling around me, and sat down

in the wheelchair. "Stoker wants his son to join an SCI trial at UCLA?"

"Stoker needs his butt kicked. Buddy's not strong enough yet, and he doesn't even fit the clinical criteria. They want people with incomplete injuries, at least two years post."

"You didn't throw away the application."

He grabbed the soap and ran it over his chest. "Nope."

"Are you thinking of applying?"

He ran his head under the water.

"Blackburn? You're going to have to tell me, because your Jedi mind trick isn't working."

He looked my way. I felt a jolt.

He was long legged, with swimmer's shoulders, and had always been lean, lithe, and tan when he'd been training. His hours in the pool were a journey along a pure shore, and in the past few months he'd been training hard. And I had not appreciated the results.

He was ripped. Under the lights, the water shone against his skin. The planes of his back and arms were sharply defined. I realized that I was gazing at him with a kind of awe.

A crooked half smile spread across his face. But this time there was nothing lost or broken behind it. Nothing wistful, no regrets, no worries, other than for me.

How long had I been taking him for granted?

A lump formed in my throat. For so long I had seen his scars, had watched him battle himself, his demons, and a world that considered him invisible. I had missed, somehow, a victory.

He pushed open the shower door, held the grab bar, and stood up. He reached out a hand to me.

"Come here."

He hauled me up and pulled me straight into the shower. His grip was intense.

The water hit me, hot, soaking my camisole. He tugged me against him and pressed his mouth to mine. I closed my eyes and kissed him, putting my hands against the sides of his face. My jeans clung to my skin. I felt my heart thrumming.

Lips close to mine, he lowered his voice. "Fucking Fact of Life Number Two: Don't think. Let go."

"I'm not letting go of you."

His skin was hot. I ran my arms around his back, closing my eyes and kissing him again. Then I tilted my head back and let the water pour over my face, and he kissed my neck. His free hand slid around my ass and he pulled me up, harder, and he was sucking on my skin. I tried to speak but raw longing flowed through me. I raised myself up on my toes and grabbed the showerhead and said, "God Almighty," when he worked his way down my neck to my chest and to the thin wet cotton of my camisole, and I didn't have time to pull it off before his mouth closed around my breast.

Getting wet has never thrilled me. Getting dirty is something else.

Later, sitting on the bed hugging my knees, I watched the clouds tumble by outside. Beside me Jesse sat cross-legged, barefoot in jeans. The clouds split and for a moment the sky turned cobalt, shining all the way out, beyond time, beyond peace. Again I thought of the baby we had lost, the spark that flared before dimming beneath the background glow of creation. Gone, beyond.

I turned my head. "Are you going to do it?"

His eyes were the startling blue of the sky. "You think I'd be running down a blind alley?"

To a dead end, where he could tear open his wounds all over again. "What does the clinical trial involve?"

"Gait training. Intense physio, walking with your weight supported by a harness. It's about finding what mobility you really have and taking it to the end of the line."

I held his gaze. God, I yearned that this whole reality could be swept away, that he had never climbed on his bike that day, that he had worked late or gone running and never had to learn how to get in and out of a wheelchair.

"I only wish . . ."

I stopped myself. *If only* was a phrase he rejected, forcefully. Fucking Fact of Life Number Three: *Might have been* will make you insane.

"Ev, I've been up against the wall for a long time. Maybe it's time to see if I can break it down."

"Just tell me you aren't thinking of doing this because Stoker goaded you. Or the cops last night."

"Let someone goad me? Never. If disability's taught me anything, it's patience and humility."

I gave him a look.

"Okay, forget humility," he said. "But I have patience to spare."

This was a reference to our wedding, which I still hadn't planned. I mock-kicked him off the bed. "Get it in gear. You're going to be late."

He got up. "And gratitude. I'm a grateful person."

I stood up, planning to head for the shower. He pulled on his shirt, checked his watch, and started moving faster. He took some papers from his wallet and muttered, "Shoot, I left my notes at home. I have to go get them." I walked past him and he caught my hand.

"I am grateful, you know. For a hell of a lot," he said.

"But it's not enough, is it?"

"It may have to be. But I'll never know unless I take the chance. If you can't face the possibility of loss, you end up hiding from life." He froze, chagrined, realizing how that sounded. "I didn't mean . . . Damn. Your dad's going to turn up. Forget what I just said."

I touched his face. "Done."

But I couldn't forget it. I would never forget it.

"Peaceful city. I hate places like this."

It was two p.m., and the white Mercury was parked at the curb on a sleepy Santa Barbara street.

"You have more chance of getting laid in Disneyland than this town," Christian said.

Boyd Davies grunted. "People like downtime."

"Downtime makes me no money. Home on the couch with wifey."

Behind the wheel, Davies slouched against the headrest, biting down on a toothpick. He didn't know why Christian was complaining, so nervous he was actually grinding his teeth. The house up the street was quiet. Quiet was good. It meant the target had no clue.

This entire street was comatose. They'd seen just one guy on the road, fifteen minutes ago as they pulled around the corner, black pickup cruising away with the stereo cranked up. Boyd guessed that Christian needed bright lights, Vegas wattage, a chick in a shiny miniskirt shaking her ass in his face, or he got antsy. Dead quiet on a cloudy day and the guy was sitting here wearing sunglasses, actual Armani shades, as if this place were lit like the Strip. But then Christian was also amped on speed, so maybe the sunglasses kept him from seeing quite so many snakes.

"How much longer you want to wait?" Boyd said.

Christian didn't answer but kept playing with the cartridges from his SIG Sauer, lining them up on the dashboard. He set the last one down and touched each in turn.

Jee-zus. "There's still nine, same as last time you counted. How long?"

He kept counting. "She's not going anyplace in the next five minutes. After that, going places doesn't begin to cover it." And he smiled.

Boyd's balls shrank. This guy Christian, he wore rich man's clothes, he had romance-novel long hair, everything screamed male model, and the smile was cold-blooded as a scorpion. Empty and calculating, and maybe injured. Like something was missing. It put a metallic taste in Boyd's mouth. He grabbed his smokes.

Christian scowled. "You don't smoke when you're on surveillance. People see."

"People see? Like we're Delta Force? This ain't fucking Tehran, man." He lit up.

Christian plucked the cigarette from his fingers and stubbed it out in the ashtray. "I have my health to worry about."

Boyd colored. "Know what you are? You're a brat."

"Know what I am? I'm the boss."

Yeah. Man in charge and acting like a ten-year-old who never in his life heard of limits. But then, that was the guy's business. Getting people anything they wanted, no matter how far over the line it went.

"Then be the boss. Do this thing," Boyd said.

Christian sat for a moment, sleek and mean behind his shades. He took out his phone and made the call.

"Rio, where are we?" He listened for a while. "Then we'll kick it into gear." He flipped the phone shut. "No chance of getting it from the old man. The daughter's got to convince him to give it up."

"Right." Boyd put his hand to his ear, listening to the feed from the microphone. He heard nothing. He turned off the equipment and checked his holster.

Christian took the bullets from the dashboard one by one and began loading them in the magazine. Then he smiled that insect grin and put on a quavering voice.

"The girl is mine," he said. "Mine mine mine, all mine."

The wack job was singing Michael Jackson. He slammed the magazine into the butt of his pistol.

"I've been waiting half my life for this, Boyd. We do it in my time."

5

Five seconds, that was all the time it took.

I came out of the bathroom with my hair in a towel, half-dressed, skin warm from the shower, and began making the bed. The sun was slanting through the clouds. I tossed a pillow into place and a breeze swept through the window. The light seemed to alter. I smelled cigarette smoke.

Without warning a hand covered my mouth and *boom*, I was facedown on the bed with a man lying on my back. My heart flipped. I jerked my head back, trying to butt him in the face. He pressed his weight against my shoulders, pushing me into the mattress, and put his lips to my ear.

"Don't be dramatic."

Even at a ten-decibel mutter, his accent sounded menacing: the feral growl I connect with British gangster movies. His hand was rough, his breath hot against my neck. Lying beneath him in nothing but a camisole and panties, I felt completely vulnerable. I forced myself to stop fighting.

"Good," he said. "Quiet. They have men outside. Get dressed."

He let me go and stood up. I scrambled off the bed, grabbed a T-shirt, and pulled it on. He watched, eyes calm in a dog-pound face.

"Who's outside?" I whispered.

"Later."

I found some jeans and turned toward the bathroom. I

felt a visceral need to reclaim my privacy from Tim North. He blocked me.

"Don't waste the time. We have to go get the dossiers."

I continued dressing. "No, you don't."

"Yes, I do." Without seeming to move, he was nevertheless right in my face. "Jax is missing."

I opened my mouth to speak. His finger appeared in front of my nose.

"Talk comes later."

He was a hot negative looming before me, black body radiation. "We'll leave through the window. Bring cash, credit cards, a phone, and ID. Passport, preferably."

I murmured, "Your dossiers are here in the house."

His head swung around. "Where?"

"Tell me where we're going first."

Again he moved soundlessly to within inches of my face. "We're going out of range. Where are the dossiers?"

"The fire safe in my closet."

"Key?"

I got it from the nightstand and gave it to him. He grabbed my arm, hissing, "Quietly," and while I gathered my things into a backpack, he extracted the manila envelope from the small safe. He grabbed my laptop, came back, and whispered, "Count with me. On ten, you flush the toilet and we'll go."

"Why do you need sound?"

"They have a parabolic microphone. We'll cover our tracks with white noise."

"I want to call the police."

"Do that and I'll be gone."

For a second, all my worries went out the window with that idea. Yes, Tim: Take your dossiers and be gone. Get this load off my back. Remove yourself and your dirty secrets from my life for good.

But if he did that, I knew my best chance of finding out what had happened to Dad would go with him. And he'd leave me to face whoever was out there alone.

I took my cue. Tim slipped over the windowsill, landed soundlessly, and turned to offer me a hand. With much less finesse than he, I hauled myself out.

Eyes panning the property, Tim moved smoothly toward the hedge at the back of the yard. He knew exactly where to squeeze between the two poplars. We scraped our way between them and jogged across the lawn of the house behind mine. Nobody was home. The gate was already open.

Out on the street, we slowed to a walk. White oleander thrived along the sidewalk. Tim was wearing a light jacket, jeans, and hiking boots, striding with his hands loose at his sides, eyes front. The air seemed to crackle around him.

"Start talking," I said.

"Two men are sitting in a white Mercury, eighty meters down the street from your front gate. One has a Nikon with a telephoto lens. He was taking photos of your car and your neighbor's house. The other strolled past the front of your property ten minutes ago."

"Who are they?"

"Bad."

"Can you be more specific?"

"Very bad." His gaze swept the street. "I lost contact with Jax five days ago. She should have checked in on Wednesday. She didn't."

"You're sure she isn't simply . . . out of range?"

"She missed three consecutive call-ins. She hasn't responded to my attempts to contact her on any band. She hasn't sent a mayday. I'm sure."

I nodded, too chicken to ask where she had been, or what she was doing. "How'd you get here so fast? I left the message two hours ago."

"Message? I monitor the news feeds. The *News-Press* published a bulletin about the car wreck at eight thirty this morning."

I looked at him. "You monitor the news feeds for information about my father?"

"Since he decided to play the hero last year, yes." He

turned the corner on Pedregosa, heading for the hills. "Putting himself in the spotlight, standing up in front of television cameras at a press conference. It triggered everything. Bloody fool."

His tone made me flinch. "Triggered what, Tim?"

He took car keys from his pocket and jabbed a remote. At the curb ahead, a black BMW flashed its parking lights.

"Get in," he said.

"Cut to the chase. What's going on?"

He gave me a glance, all portent. "Somebody has taken my wife and your father. The key to getting them back is in that envelope you have in your backpack." He opened the car door. "We're going to find it, and then I'm going to find out what those men outside your house know about it. And it's going to be ugly."

"I know Dad was an intelligence officer. And that he knew Jax. I can deal with clandestine ops."

He stared at me across the roof of the car as though about to deliver the punch line to a tasteless joke. "Forget clandestine ops. This is about hookers, guns, and money."

On the ocean behind Jesse's house, sunlight fell piebald through the clouds, and whitecaps sizzled in the wind. He opened his front door and saw the mail heaped on the floor in the entryway, noticed the message light blinking on his answering machine, and left it. He found his notes for the colloquium on the kitchen table. He sorted through them and stopped, leaning on his knees.

His back was killing him. It had been since last night, when he spilled. When the cops drove up. And he hadn't told the half of it. Goading him didn't cover it.

He had hotdogged it and lost his balance showing Buddy how to hop the curb. Their headlights caught him slap-bang flat on the ground, and by the time he got up they were out of the patrol car. *What are you two doing?*

It's okay, Officer, I work here.

Sure. How about we give you a ride home?

No, we'll be a while. We're practicing penalty shots.
Buddy laughed. The cops didn't.
Is there somebody we should call? A caregiver or doctor?
No. Why would you do that?
Blank disbelief. *Because you can't walk.*

And in their eyes, living his life in the face of that fact proved him crazy for sure. They had no idea—not walking wasn't the worst thing.

Indignity was. And pain. And loss of independence.

He poured himself a glass of water and tipped pain-killers from the prescription bottle into his hand. That was what the clinical trial would be about: freedom. To live without the hurt raking into him. To stand up for a few minutes longer, to reach things on a shelf, to talk eye-to-eye, to go places without worrying about accessibility. Without strangers giving him that you're-so-brave look. Without having to ask for help with simple things from the woman he wanted to marry.

He gazed out the plate-glass windows at the beach. Free-dom, right. He didn't want to spend the day sunk in a drowsy trance, in thrall to drugs because of legs that barely worked. Especially not if he was going to talk to P.J. Drugs had helped send his brother to jail. How could he help P.J. stay clean if he retreated into his own pharmaceutical haze? He scooped the pills back into the bottle and put it away.

He headed for the front door, hitting *play* on the answering machine as he went past. He grabbed the mail, ripped open an envelope, and heard a hardpan Oklahoma voice on the machine.

"It's Phil. I'm in trouble, so you've got to do this for me."

He looked up.

"I've been ambushed. Highway One, north Santa Barbara County."

Oh, Christ.

"These people want something Jakarta Rivera stashed away. The trail that leads to it is in those papers Jax left with Evan. We can't let them get it. If they get that information, they'll use it to track and target and . . ."

A ragged pause, noise in the background. "That information can never come to light. If they get hold of it, they'll start killing. Jesse, you have to get those papers and destroy them."

The blood drained from his face. Evan had the dossiers at home. She'd already sent out word to Jax and Tim.

"Destroy them. Do whatever it takes."

Phil's voice dropped further, and Jesse listened to the rest of the story, disbelief draining into shock. He understood why Phil was telling him to do this. What would happen if he didn't. Evan, all of them, at risk.

"Do it tonight. Tomorrow will be too late. And . . ." Pause. "You have to keep my daughter out of this. Evan cannot know. Keep her clear. Do you hear me, Jesse? If you don't, my family becomes part of the kill chain."

"Oh, fuck."

He grabbed his phone and dialed.

Sitting in the parked car, I handed Tim the manila envelope. "Explain that remark."

He pulled out the thick bundle of documents. "Sexual blackmail is an enduring espionage technique."

"Yes. Catch Ivan with his pants down and force him to steal the blueprints for the ICBM; I get it. If you're saying my father used a honey trap to obtain information, I guess I can't be surprised."

His gaze ran across my face like a splash of ice water. "No, you're not surprised. You're repulsed and think it's not true."

Flushing, I looked away. Clouds were lowering over the mountains again.

He returned to the dossiers. "Jax worked for the agency back when they were just sussing out the connection between drug cartels and paramilitaries. Asian colonels selling heroin to build private armies. That cartel in Ecuador funding Hezbollah weapons deals, the IRA training FARC rebels in Colombia."

"Get to the part about hookers."

His eyes cut my way. "Jax managed an extensive honey trap. She bought information from the madam who ran a prostitution ring."

"A madam?"

"Her name is Rio Sanger. She's behind this."

I gaped at him. "You're saying the owner of Miss Kitty's House of Pleasure has kidnapped my dad?"

"Jax and your father worked only one operation together. If they're both missing, that op is the reason. And Rio is the connection."

"Madam Bang-Bang grabbed him off the road? Why?"

He stopped rifling the papers. "The operation ended badly. Rio got burned on the deal. I imagine she wants restitution."

He meant payback. I ran a hand over my forehead. "What happened?"

"Jax was tracking the drug money. Phil came in to assess the weapons angle, to find out who was buying what kind of firepower." He lifted a scrap of paper to his face. "Rio ran a club that catered for exotic tastes. Her clients didn't know she was getting it all on film."

"Which she sold to Jax."

"Turned out the arms dealers and moneymen weren't as dangerous as the whores." He smiled, unamused. "Customers who were flunkies twelve years ago are power players today. Military brass, captains of industry. If these people could be blackmailed or turned, the take would be huge."

"So she's after money."

"She's after power. Money is a happy side effect."

"What went wrong?" I said.

"You recall why Jax left the agency?"

"She told me she got involved with an asset who betrayed her, in Medellín. She killed him." My eyebrows rose. "That was this operation?"

"Riverbend. And the key to it must be in here some-place." He pored over a précis and several grainy photographs. "How much of this material have you examined?"

"None."

He looked up. "Really?"

"Perhaps I'm not the curious cat you imagined. How much of it did I want to know?"

He eyed me for a second longer and went back to pawing through papers. Across the street, a door opened. A jogger came out and headed up the hill.

"Understand something, Evan. Some men don't care if they get caught with hookers. Rio went to extra lengths to capture them on film committing ... acts that would humiliate them culturally." Finally he looked at me. "We're not speaking about ten minutes in the missionary position. And we're not talking about consenting adults."

The truck barreled along the freeway toward town. Jesse couldn't get through on the phone. He glanced at the speedometer—ninety, too slow. Her home phone clicked to the answering machine, and calling the cell phone got a recording: "The person you are calling is unavailable. Please try again later." She was home; she had to be there. If she wasn't answering, something was wrong. He closed on the car in front of him and flashed his lights. It pulled into the right lane and he screamed past.

You have to keep my daughter out of this ... Do you hear me, Jesse?

He heard. He heard hard-nosed, wily Phil Delaney sounding ragged and desperate. He heard, *Tomorrow will be too late.* He swung off the freeway toward her house, trying her number again.

Tim continued hunting through the files. "Rio promises the rich and powerful anything they want. That was why her client videos proved so valuable. Because she traded in the only currency that counted with these men."

I sat with my hands clenched. Trading in depravity. Realpolitik worked like a two-by-four to the head.

"How will this Riverbend information help get Dad and Jax out of trouble?"

"We'll trade them for it."

I barely knew Tim North, and didn't want to know him. His résumé included the British Army sniper school, dirty ops conducted in the planet's worst sump holes, and a second career doing a sociopath's dream job—killing people for money. He was a pit viper.

I didn't think he would take this outrage lying down.

"I don't believe you," I said. "You don't plan to pay this woman off, chalk it up as a loss, and walk away."

"Getting my wife back is a win."

"But that won't be the end of things."

He flipped a page and turned his head. His eyes said no.

I jumped. My phone was ringing. I grabbed it, seeing JESSE on the display. "Babe?"

"Ev, I'm in your driveway. Where are you?"

My pulse jumped. "What are you doing at my place?"

"Your dad—"

Tim grabbed the phone from me. "Get inside the house." Impatient. "Yeah, that's me. Get yourself inside Evan's house as if everything's normal. And—" Eyes heating. "Mate, shut up. Give me a yes or no. Is a white Mercury parked down the block?"

Tim had spirited me away from bad men lurking outside the house, but was sending Jesse inside?

"What do you think you're doing?" I said.

"Bloody hell." He hit the power button, shoved the phone back into my hands, and fired up the car. "The Mercury just started up and drove past Jesse."

He threw the BMW into gear. We leaped away from the curb and roared down Pedregosa.

"Why didn't you tell him to watch out?" I said.

The street bled by. I started to turn the phone back on. Before I could flinch, Tim slapped it from my hand.

"Presume they can intercept or triangulate any calls you make," he said.

Hand stinging, I stared at him. "He doesn't know there's trouble. We have to go back to my house."

In answer, he gunned the car around a corner onto a side street heading toward the Old Mission.

"What are you doing? You're going to leave Jesse to face—"

"They're not after Jesse. They're after you."

He poured straight through a stop sign. The street was narrow, cars lining the curbs, live oaks hanging overhead. He powered around another corner.

He didn't know where he was going.

"Tim, the streets only get tighter this way. You have to get out of this neighborhood or we'll get stuck in a dead end."

He shifted again, pushing the car to sixty. His face was set, his eyes bouncing between road and rearview mirror.

"How?" he said.

I fumbled for my seat belt and buckled up. "Left at the corner."

He kept his foot down and we half slid around.

"Jesus." I threw myself back and jammed my feet against the floor as if braking.

Dead ahead a garbage truck was stopped in the middle of the road. Yellow lights flashed on the roof of the cab. Two crewmen were jogging toward it, pulling trash cans. Tim slammed on the brakes, snapping me forward as we shrieked to a stop. The crew bolted for the sidewalk.

We couldn't get around the truck. Tim tossed the car into reverse and screeched back up the street through scorched rubber and the shouts of the garbagemen. At the corner he threw the wheel, spun us around ninety degrees, and barreled off in another direction.

"Get off this street," I said.

"Where? Get me out of this labyrinth."

We were heading downhill back toward my house. Laguna Street would work, and if we could hit Anacapa, it would be a four-minute drive to the police station.

"Second left."

Tim downshifted and swung wide, preparing to shave the corner.

Ahead, a white car came into view, heading for the intersection from the right. Maybe not, I thought, maybe that's not the car—

Tim hissed and spun the wheel. The BMW snapped into a power slide. We swung around and I hit the door. Ahead, the white car stopped in the intersection, blocking us, and all at once I found myself in a movie where you know what's coming next, except that at the theater I could stand up, walk out, throw popcorn at the screen, and say, "This is bullshit—"

The BMW plowed over the curb onto a front lawn. Green turf thudded into the air and across the windows and hood of the car. The car clipped a fire hydrant with a huge clanging sound and bounced to a stop.

The white Mercury was directly ahead of us. In front of it stood a pale man with a black goatee, long hair flying in the wind. In the stormy light, I saw a dark object in his right hand. He raised his arm.

Every hair on my body stood up. He was going to shoot us.

Hands out, I screamed, "Don't!" Tim shouted, "Get down!" and gunned the engine, spinning the wheel. The back of the BMW pinwheeled, and as I ducked I saw a flash erupt from the muzzle of the gun. Above my head the window shattered. Below the roar of the engine, the report came like a pop.

Clenching my arms over my head, I tried to hide but had no place to go. I heard metal drumming into the front of the car. Jesus, more gunfire. The car kept doing a doughnut, and *whang,* we hit something solid and stopped dead. I heard a spewing sound, and the sky seemed to cut loose with rain.

I felt paralyzed with fear. If I moved, the gunman would see me. But the car wasn't rolling, and if I didn't move I was a stationary target, and I knew I had to move, had to get out of this car. I turned my head, trying to see what to do.

"Stay down," Tim said.

He was above me, leaning across to the passenger side. Outside the window a shadow appeared. Pure, bright terror flew through me. The gunman was right there.

The report was deafening, incredible noise right above my ear. I screamed again. The tang of cordite filled my nose.

A heavy weight landed on me. Oh, God, Tim had fallen over. Was he hit?

But he hadn't collapsed; he was climbing over me, shoving open the passenger door, and lurching out into the street. The rain thundered, a waterfall. Deep in my gut, admiration told me that Tim had put himself between me and the gunman. I moved, feeling abject mortification that it had taken this to free me from my paralysis. I was covered in glass. Unbuckling my seat belt, I peered out.

Water was cascading onto the car, obscuring the view out the rear window. The fire hydrant was geysering.

Through the door frame I saw Tim standing in the street. In his right hand he held a pistol aimed at the ground. Gingerly I pulled myself up, glass nicking my palms.

The gunman lay wounded on his back in the road, staring up past the barrel of the pistol into Tim's eyes.

Tim kicked the man's own gun from his hand. "Where's my wife?"

Water from the fire hydrant sluiced down on the roof of the car. The man's reply was inaudible.

"Fuck money. I don't want money. Where's my wife?"

Mist flew from the edges of the hydrant geyser, spinning into rainbow. Blood flowed from beneath the gunman's back, mixed with the water, and ran toward the gutter.

He raised a hand, feebly, palm out to ward Tim off. " . . . don't know."

"Where?" Tim said.

"I don't know." His hand hovered in front of his face.

Tim stared down at him, heedless of the water raining on his shoulders.

He blew the man's brains out.

6

Water continued spewing from the fire hydrant. In the street, blood pooled under the gunman. From beneath his head a revolting spatter fanned out.

Tim kicked a lifeless arm off the man's chest, the arm that three seconds earlier had been raised to fend him off, and bent to rifle through his pockets. He took the man's phone and wallet. Stepping back from the body, he glanced around at the asphalt. He picked up a shiny object from the road, searched some more, and picked up a second one. He was collecting the spent brass from the cartridges he'd fired, getting rid of the evidence.

He looked up at me. His face was emotionless, his eyes analytical.

I scrambled like a wildcat across the gearshift and driver's seat and shoved open the driver's door and stumbled out of the car. Water from the busted fire hydrant cascaded over me. I bolted, eyes on the far end of the street, thinking, *Get there,* and not even pausing to breathe. Ten yards, twenty, sprinting like hell.

Footsteps closed on me from behind. Tim grabbed my wrist. I shouted, just shrieking, and tried to pull away. He got his other hand around my waist. The gun was in his right hand.

"Let go. Let me go, let go, God—"

"Shut up and get back in the car."

I fought him, writhing, but instead of stopping me he

kept running, swinging me around with his momentum and angling back toward the BMW.

Toward the body of the man he had just executed. I dug my heels into the road.

"Bloody idiot, if you want to get out of here, get in the car. The other one's still out there."

My mind wasn't working linearly; my feet were still digging in. Damn, damn. "The second man?"

"Will be coming on foot."

I stopped fighting. Hanging onto me, Tim rushed back and bundled me into the BMW. I scanned the scene.

"What if he's at my place? What if he went after Jesse?"

He jumped in and turned the key in the ignition. "I'm not going back to find out." The car didn't start. He tried again. "Come on."

My phone was on the floor. I grabbed it and turned it on. Tim tossed me the wallet and phone he'd taken from the gunman.

"See who he is." The engine struggled to catch. "Start, you piece of German *scheisse.*"

Up the street a front door opened and someone peered out. Down the road, traffic had stopped. One car was turning around, bugging out of here. I pushed speed dial, put my phone to my ear, and fumbled the wallet open. The engine caught. I heard Jesse's cell phone ringing.

Tim yanked the phone from my hand. "I told you to shut that off."

He smashed it against the dashboard. I recoiled. He tossed the phone on the floor, jammed the car in gear, and gunned the engine. The tires spun in the mud.

"The wallet," he said.

Dazed, I opened it.

Tim muttered under his breath. "Oh, no, you don't."

I looked up. From the far corner of the intersection a man was running toward us. He was young and sleek, dressed in a black coat and sweater and jeans, dark hair swirling in the wind. He caught sight of the mayhem in the street and windmilled to a stop.

Tim gunned the engine again. The car clawed its way out of the mud, jerked over the curb, and leaped forward. The man in black stared openmouthed at the gunman's body. Tim aimed the BMW straight at him.

For a second the man continued staring. Snapping out of it, he reached to the small of his back and drew a gun. Tim aimed the car at the sidewalk, putting the man dead in his sights.

The man broke, sprinting out of our way across a lawn and around the corner of a house. Tim sped past. Looking back, I saw a black coat disappear through somebody's gate. A horn blared. Tim swerved and careered down the street. Things were collapsing, my heart shrinking in my chest.

Tim's voice cut through the wool in my head. "Who was he?"

Trees and houses and parked cars streaked by. I looked again at the wallet. Inside I saw the face of the dead gunman, glowering from his official photograph. I saw the badge, with the acronym ICE and the golden eagle atop the U.S. government seal.

"Immigration and Customs Enforcement," I said. "You killed a federal agent."

When he hit the top of the hill Christian glanced back down at the neighborhood. Cop cars everywhere, and Boyd with his head sprayed across the intersection. He kept running, getting it straight in his mind. When he neared the hotel he made the call. Hearing the number ring, he slowed to a walk, grinding his teeth.

"Christian? What is the status?"

She was impatient; he heard the tone.

"Christian?"

He put a hand to his stomach. "Boyd Davies is dead."

He strode into the grounds of the hotel, waiting for the eruption. It didn't come.

"Tell me," she said.

He talked, making sure to describe his part, how he chased the Delaney woman on foot, catching up too late.

"Davies was dead when I got there," he said.

"Does Bliss have the Delaney girl?"

Steady, he had to be rock steady. "I sent Bliss back to L.A. beforehand. It was just Boyd and me."

Silence throbbed from the phone, but the lid stayed on. He strode across the grounds. "Bliss installed the tracking program on Boyd's phone. She thought that would be enough for her to stay on his trail if—"

"So the Delaney girl got away."

And instantly he felt four feet tall, ten years old, standing in the middle of the room in a puddle of his own urine, grown-ups staring at him.

"You let her escape. Our best chance to get the information."

"This BMW nearly ran me down. I had to dive out of the way. Rio, she tried to kill me."

"Did she hurt you?" She went quiet. "You sound winded. Christian, sit down; take your pulse."

"No, I'm fine. Rio, she was with a man. White guy, ugly. And there was another guy, outside her house. In a wheelchair."

He crossed the hotel grounds to his villa. Manicured lawns spilled down the hillside, and middle-aged bikinis lounged around the pool, all Botox and mimosas sipped through tiny straws—El Encanto had the whole quiet-money thing going on.

Her voice stayed level. "Forget the men. We don't have the Delaney girl. We have to go to our fallback."

He knew already; she didn't have to tell him. Get Evan Delaney and use her as leverage to force Phil to give up the information. But now that was blown. The glossy sunlight irked him.

"Christian, we cannot miss again. Do I have to remind you what is at stake? What she and her family owe us?"

"We're owed a death. And we'll get it." He unlocked the door to his villa. "What do you want me to do?"

"I will take care of it. Get out of Santa Barbara."

The villa felt chilly. Its adobe walls were good and thick; you could screw at top volume all night long, service the Santa Barbara polo team or whoever stayed here. Rotate two or three of the girls in and out—ten-thousand-dollar night if you worked it right. He tossed his hair out of his eyes.

"If Boyd is dead," she said, "the police will be after her. We must get the information as soon as possible. Every hour that passes gives them time to shut this down."

In the ornate gilded mirror over the fireplace, he saw stress lines around his mouth. His eyes looked wan. He needed to redye his eyelashes.

"Evan Delaney is our one chance to get what we need. What you need. We cannot miss again."

The threat was behind her words. Always: or else. His reflection seemed to flatten, as if he were transparent. His hands were cold. His hematocrit was dropping.

"Christian, I know you want to handle Phil Delaney yourself. But get the prize, and he will die knowing that everything he fought to protect is ruined." Her tone lifted. "This is our future, the Sanger name. I'm counting on you being at my side."

He breathed out. "I understand."

"Excellent. Hurry back, Christian. I love you."

There was lint on his sweater. Seven-hundred-dollar cashmere, the thing should repel lint. He picked it off and flicked it away as if it were larval.

"I love you too, Mom."

Wind poured through the shattered window of the BMW, whipping my hair against my face. Outside, an upscale neighborhood blurred by, the white walls of Spanish-style homes dappled with stormy light. The noise of the engine drilled through my head. I wanted to be sick.

Tim drove with one hand on the wheel, one on the stick, eyes dead. "What's the quickest way to Bautista Street?"

My thought processes seemed to be coagulating into a gelatinous mass. I stared at the badge in my hand, the photo of the federal agent whose head Tim had emptied onto the road.

"Bautista. Evan, for fucksake."

His tone brought my eyes up. He was sweating.

"Left. At the corner, and down three blocks." Thinking: We need to get to the police station. "Why Bautista?"

"Dump this car."

With that, I snapped. "Dump this car? It's not enough you just murdered a man—now you want to commit grand theft auto?"

He took the corner hard, grimacing.

"Why stop there? How about committing some other felonies? Maybe arson? Bribery? Robbery? Wait, I forgot— you already robbed the corpse of the man you *shot in the head*."

I hit him in the shoulder with the wallet. Over and over.

He reached out and shoved me by the face toward the shattered window.

"Get this through your brain. That was no cop on duty, performing an arrest. Mr."—he snatched the wallet and glanced at the name—"Boyd Davies was two seconds from putting a round through your temple."

"You executed him."

"He was working with the people who ambushed your father. That tells you the kind of cop he was."

The wind whistled around me. My clothes were wet, cold, and studded with glass. I needed help, needed somehow to pull out of this catastrophe. I had to get to the police.

Tim would never do that. I had to get away from him.

He heaved the BMW around the corner onto Bautista, swinging wide and overcorrecting sharply. The road was winding and empty of traffic. Two hundred yards along he swerved to the curb behind a parked red SUV.

He turned off the engine. "Get out. Bring everything."

I stuffed the dossiers inside the manila envelope and put Davies's phone and wallet, along with my own smashed phone, in the backpack. The spent cartridges rattled in Tim's pocket. Distantly I heard sirens.

"And so you know," he said, "I'm not going to add auto theft to the list."

"No?"

"No. I already stole this BMW."

I put the heel of my palm to my forehead. He opened his door, turned to look at me, and sank back against his seat.

"You want to go to the police?" He jerked his head in the direction of the sirens. "They're on the scene. Go ahead. Get arrested."

"You want me to keep your name out of it?"

His gaze had a serrated edge. "Boyd Davies was a U.S. special agent. Nothing else will—" He looked around, frowning. "What's that sound?"

Inside my backpack, a phone was ringing.

"I told you to turn the bloody thing off; they're probably triangulating the—"

"It's not mine." I opened the pack. "It's his."

I took out Davies's phone. The display said PRIVATE CALL. Tim and I exchanged a glance.

"Answer it," he said.

With trepidation I flipped it open. "Yes?"

"If you let this situation run out of control, things will go badly. Your father isn't feeling well, and if you lose it again, he'll die."

The voice was silken and smutty. I looked at Tim, my heart thumping. He mouthed, *Them?*

I nodded. "Who is this?"

"Tell that ugly maniac with you, he will pay for Boyd. And if you ever again come close to hurting my son, I will kill you myself."

A sour taste bloomed in my throat. The voice was plummy, like fruit so ripe it was beginning to ferment. The phone made a new sound, the chirp of a photo arriving.

"Take a look." She hung up.

Heart racing, I brought up the photo on the screen. My stomach hollowed. I squeezed my eyes shut, then opened them again. The picture was still there.

It was Dad. His hands were bound behind his back, and a gag was drawn tight in his mouth. Tears swam into my vision. His face was battered, one eye swollen purple. Blood was matted in his white hair.

Tim gestured. "Here."

I handed him the phone. He grunted.

"Dark background, no way to tell where he is. And no time stamp. You can't tell how recent it is."

A drone rose in my head, and my brain shifted from overdrive to neutral, losing traction. The phone rang again.

Tim put a hand on my arm. "No tears. No begging. Hold your bottle." He handed me the phone.

I blinked away tears, cleared my throat, hard, and answered, "Bitch."

"If you want your father back you will not involve the police, because the second you do, they arrest you for killing a federal agent. Then you go to jail and your father dies. Cunt."

"I want to speak to him."

"Let's skip the clichés. I want the Riverbend file. Every record Jakarta Rivera kept on the operation, from Colombia and Thailand."

Gooseflesh crept across my arms. Her voice felt like mud sliming over me.

"If I turn over this information, you'll release my dad. Correct?"

"I do not mean memos or handwritten notes. I mean DVDs. Video records."

I glanced at Tim. "I don't have DVDs."

"Get them. You have seventy-two hours."

"Deadlines are a cliché. Forget it."

She laughed. "You misunderstand. This is not my deadline. I am finished with him. It's up to you to get to him before he dies of dehydration."

I stared vacantly down the road. The voice carried the ripple of a distant shore, and sounded even more smug and self-satisfied than it had before.

"You deliver the Riverbend files and I'll tell you where Phil is. This is simple. You're already running out of time."

Blood and bruises, gag in his mouth. Hands bound, no food, no water, no way to even wet his mouth without that dirty cloth absorbing all the moisture. He'd been ambushed yesterday. He could be anywhere from a cave in the mountains to a stifling shack in the Nevada desert, sweating out his life under a baking sun.

"How will I get the information to you?" I said.

"Write this down."

She rattled off a phone number. I grabbed a pen and wrote it on my wrist.

"That's a message phone, and untraceable to me. And so you won't go shouting to the authorities, let me tell you: Your father is no angel."

"I don't care."

"You need to care. When you get a look at Riverbend I don't want you freaking out. And I want you to understand why you don't want the cops obtaining the file. Phil is no Mr. Clean."

"Fine."

She laughed, a sound full of sex and malice. "You think he was John Wayne. He was a procurer. Back when your big thrill was letting some high school boy stick his tongue in your mouth, Phil was using whores to gather intelligence for him."

I stared out the windshield. "Tell me something useful, or I need to go."

The laugh sounded worse this time. "Your father is in enough *mierda* without the world learning he had women work on their backs for the CIA."

I pinched the bridge of my nose.

"Seventy-two hours. Your daddy is getting thirsty."

She clicked off, leaving me gazing at roiling clouds and the empty street. Tim put a hand on my arm.

"DVDs," he said.

"In seventy-two hours or he dies."

"What about Jax?"

He looked pale and seemed to have honest-to-God pain in his eyes.

"She didn't mention Jax."

He slumped lower in his seat. Then he blinked, shoved his emotions back behind the wall, and pointed at the dossiers. "I've never seen any DVDs. But there's a small envelope in one of those folders. It has a key inside."

Rifling through the material, I found it. The envelope was labeled SINNER'S PRAYER. Inside was a handwritten letter. Taped to the letter was a small red key with the number 357 stamped on it.

"Where's the safe-deposit box?" I said.

He gestured to the letter. I unfolded it.

> Looks like I got a losing hand.
>
> I tried to rise, baby, to ride it right to the top. But you win again. If I've done somebody wrong, it's myself.
>
> Maybe one day I'll see you, but for now I gotta hit the road. Let me be.
>
> > J.R.
> > 1821 Century Park East
> > Los Angeles

"It's a code, isn't it?" I said.

He leaned on the steering wheel, peering at the letter, his face rough with concentration.

"Is it encrypted?" Anxiety began spinning up. Did we need a mainframe computer? A linguist? Indiana Jones?

He shook his head. "It's a simple code. The address is real."

"Century Park East is Century City. It'll be an office building."

"Then it will be a private bank." He reread the letter, half-aloud. Though he looked focused, his intensity seemed to be ebbing. "Got it." He blinked, grimacing again. "We go to the address and decipher the rest from there. The second sentence is the key." He glanced at me. "Unless you can think of a title I'm missing."

"I'm blank."

He tapped the letter. "The second sentence is the only one that's not a song title or lyric." Nodding, almost smiling. "Jax, you beauty." He looked at me. "Rhythm and blues. Don't you know Ray Charles?"

"Obviously not well enough."

" 'Sinner's Prayer.' 'Losing Hand.' 'You Win Again.' All his songs." He gave me a look of disbelief. "Come on—'Hit the Road, Jack.' "

"Okay, that I know."

" 'Let me be'—that's a line from 'Unchain My Heart.' Simple. You just have to know Jax. The only one that doesn't fit is the sentence about rising, riding to the top. That'll be the clue."

I looked at my watch. Four ten p.m. Without traffic, Century City was ninety minutes in a fast car. During rush hour it could be a nightmare.

"Let's go." He got out of the car, grunting. I got my backpack, stuffed the manila envelope back inside, and followed him toward the red SUV.

"Tim, you go get the file. I won't run. And certainly not in a stolen vehicle."

He took keys from his pocket and flicked a remote. The lights flashed on the red SUV. "This isn't a stolen vehicle. It's mine."

"I have to go to the police."

"That's not going to work."

He turned all the way around to face me. Shock twanged down my arms. He had unzipped his jacket, and beneath it he was bleeding.

"Oh, no."

I walked toward him. Gingerly he pulled his jacket farther open. His shirt was sticking to his left side, and there was a ragged hole in the fabric. His serrated expression had worsened, and I saw that he was very pale. I put my hand under his elbow.

He held out the keys. "You drive."

I helped him into the car. "We have to get you to the hospital."

"This is how it is, love. I can't possibly go into a private bank like this. You have to do it."

"You need immediate medical attention."

He glanced again at his shirt. It was sopping. "The shot was through-and-through. It didn't hit anything vital."

"I don't believe that."

"If you take me to a hospital and turn yourself in to the police, Jax and your father will die."

"Why?"

"The only way to get to Rio Sanger is through Riverbend, and the police must never see that file. The information it contains could prove deadly to Jax and your father."

"We need to trust the cops. Tim, the entire law enforcement apparatus isn't corrupt. You may have gone freelance, but that doesn't mean that everybody else is a bad guy."

He gave a brief, eerie smile. "Your faith in democracy is touching."

"So's your cynicism. But right now you're being unreasonable. And you're bleeding to death."

"There's no time to argue. You need the Riverbend file." He grabbed my wrist, his grip fierce. "You have to do this. You can't fail. If you don't get the information to Rio, we'll never see Jax or your father again."

I blinked back the stinging in my eyes.

He held hard to my wrist. "You only have a few hours before the cops figure out who you are. I don't know how they'll play it—accomplice or my hostage. Either way, they'll issue a BOLO with your name and photo. Once they do, your room to maneuver shuts down."

He turned my wrist so we could see my watch. "Six p.m. Get the information by then or you won't get it."

Nodding in distressed assent, I jumped in the driver's seat and fired up the SUV. I peeled away from the curb and tore down the winding street. Live oaks blurred by.

"When I get this file, we won't simply hand it over to the kidnappers, will we?"

"No. We'll do more."

He eyed me. He didn't need to say the word he was thinking.

Revenge.

7

Police cars blockaded the street. Black-and-whites, officers and detectives moving around beyond them, and an ambulance, lights flashing. People clotted the sidewalks. Jesse screeched to a stop and clambered out of the truck.

Damn it to hell. He pushed through the crowd. Beyond the patrol cars in the intersection sat the white car he'd seen gunning away from Evan's house. Cops and paramedics were working on someone in the road. Someone dead.

A policeman passed by, talking into his radio. Jesse called, "Officer." The man didn't look up.

His head was pounding. He had heard Phil's message too late. He couldn't see past the patrol cars. Who were the cops working on in the street?

He knocked a fist against the patrol car. "Hey. I need to get through."

The cop on the radio turned around. The man's eyes pinged with recognition. "What are you doing here?"

Great. It was Officer You-can't-walk, from last night. Jesse pointed at the scene. "My girlfriend's in there."

The cop walked toward him. "Back up, buddy. What are you talking about?"

He heard somebody call his name. Drew Farelli, from the U.S. Attorney's office, was striding toward them, phone to his ear.

"Drew." Jesse pointed at the intersection. "I saw that Mercury outside Evan's house. It went after her."

Farelli nodded at the cop, pulling out an ID. "It's okay, Officer."

The cop jerked his thumb at Jesse. "You know this guy?"

"Yes." Farelli squeezed his pudge between two patrol cars, catching the cop's mistrust. He nodded to his phone call. "Yes, Nicholas. Right away." He hung up. His expression was harsh. "Let's get away from this crowd."

Jesse felt completely cold. Farelli put a hand on his shoulder. He shrugged it off.

"Stop it. Drew, is that her?"

"No, it's not."

Relief lit his vision like a magnesium flare. He nodded and rubbed his knuckles across his forehead, momentarily mute.

"Evan's not here," Farelli said. "She drove off with the shooter."

He looked up. "What?"

"You saw that car chase after her? Why did it do that?"

"What do you mean, drove off with the shooter?"

Farelli's cocker spaniel face was bright red. "The driver of that car was shot in the head. Your fiancée not only witnessed it, she got in the killer's vehicle and drove away with him afterward."

He blinked. Hell. Tim North.

"There's more. SBPD found something in the victim's car." He walked around the front of the patrol car with Jesse following, and called to a member of the forensics team. "Higgins. Got that jacket?"

The forensic tech nodded and held up a sealed plastic evidence bag. Inside was a blue windbreaker with big letters printed on the back: ICE.

"Know what that means?" Farelli said.

He knew, but there had to be an explanation.

Yeah. Tim North was a stone killer. Phil Delaney had lived a black life that led to this. He himself was too late. And Evan was screwed.

Farelli crossed his arms. "Till now I thought Evan was

just being loyal to her dad. I gave her the benefit of the doubt because I thought you were a straight shooter. That'll teach me."

"Drew, Evan's in danger. We have to find her before she gets hurt."

Farelli shook his head. "People saw her get in the car, voluntarily, and flee the scene of a murder."

The street was wet, gleaming with sunlight. From this angle he could see the victim's legs. Dirty jeans and heavy boots, splayed on the road. Meat puppet. He looked away.

"That's a federal agent over there. One of us." Farelli pressed his lips together, fighting emotion. "This one we take to the wall. Murder and unlawful flight to avoid prosecution. The DA's applying for a warrant. In about half an hour Evan is going to be a fugitive."

"Farelli, that's ludicrous."

"This won't stay local, either. That was Nicholas Gray on the phone. The U.S. Attorney's office will seek to charge her with murdering an officer of the United States government. You think you've seen my boss on the warpath, you have no idea."

"Drew—"

"Find Evan." Farelli turned and walked away. "This afternoon. She turns herself in or she's toast."

Jumping lanes on the 405, I hopscotched through afternoon traffic heading up the hill through the Valley, nearing Century City but not nearly fast enough. Tim coughed. Barely audible, he muttered, "Bloody hell." His skin was the color of candle wax and sweat was beading on his forehead. He had the phone to his ear again, his fifth call since we left Santa Barbara. He was arranging for someone to get him medical treatment, out of the spotlight.

He hung up again and dropped his hand to his lap. The Percodan he had taken from his first-aid kit seemed to have soothed his nerves but not his pain.

"Time to talk about when we get there," he said.

"I go in, get the file, we call Rio."

I glanced at his phone. He was holding it tightly, keeping the line open for his contact to phone in. I was itching to grab it. The sun, smearing through hazy air, popped against the sea of vehicles slurring along the freeway. The SUV rumbled up the Sepulveda Pass out of the Valley.

"If things go wrong"—he grabbed a breath, pain pricking his features—"there's five thousand dollars cash stashed in the spare tire. You take it."

"Why?"

"If you have to run."

I wrung my hands on the wheel, foot heavy on the accelerator.

"And dump Davies's phone. Use pay phones, or get some new mobiles if you have time. Pay-as-you-go, and use top-up cards."

He shifted in his seat. A coppery smell reached me, the odor of blood.

"When you get out of this car, trust nobody. And I mean nobody. Rio has more thugs like Boyd Davies. Presume she'll try to track you and get the information from you, violently if necessary."

I nodded, my stomach tightening. "Rio's son is in on this too. That must have been him in the black designer outfit."

"Christian. Heir to the family empire."

"When I spoke to Rio it sounded like she has a foreign accent."

"She's not American, but she operates here now."

"What do you know about them?" I said.

"What I've told you. I've never met them. Riverbend happened before Jax and I met."

"What's in the file?"

"I don't know. Just that the operation ended disastrously. And that your father is the one who got Jax involved in it."

Traffic flowed sluggishly through the afternoon sun. We needed to go faster.

"I'm not dumping Davies's phone yet," I said. "That photo is the only evidence we have that Dad has been kidnapped. And I want to get a look at his phone book and call records."

"Don't get caught with it on you."

"I won't. But I need to do something right now." My face was heating; he wasn't going to like it. "I'm calling Jesse. Give me your phone."

He shook his head.

"You know how you felt when you realized you couldn't get hold of your wife?" I said. "That's how Jesse's feeling right now. I have to let him know I'm all right. And if I can't trust anybody once I get out of this car, I need a lifeline back home. Especially if things go wrong."

He sliced a look my way, but handed it over.

Jesse slammed through the door into the foyer at Sanchez Marks. He needed to talk to Lavonne. They had to form an assault plan, deal with the cops and the U.S. Attorney's threats. And find out what the hell was actually going on.

"Jess."

He glanced over his shoulder, past the big window that looked down onto the street, at the sofas in the reception area. "P.J."

His brother stood up, rubbing his palms against his legs as though wiping off sweat. "Got a minute?"

Not even a second. He opened his mouth and closed it again. P.J.'s face was earnest, searching him for signs of annoyance.

"Sure, a minute. Come on."

P.J. jogged to catch up. He jammed his hands in the pockets of his jeans, seemed to hunch into his shirt. Along the hall people walked past, staring. Jesse knew it wasn't because he and P.J. looked alike, or because his colleagues were pleased to see his brother.

He paused at Lavonne's corner office and rapped on the

door. When she called, "It's open," he pushed on it. From her desk Lavonne peered at him over her half-glasses.

"You missed the colloquium. I presume there's a reason," she said.

"We've got a cyclone."

She caught sight of P.J. and raised an eyebrow.

Jesse shook his head. "Something else."

Her riot of black curls was falling in her face. "I'll be here."

In his office, he closed the door. P.J. walked over and gazed out the window.

"Sorry, I'm pressed for time. Is something wrong?"

P.J. laughed humorlessly. "Didn't occur to you I came by to take you out to lunch, huh?"

"Did you?"

Long, nervous glance. "No." He wandered to the desk and picked up a pencil. "I was, ah . . ."

Jesse spread his hands. "P.J., what?"

He poked the pencil into the desktop blotter. "I thought maybe I'd apply for a job."

"Oh. Yeah, well, good. Glad to hear it. Where?"

He poked the blotter again. "Here."

Jesse felt his hands go cold.

"I thought you might put in a word for me."

With the firm? Last time he got P.J. a job, it was with one of the firm's major clients. That ended with the client ruined and P.J. in jail. Was he serious?

P.J. gave him a sidelong glance. "Evan works here."

"Evan does freelance work for us, and . . ."

Forget it, he thought. Mentioning Evan was politics, a guilt trip, a tomato thrown in his face. A masterstroke.

"It doesn't have to be anything big," P.J. said. "I can make coffee. Deliver the mail. Courier things to the courthouse; I don't know. But I want to get back on my feet."

Jesse pinched the bridge of his nose.

"Part-time. Anything. Come on, dude, I'm trying here."

Couriering things to the courthouse—as if the firm

would let him touch, or even see, contracts, confidential attorney–client communications . . .

P.J. dropped the pencil and headed for the door. "Never mind. I don't want to put you on the spot."

"No, wait." Jesse caught his arm. "Look, you got me at a bad time."

P.J. tensed under his grasp, skittish. Jesse let go.

"Just . . . let me think about it. I need to check some things out."

P.J. gave him a look, hard and wary, that caused Jesse's breath to catch. Before he went to jail P.J. couldn't possibly have worn that expression.

Then he recovered, breaking into a big-kid grin. "Really?"

"No promises."

"Sure. Tomorrow?"

"No, that's too soon."

"But maybe I could help prep people for trials. You know, you practice grilling a witness and I'd be the jury, telling you how it played."

Trial prep. Jesse felt cold sweat forming.

"Fine; I'll wait. But I'm ready for anything," P.J. said.

With a knock, the door swung open. Lavonne jerked a thumb over her shoulder.

"My office. Right now."

She was gone by the time he turned to his brother. "Sorry."

"No, you're busy. Just let me know. And . . ." He looked at the floor before finding the word. "Thanks."

Lavonne was pacing behind the desk, her face brooding. Motioning for him to shut the door, she nodded at her speakerphone and said loudly, "Jesse Blackburn is joining us, Nicholas."

He managed not to flinch. Nicholas Gray's voice echoed from the speaker.

"This is more than an appalling coincidence. This is an outrage."

Jesse kept his voice level. "Nicholas, yes. Evan's in danger. We need the police to help get her home safely."

"Save the ham for the company picnic, Blackburn. A federal agent was executed in the middle of a city street, and your girlfriend's in on it."

Lavonne grabbed a pen and scrawled on a legal pad, holding it up for him to see: *Cyclone? No—blindsided.*

Gray said, "Phil Delaney is on the run and now so is his daughter. And Sanchez Marks is in the middle of it."

He felt Lavonne's eyes on him, hot. He took the legal pad and wrote, *Phil D—not car crash. Ambush.*

Lavonne stared at the legal pad. "How do you know that?"

"What?" Gray said.

"Nothing." She stabbed a finger at the pad. Jesse scribbled, *Can't tell cops yet.*

"Are you paying attention?" Gray said. "I'm not playing games. You need to give up Phil Delaney."

"We can't," Jesse said. "We don't know where he is, and we're not in contact with him."

"Is that so?" Gray said. "We've obtained Delaney's cell phone records. He phoned you last night at nine forty-six p.m."

Lavonne's head came around, slowly.

The door opened with a knock, and a secretary came in. "Line two. It's Evan."

Jesse's head swung up. Lavonne dived for the phone.

Gray's voice sharpened. "What's that? What did I hear?"

Lavonne punched buttons, said into the phone, "Hang on," and hurried out the door to take the call at the secretary's desk.

"I heard that," Gray said.

Jesse stared at the door, but Lavonne had closed it. "Nicholas, I'm going to have to get back to you."

"Don't brush me off. I don't think for a second that she slipped away on her own. You know where she and her father are."

"Stuff the conspiracy theories back down the hatch. You're out of line."

"I'm out of line? You were a crime victim. You should be grateful that men like Boyd Davies are out there protecting you."

"Stop right there, Nicholas."

"But you're willing to let his killer get away. Screw the cops, huh? Is that because of your brother?"

Colder now, Jesse said nothing.

"I see that a plea bargain let him do county time. He slid right out from under what could have been a long prison sentence. Did you help him with that?" His voice went smooth. "I wonder whether federal charges were ever fully investigated. Mail fraud, for instance."

He fought to keep his voice even. "Do not even think of leaning on my brother."

"I'm doing no such thing. That's a paranoid accusation."

Jesse stared at the phone. "If you go after him I will take you apart."

A long, electric silence filled the room. When Gray spoke again, he sounded pleased.

"Hear that noise, Blackburn? That's the sound of your career being flushed down the toilet."

8

I kept the cell phone to my ear. "Lavonne, I'm alive, I'm uninjured, and I had nothing to do with that man's death."

"Where are you?"

"Off the grid." She wouldn't like hearing that, but I was beyond letting her intimidate me. "Please put Jesse on the phone."

Traffic on Santa Monica Boulevard was loud and flashy. In the distance the Hollywood hills rose green through the smog. Ahead of us, the skyscrapers of Century City reflected the late-afternoon sun. I drove toward them, my stomach knotting, desperate to hear his voice. Finally the phone clattered.

"Evan? For chrissake—"

"I'm in one piece. Jesse, listen to me for a minute."

"What's North doing to you?"

"Thirty seconds, Blackburn. Be quiet and let me talk."

He shut up. I talked, phone scrunched between my ear and my shoulder, running him through it while I drove with one hand and fired up Boyd Davies's cell with the other.

"I'm sending you a photo." I forwarded the image of my father.

"Do you know who the dead man was? You're in trouble up to your eyeballs."

"I know this is—"

"Your thirty seconds are up. Every law enforcement

agency in Southern California is going to be gunning for you by the end of the day. You need to come in."

"Not yet."

"Yes, right now. You . . ." His voice trailed off. "Oh, man."

"You got the photo?"

"Jesus. Evan, I'm sorry."

"Jesse, I have one chance to get Dad back. If I'm under arrest, I can't do that."

The sky was blue behind the scrim of smog, the sun reflecting off the windshields of vehicles coming toward us. A police car approached and drove past. I glanced in the wing mirror and saw his brake lights come on.

"Evan, listen carefully. Your dad called me last night."

I nearly hit the car in the next lane. "What?"

"Right before the kidnappers grabbed him. He left a very specific message saying to keep you clear of this."

I clutched the wheel, emotion welling up. Dad had used his final moments of freedom trying to protect me. "If I stay clear, he has no chance."

"Do you have Jax and Tim's dossiers?" Jesse said.

"Yes."

"You have to stop what you're doing and bring them to me. Asap."

"The dossiers?" In the mirror I saw the cop make a U-turn and fall in four cars behind me. "Dad wants me to give them to you?"

"He told me to destroy them."

"What? Why?"

The cop was keeping pace with us. Jesse didn't reply.

"If Dad was afraid that classified material will be exposed, then . . ." I glanced at Tim. He didn't plan simply to hand over the information. He planned to kill the kidnappers, if he still had any blood in his veins. "I don't think that will happen."

"That's not it. Your dad said if I didn't destroy the dossiers you'd become part of the kill chain. If the Sangers get the information they'll come after your family."

"They're already coming after us. Dad, now me—what if the next person they go after is Luke?" I didn't know how far they'd go to put us under duress, but the thought of them hurting my little nephew gave me chest pain. "The only way to prevent that is to get this Riverbend file and use it to free Dad."

"Delaney, will you pay attention to me? Phil said I had to get those papers last night or it would be too late."

I felt ill. "It is too late. They've got him."

"That's not what he was afraid of."

"Then what exactly did he mean?" Something wasn't firing on all cylinders here. "Jesse, if you know something I don't, you need to tell me."

He exhaled but didn't answer. Was he holding something back, something concrete that could help me?

"What is it?" I said.

"Your dad, he . . . Damn."

"Things have changed. When Dad told you to stop me, he was still free. He didn't know what was going to happen next. Now all bets are off."

In my ear I heard a beep, the sound of a call coming in. It had to be Tim's contact. He gestured for the phone.

"Jesse, I have to go."

"Evan, don't. Don't. Your dad wanted to protect your family, wanted me to keep you out of this."

"Of course Dad wanted to keep me out of this. *I* wanted to keep me out of this. But now I'm in it, and Dad's depending on me."

"Ev, you're making a mistake."

"I know you're trying to protect me, but this isn't about me. It's about Dad."

The call beeped again. Tim grabbed the phone from my fingers.

"Sorry, mate." He clicked to his call. "Yeah."

Stomach churning, I looked in the rearview mirror. The cop was still there.

*   *   *

"Damn it. Damn."

Jesse slammed down the phone. Out in the hall, two paralegals stopped talking and turned their heads. Lavonne bustled in.

"Control your volume. The clients think we've just lost a big case."

"Evan doesn't know what's really going on," he said.

"But you do, and you're going to tell me. Now."

"Phil's message. He swore me to confidentiality about what the people who ambushed him are really after." He shut the door. "It's not money. It's worse."

The LAPD car cruised along behind me. In the mirror I saw the officer, dark blue shirt tight on his shoulders, hair cropped, sunglasses obscuring his eyes.

"Did somebody see us switch cars back in Santa Barbara?" I said.

"Possible."

The boulevard clicked by, strip malls and squat apartment buildings. The skyscraper canyon of Century City rose ahead. Dammit, why wouldn't Jesse listen to me? Didn't he get it? Arriving at the street I wanted, I signaled and turned onto Century Park East. Again I checked the mirror.

"He's following." The cop had his radio transmitter to his face. "He's calling in the license plate."

Tim watched in the wing mirror. "A plaza runs behind these office towers. Carry on past eighteen twenty-one and go into an underground parking garage. I'll take over the wheel."

"And I'll double back through the plaza?"

"We'll rendezvous in forty-five minutes. Century Plaza Hotel."

I cruised past 1821, a black tower soaring thirty stories high, and turned in to the garage beneath another skyscraper. I squealed down the ramp and parked. In the SUV's spare tire I found the hidden cash. The packet of pristine hundred-dollar bills weighed no more than a flimsy newsmagazine. Cradling his side, Tim edged into the driver's seat.

I went to his door. "Forty-five minutes."

"If you don't show, I won't wait."

I took the stairs two at a time and came out into a lobby bouncing with sunshine, marble, and conversation. The cop had parked at the curb outside and was walking toward the entrance. I strode in the opposite direction, out into the plaza behind the building. Eyes front. After a hundred yards I shoved through the door into another gleaming lobby and finally looked back. No cop, but he was looking for me.

I found a building directory. The list ran to fifty names. I pushed a hand through my hair, repeating the cryptic line from Jax's letter. *I tried to rise, baby, to ride it right to the top.*

Alliance Mortgage. Westside Ventures. Robinson & Niebuhr LLP.

Crescendo Ltd. Eighteenth floor.

The elevator doors slid open to a lobby with seductive lighting and a shining parquet floor. I double-checked the floor number: eighteen. Whatever I thought a private bank would look like, this wasn't it.

This wasn't a bank at all. Behind the rosewood desk, there was just a receptionist with a headset mike. She was about fifty, wearing a long linen dress and a turquoise turban, tied African-style. Unlike the women who fronted other Los Angeles foyers, she wasn't chewing gum or filing her nails. Or handing me her demo recording in hopes that I was a record producer.

Gospel music was playing. Call-and-response, four-part harmony, with a funk band backing a choir singing heavy-duty, go-down-Moses-type lyrics. This most definitely wasn't a law firm.

The receptionist glanced at me with polite interest, and I

became aware of my rumpled shirt and worn running shoes. In light of the music, she looked like a church secretary for a serious Baptist congregation, warm and formidable.

"May I help you?"

Crossing to the desk, I set the red key in front of her. I could think of nothing else to do. If she asked me to sign in to access the safe-deposit box, I was in trouble. The dossiers had contained a couple of examples of Jax's spiky autograph, but I doubted I could copy it. Maybe. Perhaps if I pretended that I had a broken hand, or a neurological condition.

If this redoubtable church lady asked me for identification, or if Jax had set up the account under an alias, I was hosed.

She took the key, saw the number etched on it, and made a phone call. "There's a woman here with a key. Three fifty-seven. Will you check?" She glanced up. "Just a moment."

Her expression was amiable, and she seemed unperturbed that a gal in grubby duds had walked into this elegant lobby. However, I wondered exactly how good I was going to be at convincing her that I belonged here. This lady was African-American. So was Jax. Gospel music was playing. If there was a trend here, I would have a hell of a time catching up with it.

Her gaze remained on my face, and I realized that I hadn't spoken. I didn't want to be any more memorable than I already was. *Yes, Officer, she's here. Unfashionable white woman, completely mute. Has a suspicious twitch in her writing hand.*

Trying to sound nonchalant, I said, "Great music. What is it?"

"Sounds of Blackness."

"Right." I smiled, feeling idiotic. What was taking so long?

Into her mike she said, "Okay, I'll tell her." She looked up. "It's in the vault, not the archive. Kani will escort you there."

Vault? On the eighteenth floor of a building? "Thank you."

A moment later a young woman opened a frosted-glass door in the far wall. She was no bigger than a leaf, wearing a bandanna tied around her chest as a top and hip-huggers so tight on her frame the size had to be somewhere below zero. Probably at "Barbie." Spiky hair, horn-rimmed glasses, sparkly flip-flops. East Asian face. She looked like an anime drawing given life.

She stuck a pencil behind her ear. "Follow me?"

Thanking the receptionist, I followed her through the door.

Abruptly we departed Gospel Land and entered the Matrix, sound track by the Red Hot Chili Peppers. We were in a music archive. On metal shelves all around us, floor to ceiling, were reel-to-reel tapes, labeled with the artist's name, album title, and date of recording. The shelves ran in narrow rows to the windows. Around us scampered other manga characters, pierced and colorfully tattooed, looking eager and purposeful. Some were wearing headphones and handling recording consoles, others working at computers with cinema displays. Doing what, I wasn't sure.

"Can I ask you something?" Trying to think of an oblique way to phrase it, I gestured across the room. "About your storage practices."

Manga Barbie followed my gaze. "The windows?"

"For starters."

"Tempered polarized glass, absorbs full-spectrum UV, reduces the possibility of degradation. Of course, all these masters are stored here temporarily, until we can transfer them to digital media."

"I see." Sensing that she was watching for my approval, I declined to give it. "What about heat and corrosion?"

"We're temperature-controlled, 'round the clock. The canisters are acetone-free."

"Good." I kept my expression flat. "I guess my basic question is about overall security."

"Oh." She tilted her head, puzzled. "If you're worried about theft, it isn't really a problem. Most of our work is rescuing or remastering old recordings. I mean, they're primarily out of copyright. With compilations and spoken-word recordings, piracy isn't a big issue. Really delicate or rare stuff, like live performances by famous jazz artists—that's why we have the vault."

"Naturally."

I thought I got it: This outfit archived luxury and specialty items, things that rich investors or well-endowed museums would pay a lot for—which explained why it was here in a swanky skyscraper instead of an industrial building in the burbs.

"And as far as the vault—I guess you don't worry about robbers jackhammering through the floor above to gain access," I said.

"I see your point. But we don't hold cash or bullion. It's a fire vault. Metal floor with seismic reinforcement. Protects against flame, flood, or earthquake." She looked at me askance. "Wasn't all this explained when you signed up for archiving services?"

"I didn't take a tour." I kept the suspicious face, relying on attitude. "When you store something contentious you want to make sure it's properly protected."

"Contentious?"

"Disputed. That's part of your service. Right?"

"The escrow service, you mean?"

"As it was explained to me, you'll hold things that are contested in inheritance or ownership disputes. . . ."

"Yeah. Or things that might be used as evidence in a court case. So we're careful to maintain chain-of-custody procedures."

"Good."

We reached the vault. Manga Barbie put herself between me and the door. "We typically provide vault services to law firms and auction houses. And excuse me, but if that's your key, how come you don't know squat about Crescendo?"

So much for bluffing. I didn't have time to try anything else.

"Because it's not my key."

Her eyebrows shot up behind her horn-rims. "What?"

"The box is a friend's. I'm here at their behest."

"This is irregular. How come your friend isn't here?"

"I appreciate your caution, but I presume that the services Crescendo provides its clients include discretion. And privacy."

She blushed. After looking at the floor for a moment, she pulled the door wide.

Lockboxes filled the vault. I handed over the key and she unlocked box 357, slid it out, and handed it to me. It was the size of a manuscript container. I set it on a table in the corner.

"Call when you're finished," she said, and left me alone.

Palms sweating, I sat down and opened the box.

9

Sitting in the vault staring at Jax's safe-deposit box, I told myself to stay cool. Outside in the music archive, Manga Barbie stood drinking a Starbucks coffee. "Give it Away" was cranking on the sound system. Resting in front of me was a fat manila envelope. Inside it was the ticket to my father's freedom.

I tore the envelope open and pulled out a heavy paperback book.

I stared at the stone graveyard statue on the cover, baffled. She had to be kidding.

Midnight in the Garden of Good and Evil.

The book was dog-eared, the spine cracked, the cover held closed by thick rubber bands. I peered in the envelope. Nothing else was inside.

I pulled off the rubber bands and opened the book. Title page, table of contents: "Destination Unknown," "Gunplay," "And the Angels Sing" ... No note, no remarks scribbled in the margins, no letters highlighted. If a code lay hidden in this four-hundred-page Southern gothic tale, I was in trouble. Jax had a degree in linguistics. I figured that meant she was more adept than I at manipulating language. And I earn my living manipulating language. I picked up the book and fanned the pages.

Oh.

There in chapter seventeen was a chunk of hollowed-out pages. Just big enough to hide the tiny computer flash drive.

I tipped it into my palm. Smaller than a stick of gum, according to the marking on the silver case it had eight gigs of memory. That was plenty to contain DVD-quality video. It was strung on a chain, together with a religious medallion. The sight of the Madonna and child was as disconcerting as anything. I pulled my computer from my backpack. Manga Barbie, now talking on the phone, shot a glance my way.

A hollowed-out book; I half smiled. Jax was old-school.

Or a joker. Chapter seventeen: "A Hole in the Floor." My computer fired up.

Lavonne paced. "The kill chain."

"It's the target cycle. Find, track, target, and kill," Jesse said.

She glowered out the window. "And he meant—"

"Nothing good."

Her expression said, *No kidding.* "Keeping Evan clear is no longer an option."

"So I have to stop her."

His tone was measured, but she raised her hands, trying to slow him down. "You can't tell her."

"If I do, I can get her to—"

"No. This information is privileged. You cannot disclose it. Period."

He raked his hands through his hair. "Then I have to get her off the street somehow, because I don't know if I can reach her again."

"This is a raw, gut reaction. Aside from whether you can actually stop Evan, do you—"

"Nobody can do it but me. Not and keep Phil's message confidential."

She shook her head. "You're setting yourself up for disaster. You have a huge potential conflict of interest."

"Phil spent his final seconds of freedom sending me this message. No way am I going to sit here pondering the niceties of conflict-of-interest law." He spread his hands flat on her desk. "He was clear. Do this to protect his family."

"He's your client, not your commanding officer. You don't take orders from him."

"It's not an order. It's a call to action."

She held his gaze.

"I know Evan's trying to save her dad, but she doesn't understand how bad things are," he said. "I have to stop her from getting this information."

She took off her glasses and tossed them on her desk. Rubbing her eyes, she said, "I know."

Gratitude and adrenaline hit him all at once. "What do you want me to do about Nicholas Gray?"

"Let me make the next move." Her expression soured. "Threatening your brother will not stand."

Lavonne called herself a tough little broad from Philly, but tough and righteous was the crux of it. She would go to the mat for Jesse. He nodded his thanks.

"Get out of here," she said.

My computer booted. With luck I could not only examine the information on the flash drive; I could copy it and even forward it—to Sanchez Marks, and to Rio Sanger. I was willing to bet that Crescendo had a wireless network. I wouldn't have to spend time driving someplace to deliver it. One click and I could get to Dad.

My screen came up. I jacked the flash drive into the computer. The drive lit red, flickering on and off.

And in less time than it took to inhale, the red light vanished and my screen went black.

Jet black. No cursor. Nothing at all, except . . . at the top left corner of the screen, in tiny white machine-script letters, a single word.

*Root_*

This couldn't be good. I ran my hand over the track pad. I hit *escape*. I hit *return*. I tried to quit. Nothing happened.

Damn. Computers aren't my métier. They're great for

online research and for finding high-resolution photos of
the U.S. men's Olympic swim team, but when they go hay-
wire I'm useless. Fix one? I stood a better chance of landing the space shuttle. I smacked the side of the monitor
with my hand.

*Root_*

Jax, what did I do? What do I do now?

Peering out the door, I waved to Manga Barbie. "Kani?"

She looked up from her phone call. "Done?"

"No, computer question. What do you do"—when
you've totally screwed yourself?—"when your screen goes
black and you get the message 'Root'?"

Looking nonplussed, she adjusted her glasses and called
the question to a colleague across the room. "Try typing
'Logout.' "

"Thanks." I did it.

For a moment the screen stayed black. Then text
bloomed, the tiny white machine letters multiplying in long
strings of script, filling the screen and starting to scroll. I
blinked, fingers hovering above the keyboard. The letters
multiplied into words and nonsensical verb strings, scroll-
ing faster, as if they were alphabet bacteria running amok.

Abruptly, the letter train stopped running. Below the
profusion of text, at the bottom of the screen a single word
winked at me.

*Loading_*

I held my breath. The machine script vanished and on
the screen a video faded in. Staring straight at me was my
not-friend Jakarta Rivera.

"If you're watching this, then you're after the Riverbend
records."

She spoke with an arctic calm that sent a needle climbing my spine. Manga Barbie looked my way, curious. I
grabbed some headphones from my backpack and plugged
them into the computer so she couldn't overhear. Jax's
voice came in, blade-smooth.

"In that case you'd better be damned sure these records

are what you want, because from this point, it's the whole shebang."

She was sitting in a teak-paneled room with amber light flowing from the sconces in the wall behind her. Hands folded on the desk in front of her. Pearls on her ears and at her throat, dressed as if for a diplomatic negotiation in a severe black suit with a daring neckline. Feline self-assurance. Heat in her eyes so primal, it approached blood-lust. The effect was Condi Rice meets *Kill Bill.*

"If you want to stop now, eject the flash drive," she said. "You have ten seconds to consider it. After that, you're in."

Slowly I breathed. Riverbend: I'd heard the word repeatedly. From Tim North. And from the slutty voice on a dead man's cell phone. I was in.

Jax said, "All right. You want it, you'll get it. The whole shooting match."

Her expression hadn't changed, but her tone seemed tinged with regret. It occurred to me that she didn't know it was me watching this video.

"When I went to Colombia twelve years ago, I didn't expect it to be my last federally funded assignment. Even if I was a NOC, out there on my own."

She pronounced it *knock*—nonofficial cover, a covert operative posted abroad without any diplomatic protection. The needle pricked its way along my spine.

"And for so many months the mission went well. Gathering information, cultivating assets. Pure humint, highly valuable. I was damned good. The film footage and still photos back me up on that. Doing my part in the war on drugs, right up to the moment it turned into a tactical cluster fuck."

Her face remained glacial. "You're going to see all the footage. But you have to work for it."

I sat forward.

"As soon as you typed 'Logout,' the flash drive loaded a program into your hard drive. When the ten-second mark passed, it activated."

Uh-oh.

"Right now, it's building the program it needs to decrypt and display the Riverbend file. However, the flash drive has only part of the information you need to do that." She refolded her hands. "There's more, and you have to go get it."

No. I didn't want to go anywhere else. I wanted this to be over, now. Before Dad died of dehydration, before the cops figured out that I'd taken the elevator up here and came storming in to arrest me.

"Jax, don't do this."

"A second flash drive will supply another chunk of source code. But you have to get it in time, or everything you've just downloaded will be corrupted. You won't be able to reload it. Once this program launched, the flash drive attached to your computer was wiped and overwritten. Every bit of information it contained is now on your machine. It can't be copied. It can't be attached and forwarded to somebody else."

"Dammit."

The heat in her eyes was unnerving. *The whole shooting match.*

"And it can't stand on its own. You must get the next portion of source code or everything on your computer will be erased."

"No. Jax—no."

"I told you. In all the way."

The machine script that had infested my screen was not lingual bacteria. It was a virus. And it was demanding, *Feed me.*

"The program is still building. The first chunk of footage will be available from this download in twelve hours. Get ready for Riovision."

Twelve hours, not good.

"And before you try to hack this—don't. You load the next section of code or you'll be frosted out. You have to get all the flash drives in the right order, under the deadline. You can't crack the program. Don't try it. You don't have time."

I leaned on my elbows, clawing my fingers into my hair. Get them *all*?

"So saddle up. You want to know where you're going?"

"Don't screw with me any more than you already are," I said.

"Look at the back cover of the paperback."

I flipped it over.

"Bottom left, there's a photo credit."

My eyes ran down the page. *Cover photograph: Bonaventure Cemetery, Savannah.*

"No," I said. "No way. Don't send me three thousand miles across the country—"

"Hit the *escape* key and type those words in. You'll get the location."

I did. My fingers felt numb.

> Ajahn Niram
> 2 Sanamchai Road
> Bangkok 10700
> Thailand

"Take the book with you. Hang onto the medallion of *La Virgen*. You'll need her."

On the screen a new window appeared. It was a timer and it was running down: 29:59.00, 29:58.59.

Jax's voice went flat. "Hit the road, Jack."

10

Jamming everything into my backpack, I bolted out of the vault. I felt as though I were breaking out in a rash. Thirty hours to get a computer flash drive in Bangkok. Was Jax crazy?

I wanted to call somebody on the ground there, tell them to get this damned flash drive and FedEx it to me. But who was I kidding? I knew nobody in Southeast Asia. I had to go.

Thirty hours. In the background, the music segued to "Can't Stop." I glared at the speakers.

The thought of going halfway around the world gave me vertigo. I'd never been to the Far East. For all I knew, west of Hawaii the earth ended, and everything I'd been told of this continent called Asia had been invented from whole cloth by jokers at *National Geographic* magazine. What the hell did I know about Thailand? Not a word of the language. Not a clue whether Bangkok was a safe place for an American woman to travel alone. Nothing. Watching *The King and I* six times didn't count as a mission briefing.

By the windows the Barbies and Kens were gathered, peering down. One pointed, and another stood on her toes for a better view. Passing by, I glanced out. The psychic rash reached my hair and fingertips.

Two police cars were parked farther down the block. A cop was walking up the sidewalk in this direction.

At the phone, Manga Barbie looked up sharply. "All set?"

I backed away from the window and hurried for the exit. "Yes. Thanks for your time."

On the way through the lobby, the church lady smiled from beneath her turquoise headdress and wished me a blessed day. "I'll Fly Away" was playing.

Easier said than done. Riding the elevator down, I felt the weight of my infected computer in my backpack. The spent flash drive hung along with the religious medallion on the chain around my neck. The Virgin Mary, bearing the Christ child: It was an image that beamed from plaster statues in ten thousand parish churches. What it had to do with Jakarta Rivera, patron saint of the devious, I couldn't fathom. I checked the time: thirty minutes to the rendezvous with Tim.

The rest of my family had been to Thailand—my brother on R & R from carrier duty, my mother when she had worked as a flight attendant. And Dad, as the U.S. Attorney was wont to remind me. That thought had been catching in the back of my mind for the past few minutes. Dad had keepsakes from his trips there during his navy days. I recalled photos of him with service buddies, all with crew cuts and beers, smiling against a backdrop of coconut palms. A ceramic Buddha had occupied a place of affection on an end table in our living room. He was a jolly little guy. When Dad would come home at the end of the workday he unloaded his wallet and coins from his pockets next to it. I remember asking about the Buddha when I was little.

"He's Thai," Dad said. "From Siam. You rub his belly for good luck."

Siam. As a child I had regarded it as so exotic it was almost magical.

All children grow up to comprehend that their parents aren't who they think they are. That's Freud for Dummies. But now I wondered if R & R on a white-sand beach was Dad's only experience of Thailand. How many times had he been back, and what had he done there?

The elevator reached the ground floor. The doors

opened to clacking heels and echoing conversation. Five feet into the lobby, I heard the scritch of a two-way radio. Fighting near-irresistible impulse, I kept my pace even. I cut my eyes left. Two LAPD officers stood talking to a security guard. I heard "woman" and "CCTV footage" and my blood pressure jumped. Don't run. I focused on the far door and strode straight toward it. I walked out into the sunlight, one hand clutching the strap of my backpack, eyes on the path through the plaza gardens. I had made it. Now all I had was twenty-nine minutes to get through Century City and meet Tim at the Century Plaza Hotel.

Kani scratched her head with the tip of her pencil and wandered to the window to observe the commotion outside. LAPD cars were bunched in the street below. She got a funny feeling, intuition creeping up on her. It calmed her stomach.

She'd done the right thing; she felt sure of it now. This wasn't coincidence.

Three fifty-seven was a red-key box. That meant there were special instructions on file. When she checked, the protocol was specific: Should the box be accessed, Crescendo was to notify a voice mail number back east. Made her feel like a narc, but now her conscience was eased. She had followed procedure. Something hinky was going on with box 357, but the people who got the message would deal with the problem.

Bliss scratched her cheek and stared out the window of the Porsche at Century City. The woman had to be nearby. Middle-class, white, gotta be soft and slow to react—the hole who took Boyd's cell phone was around here someplace.

She pulled to the curb on Little Santa Monica and watched the red dot on the screen of her handheld. The tracker program was true to within fifty yards. The phone was there in the maze of skyscrapers.

She played her fingers over the studs in her ear. Things

had gone badly with Boyd. She took her gun from the glove compartment and set it on her lap.

Her cell rang and Christian said, "Give me the location."

"You'll be two hours. I'm here now."

"You sure this thing will work?" he said.

"I programmed the phone to broadcast a beacon, so unless they smash it, we're good."

Boyd never knew she had set up the tracker. After thirty seconds of banging her doggy-style, he had to go take a long piss in the woods, and didn't notice her slipping the phone from his jacket on the backseat of the car.

"If she's got the Riverbend file, get it, Bliss. I've waited too long to mess around waiting for her to deliver a ransom. Everything got screwed up with Boyd. I can't have anything else go wrong."

"Lot of cops buzzing around here."

"This has to stay off the radar," he said. "Do it quiet and clean. No gunfire, no blood."

"I'll do what I have to do."

His voice rose. "This isn't you taking off the top of your old man's head with a farm hoe in the barn back home; this is Century City. Gunfire will bring the LAPD down on you like rain. If they get the file, I'm dead. Hurt her some other way."

"You always throw the hoe thing in my face."

"Do it right."

He hung up. She scratched at the scab on her arm, looking out the window at the skyscrapers and a plaza and a pedestrian bridge that crossed the avenue, linking up with the shopping center. Fine, she'd do it his way. She put on her shades and got out. Show yourself, hole.

I crossed the plaza and climbed the stairs to the pedestrian bridge that soared across Century Park West, heading for the rendezvous. The hotel was on Avenue of the Stars, beyond a rank of skyscrapers and the chic Century City Shopping Center. Traffic coursed below, a shiny river of noise. Men walked past, bankers with their ties batting in the breeze. The back of my head was itching, but I didn't dare look back. If I did that, I might as well take out an ad in *On the Lam* magazine.

I had to get myself organized. I couldn't show up at LAX like this. Right now I was a walking checklist of security warning signs. Ticket to Thailand? Bought on the spot? No luggage? I could already hear the snap of the guard's latex glove as she told me to bend over and enjoy the cavity search. I needed a change of clothes and travel gear, but I had to do it quickly.

I jogged down the steps on the far side of the bridge and cut between office towers to the shopping center. I dared to look behind me. No cops.

I found a Starbucks with wi-fi. The down-ticker was running in the corner of the screen: 29:53.41. Aside from that, the computer was now operating normally. I logged on to a travel site, typed in, *LAX-Bangkok,* and a lump of clay formed in my stomach. The shortest journey time was sixteen hours.

For a moment I stared at the screen. The ticket price was ghastly, but money didn't concern me. Because my mother worked for a major international airline, I got the world's greatest perk: I flew virtually free, worldwide. Money wasn't the problem. Covering my tracks was.

I considered phoning Mom, but quelled the thought. A warrant was sooner or later going to be issued for my arrest, and asking her to book me a flight would expose her to charges of aiding my escape. More to the point, if I told her I was doing this for Dad she would likely refuse my request, tell me to haul my keister home, and go after the file herself. My parents' divorce was as combustible as their marriage had been. She'd probably rescue him, hold it over his head, welcome him passionately, and then strangle him for getting kidnapped in the first place. No, I had to keep Angie Delaney out of this.

Crossing my fingers, I called the airline's family reservation number and booked a round-trip ticket on a flight leaving late that evening. I said I'd pay cash at the airport for the ticket tax. I hoped that this would keep me out of the security system at least until takeoff. I wasn't using a credit card. I wasn't on a no-fly list. I didn't know if a warrant had been issued for my arrest, but if I could get aboard the plane I would be okay.

Another glance at my watch. I had eighteen minutes to get rid of Davies's phone and make myself look like something besides a fugitive drug runner. I forwarded all the information the phone contained to my laptop: calls dialed and received, calendar, notepad, and phone book. He had perhaps forty numbers listed, none of which sounded terribly official. That gave me a funny feeling.

I rushed out of Starbucks. My first stop was a courier service. Then I ducked into a clothing store, grabbed the first ten things off the rack with tags saying they were my size, and hustled to the dressing room.

When I pulled off my grungy shirt I felt instant relief. Specks of glass from the shattered window of the BMW had been nicking me since Santa Barbara, minuscule gremlins telling me my world was wrecked and heading for hell. I brushed my skin clean, shook out my hair, and got a good glimpse of myself in the mirror. Call the pound: I looked like a stray dog.

Out at the register I threw down a pile of clothes, tossed pairs of socks and underwear onto the stack like grenades, and headed for the accessory section. Nobody flies to Asia with just a small backpack, so I grabbed the biggest carryall they had, a suede bag the size of a warthog. The saleswoman smiled and asked how I was doing today, ringing up my purchases meticulously so as not to chip her long scarlet nails. I checked my watch: four minutes. She asked if I wanted to sign up for a store credit card. I didn't. Did I have their new catalog? Did I want anything gift-wrapped? She took out tissue paper and prepared to wrap each item separately, moving as though conducting a ritual Japanese tea ceremony. I opened the carryall, told her to shove everything inside, threw down cash, and strode out of the store toward Avenue of the Stars. I wasn't disguised; I was barely presentable, but this would have to do.

Still trying not to run, I approached the road. Across the street, parked on the curving drive in front of the Century Plaza Hotel, I saw Porsches and Mercedes but not Tim's red SUV. Had I missed him? I dodged across the street and jogged past hotel guests who were scented with perfume that probably cost more than my mortgage payment. Then I saw Tim behind the wheel of a blue Volvo wagon. He winced out of the car, face sallow, favoring his left side.

"You drive," he said.

I dumped my things in the back, hopped into the driver's seat, and started the engine. In the wing mirror I saw Tim inching his way to the passenger door, hand on the car to steady himself.

People were watching. A blonde walking up the driveway behind him pulled off her shades and stared. She had big eyes and a ripe little mouth. Her blouse was low-cut on a frame so boyish that a heroin addict could only aspire to it. If she bent over, one of her free-range breasts might poke a nipple out for air.

She was close, too close. Tim opened the door, looking at the car. With a single swipe she raised her arm. He turned, elbow swinging up in defense, but she hit him in the back of the neck. He slapped his hand over the spot. A second later, he went down.

11

Tim staggered against the car and slid to the ground. Reflexively I reached toward him. The woman's hand retreated, but not before I glimpsed the shiny object in her palm. She looked at me through the open passenger door. Her eyes were too bright, weirdly oily. My confusion sloughed off to straight-up fear.

She flew into the car, hands out, going for my neck. I put up my arms but she was on me, a pungent smell of perfume and dried sweat and sex rolling off her. I cocked an arm, but in the close confines of the Volvo I couldn't get a punch in. Her hands scrabbled for me. Beneath the filmy blouse her arms felt as ropy as beef jerky.

"Shit." I clawed behind me for the door handle.

People were staring, but nobody came to help. I flailed and brought up my knees, still scrabbling for the door handle.

And behind her in the doorway, Tim clawed to his feet. He grabbed her by the ankle and hauled her out. As she slid backward that oily sheen in her eyes focused on the flash drive. Slicker than an eel, she grabbed it and tore the chain loose from my neck. The medallion bounced onto the console between the seats.

Tim pulled her out of the car. She turned, lunged, and sank her teeth into his cheek. He roared in pain and fell against the car, hand over the bloody wound.

She turned and looked at the medallion. Her teeth were

filmy with blood. Her gaze jumped to me. "She won't help you."

She ran. I scrambled out of the car, but by the time I got around, Tim had pulled himself into the passenger seat. I grabbed the medallion.

Finally, somebody said, "You all right? What happened?"

Tim said, "Drive."

I jumped behind the wheel and squealed away from the hotel, swerving as I tried to get a look at him. "What did she stick you with?"

"Not sure. She didn't give me a full load." He grabbed my arm. "Never do that again."

"What?"

"The car, you daft idiot. You had the advantage and abandoned it. You should have driven away before she got inside."

I flushed. "And leave you?"

"Yes." He fell against the door. "No pity, only the goal."

I poured down the avenue, seeing the bloody mess that he had become. I blinked down embarrassment and fear, and tightened my hands on the wheel.

"In that case, I'm going to the airport. You can ride along or get out."

He cut his eyes at me, breathing heavily. "Pull over."

I left him at a gas station on Olympic Boulevard, waiting on a stack of used tires for his contact. Before I turned to go, I held out my hand. He took it and said, "Only the goal."

I nodded. He pulled my hand to his lips. His kiss was cold.

"Got it. Bliss, I've got the signal. I'm on it."

Christian gunned the Viper up the freeway, his pulse beating in time with the engine. He glanced at his handheld. The map displayed a red dot heading up the freeway ahead of him: Boyd's cell phone.

Bliss had let the woman get away. He would catch her.

Her father had taken everything from him. He'd been so young, so helpless, and Phil Delaney had destroyed his world. Left his mother to face whoredom. Set the course for all that followed, to his desperation, to time running out. His heart was going like a chain saw, chuddering in his chest. He caught sight of his face in the mirror. He was pale but no longer transparent. They were going to get the Riverbend file and then the Delaneys would finally pay.

The computer display refreshed, and the blip moved off the freeway. He screeched into the exit lane and onto the off-ramp, honking at the car in front of him. Come on, cocksucker, out of the way. At the light he roared past and gunned away, resting his thumb on the SIG in his lap.

He followed the tracking signal along the frontage road. She had to be just up ahead, past a package delivery truck and an overloaded pickup. Traffic slowed while the trucks made a left turn. He sounded his horn, ground his teeth, shifted, and flew down the road again, closing on the car ahead.

The screen refreshed, and the pinging of the locator changed pitch, dropping lower. He glanced at it—no.

The signal was now behind him. He'd passed her somehow. He skidded into a U-turn and raced back the other way. Quarter of a mile along, he slowed, checked the signal, and turned onto a side road. He punched it up the hill, around the curve, and hit the brakes.

The unmitigated bitch. The signal from Davies's cell phone was coming from the package delivery service truck. It was parked in front of the Santa Barbara sheriff's department.

The check-in agent peered at her computer monitor. "Did you pack your bags yourself?"

"Yes." Five minutes ago, in the women's room near the entrance to the terminal, but she didn't need to know that.

She ran my passport through the magnetic strip reader on her keyboard.

Behind me, a long line snaked back from the counter. The flight to Bangkok was nearly full. Foreign words bounced around me, sounding to my ears fast-paced and nasal. The ticket agent kept hold of my passport, staring at her screen.

Boyd Davies's phone should be at the sheriff's department by now. Before I left Century City, I had stuck it in an express envelope at the courier service and sent it urgent, same-day delivery to Detective Lilia Rodriguez.

The blonde had used Davies's cell phone to track me somehow, even when it was turned off. The moment the Sangers thought that I possessed what they wanted, they sent somebody to steal it from me. They had no intention of telling me where Dad was. They were going to leave him to die.

To rescue him, I would have to turn that around on them. Somehow I had to find some leverage against them, something they needed, some means of withholding the information they were after until they led me to my father.

The ticket agent frowned at her screen for a second longer. Near the terminal doors, two well-armed policemen were scanning the crowd.

The agent smiled and handed me my passport and boarding pass. "Have a good flight."

Beyond security, I found a wireless hot spot. Surrounded by a loud TV sports channel and business travelers hunched over beers, I logged on and set up a new e-mail account. Then I wrote a message to Jesse.

Check these out.

I attached the data I'd taken from Boyd Davies's phone, and told him I'd couriered the phone to Lily.

What's weird? Calls received look like L.A. and Santa Barbara numbers. No federal agency numbers.

No police, no Wash D.C. nos either. The number labeled Office clicks straight to voice mail. Something's
not right.

I sat for a moment staring at the screen. I knew I'd an-
gered him earlier. And if I told him where I was about to
head, he would go ballistic. I couldn't face that, not yet.
That was why I wasn't phoning him, even though I had just
purchased a new cell phone. And I deeply, deeply wished
that he were here with me, that we could take this on together.

And it hit me how truly far off the chart I was going.
Here in the cavernous terminal, holding a boarding pass
that would send me nine thousand miles away from home,
I felt unutterably off balance. Alone.

Babe, I know where to find the information that I
need, and I have to go get it. Please trust that this is the
way it has to be. I love you. I wish you could say a
prayer for me.

At the bar, glasses clinked. I sent the message and sat
rubbing my temples. On-screen, the ticker read 25:09.17.

I heard the television go to the news. Glancing up, I saw
my fears realized.

They were reporting Boyd Davies's death. I sat bone
still, seeing footage from the scene, police cars and an ambulance, cops, and Jesse's old classmate Drew Farelli, the
U.S. Attorney's cocker spaniel.

Man and woman wanted for questioning.

Nothing about my name, but that wouldn't last long.
Soon I'd be on television, wanted posters, and airline computers.

The bartender was wiping the counter. A few people at
the bar were casually eyeing the TV. I gathered my things.
Hoisting my pack onto my shoulder, I stood and strolled
toward the gate.

Forty-five minutes later my flight heaved itself skyward, engines at a hard drone. The lights of the coastline swept past below us. In jerks I let out the breath I'd been holding. We climbed over the black ocean and banked northwest on the great circle route toward Asia. But as we rose I felt that I was falling. That the world was dropping out from under me. That I might never see my father again.

12

Tuesday

Salt and iron. Cry of gulls. Smell of rust.

Phil crossed the boundary to consciousness. Beneath his back lay cold metal. Creaks on the wind, a swaying. He was at sea.

Dark out. He breathed, eyes open, seeing nothing. Concussion or heavy tranquilizers had put him down; he didn't know which. He blinked, beginning to discern shapes. The ship was swaying.

No, he was. His head was spinning. One eye was punch-swollen. Blood had dried on the side of his head, and he ached. Did he ever, balls to bone. Fifty-nine was bitch enough without the beating. He inched his fingers down to his knee.

One touch and he shouted in pain.

His voice bounced and disappeared, swallowed by the darkness. He lay still, absorbing the hurt. The metallic creaking resumed. Salt air but no water rushing past. No engine sounds.

Where was he?

He pressed his hands to the rough iron beneath him and sat up. It was heavily oxidized, needed painting or it was going to rust right through. This vessel could only barely be seaworthy. Gingerly he turned his head and saw a vertical shaft of light no wider than a filament.

Was he in a cargo hold? He listened again to the sounds of the ship, and the absences. No water. No engines. He should hear the engines, that deep rumble of diesels. Were they at anchor?

His jeans felt stretched tight over his knee. He let his hand hover above his kneecap, feeling a pulse of heat off it. He touched it just for a split second. It felt like a swollen and decayed old gourd. He wasn't going anywhere, least not fast.

He looked at his watch, pressed the light, and saw the dial: one seventeen a.m., Tuesday April 14.

More than a day had passed. Hell. He fought to remember the chain of events. Biker white trash. Speed-freak hooker booting him in the skull. Running, dialing his phone, and praying for Jesse to answer.

His phone. He patted his shirt pocket.

Gone. He leaned on his hands, remembering headlights on the highway and Christian Sanger stepping out of the vehicle. The Queen of the Damned inside, smiling as her son strutted toward him.

That creaking came again, wind-driven. He listened harder. Far away he heard a motor running. He clapped his hands. "Hello."

The sound came back at him from his left but suffocated in front of him. Something was absorbing it. Digging into his jeans pocket, he found his lighter. He flicked it and a bolus of light bloomed before him.

He saw corrugated metal walls crawling with rust. Dirty floor. A huge padded furniture blanket hanging from one wall, another slumped in a corner. Then he understood about the creaking, the wind, the absence of engine sounds.

The motion he was feeling wasn't anything like the pitch of a ship driving through blue water. It was the creaking of a big block of metal stacked amid others. He was in a shipping container.

The slit of light in the wall was a crack in the container doors. Biting down against the pain in his knee, he pulled himself along the floor and pushed against them. Bolted from the outside.

For a minute he slumped, breathing hard. He hadn't eaten or drunk anything in two days. His mouth was parched, but discomfort wasn't the danger.

What the hell was he going to do? What were they going to do with him? He breathed deep, smelling something more than rust and metal. Water: The container was wet somewhere inside. From rain, or being hosed down. And he smelled other scents now. Sweat. Old fruit. Rank urine.

He held up the lighter again. Candy wrappers were piled in a corner. Beyond them lay an apple core. Near the crumpled blanket was a shoe. He lugged his way over and grabbed it. His heart went south.

"Son of a bitch."

It was a girl's tennis shoe. Bedecked with red and white daisies, beads worked in among the laces. The beads spelled out a name: Lita. Glancing around again, on the walls he saw marks, notches scratched into the metal. He knew they must signify days. Below them words were scratched, some in English, others in the baroque alphabet of the Thai language. And one in Spanish.

He had to get the hell out of here, and soon.

The container was stacked with others on a dock. The sounds outside were forklifts and cranes. They were loading these containers into the hold of a ship. If that happened, if he were sent out to sea without food or water, he would die.

Perhaps like little Lita. He glanced again at the Spanish writing scratched into the wall. *Ayúdame.* Help me.

13

Christian parked the Viper on the drive behind Bliss's Porsche and stalked into the house. The electric glow of L.A. lit the night, feverish, like his mood.

Going through the arch into the courtyard, looking past the trellis down the precipitous hillside, he heard music, the Callas recording of *Tosca*. Bliss was going to get one across the side of her face. Propping his shades on top of his head, he threw open the door.

The aria cut the air like a blade. Across the entryway and living room, he saw Bliss slouched by the windows. The five-million-dollar view tingled behind her. She was wearing six thousand bucks of designer clothing, but with a dozen studs in her ear and scratching at scabs on her arm, she looked like the sullen backwoods runaway she had been.

He stalked across the room. "She shipped the phone to the Santa Barbara sheriff. You let her get away."

He raised his hand. She scratched her arm, gave him an eyeful of scorn, and shifted her gaze to the far side of the room. He stopped himself, catching a whiff of perfume.

He turned his head. "Rio."

His mother was sitting on the divan, arms draped across the back, legs languorously crossed, sculpted into a vermilion suit. She proffered her cheek. He breathed, crossed to the sofa, and kissed her. Her perfume hinted at incense. They must be working an Asian group tonight, one of those horny trade delegations from the Chinese consulate.

"Rivera was cautious," Rio said. "She didn't simply put the file on disk."

Bliss held up a flash drive. "It's fried. Self-destructed."

His scalp pinpricked with sweat. "The information's gone?"

"Of course not. Transferred."

"Where?"

"Delaney's daughter," Rio said.

He gestured at Bliss. "Who she let escape."

Rio gave him one of her looks and recrossed her legs. That Sharon Stone thing, it was a tic with her.

"Christian," she said, probably for the second or third time. "We know where she is, and Shiver is on it."

"Shiver?"

Bliss scratched at her arm. With her skinny frame, her inch-long blond hair made her look like a boy. "Delaney doesn't know she has a second tail."

"Why hasn't Shiver stopped her?" Christian said.

"She's on her way to Bangkok. And so am I."

"What?" He didn't bother to hide his surprise. Turning to Rio, he said, "What's she going there for?"

"Obviously, to get more information," Rio said.

Rio's hair gleamed in the light, black curls piled high. It was the hairdo she had worn for the latest portrait, which hung behind her on the wall, the one modeled on the painting of Caesar's wife. Though his mom wore more jewelry, and stilettos, and breast implants. Thai breast implants.

Bangkok . . . he hated that place.

Even though he thought that maybe it was where Rio's mother, his grandmother, had come from. Rio's father had been a U.S. serviceman; he was pretty sure of that. Her mother . . . Rio said she was a Thai city girl. She also said she was a Casablanca runaway. Or, on nights like tonight, when Maria Callas was rending the air, she might have been Italian. It didn't matter now—they all had American passports.

But Bangkok, that was where their lives had gone

wrong, when his own father was working there. It was the place where Rio got the idea for the growth hormone, and for keeping her stable looking young. And where everything turned to shit.

"Christian," she said.

"How do you know for sure? What if she's just running away?" He heard his voice rising and couldn't stop it. "We have to get it."

Bliss slid up behind him. "The flash drive was on a chain with a medallion. You know who?"

Christian rubbed his hand over his chest. His bones were aching. The fatigue was sinking into him, overcoming his jitters. He eyed Bliss more closely.

"Maria Auxiliadora?" he said.

"Herself. La Virgen."

He nodded, still rubbing his sweater. From one of the bedrooms, feet padded along the tiled floor. Eden came into the room wearing a man's dress shirt and bronze legs, looking half-asleep. She stretched her arms over her head, running her fingers through her tousled black curls.

He snickered at her. "What the fuck is that? A beaver 'fro?"

She hoisted the shirt around her waist and peered at her pubic hair. It was shaved in the shape of a lightning bolt. "Like it?"

Rio stood up. "Do you have the game worked out tonight?"

Eden dropped the shirt. "Yeah. The uniform's Culver City PD, the car's old LAPD. I'll stop him on his way home from the country club." She explained for Christian. "Fortieth birthday role-playing. A kidnapping."

Rio smoothed her skirt. "You do not beat him at the roadside. Take him to the Valley house before you get busy with him."

"Of course."

"And, Eden, he turns the tables. You let him get the upper hand."

Eden tightened. "I don't play the submissive; you know these guys don't have limits—"

"You do it, or we don't get their repeat business."

"He's a venture capitalist. His partner set this up—you remember the guy last year, Rio; he cut me—"

Rio snapped her fingers. Eden went quiet.

"And this man may cut you too. And you will scream and come, and then you will clean it all up."

Eden looked at the floor.

"It will all be recorded," Rio said. "Stop worrying. I take care of you. I always do."

The cameras would catch everything. Though, of course, the clientele didn't know they were being put on video—they discovered that only if they went too far. But anybody who messed up one of the girls from Elysium Concierge Services paid for it. Dearly, sometimes for years, generally to the Caymans account.

Rio tilted her head, waiting until she got a nod from Eden. She turned to Christian. He rubbed his chest again, the tightness returning.

Rio looked like a million bucks in that red suit. She was exceptionally proud of her body, and always dressed to show off. That was something she'd learned in France. Make them appreciate. Demand it. She angled her shoulders back, waiting.

"You look fabulous, Mom."

She glanced down at her breasts approvingly. "Have you talked to that actress's agent yet?"

"I will."

"These Russians really think they can nail an A-list movie star. Offer more money."

His chest squeezed. "I'm working on it."

COO, that was what she called him. Chief operating officer. He felt like chief operating orifice. Elysium: your every desire fulfilled. That was what she promised. Plow the first lady? No problem. Get on it, Christian. He felt his energy seeping out as if he'd cut himself.

"What if we're too late?" he said.

She blinked at him, her gaze softened, and with a beckoning finger she drew him near. He sidled over and she took his hand in hers.

"We will get this. They will pay." She squeezed his hand. "Do you hear me?"

"Yes."

"These people ravaged us, but that has made us survivors. Your father died, but we coped and overcame. And now look at us."

The voice of Maria Callas soared over the room. He looked past his mother, at her portrait above the mantel. Rio was like Callas, a champion.

She ran a hand over his flowing hair. "You're pale."

On his wrist, her grip shifted. She checked his pulse and looked at his nail beds, his hands so white.

"Go take your medication."

"Bliss and Shiver cannot get this wrong, Mom."

Her eyes went bright with tears. She pulled him close, clutched him to her. "Be strong. We're going to fight. The two of us, we're fighters."

He stood rigid, arms at his sides. "Sure."

She leaned back and patted his shoulders, her face red. "Yes, Christian. Good. You stay tough. It's . . ." Hand through his hair, looking away. "It's okay."

He waited for her to let go, then stalked toward his bedroom. At the front door Bliss was zipping her jacket. She had a suitcase packed.

Bangkok. Rio had all her plastic surgery done in Bangkok. U.S. board-certified surgeons, deluxe hospitals, Asian prices. She got all her treatments there as well, the hormones that kept her skin so smooth and supple—why she looked so fabulous despite the struggles she had lived through. Bangkok was one of her favorite cities. She went there on regular scouting missions, looking for talent to import.

• He paused, and when Bliss looked at him he pointed his

hand at her, making a gun with two fingers and his thumb. He fake-fired at her.

In his bathroom he got his works, filled the syringe from the bottle, and injected the EPO. Erythropoietin—it would get you busted for blood doping in the Tour de France, but was prescribed to keep up his red cell count. It staved off the worst effects of the anemia, though it wouldn't for much longer.

Eden found him sitting on the bed, field stripping the SIG. He had removed the cartridges from the magazine and lined them up in front of him. Nine—he touched them one after the other. She climbed on the bed beside him.

"Rio told you to come take care of me?" he said.

They always seemed so comfortable with him like this. They never looked worried that he would try to fuck them. He reassembled the slide, put it back on the frame of the SIG, counted the cartridges again, and loaded them in the magazine. Eden touched his shoulder.

He shoved the magazine into the pistol, pushed her down onto her back, and slid the SIG between her legs. She stared at him. He rubbed the barrel back and forth on her pussy. She smiled. Carefully she took the gun from his hand, ejected the magazine, and gave it back.

"Sorry, hon. I only have safe sex."

Above his empty hand, in the crook of his elbow, blood was running from the needle mark. That would change. Soon the blood would be running the other way. From other people. Down to the marrow.

Wednesday

The plane swayed through the deep night. Beneath us eastern Russia slid by, lights scattered along its coastline like lonely stars. Twelve hours had passed. So had Tuesday, cut short when we crossed the international date line.

It was time. I fired up my computer, put in my earphones, and angled the screen so my seatmates couldn't see. Jax appeared in her sleek black suit, eyes heated. The down-ticker read 18:01.33.

"When I went to Colombia, I didn't intend to embed myself with a bunch of gunrunners. My brief was to track the drug traffickers who were financing them. And it's my endless regret that I did it by buying information from Rio Sanger."

Though her voice was smooth, the energy behind it radiated anger.

"Rio liked to watch sex and knew others did too, and would pay for it. People at the CIA. She approached us. And I dug all that shiny, happy footage of government ministers cozying up to her hookers. Those videos are what made them flip harder than bugs in a skillet." She glanced at her hands. "But that's not what this is about."

Her face faded out, replaced by a set of black-and-white photos.

"Rio's junior varsity squad."

"Oh, my God," I said.

They were hardly more than children. Girls riding the cusp of puberty, they were slim, faun-eyed, and terrified. One waif with raven hair and a soft mouth stared at the camera with a need to please so patent it was excruciating. I had to look away.

"First clip," Jax said.

The footage segued to grainy video. A bedroom, the camera apparently hidden in a ceiling light. The door opened and in came a man, obese and half in the bag, accompanied by two girls who looked about fourteen, one East Asian, one blond. The man dropped onto the edge of the bed. One girl knelt at his feet and untied his shoes. The other began unbuttoning his shirt. He put two fingers on her neck and ran them down the midline of her chest. Nausea rolled through me like a wave of heat.

"He was a salesman for an arms firm," Jax said. "This was the next morning."

Cut to the disheveled bed, the man pulling on his

clothes, cigarette in his mouth, face hungover. The girls were sleeping spooned together. With a knock, the door opened.

The man glanced up. "Rio."

My skin tightened. She was dazzling, in a Roman-orgy way. Bronze skin, exotic features, helix coils of black hair, skirt highlighting a magnificent ass. She smiled, rested her fingers along the man's forearm, and said something so soft and soothing that it was a mere stroke of the air.

She snapped her fingers at the girls. "Wake up."

The girls scurried awake, got up, and pressed their palms together in front of their faces, as though in prayer. It was a distinctly Asian gesture, gentle and respectful. Thanking their defiler: holy God. The man dug in his pocket and handed them each some cash. Then he smiled at Rio and sauntered out the door.

Rio snapped her fingers again, pointing around the room. "Clean it up. Spick-and-span." She swept out. I wanted to punch a hole in the computer screen.

Jax reappeared, eyes shining with either defiance or shame.

"Those girls—I never got them out. They're lost. When things went bad . . ." She looked away and back again, fierce. "Watch out. Rio still has them. There are three of them, and hooking isn't all they do for her now."

She touched a keyboard on the desk. "In the end, this is all about lost kids."

A photo popped on-screen: a girl of about seven, whose dark curls caught the light like a halo. Her brown eyes were impish, her gaze precocious. She was perched in the crook of a tree.

"This one too. Lost. And . . ."

The energy drained from Jax's voice. "You really wonder why I quit the Company?"

The photo segued into a video clip, the brown-eyed girl playing on a beach, and the air full of sweet laughter.

"Lives ruined, what might have been, I can't even . . ."

Her voice was rough, her coolness and aloofness gone. The plane rocked, and disbelief crept over me. Jax cared.

After a moment she straightened and lifted her chin. "You're laughing and shaking your head, aren't you? Rule number one: Don't get involved. But I certainly did."

Her expression turned piquant. "Let's get down to it. The op went wrong because I got involved with Rio's man. So here you go, for posterity."

She leaned toward the camera. "Hank Sanger was an asset. American, ex–Green Beret." Chilly smile. "I have a fatal weakness for military men."

I ran a hand over my face, wondering if she was addressing this to Tim North.

"Hank was a mercenary, loosely connected over the years to the CIA, the contras, ran guns to private armies in Southeast Asia. I met him in Thailand. I thought he was helping us, getting information on some of the guerrilla types who were selling guns to the paramilitaries."

New film footage loaded. A bar: neon beer signs on the wall, the crowd smoking and drinking, jukebox in the corner where a man dropped coins and an old tune swelled to life, the gravelly voice of Ray Charles singing "Georgia on My Mind."

Jax said, "Aren't we lucky that Rio puts cameras everywhere, just in case someone exciting shows up? She was always willing to sell us this club footage, at a discount."

A mix of Asian and Caucasian men filled the club. The girls were dancing, flirting, sitting on laps. The front door opened and in walked a husky man, handsome, crew cut, tucking aviator shades into his shirt pocket, eyeing the scene like a linebacker hunting for a quarterback to sack.

"I knew Hank was mixed up with Rio. He was a bon vivant. But I didn't care. He helped build the conduit, getting Rio's film footage to us."

She seemed to consider her words.

"I didn't know he'd been crazy with lust for Rio for fifteen years. For too long I didn't know they had a child, Christian. I was a fool," she said. "I convinced myself he would help me get the underage girls out of her cathouse. I didn't know Rio was splitting her take with him."

She focused on the camera. "He decided to shop me to the gunrunners. Apparently they paid better than the agency."

Hold on. This was the tale she'd told me when we first met: that she became involved with an asset, and killed him when he tried to shop her to drug traffickers. Except it wasn't. It was Jax version 2.0, a new spin on the mythology.

"But I found out. That's when things got ugly."

In the club, Hank was ordering a drink. The music rolled over the top of the crowd. The man at the jukebox turned around.

It was my father.

"Real ugly," Jax said. "And I know there are only two words to explain why I'm alive and here to tell you all this. Phil Delaney."

He was younger, mid-forties, raw and coiled even as his slow stride took him to the bar. I reached out and touched his image on the screen.

"It wasn't the agency that extracted me. It wasn't State. Those prigs wouldn't rescue Jesus from the cross unless they cleared it with the legal department first. It wasn't naval intelligence in D.C., or the Senate Select Committee on Intelligence. It was the man on the ground."

One of Rio's girls approached Dad—the raven-haired waif with the hungry eyes. She put a hand on his chest.

He removed it. The waif looked over her shoulder and slipped away into the crowd as a woman approached Dad.

When Rio Sanger put her hand on my father's chest, he didn't push it away.

He spoke to her, standing absolutely still, hands loose at his sides. His gaze slid past her shoulder as Hank Sanger came toward them down the bar, plowing through the crowd like an icebreaker.

The video faded, the song lingering from the jukebox. *Still in peaceful dreams I see the road leads back to you . . .*

Jax appeared. "Phil, Tim—you're the reasons I'm alive. Got me out, saved my soul. So this hatred . . ." She looked away, shaking her head. "It's wrong."

I jerked upright and grabbed the sides of the computer.

"We couldn't rescue all Rio's girls. But you did rescue me."

Hatred—between Tim and my father?

"And having Hank Sanger die didn't turn out to be the end. It was only the beginning. Which is why you'd better be across the date line by now."

She hit a key. "Remember, there are three of them. Watch out." The screen went dark. "Eighteen hours. Hope you're hauling ass."

We descended into Bangkok from the north, bouncing over a city that spread from horizon to horizon. The airliner's cabin looked like a college dorm the morning after a party. Blankets, trash, the lingering smell of noodles, a waft from the bathrooms. My eyes felt gritty, my legs stiff. With sunrise the earth had gone green, and through bright haze flecks of light gleamed up at us like mirrored tiles. Bumping lower, I saw that they were tin roofs amid lush foliage.

I felt wired. In my backpack I had a Bangkok guide and several hundred dollars' worth of crisp, psychedelically colored Thai baht. The address Jax had given me was carefully written on a slip of paper in my pocket. I had five hours to get the next flash drive. The jet strained, wings bouncing. It flared and hit the runway.

With three hundred other passengers, I hustled out into the airy terminal. The first thing that struck me was the signage: The Thai alphabet looked rococo, like scrollwork. Around me, conversation sounded chopped and full of intonations. It hit me exactly how foreign I was here. This wasn't Mexico or France, where I could decrypt familiar phrases.

At passport control, the woman behind the desk scowled at my photo, and my face, and her screen, and whacked my passport with her stamp. My luggage came and I humped outside. Into a day of buzzing tourist vans, shouting drivers, gushing purple orchids, smog, and humidity. A hot breeze scudded over me.

Welcome to Thailand.

At the taxi rank a driver got out and sauntered around to the curb, greeting me as he popped the trunk and tossed my bag inside. *"Sawatdee."*

"Sawatdee." Peering at my little Thai phrase book, I stuttered, *"Bpai tee yoo nee."* To this address. I read aloud the name of the guesthouse I'd booked online from LAX, adding, *"Ga-ru-na."* Please. He nodded and climbed in the car.

Even if I was here for only a few hours, I needed someplace to park my luggage while I chased down the next flash drive. The guesthouse cost seven dollars per night and had taken my reservation without asking for a credit card number. I got in the taxi, feeling spacey. The driver pulled out and screeched away.

Down the wrong side of the road.

Whoa—they drove on the left here? I thought this only happened in England. I gripped the door handle, feeling freaked out.

Within minutes he accelerated onto a freeway and sped along, windows down, through thick traffic. Apartment buildings swept past, and thick greenery, lacy tall trees, and random skyscrapers. Shine, dirt. New, old. Decrepit, gilt-laden. Thai talk banged at me from the car radio. The sun was orange in the morning sky. We streamed on, mile after mile, the city so vast that I couldn't see any discernible skyline on the horizon, just sprawl.

When the taxi lurched to a stop, my eyes popped open. My hair was stuck to the side of my face with sweat. Shoot. I'd fallen asleep.

We were stopped at a red light on a congested surface

street. Noise bounced off buildings, smoked-glass offices and old plaster-walled shops painted bright blue or yellow. Greenery gushed from the sidewalks and from every space between buildings. Hawker carts lined the sidewalks, selling clothes, souvenirs, and food from steaming woks.

A traffic cop was directing cross-traffic, wearing a helmet and a surgical mask. Trucks and buses spewed exhaust through the open windows of the taxi. A beggar was working his way down the middle of the street between stopped vehicles. All around, waiting with us at the lights, were motor scooters. A horde of motor scooters, bearing cute teenage girls and boys, middle-aged women, entire families—mom, dad, and grandma packed aboard, a toddler, nut brown and wiry, squirreled on the driver's lap.

There was a knock on the frame of the car. I turned and went still. The beggar stood at the window, one hand out. His other arm was paralyzed, hanging like a sock full of laundry. The driver turned up the radio and ignored him. I stared. Santa Barbara has some shameless panhandlers, mostly alcoholics hustling cash for booze, or mentally ill homeless people arguing with the sky, which is why I give my money to the shelter run by Catholic Charities. But the man outside my window was sane, sober, and awful, and perhaps the head of a household. He leaned toward me, swinging the useless limb in front of my face.

All I could think was how the sight of this beggar would incite Jesse to sulfurous anger, and how thankful I was that his life didn't demand such abasement. I jammed money into the man's hand.

The light turned green. The motor scooters revved, buzzing like a host of demented frogs. The air turned blue with exhaust. The taxi pulled out, leaving the beggar behind.

The guesthouse proved less dicey than I had feared. It was dim, hot, and full of Australian backpackers, rugged guys and gals with white-folk dreadlocks and faded bandannas tied around their necks. Hearing English, that tangy Aussie accent, gave me a boost. Once I checked in, I ran up three flights of creaking stairs. The slat windows in my tiny room overlooked an alley lined with cafés and overhung with electric wires. I dumped my luggage on the linoleum floor, changed my socks, and jogged down the hall to the bathroom to wash my face with cold water. I dried my hands on my green combat trousers. Grubby though I felt, I had no intention of showering. This bathroom did not have a floor where I wanted to set bare feet, even if somebody dared me or paid me. Big money.

Back in the room, I turned on the cell phone I had purchased at LAX. It was pay-as-you-go, meaning I hadn't had to register for the phone network with a credit card. And it was triband, so it was supposed to work worldwide. Now I waited, hoping that "worldwide" included this humid, dingy corner of Bangkok.

The phone chirped and the network signal came in strong. I put it in my backpack along with my computer. That was staying with me, no matter what.

Ten minutes later I was striding down the crowded street with sweat and grime working into my pores. Above my head, laundry hung on poles outside apartment windows. Music poured from boom boxes. Tuk-tuks droned past, open-air taxis that were basically rickshaws bolted to mopeds. Signs said McDonald's, 7-Eleven, Tiger Beer. Everybody else was having a great time. Everybody else was smoking. Outside a souvenir shop, vividly colored sarongs waved like palm fronds. Nearby, the shop's proprietor squatted in the shade. Thais and Western tourists packed the sidewalk cafés. I must have looked like the grimmest ratty backpacker in town.

The down-ticker on my computer read three hours and two minutes.

At the corner I hailed a taxi. I showed the driver the address and pronounced it for him: Ajahn Niram, 2 Sanamchai Road.

The road was jammed with Toyotas and scooters and tuk-tuks struggling to accelerate. My hair batted around my face in the wind. I had no idea what kind of place I was going to. We drove for twenty minutes, until we reached a broad boulevard that edged a vast plaza with a park in the center. Museums and elegant temples lined the exterior. Two billboards bore photos of the king and queen. They looked noble and resolute in their formal regalia and thick spectacles.

Traffic thickened, and the driver crawled down one side of the square under a leafy canopy of trees. He pulled to a stop alongside the whitewashed walls of what looked to be a fortress.

He pointed at a gate in the wall. "Wat Po."

My slip of paper said nothing about Wat Po. "Ajahn Niram?"

Again he pointed, speaking syllables I couldn't grasp. I got out into the broiling sun and paid him, saying, *"Kop khun."* Thanks. The walls, reflecting the light, were whiter even than the glazed surface of the sky.

I walked through the gate, into the grounds of a Buddhist temple.

14

My shoulders slumped. Wat Po was more than a temple. It was a city within the city, an expanse of monuments and cloisters and museums—a university campus, essentially. How on earth was I supposed to find the flash drive in here?

Paying the entrance fee, I wandered into the grounds. There was a sense of elegance and grandeur, and about a million tourists. The buildings were of a classical Thai style, whitewashed with orange-and-green tile roofs and gold spires along their gables. Imposing and ornate, they stretched along tree-lined walkways. Near the walls, kiosks sold knickknacks, maps, incense, and ice cream. Bands of monks strolled by, shaven headed and swathed in saffron robes. Where there was open space, round spires rose from the ground like stalagmites, covered with bright mosaic tiles. The whole place shone in the sun like a solar-collecting system.

"It's called a chedi."

I looked around. "Sorry?"

The young woman had an Australian accent and a generous smile. She nodded at the ornate mosaic spire I was staring at. "They're pagodas. Shrines." She strolled over, propping a pair of sports sunglasses on top of her head. "Saw you at the guest lodge, didn't I?"

She did look familiar, but that may have been the backpacker's clothing and sense of ease and adventure she exuded.

"You seem lost," she said.

"Jet lag." Hopefully I asked, "Are you a tour guide?"

"Nah, tourist. I'm waiting for Russell; he's my boy-friend? I'm Terry."

"Hi." I felt disconcerted, but that could have been the sleep deprivation. I glanced again at the slip of paper with this address written on it.

Her perky look evaporated. "You all right? You don't look so great."

I needed guidance, a clue, and I needed it now. And all at once I knew that I was on the verge of losing it: too hot, tired, and depleted.

"You're dehydrated. Come on; let's get you some water."

I let myself be pulled along to a stall selling drinks. Speaking some loud combination of Thai and Aussie, Terry got me a large bottled water. We wandered over to a planter and sat down in a shred of shade. She twisted the top off and handed the bottle to me. I downed half of it.

"Thanks," I said.

She took off her bandanna, poured some water onto it, and pressed it against the back of my neck. I felt immensely grateful.

"Not to pry," she said, "but are you in trouble?"

I shook my head. "Thank you for your help." I showed her the piece of paper with the address on it. "Does this mean anything to you?"

She tipped her head. "Ajahn Niram."

"Know how I can find it?"

"Not it. Him. Ajahn, that's like . . . teacher, or reverend. It's a title for a monk."

The *duh* landed on me like a lump. With a concerted push, I stood up.

And felt a rush in my head. I waited for it to subside. "Can you do me one more favor?"

She accompanied me back to the food stall. A group of twelve-year-olds was crowded around the counter eating snow cones. The food coloring had turned their lips turquoise and purple. The woman in the stall glanced at me, barely moving in the heat.

"Ajahn Niram?" I said.

She kept serving the schoolkids but nodded at some buildings in the distance and spoke rapidly, words that meant zip to me. I glanced at Terry.

"She said something about the main temple," Terry said.

The woman repeated the monk's name and tapped her cheek. She pointed toward the center of the temple grounds and said clearly, "Wat Phra." When I repeated that, she nodded and said, "You go. He come there."

I thanked her and walked toward the temple. Terry came along.

"Listen, I'm feeling much better now," I said.

She continued along with me. "No worries. You gonna tell me what this is about?"

"Long story."

"I got time."

"Where's your boyfriend?"

"Probably went to find something to eat. He likes noodles more than Buddhas."

I didn't want to be rude, but I didn't want her along either. "Thanks for your help. I'm fine now."

"Glad I could give you a hand. Wat Phra's up ahead." She pointed and led the way.

The temple was in the center of a cloister, surrounded by green grass, high walls, and a cocooning quiet. Seeing rows of sandals and boots outside the doors, I removed my hiking shoes and went in.

I'd never been in a Buddhist temple. There were no pews, no music. Columns inlaid with ornate tilework rose to the dark recesses of the ceiling. At the far end of the room, a towering altar bore a golden Buddha. Offerings were set out on the floor before it—photos, flowers, food. On the carpet, twenty monks sat cross-legged in prayer.

Terry appeared beside me. "You can kneel or sit, but don't show the soles of your feet to the Buddha. That's very rude."

We knelt. It was calm and blessedly cool, but I gazed at the monks with dismal anxiety. In my head I heard a ticking sound.

Five minutes, ten—finally the monks stood to leave. I scanned each of their young faces, hoping for some flash of inspiration. And I saw him.

His glasses were thick, and the stubble on his shaved head showed gray. Beneath the one-shouldered saffron robe, he had the body of a blacksmith. The scar ran from the bridge of his nose across one cheek and back to his ear.

Quietly I said to Terry, "Excuse me. I have to go."

I stood and walked over to him. Putting my hands together in front of my face the way I'd seen the local people doing, I said, *"Sawatdee."*

He did the same.

"Ajahn Niram?"

His gaze was old and ferocious. The scar was lumpy, as though the wound had not been repaired so much as bundled back together under rough conditions. He seemed to be waiting. I took Jax's religious medallion from my pocket and handed it to him. He eyed the Madonna. Closing his hand around it, he walked outside.

I followed, retrieving my hiking shoes and jogging after him. He rambled into the sunshine. His robes lit like a sunset.

"Do you have a name?" he said.

"Evan Delaney."

He gazed into the distance. "You have your father's way."

My throat closed up. "You know Dad?"

"I knew him. And I know what you want."

"Do you have it?"

From the folds of his robes he produced a cell phone. He

made a call in rapid-fire Thai, flipped it shut, and said, "Five minutes."

Though he continued staring into the distance, his bearing seemed not meditative but eager. I felt a strange conviction—that he, like I, had been given something dangerous for safekeeping by Jakarta Rivera. And now he was relieved to be getting rid of it.

"How do you know my father?"

He turned the medallion over in his palm. "That was another time. Not literally another life, but morally and physically it might as well have been."

As he turned the medallion in his palm, I got a clear view of the tattoo on his forearm: wings unfurled around an open parachute.

"You were a paratrooper?"

"Yes. I got this at jump school, Fort Benning."

I looked at him anew: Not only had he served in the army, he had served in the U.S. Army Airborne.

"You are surprised?" he said.

"No. You used to drop out of the night sky to bring fire on your enemies. Now you cloister yourself behind these walls. Either way, you're quiet and evasive."

Below the scar, his mouth bent into a smile. "It isn't your face. Your walk, perhaps. That long stride, though yours has less swagger." He surveyed me. "Your eyes, I think. You Delaneys are like heat-seeking missiles. Once you launch, you can't be called off."

"Dad's in trouble," I said.

He adjusted his robes. "Phil has always been driven as much by desire as by duty. And desire is the cause of all suffering."

Karma 101. I shoved my hands in my pockets, trying to maintain a semblance of Buddhist patience. Ridding oneself of desire, that's the trick to reaching nirvana. Tough when the down-ticker was down to the dregs.

"Your father walks his own path, and now you're walking after him. If you're going to do that, remember—life is like a narrow bridge. The most important thing is not to be afraid."

"Is that a Buddhist tenet?"

"Jewish. A saying of Rabbi Nachman. The point is, let go of your fear. Cross the bridge. Your father will be all right."

"That's easy for you to say. When you were falling, you had on a parachute."

Exhaustion and heat and emotion rolled over me like a wave, dropping me into a trough. I rubbed my fingers across my forehead. "This is about Rio Sanger."

"I had no doubt. She's a feeder."

"What do you mean?"

"People come to her seeking pleasure. They want. They long to take, to get, to wallow in desire. But in the end they surrender to her, flesh and spirit. They're sucked empty." Something—sadness or disgust—crossed his face. "Outside these walls, you can get almost anything. Rio Sanger knew that, and spent some time doing business here. She excelled in trafficking women and girls to the West for prostitution."

"Girls?" I said.

"Country girls, Thai, Lao, Burmese . . . some, the ones most pleasing to the western eye, she would send abroad." He took off his glasses and cleaned them on the hem of his robe. "Exporting them like cheap shoes."

"She sent these girls to the U.S.?"

"Some. That's where she now works, I believe."

Import-export. That involved Immigration and Customs Enforcement. I wondered about Boyd Davies. Did Rio use him to help her slip trafficked girls past the authorities and into the U.S.?

He put his glasses back on. "Of course, Rio has been savvy about peddling the evidence of her perversions to those who can use it to their own ends. Intelligence agencies, organized crime, those seeking revenge. She feeds herself, she feeds her son, on hatred, and she feeds the cycle of suffering." He glanced at me. "This is about the blood feud."

I stopped. "What blood feud?"

He turned, eyes remote. "If Rio Sanger has done something to your father, it is because she is engaged in revenge. She seeks to punish your family for something done to hers."

Tim North had implied the same thing. "The death of Hank Sanger?"

"The blood feud calls on you to kill some of your enemy's people in revenge for past injuries. It doesn't matter who. The feud is eternal. What matters is the wheel of vengeance."

"You're saying the Sangers won't stop."

"No."

He began strolling again. My head was pounding. Rio and Christian already had Dad. What else did they want? What would be worse?

"Jakarta Rivera," I said. "Did you work with her and my father?"

"Do you know who she is?" he said.

I frowned. "Yes. She's the reason I'm here. What I've never understood is why she drew me into this . . . netherworld she inhabits."

"You never know whether she's endangering or protecting you."

"Exactly."

"Miss Rivera is expert at playing both sides in a game. But remember, most motives are not Byzantine. They're deep and basic, and driven by desire." We rounded a corner onto a plaza crowded with chedis, shrines, and tourists. He stopped. "If you wait at that temple, you will get what you have come for."

"Thank you."

He handed me the medallion. "When I asked if you knew who she was, I did not mean Jakarta Rivera." He nodded at the image on it. "That woman."

"The Virgin Mary."

"This specific image is known as Maria Auxiliadora. Our Lady of Christian Help."

"Sounds like I want her on my side."

"Perhaps not. In Colombia she has another name." His smile was only a hint, and beyond cynicism or irony. "Our Lady of the Assassins."

15

At the top of the temple steps I turned and glanced back. The old monk was distant, walking back to his seclusion. I headed for the door, removing my shoes again and setting them on a rack.

"There you are."

I looked around. Terry was climbing the steps. I raised my hands.

"No offense. But I need some space."

"None taken."

"What's going on here?"

The crowd eddied around us, a mix of wilting tourists and devout locals. I gave the Aussie as cold and inquisitorial a look as I could muster.

She sighed. "Okay. Russell took off. I just thought . . . you're another girl on her own, maybe we could join forces, seeing that we're staying at the same place. Strength in numbers, all that?"

I tried to gauge whether she was on the level, and decided it didn't matter. What was I going to do, make fun of her until she cried and ran away? I shrugged and walked into the temple.

And took a deep breath. Wow. I'd been expecting another big open space. Instead, filling the building—floor to ceiling, wall to wall—was a colossal golden statue.

"The Reclining Buddha," Terry said.

This Buddha wasn't like the jolly little guy who sat on

my parents' table. This Buddha lay on its side with one arm propped under his head. It was about a hundred fifty feet long and fifty feet tall. And gold, so gold that it seemed to throb with light.

The crowd was slowly processing around it. I joined in, feeling a hush come over me. This was like nothing I'd ever seen.

Smaller Buddhas were spaced along its length, surrounded by flowers and stippled with gold leaf that had been applied in postage-stamp amounts. Tourists snapped photos and lit incense. Thais stood praying, hands steepled in front of their faces. The schoolkids who'd been at the food stand came jostling in, mouths Day-Glo colors from their snow cones. The scent of incense hung thick in the air.

I strolled along the Buddha's length, keeping my eyes open. The soles of its feet rose high above my head and were inlaid with mother-of-pearl. Along its spine a row of begging bowls was set out. Some westerners were walking along dropping coins into them. From the chirpy smiles on their faces, they regarded this like tossing pennies into a fountain for good luck: karma collection. I didn't join them. You don't treat religious rituals as a game. When you partake, you open yourself to a power beyond yourself.

Near the entrance stood a young man with a package in his hand, eyes on me.

I walked over and showed him the medallion. He handed me the package. It was the size of a brick, wrapped in brown paper, and weighed a couple of ounces.

"Kop khun ka," I said. Thank you.

He left. I felt breath on my shoulder. Terry was standing behind me.

"I'll contribute," she said.

"What?"

"I'll pay my share." Dark excitement was in her eyes. "It must be really good stuff. Come on, I'll pay top dollar."

Oh, great. She thought it was drugs. "No. You're way, way

off base." Shaking my head, I pushed past the snow-cone kids and headed for the door.

The girl separated herself from among them with the speed of a knife slicing the air. She was the only one without food-color lips, about twelve years old with hair to her waist. Reflexively I tucked the package under my arm.

Her eyes lit and her bearing changed. The girlishness ablated to sinewy purpose. She seemed to uncoil like a whip. Silent, she flew at me.

Her hands were out, fingers rigid, reaching for the package. Without even seeming to jump, she was in midair and on me.

She clawed at my hand. "Give it up, bitch."

Her voice was pure, trashy American. Her teeth were decayed. Though her frame was a child's, her eyes were stained with age. She clung to me, arm around my neck, fingers grabbing for the package.

From beyond my field of vision a dark object came swinging. Terry smashed her in the side of the head with one of the begging bowls.

Coins flew. The bowl rang against the girl's skull. Her eyes glazed but she held on. Terry grabbed a cluster of burning incense sticks and shoved them down the back of the girl's shirt. Faster than a scorched bat, she let go of me and dropped to her knees, flailing at the back of her shirt.

I grabbed Terry's sleeve. "Come on."

We sprinted past horrified tourists and out of the temple. Terry veered off to retrieve her shoes. I snatched mine, but no way was I going to stop and put them back on. I jumped down the steps three at a time.

"Wait," she called.

Glancing back, I saw her fumbling with her boots. Behind her, materializing from the shadows in the doorway, came the girl. Except it wasn't a girl but a hobgoblin, something stunted and freakish. I saw an object in her hand, shining and sharp.

Just like back in Los Angeles, when the blonde attacked Tim.

"Run, Terry."

I kept going. Twenty yards farther on, I looked back. Terry was sprinting, boots clenched in her hands, the goblin hard behind her.

I careened around a pack of Japanese tourists, feeling the heat of the concrete scorching my socks, and sped around a corner. I ran straight into a group of young monks. I stopped short. They adjusted their robes, startled.

I raised my hands. "Sorry."

And had a better thought. Monks. Sanctuary. "Could you . . ."

From down the way came a keening voice. The goblin was running at us, chasing Terry, wailing. She had a hand to her face. It hid her eyes and her age. The monks frowned and glanced at me askance. She yelled again, undoubtedly *thief* or *pervert*.

It didn't take a genius to see how it looked: two scuzzy westerners fleeing from a singed, wailing child, me clutching a package that must be drugs. When I write *Top Ten: Thailand,* getting my ass kicked by irate holy men will not make the list. I ran.

Hard, dodging tourists, slaloming around chedis, rounding corners, and crossing a courtyard, heading deeper into the temple grounds with no idea where I was, running blind. Behind me I heard the goblin crying, and men sounding angry. I ducked at a corner and found myself in a courtyard with a long gallery of Buddhas and no place to hide. The monk mob would be approaching any moment.

I scanned the area for an escape. And, deep in my backpack, my new cell phone rang.

The hairs on the nape of my neck jumped up. I stopped, jammed my feet into my shoes, unzipped my backpack, and shoved the package inside. The phone continued ringing. I dug it out. Unless I'd just won a fabulous cruise to

Bermuda, it could be only one person. I answered breathlessly.

"Ev? Finally. I have to tell—"

"Jesse, oh, my God." Gripping the phone, I took off again.

"I can barely hear you. Where are you?"

I cut around a corner. "Bangkok."

The silence on the other end was thicker than mere static. "Doing what?"

I heard feet beating behind me. Looking back past a family strolling along the Buddha gallery, I saw the goblin sprint into view. She knocked into the family's little girl. The child slammed to the concrete, her bright orange flip-flops flying.

I stopped, turning to check the child, but her father barked and grabbed the goblin's arm. I took off again.

"I'm in trouble. It's . . ." Running around a corner, seeing another courtyard. "Dammit, how do I get out of here?"

"Where?"

"This temple. Wat Po."

The silence this time was longer and angrier. But when he finally spoke, his voice was dead even.

"Are you by the Reclining Buddha?"

"What?"

"Big gold dude, lying on his side."

"I don't . . ." Angling around a corner, I came out onto the crowded plaza where I'd started. I had run in a circle. "Yes."

"Go out the gate."

I pulled the phone from my ear and stared at it. "What are you talking about?"

"A gate. In the wall, under an arch, there should be a gate out to the street, where the cabs and hawkers are. Phong Chat Road, Chan Chick, something."

I saw it. "Chetuphon Road?"

"That's it."

The crowd was thick. I shot one more glance over my

shoulder, seeing neither the freak nor Terry. I passed through the gate onto a busy street where buses belched along in traffic and trees struggled for air. Tuk-tuk drivers beckoned to me. I rushed to the nearest one and jumped in.

"I'm out."

"Good. Keep going, and stay out of those tuk-tuk things. They'll get trapped in traffic."

Exhaling, I jumped out again. "What, then?"

"Run."

I took off down the sidewalk. Heat radiated up through my feet. The sky was white, the sun beating on my back.

His voice had an edge. "Are you clear?"

"Maybe." Another glance; still nobody behind me. "Are you online with a Bangkok map?"

Hesitation. "Good idea. Hang on—it'll take me a minute. Keep running."

"Which way?" More perplexed by the second, I said, "Jesse?"

"Give me a second to get the visual clear in my mind. Been a few years since I was in Bangkok."

"You gotta be shitting me."

"Left. Should be a market."

I cut around a corner and pulled up, faced with a wall. "No."

"Straight, then. West."

Back on the street I ran toward an intersection. "Traffic lights."

"Keep going."

I stopped at the street corner, checked left for traffic, and—wrong. Everything was whizzing away from me on the left side of the road. Check right—buses, tuk-tuks, and four hundred motor scooters were coming like a rockslide. I looked back toward Wat Po. Deep in the distance, I saw Terry running.

And behind her, the goblin. Quick as teeth sinking into a prey animal, she leaped and brought Terry down.

I stood frozen. The goblin smacked Terry across the face, ripped off her backpack, and rifled through it. Terry struggled to get up. The goblin threw down the pack and kicked Terry once, twice, sadistically, driving her to the pavement.

"Oh, my God," I said.

Pedestrians stopped, and a tuk-tuk driver yelled and started toward her. She dropped the pack, looked up, and saw me.

"Oh, no."

"What's wrong?" Jesse said.

She began walking toward me. Behind her Terry lay limp on the concrete. The pedestrians gingerly approached her. The goblin lit into a run, pointing at me.

From the north, I saw a second figure dashing across the street, darting between the buses and scooters.

"There're two of them," I said.

My light was still red, but I saw a break in the traffic and dashed out into the road. Taxis honked. A bus loomed, my sphincter tightened, and under a cascade of noise I reached the far side of the road.

"Where to now?" I said.

"West, toward the river."

River? Fatigue was hitting hard. "How far?"

"You can make it."

I aimed myself down the street, working to keep up my pace. "Blackburn. What were you doing in Bangkok?"

"Where are you now?"

Fine, don't tell me. "Heading"—I smelled it—"through a fish market."

"Yeah," he said, and with more certainty, "I knew there was a market. Keep going."

Dried squid lay in crates on the sidewalk. The odor scorched my nose, a powerful sweet-salty mix. The squid were gray and desiccated, shiny, roadkill flat. Old folks stood around eating them on sticks. Jeeminy. Squidsicles.

Beyond the fish market I ran past tiny shops and stalls, sensing a faint whiff of water and a cooler patch of air.

"I think the river's up ahead."

With each step I grew more certain, and now between buildings I caught a broad shine from the water beyond, a pewter green glare. I described it to him.

"Chao Phraya River. You're there."

"Now what?"

"Get on a boat."

Out of breath, I rushed out on the riverfront. The river was massive. About two hundred meters across, green as a bottle, shrieking with sunlight. Along its banks ran swank hotels and businesses and thick stands of trees. Traffic on the water was busy. Nearby, a cluster of boats bobbed alongside a wooden dock—hotel shuttles. They looked as ungainly as hippos.

I stared, dismayed. "These things? They're tugboats. I might as well try to escape on the Jungle Cruise at Disneyland, and, Jesse, if I haven't made it clear, people are *chasing* me."

"No—the longtail boats. Look around; there'll be a guy ready to dicker to give you a ride up the river."

Past the hotel shuttles I saw them. A couple of boats edged up against the dock like gondolas at a Venice pier, they were thin, slick, and weirdly fast-looking. Behind me came the sound of feet tattooing the wood. I ran down the dock.

The first boat was loading a tourist group, German by the sound and strudel-fed look of them. I ran to the second boat, where a driver in a Pepsi T-shirt was lounging on the dock, smoking and chatting with a friend.

"Get me out of here," I called.

He roused himself and said something in Thai. I had no time to find my phrase book. No time to dicker. From my pocket I dug a wad of baht. I shoved it in his hand and ran to the boat. Heard him calling me, saw him sneering at the money and shaking his head. I pulled out another, bigger wad of baht and practically threw it at him. He nodded. I jumped aboard. The boat rocked precipitously, and I grabbed one of the slat seats to steady myself. With my computer zipped in my backpack, falling into this deep water would be disastrous.

Looking down the dock, I saw two female figures skittering this way, one Thai, one fair, faces blank and eerie.

I beckoned the driver. "Go. *Ga ru na.*" Please.

Why hadn't I memorized the phrase for *right goddamned now, before those freaks get me*? He tossed his cigarette into the water and climbed aboard, moving without hurry.

Combine a covered wagon with a top-fuel dragster, and that would approximate the look of the longtail boat. At the front it rose to a curving prow bedecked with garlands and orchids. At the stern was the biggest fricking engine I had ever seen.

I put the phone to my ear. "Jesse, you there?"

"Here. Are you gone?"

"Will be." Come on, man, light this sucker up. "The engine on this thing, it looks like a V-eight."

"Probably a truck engine pulled out of a big rig. I don't hear it."

The motor was mounted on the deck and rigged to swivel. Hooked to the front of it was a metal tiller. Running out the back was an extended drive train leading to the propeller: the boat's longtail.

The goblins came speeding along the dock. The first one called out in Thai, pointing, clearly indicating that they wanted to get aboard my boat.

"Come on," I shouted. "Go!"

The driver started the engine. My world turned to noise. Hot fumes bellowed into the air, shaking the exhaust pipe, and we eased away from the dock.

In my ear, Jesse said, "Talk, Delaney."

"We're going too slow." The goblins were now dickering with the other boat driver. "Come on, bro, let's haul."

"That's not what I mean." Jesse's words were nearly swallowed by the roar of the engine, but his pitch came through clear enough. Any clearer, he would have turned the river to ice.

"The stuff I need to help Dad is here in Bangkok. But if we don't get going, I'm hosed."

The driver edged the boat past a hotel shuttle, bobbing up and down. He swiveled the engine on its pivot, throwing his shoulder into it, and drove the longtail out into the river.

The goblins were scuttling aboard the first boat, moving among the German tourists as though weightless. They shouted and pointed at us, plainly telling the driver to skip the scenic tour and give chase. He seemed unmoved. Then one of them flashed what, even from this distance, I could tell was a platinum card. He took it. Shit. Plastic beats wads of baht.

"Fast," I shouted at the driver, aiming my arm downriver. "Please. *Now.*"

He gave me a look, mostly indecipherable, and opened it up.

The roar of the engine went from loud to overwhelming, and the longtail accelerated with a huge rush of power. I whiplashed backward, gripping the edge of the seat. The bow rose, garlands and orchids flying. Behind us in the ferocious wake of the engine, a rooster tail of water curved white into the air. He powered into a sharp turn and we screamed downriver.

I glanced back. The second boat was pulling out and following us.

We roared through spangled sunlight, skipping on the green chop like a stone flung across the water. Along the riverbank, trees and shining restaurants and crumbling nineteenth-century warehouses streaked by. The wind, the speed, and the power of the engine felt exhilarating. But to get away, I had to get off this boat without Rio's trolls spotting it, which meant getting around a curve and out of their sight. And now when I looked back I saw a second rooster tail. Bigger than ours, if possible, and gaining on us.

How could they be gaining on us? They were carrying an oompah band. Damn, I needed one of those platinum cards—they truly had no limit. We slewed past traffic. Spray flew across my face like mist.

I needed cover. A bend, a ship, something. Ahead in the distance, an enormous barge was lumbering our way. It was bigger than three buildings and could hide my flight, but I didn't know if we could get around it before the other boat caught us. We roared toward it, flinging up spray.

Vaguely, from my cell phone I heard Jesse shouting at me. I put it to my ear. "What did you say?"

"You've got to be careful, Ev."

We closed the gap to the barge. It was dirty black and four times as tall as the longtail. The driver hauled on the tiller to angle around it. We banked, the back end sliding out, and sliced toward midriver. The barge rose ahead, huge engines droning, tires nailed to its flanks, bow wave spreading out in a V.

The second boat edged up behind us. The goblins were perched at the bow. With the wind batting through their hair and flattening their clothing against their bodies, they looked wasted and ropy. The Thai waved her driver to close on us. And . . . I didn't believe it. The second one, the blonde—it was the woman who had jumped Tim outside the Century Plaza Hotel.

They swung to our inside, between us and the barge, and pulled ahead. They were preparing to board us. The barge began droning past.

The goblins crouched, eyes on us. And their boat slammed into the bow wave of the barge. The longtail pitched up and, with a shriek, one of the German tourists tumbled overboard. The driver decelerated and broke off, circling to retrieve her.

I laughed out loud, seeing the German break the surface. The goblins shouted at their driver but we sped away. I turned my face into the wind.

Hell.

"Can you hear me?" Jesse shouted. "Bangkok isn't Santa Barbara. No matter what, remember—"

We hit the bow wave. In a confusion of water we skipped from the surface and slammed down in a trough. I saw the sheet of green river coming at us. The wave hit me full in the face.

Jesse shouted in my ear, "Don't drink the water."

16

The people under the awning at the restaurant glanced up from their cool drinks as I walked by. The fish stacked on ice in the display case glared blindly. My hiking shoes were squishing, my clothes sodden, my hair dripping. I gestured that I'd like a table for one. The waitress showed me to a hot corner by the kitchen, and I headed down an airless hallway to the bathrooms.

The toilet was dim and pungent, but no matter; I needed a door I could lock. My cell phone had drowned, I smelled like river, and my backpack was wet. Our Lady of Christian Help, grant that my computer be dry.

I ran my hands under the air-dryer, set the laptop on the sink, and pressed the power button. Ripping open the package I'd been given at Wat Po, I found a smaller parcel inside, wrapped in newsprint. When I unfolded it I mentally scratched my head. It was a map, of the Battle of Jonesborough. Fought in 1864, part of Sherman's Civil War campaign through the south. The flash drive was inside.

Lovely as a lullaby, my laptop chimed. I waited for it to boot.

I leaned back against the wall. Rio's people had found me. I wasn't even a half-assed spy. They'd been on my trail the whole way from Los Angeles.

So they must know that I was registered at the guesthouse. Thank God I'd kept the computer, passport, and cash on me. The little room I'd rented would be tossed. And they'd be watching for me. I couldn't go back.

My screen came up. In the corner, the ticker read 1:08. I inserted the flash drive.

The screen lit white, skewed with streaks like veined lightning, and dimmed again. That wasn't good. The ticker disappeared.

This time there was no preamble from Jax. Only the grainy view of a bedroom: rattan furniture and French windows opening onto a veranda, overlooking a lush garden. Through another door, a living room was visible. A ceiling fan lazed overhead.

Voices approached, sounding scratchy through the cheap microphone in the video system. In the living room Hank Sanger brawned into view. He dropped a baseball cap on the coffee table, headed to a sideboard, and screwed the top off a bottle of whiskey.

"Want one?" he said.

"Two fingers."

As he poured, Jax sidled into frame. He handed her a glass and they drank.

She was young. She looked supple; she had the same dancer's posture, but the clothes fit around yielding curves. Hank came into the bedroom, bringing his glass. Unzipping his jacket, he removed a silver gun from a shoulder holster and set it on the dresser.

He opened the French doors out to the veranda. "How about you rustle us up some steaks? We don't have to go to the club till ten."

Jax sauntered into the bedroom. She drank a swallow of whiskey and took a cigarette case from her back pocket. "How about we get high? We'll be fine by ten."

"Sounds good."

I was wrong. She wasn't yielding; she was petrified. Hank's back was turned, and her gaze was shifting between him and the gun.

"God," I said.

This was it. She was going to kill him.

I hunched against the wall, nauseated. She was going to murder him and make me watch it.

Hank turned from the window. "Something wrong?"

She looked up with a nervous smile. "Just wound up about the meeting."

"Don't worry. You're going to wow them. And you'll get the information you're after, so you can go back to D.C. with a big notch in your belt."

She nodded, but looked unconvinced. Because she knew that he had betrayed her—that the meeting was going to be an ambush. The people she was to meet were going to tear her apart.

He wrapped a hand around her rear end and kissed her roughly on the neck. "Course you will. Now come on, *mija,* I'm ravenous."

She pulled out of his embrace, took a joint from the cigarette case, and lit up. She handed it to him and slipped a hand around his waist as he toked, her eyes on the flame, watching him inhale.

For a second I thought I was wrong. This was going to be something other than a snuff film. But no: He wanted the high more than the sex. Turning away from her, he took a deep drag and walked out onto the veranda. She stood by the dresser, eyes on his gun.

She made the sign of the cross and, in a whisper, began to pray.

"Hail Mary, full of grace, the Lord is with thee."

Staring out the veranda doors at Hank, she clutched the medallion hanging around her neck. Our Lady of the Assassins. My flesh contracted.

"Holy Mary, mother of God, pray for us sinners, now and at the hour of our death. Amen."

Bewitched with dread, I couldn't turn away. This was what Rio Sanger wanted. Film footage of Jax Rivera killing her husband.

Hank stood on the veranda smoking the dope, leaning on the balcony railing. He lifted his glass and sunset turned the whiskey golden. He smoked the joint down to a roach and came in from the veranda, bumping the door as he passed through. He stared at his glass, and at the roach, with confusion.

Jax took it from him. "Easy, big guy."

"This shit packs a punch. Where'd you get it?"

He swayed. The whiskey glass slipped from his fingers and cracked on the floor. He put a hand to his forehead.

"What's . . . ?"

"Sit down, honey," she said.

She eased him onto the edge of the bed. He reached for her, languidly, and smiled. She straddled him. He lay back and surrendered to the narcotic embrace.

She held herself motionless, eyes on his face. "Hank?"

He lay there like a slab of dough. After a minute she slid off him, moving like a cat, and pulled herself upright. Without a word she picked up his gun from the dresser.

With balletic precision she turned, raised the gun, and centered the barrel on his forehead. She held poised, staring hard at him, arm stiff.

I couldn't even breathe. "Don't do it, Jax."

On my computer screen a warning flashed: *Low battery. Your computer will automatically shut down in two minutes.*

Not now. I dug in my backpack for the power cable and adapter plug, and kept watching.

Jax stared at Hank. She said, "God forgive me."

And lowered the gun. Her shoulders heaved.

Her arm dropped to her side and she turned away from him. She had tears in her eyes.

Then she drew herself up. She turned back around to face him.

Hank was awake.

He was up off the bed. He was right there, ripping the gun from her hand. He backhanded her across the face, and sent her keeling.

And then he shot her.

The shot blew Jax off her feet, flat to the floor. I gaped at the screen, seeing the blood turning to a wet rose on her thigh. She struggled to sit up, horror on her face.

Warning: Your computer will shut down in one minute.

No, no. I looked around. Where was an electrical outlet?

Hank stared at the gun, and then he began to lift it, getting ready to fire at her again.

"Don't," Jax said. "I have to tell you something."

"You got nothing left to say to me."

"It's about Christian. Something's wrong with him. Kill me and you'll never find out."

He kept the gun on her.

My computer went black. "Dammit."

The outlet was at the baseboard near the door. I jammed the adapter into it. Come on, come on. Karma, please come on. The screen streaked again, shot wild with colors, and warped back into view.

The video clip was gone. In the bottom corner there was only a line of text and a blinking cursor.

Victorious commander?

"Goddammit." I ran my hands through my hair. Then I forced myself to think. I got the map the flash drive had come wrapped in. I typed, *William Tecumseh Sherman.*

A new line of text appeared.

328 North Bridge Road
Singapore

In the corner of the screen, the down-ticker reset: 10:00, 9:59.59.

Slamming the computer, I hurried out through the restaurant and into the muggy day, winding between the sidewalk tables onto the narrow street. I felt numb. I waited for a couple of motor scooters to buzz past and stepped off the curb.

What the hell had happened during Riverbend?

Two steps into the street I heard a motorbike shift gears and rev up. I looked, saw the bike gunning along the street toward me. The driver was swathed in black leathers. Sunlight refracted off his helmet visor. I stepped back. The bike veered in my direction. Another step back, and the bike angled again to take aim at me.

I was so tired.

Damned tired. Past-the-point-of-putting-up-with-this-shit tired. I turned to a tourist couple at one of the sidewalk tables.

"May I borrow this chair?"

"Certainly." They gestured for me to take it.

The bike sped along the curb. I hoisted the chair and swung it around like a drunken dance partner.

It hit the driver in the face and flew out of my hands. The driver sailed off the bike. My arms rang from the blow and the bike kept going. The driver hit the ground like a crazed bowling ball, flipped onto the opposite curb, and smashed into a rack of trinkets outside a gift shop. The bike jerked its way along the street and crashed over.

The tourists at the table leaped to their feet. "Bloody hell, what was that for?"

The driver lay in a heap with trinkets and toys dribbling off the rack across his leathers.

The shopkeeper rushed to the doorway. Diners stood up. The biker sprawled under the avalanche of baubles. The bike lay twenty yards farther down the street, motor revving. I walked toward it.

Screw the airport. I'd drive to Singapore. I pushed the bike upright, straightened the handlebars, and swung a leg over the seat.

Feeling a shift in the air, I turned my head. The biker grabbed me by the shoulders, hauled me off the motorcycle, and shoved me onto the sidewalk. Flinging his leg up, he threw a roundhouse kick that caught me in the midsection. I slammed backward through the door of the tourist shop and crashed into a display case. I slid to the floor. When I looked up, I saw his arm cocked to hit me.

Before I could raise a hand, the biker swung an arm and slapped me across the face. It stung like crazy. I thrashed to get up but was tangled in trinkets and strings of beads. The biker dropped down, straddled my rib cage, and clamped a leather glove around my neck. He raised his other hand. I tensed for his punch.

He flipped up the visor on his helmet. His eyes were dark and infuriated. And familiar.

Jax? I mouthed.

She lifted her hand from my throat. "That hurt. Like hell."

"How did you—"

"You could have killed me." Sinking her gloves into my shirt, she hauled me to my feet.

"I didn't know—"

"And you were going to steal my bike? I don't think so. Move."

She shoved me toward the door. The shopkeeper was waving her arms and yelling. Jax shouted back in Thai.

"Give her some money," she said.

Head zinging, I fished a hunk of baht from my pocket and held it out. Jax handed it to the woman. I brushed broken plaster from my chest. Jax grabbed my shirt again, yanked me out the door, and pulled me toward the still-revving bike.

"Get on."

She righted it and swung a leg over. Dumbly I climbed on behind her and wrapped my arms around her waist, feeling the heat swarming off her leathers. Without another word, she took off down the street.

17

I clung to Jax, my skin so slick with sweat that when she banked the motorcycle I slipped to the side. The street scene sped by, crammed with cars; tacky shops; ripe, damp smells; and hot people seeking shade. She shifted her balance and leaned into a turn. We careened around a corner. I gripped her waist, squeezing my thighs against hers. She rode the bike as if it were a metal extension of herself.

She gunned down an alley, sweeping under a line of trees, and all at once we were driving in gentle shade up a spotless driveway, through lawns and palms and lush ferns, toward a hotel that loomed like a pagoda. I saw the sign: SHANGRI-LA.

She stopped beneath a cool portico, and a doorman came smiling forward to welcome us. Awkwardly I climbed off the bike, legs chattering. Jax pulled off her helmet and strode toward the entrance.

"Wait," I said.

She swept into the lobby. I followed on her heels, seeing marble, chandeliers, and orchids. Behind the front desk, slim young women put their hands together in that prayerful gesture and greeted her, *"Sawatdee."* The view out the windows showed coconut palms, a sparkling swimming pool, and the river. I wanted to sit down and stay forever.

It was air conditioned. Blissfully, extravagantly, Norwegian-fjord cool. Forget karma—take my soul. Just give me thirty more seconds here.

Jax strode to the desk with breezy élan, as if hard-assed African-American women roared up to this place on a 500cc bike every few minutes. She gave a gleaming smile, spoke about five words, and came away with a key card.

"Walk with me," she said.

Somewhere a grand piano was playing. Any moment I expected to see Yul Brynner and Deborah Kerr sweep down the grand staircase and break into a waltz.

"And take that hayseed out of your mouth," she said.

Upstairs, she let us into a suite overlooking the river. It was every inch as opulent as the lobby, all gilded silk and lustrous teak. White orchids seemed to drip from the walls. At the wet bar by the door, expensive whiskeys were lined up. On the coffee table sat a lavish bowl of tropical fruit, a bottle of wine, and a lovely note from the manager, welcoming us. Who knew that some hotels provided hospitality beyond vending machines that dispensed stale candy bars?

Jax stripped off her leather jacket. She was wearing a skintight black top, and her shoulders looked angry where she had skidded along the pavement after the crash.

"You have sixty seconds to explain why you went to the red-key box at the music archive in L.A.," she said.

"Why'd you give me that *Crouching Tiger* karate kick?" I put a hand to my ribs. "You knew it was me."

She got two bottles of water from the minibar and tossed one to me. "Fifty seconds. Then I really start whipping your ass."

"Hell, no—I need to catch a flight to Singapore. I have less than ten hours to get the next flash drive. But then, you already know that."

"The information in that file is not meant for you. You're not involved."

"Not involved?"

She tipped the water bottle to her lips, swallowed voraciously, and ran the back of her hand across her lips. "One thing about Bangkok. Watch your gut. Don't—"

"Drink the water. Got that."

She had no idea, I realized. None at all.

I touched a hand to my forehead. I was going to have to tell her. All of it.

"Jax . . ." All of it. "Dad's been kidnapped by the Sangers. They want the Riverbend file as ransom."

As if a switch had flipped, she ceased movement. Even her breathing seemed to pause.

"She's tracking." Her gaze withdrew. "How did you get the address for the music archive?"

"Tim."

Suspicion rose in her eyes. "Tim doesn't know about the archive."

Oh, brother. Heat prickled along my arms. Tell her.

"Tim deciphered the clues that led to the address. The R-and-B stuff. He's the one who found the red key."

"That's improbable."

Tell her. "He thinks you've been kidnapped too. You didn't check in with him. He came to me to try to find you."

Her gaze clicked off to the side, as though assessing that. Her expression was opaque. "It still doesn't compute. Why are you here when . . ." Eyes back to me. "What's happened to him?"

A ball of emotion rose up my throat. "He's been shot."

She breathed, twice, and stilled so completely that she might have turned to slate. Sunlight limned her eyes.

"Is he dead?" she said.

"He was alive when I left L.A."

Despite all efforts, my voice cracked. For a second longer she held my gaze, and then she closed her eyes and tilted her head back. She kept her face neutral, but her chest heaved. I felt riven.

"Jax." I touched her arm. "He took a single shot to his side. He managed to call somebody to come and help him. He—"

She grabbed my wrist. "You left him?"

I spoke perhaps the hardest single syllable I'd ever had to pronounce. "Yes."

Her fingernails dug into my flesh. "Alone?"

"Tim told me I had to get the file. He said if I failed, we'd never see you or my father again." I kept myself from flinching at her grip. "Do you understand? He insisted—for you. So help me get to Singapore. We're running out of time."

"No. The one thing you cannot do is turn the file over to the Sangers."

"What?" I practically saw stars. "Why not? What's in the file, the blood of Christ?"

"This isn't about ransoming your father. It's about Rio punishing him, and me."

"Jax, she's already taken Dad. She's shot your husband. And I'm wanted by the police. What do we have to lose?"

Shoving me loose, she raised her hands. "Shut up. Let me think."

She clenched her fists and began pacing. If she was trying to compartmentalize the news of Tim's injury, she was failing.

"We have to alter the file. If we delete some information and change other parts to mislead Rio, it will work."

"Mess with the file? Forget it. I don't care about your agenda. I want Dad back."

She kept pacing. I checked my watch.

"Dammit, Dad doesn't have time for me to chase around Asia collecting these things like Easter eggs. He has forty-one hours left."

She stopped, absorbing that. "Then you have to do it my way. You go where I tell you and do exactly as I say. Otherwise, I'll make sure you never get the flash drive. Can you handle that?"

"Yes."

"It'll be hard as hell. You're going to have to bring your A game."

She looked as combustible as detonator cord. Her gaze was a challenge.

"Jax, I drove your husband bleeding out of Santa Bar-

bara after a gunfight. I got the flash drive, eluded the
LAPD, flew halfway around the world, and outran the
Children of the Corn on the river. I even managed to
knock you off your bike. And I had the guts to tell you
about Tim," I said. "Bring it on."

She held my gaze. I stepped toward her.

"But bring it now. We can't afford to waste another second."

Slowly, almost imperceptibly, she nodded.

"So, are you going to take me to Singapore?" I said.

"No." She unzipped a pocket in her leathers, pulled out
a flash drive, and held it up. "This is it."

Neon, beer, sequins, and chili: Bangkok after dark. Jax and
I strode past tourists and party seekers on a street near
Patpong Night Market, illuminated by flashing lights advertising everything from sarongs to emeralds to girls to
girls. Amplified music and multilingual chatter rained
sound on me. Under the gaudy blue shine of a nightclub
marquee, Jax's brown face took on the luster of sharkskin.
She had never looked so much her age, every day of her
forty-five years.

She wasn't speaking. Since leaving the hotel she had
seemingly gone into a trance. I suspected that her meditative state was working not toward Zen but retribution—
that it would resolve not with a beatific vision, but a bullet.

She rounded a corner and led me down an alley. Cook-
ing smells hung in the air and laughter echoed from
kitchen windows. A sickly odor crawled up to me.

"What is that stink?" I said.

"Glue."

Between buildings I glimpsed men squatting on the
pavement under bare bulbs, tools in hand. She glanced at
them idly.

"They're sticking labels into the Gucci bags they just
counterfeited. Don't worry; the stuff I'm getting you is
much higher quality."

I gave her a look. "And what's that?"

"Your new passport."

I couldn't say I was surprised. Getting passport photos taken half an hour earlier was sort of a giveaway. We were building the new me.

Here in the market we had been shopping. In forty-five minutes Jax had managed to get me not simply new clothes, but measured for a new wardrobe. Thanks to an aggressive seamstress, I now knew my crotch-to-ground measurement to the millimeter. Then Jax found me a hair-dresser. Fifty-one minutes: dye job, chop, scalp massage, mousse, and blow-dry, and I was a chocolate brunette. Punk rock lived. On my head. SpecWorld set me up with colored contact lenses and a pair of Eurotrash glasses. A discount chemist provided the makeup. Jax had lavished it onto my face.

Examining the passport photos under the alley lights, I perused the results: kohl and sleep deprivation gave me gothic eyes. "Will it work?"

"With enough attitude. Sophisticated security will catch your voice or stride pattern. But persona you can affect." She led me out of the alley onto a broad boulevard. "The key thing is learning your legend. It'll be simple, but you have to know it cold."

She stepped to the curb, watching the traffic rip by, searching for a taxi.

"Jax, it's time for you to start talking. There are things I need to know."

"You don't need to know. You simply want to know."

"Why did you say that Tim and my dad hate each other?"

"Want to know."

"Is it because Dad was involved in the operation that led to Hank Sanger shooting you?"

"Want to know."

"When you were sleeping with Sanger, did you know he was married to Rio?"

"Common law." She hailed a taxi. "Get in."

I hopped in and waited for her to slam the door. "Why did you say that Riverbend is about lost children?"

She leaned toward the driver and gave him an address. We pulled out into traffic.

"What do lost kids have to do with Rio Sanger's blood feud?" I said.

"Your father and I took some of Rio's girls away, got them to the police or sent them home. She regarded that as thievery."

"That's not enough to set her off on a vendetta."

"Let me tell you about Rio," she said. "American father, East Asian mother. She grew up in Bangkok, started hooking as a young teen, met Hank, had a baby at eighteen, her precious Christian." She watched the city blare by. "She used a sugar daddy to get her out of Asia. Other men got her to Europe and the Americas. She treated them as plane tickets. But she always came back to Hank. That's how she ended up running a club in Medellín, followed him down there. And then here again."

"I saw Hank shoot you."

"I turned my back. Never turn your back."

I was quiet for a minute. "What did you have to tell Hank about Christian? What was wrong with him?"

"I was trying to save myself. I would have said anything."

"What are you going to alter in the Riverbend file?"

"How's the writing coming?"

My scalp tightened. "I'm not doing your memoirs. Ever."

"No, your novel. Is your guerrilla chick coming back for this one?"

"Why did you leave the agency, Jax?"

"Rowan Larkin, I like her. Wish I could kill by telekinesis, the way she does. Very cool."

I hunched down in my seat, staring out the window. "The phrase *direct answer* has no meaning to you, does it?"

"Keep talking to yourself; I think you're getting the picture."

I crossed my arms. "I know why you keep turning up in my life. It isn't because you worked with Dad. It's because you have no friends."

Her mouth drew taut. She barked at the driver. He pulled over.

She paid, hopped out, and marched off along a swanky street of designer shops. I caught up. Her chin was in the air.

"The agency. Mediocre pay, lousy canteen. Office politics, expense reports, random drug testing," she said.

Crowds of shoppers strolled along, chatting and laughing, shopping bags swinging. Shop windows shimmered with red and blue silk.

"Fieldwork was better. Exotic travel and fine, fine weapons. Boffing for the USA was great, bringing down the narco kings or some rogue *comandante* through the power of positive shagging. But by the time I left, half the analysts at Langley had more contacts at the *New York Times* than they did in Peshawar." She scanned the shop windows. "This planet is scummy with dross. At Langley I was one more nodding head around a conference table. On my own I am like a refiner's fire. You don't like the way power works? Go home and read Noam Chomsky and howl about it online."

"Jesus, and I thought Jesse was a cynic."

"I really am the badass you feared I was."

She pushed open a door and led me into a shop. I felt a chill that didn't come from the air-conditioning.

I looked around. This wasn't a clothing boutique but something closer to a sculpture gallery. Under recessed lighting, we stood surrounded by fossils.

Slabs of sandstone hung on the walls, embedded with prehistoric ferns and small lizardy skeletons. A display pedestal bore the tusks of a woolly mammoth. On the mahogany-paneled wall at the back of the shop, a discreet logo read MESOZOICA—DINOSAUR VENDORS.

The gallery was hushed, spare, and, apart from us, empty.

I approached a varnished object on a display pedestal and leaned in to examine it face-to-face. It was the skull of a saber-toothed tiger. It was sublime.

"Unbelievable," I said.

"Be glad it's dead."

A man's amplified voice came to us from the ether. "May I help you?"

Jax spoke to the air. "I'm interested in the world we left behind. This would seem to be it."

The voice turned thoughtful. "Remnants of a simpler place and time? Have you seen the compsognathus specimen on the wall?"

"I'd have to pawn all my hopes to pay for that. What else?" Jax said.

"How much time do you have?"

"Not much. I'm leaving on the midnight train."

I shot her a look, amazed that spooks actually played this code-word game.

"One moment," the voice said.

Jax stood calmly among the predators. I murmured in her ear.

" 'Midnight Train to Georgia'? If the CIA's stuck in the seventies, the agency's worse off than I thought."

The mahogany wall at the back of the store began to move. Silently it pivoted, swinging ninety degrees to reveal another room behind it—the guts of Mesozoica, half office, half paleontology lab.

A man strolled out from behind a desk, where he'd been observing us on closed-circuit TV. He was tall for a Thai, a good six feet, with a gleaming shaven head. He gave Jax a knowing smile. She made the prayerful *wai* gesture and he returned it. Then he took her hand and kissed her on both cheeks, European-style.

"How thrilling of you to interrupt my evening," he said.

"I'm in a hurry, Pete."

"And you've lost none of your charm, either." He turned and offered me his hand. "Petch Kongsangchai."

Jax nodded at me. "This is Kit."

Which I was, Kathleen being my first name, but hearing the name caused a stab of distress. Only one person in the world called me Kit, and that was my father.

"What do you need?" he asked her.

"Do you still have root privileges on the Lawrence Livermore server?"

I gave her a sharp look. He didn't answer. Instead he led us into the secret room and closed the wall behind us with a soft swoosh.

"Pete? I need to access their archives to grab a type one crypto key," she said.

He looked peeved. "Nothing else? Perhaps the launch code for the nuclear football?"

"I wouldn't ask if it weren't necessary."

His expression softened. "Jakarta, what have you done?"

"This goes beyond me. It's . . ." Her rigid control slipped for a moment. "It's Tim." She waited for him to say something, but he didn't inquire further. "And yes, I do need something else. An American passport."

He shook his head. "I'm retired from that line of work."

"Driver's license, couple of credit cards as well."

"No. My business no longer revolves around simulations of authenticity. I now deal in genuine items only."

She held out my new passport photos and a sheet of information she had scribbled down at the hotel. "This is what you need."

He declined to take it. She grabbed his wrist. "She's Phil's daughter."

He turned to me with a new and awful light in his eyes. He took the photos and information from her. "She travels extensively?"

"Europe mostly. She's adventurous but green."

"Age?"

"Thirty-four," I said.

He scrutinized me. "I can give you twenty-nine." He examined the sheet of paper. "This will take—"

"Half an hour," Jax said.

He tilted his head. "Darling, when did you develop a sense of humor?"

"I didn't."

"An hour. And it will be two thousand."

Jax glanced at me. "Pay him."

I found that much baht in the bottom of my backpack, doing the math in my head. Even jet-lagged out of my mind, I calculated that it worked out to around sixty dollars. This town was bargain city. Maybe I should go back up the street to Glueville and grab some new luggage. And a plasma screen TV.

Jax put her hand on mine. "Two thousand U.S."

Too tired to feel stupid, I found the stash Tim had given me and peeled off a roll of bills.

Pete turned, but Jax stopped him. "This is vitally important. I cannot emphasize that enough."

His pissy jocularity ebbed. "I understand." He called out, "Daw. Need you."

At a worktable in the back of the room, a woman pushed aside her large magnifying glass and stood up from behind the thighbone of a Cretaceous beast. She was swathed in a black turtleneck dress, as sleek as any runway model in Manhattan.

Jax gave her a *wai*. "*Sawatdee-ka,* Daw."

The woman glided over. Pete handed her the photos.

"Jakarta. Kit. Would you like tea?" she said.

"Does it come with sympathy?" Jax said.

"It comes with a whole new life."

18

The teapot was empty. So were the bowls of pad thai that Pete had rustled up for us. Daw jogged down a flight of stairs at the back of the workshop and handed Jax an American passport, a California driver's license, and two credit cards. Jax took the passport to the large magnifying glass at Daw's worktable. Flipping on a desk lamp, she examined it.

"New cover, nicely bent in a couple of spots. The photos look good."

I walked over, took a look, and huffed. "Kathleen Rowan Larkin. Didn't you think I could remember an entirely fresh name?"

"Making things simple. Nobody will ever guess it incorporates the name of your protagonist."

"Exactly why it's so insulting."

"The point, as Daw and Pete will tell you, is that this passport will fool all but the most expertly trained of eyes."

Daw said, "Not even Immigration should pick up on it."

Jax turned it under the light. "The holograph is excellent. And the ink. Print method?"

"Perfect," Daw said. "One plate for each color used."

"Watermark?"

"Simulated but visible under UV light."

"Good rainbow. Excellent." Satisfied, she gave her a nod and turned to Pete. "Got the key?"

He stared at his computer screen. "I have the algorithm and the time stamp."

"Good."

He ejected a disk and gave it to her. Daw handed me the driver's license.

I smiled. "Thanks for turning back the clock on my birthday."

Looking up, Pete said, "Pleasure, darling."

Jax said, "Tell him about your run-in with Rio's goons today."

"That." I described the goblins: twelve-year-olds' height, faunlike figures, with ropy musculature and creepy eyes.

"Diminuendos?" Pete said.

"How would Rio do it?" Jax said.

He ran a hand over his shaven head. "She would have needed to induce hypopituitarism in childhood. Stop production of growth hormone to stunt their growth and physical maturation."

"How would she do that?"

"Drugs, surgery . . ." A look of distress came upon his face. "Jakarta, growth hormone is a boon. It can be life changing for children with congenital growth problems. To think that Rio would disrupt it . . ."

Realizing what they were suggesting, I felt a deep sense of nausea. "It also means that these people have been working for Rio Sanger for more than a decade." I looked at Jax, remembering her warning on the Riverbend video: *Rio still has those girls.*

Jax glanced at me. "I told you to watch out."

Pete looked at us anew, no longer interested solely in commerce or ancient spook loyalties. "Whatever you're doing to stop them, I hope that I've been able to help."

Daw came forward. "I hope things turn out for the best. And that Tim will be with you next time we meet."

"Me too," Jax said.

Christian paced on the balcony. Down the hill below him, Los Angeles was a throbbing grid of lights. This was the best time of night, predawn, postcoital, paycheck time, but he couldn't stand still. Finally Eden came out, phone in her hand.

"Shiver tossed Delaney's room at the backpacker guest-house. No luck."

"Nothing? Fuck."

He felt so cold. He rubbed his hands together to warm them.

Eden moved as though her kidneys hurt. Fortieth-birthday boy had given her a few energetic hits with the police nightstick.

"Don't worry. She and Bliss will track Delaney down," she said.

He paced past her. "How? It's Bangkok."

"They're resourceful."

She said it slowly, as though he were a child. His chest squeezed, that sudden tightness. Again he got the feeling that Eden regarded him as a weakling. This whore, her body stunted into a parody of adolescence, more and more treated him like the runt of the litter.

From the house came the click of heels. Rio swept onto the balcony. "Status?"

He shoved his hair back from his face. "We'll clear nine-teen five tonight."

"Good. What about the Delaney girl?"

"Shiver and Bliss are tracking her," he said.

Her perfume wafted between them, soaking into the fabric of his sweater. He was exhausted and wanted to take a shower. The high was wearing off.

Nothing was working anymore, not the EPO, not the meth, not anything. He had to stay awake and was so tired, so cold, and his mother and Eden were staring at him like they knew something he didn't.

"What?" he said.

Frown lines appeared on Rio's face. "You look awful. Get to bed."

"I can't go to sleep. Not till we know they've got her."

She put the back of her hand to his forehead, felt for a

second, and exhaled. "No arguments. You're coming down with something." She nudged him toward the house and turned to Eden. "What do we know?"

"There were only a few places Delaney could get off the longtail boat, so they showed her picture in nearby neighborhoods."

He walked toward the house. In the plate-glass windows he could see straight through his reflection.

Eden said, "Shiver found out that a scuffle happened, a fight with a motorbike rider."

"That black Texan bitch?" Rio said.

"I think so."

"Then they can estimate where she's gone to ground."

He watched their reflections in the windows. They had to get Delaney. They couldn't lose.

The SIG was in the bedroom. He needed to check that it was loaded and in working order. When he stripped it earlier, he had cut his finger reassembling the slide. It bled for fifteen minutes. This time he wouldn't cut himself. He stared at his hands. They were cold. He needed to busy them, to put everything in order.

Eden said, "Rivera will go five-star, we figure."

Rio nodded. "She would choose someplace where she could count on the hotel staff to have absolute tact. Good. Very good, Eden. Tell them to press it home. I want this."

In the reflection Christian saw Eden dialing the phone. Rio put a hand on the back of her neck and leaned down to her ear. "And tell them to hurry."

Jax unlocked the door and headed into the suite at the Shangri-La. "Ah. Good."

I drew up short, thinking I had stumbled into Santa's workshop. My new wardrobe had been delivered. Shopping bags were primped on the coffee table, shiny with green and gold and electric blue blouses, a tight-fitting black suit, a black cashmere sweater, and wool trousers.

Shoes, belts, earrings, and necklaces. It was a far cry from the jeans and T-shirts I wore at home.

"Kit Larkin outclasses me by a mile." Especially in the underwear department. And all the black lace went with my Goth eye makeup.

Jax booted up the laptop that had been delivered for her. "Kit Larkin is on sabbatical from her job at an advertising agency in San Francisco. She likes to make a splash and is traveling the world."

"Yes, Japan, Italy, and Spain in the last six months, according to her passport." I checked my watch. "And right now she wants to get moving."

She glanced at me out of the corner of her eye. "Cool it. You still have five hours on your computer's clock to download the Singapore flash drive. I'll have it decrypted and modified long before then."

"Dad may be running out of water and oxygen. I don't want to wait five hours." I rubbed my eyes. "Why did you have to set the file up this way, forcing me to run around chasing it?"

"Insurance. If the right person went after the file, they had to be totally committed to getting it. If the wrong person went after it, I could short-circuit them. Breaking it into pieces bought me time to recover the drives or set an ambush. I knew where they were going to be, and when."

"Yeah, like me."

She saw me check my watch again.

"It's eight p.m. We're checking out by nine." She set my computer on the desk next to her own. "This hotel isn't a safe house. I can count on the discretion of the staff, but we can't linger. Now let me do some serious work on your laptop."

She inserted the disk that Pete Kongsangchai had given her. My screen blossomed with a picture of deep space, a starlit blue nebula.

"How did you get access to a secure server at Lawrence Livermore?" I said.

"Pete worked as a security analyst at both Sandia and Livermore. Our paths crossed over the years."

That nonanswer didn't reassure me. The Lawrence Livermore laboratory certifies the U.S. nuclear weapons stockpile. The toys it's invented over the years include the Polaris missile warhead.

"What's type one crypto?" I said.

"Our ultimate encryption method. It's a code generated by recording static from outer space. Pulsars, X-ray bursts from black holes . . ." She flipped between programs, typing staccato. "The key to unbreakable encryption is to encode your information using a truly random number. Type one crypto captures space noise and runs it through an algorithm to generate that number. To decrypt, you need the algorithm and a time stamp pinpointing the exact moment when our satellites captured the noise."

"E.T., phone home."

She hit the keyboard with a manicured nail. "Who says SETI didn't pay off?"

"Please tell me you're going to stop the clock that's ticking down on all these flash drives."

"Yes."

"Good."

"I just loaded the decryption key onto your computer. Now . . ." She jacked the Singapore flash drive into my laptop. "I'm going to decrypt the flash drive, delete some information on it, and edit the rest. Then I'll load the revised Riverbend file onto a disk you can give to Rio."

"Excellent."

She cued up a video grab on my screen. It was a shot from Rio's cathouse, with the two girls thanking their customer the morning after. She refocused the shot and zoomed in on their faces. "Are these the Children of the Corn?"

"Holy mother."

The Asian girl was the thing who had leaped on me at Wat Po. Beside her stood the blonde who had attacked Tim

in Los Angeles. In the intervening years their facial structure had barely changed. Only their eyes, and the wear and
tear, gave them away.

"Why would Rio deliberately stunt their growth?" I
said. It was not only horrible, but perplexing. "Wouldn't it
be cheaper just to kick them out and replace them with
real teenagers?"

She looked up. "That's the most ruthless thing I have
ever heard you say."

Embarrassment came and went. "Know your enemy,
Jax."

"I presume these creatures had developed skills that real
teens didn't have."

"Value added. And not just in the bedroom." My gaze
lingered on the girls' young faces. "Turn it off."

She did. With all the emotion of a stone, she went back
to typing.

My gaze remained on the screen. "In your video narra-
tion, you said there were three."

"Yes. Rio kept three close to her, took them everywhere
with her. They all had ho names. One was Bliss. The
Thai . . ." She typed. "I think it was Shiver."

"You said to watch out for three of them. Where's the
third?" I crossed my arms, waiting for a response that
didn't come. "The little girl on the Riverbend video—the
one perched in the tree. Is it her?"

She looked up. "No."

"Who is she? You said on the video she was a lost girl."

She continued typing. I was tired of this.

"Jax. That little girl in the tree. What's her ho name?"

Before I could breathe she was out of the chair and in
my face. I put up my hands and stepped back, saying,
"Hey."

"Do you see her around here anywhere?" Her gaze was
searing. "She's one more life that Riverbend ended up
turning inside out for good. She's gone, all right?"

Jesus, was she about to cry? "What did Rio do to her?"

For a second I thought she was going to tell me, or smack me. But she shook her head, raised her hands, and backed away. She sat down and began stabbing at her keyboard again. I stood, arms helpless at my sides.

"Stop staring," she said.

Off-kilter, I wandered to the coffee table and stared at the pile of Christmas goodies.

Whether through training or emotional dystrophy, her voice turned flat. "I need to make a phone call. Go out on the bedroom balcony and take in the view."

"I have to call Jesse."

She pointed at the shopping pile. "There's a new cell phone for you. But keep it short. You'll be calling in the clear, unscrambled. Thirty seconds, no more."

"I can't do that to him."

"Then hook up the Webcam and talk online. The camera's that pinhole device."

I found it and the phone. Hesitantly I approached the desk to get my computer. She stopped typing but didn't look up.

"When are you going to let Jesse put a wedding ring on your hand?" she said.

"That's the least of my concerns tonight."

"Tomorrow isn't guaranteed." She leaned back. "Get married. Make a home with your man and have his babies."

Heat seeped from my throat down through my body. She didn't know about the child we had lost, and it felt like a fresh wound.

"You should have a big family, and thirty-four means you should get to work. Don't wait. The perfect time won't ever come." She let her hands drop to her lap. "I waited for that and I screwed it up badly."

She looked up. "You've got something. Grab it with both hands and hold on for dear life."

I found that my throat had gone dry. Her brown face was blotchy, her knuckles pale with tension. If she'd been anyone else, I would have put a hand on her shoulder.

"Jax, Tim's going to be all right."

"No, he's not. Not for a long time, anyhow. And if . . ." Pain came and went on her face. "Tim is my partner. He's my core. But he's not the one I loved." The pain edged into bitterness. "I blew it. Don't you do the same thing."

She ejected Pete's DVD and handed me my computer. "Go outside. Let me work."

When I stepped onto the balcony outside the bedroom and shut the door behind me, she was staring vacantly at the computer screen.

19

When Shiver walked up to reception at the Shangri-La, the young woman behind the front desk smiled softly and offered a graceful *wai*. Shiver set the envelope on the counter.

"Will you please deliver this to your guest Mrs. Rivera?"

"Of course."

Shiver kept her fingers on the envelope. "She may be registered under a married name. But she's American, a black woman, very bold in everything. Your staff would remember her."

The girl nodded. "Yes, thank you. We'll deliver it."

"Kop khun ka," Shiver said.

She walked out into the muggy night, where children were bobbing in the pool. She'd already been to the Mandarin Oriental, the Marriott, and the Peninsula. By the process of elimination, they were closing in.

Back inside the lobby, Bliss sat in an upholstered chair, listening to ballroom music. Scratching her arm, she watched the girl at the front desk take the envelope, consult with a colleague, and call to a bellboy. The girl gestured upstairs and handed the envelope to him. He headed for the lifts.

She stood up and followed him, dialing Shiver's phone as she went. "They're here. Get down to the phone room."

On the balcony, the humid night air cocooned me. I set my laptop on an end table and hooked up the pinhole Web camera. The noise of the city burbled far below, motor scooters on bridges and longtail boats on the water. The river was a sinuous black artery gold-lit with reflected light. Orchestral music floated up from a hotel ballroom. Below me, kids splashed in the swimming pool.

Heart drumming, I dialed Jesse's number. He picked up on the first ring.

"This had better be you," he said.

"I'm okay. Hook up your Webcam; I'm going online."

"Give me two minutes. And your phone number. And don't you damned move until we talk."

I told him the new phone number, hung up, and turned to my computer. My palms were sweating.

Inside the suite, Jax was pacing back and forth between the bedroom and living room, phone to her ear. She had turned on the television to mask her conversation, and over her shoulder I saw a frenetic Thai soap opera. She cut her eyes in my direction. I turned away to give her privacy and gazed over the electric gold leaf of the city lights.

My computer chirped and the video screen opened. Through all my nerves and exhaustion, I found myself, unaccountably, smiling.

Jesse was sitting at his kitchen table, hair disheveled, blinking himself awake. Through the windows behind him, I could see a blue dawn tracing the outline of the mountains.

"Are you still in Bangkok?" he said.

"Yeah, but not for long."

He adjusted the focus on his camera. The view turned so sharp that I could practically hear the surf breaking outside his house, smell the sea air, taste the salt that always lingered on his skin after he swam. The lights were low, dragging shadows across his face.

"What did you do to your hair?" he said.

"Ran with scissors."

"Very Chrissie Hynde. Sit still and listen to me."

His tone was disconcerting. "Have you heard something? Is it Dad?"

"No. There's no word."

I felt that ghostly fist tighten around my windpipe. "Then what is it?"

His face looked sober and intense. I wanted to reach through the screen and wrap myself in his arms.

"First thing. I checked out those phone numbers you e-mailed me from Boyd Davies's phone. You were right about him being hinky. He wasn't who he claimed to be."

"Who was he?"

"He wasn't with Immigration and Customs. He ran the Davies Bail Enforcement Agency of Las Vegas, Nevada."

Shiver pulled her burglar tool from the door to the telephone and computer room in the hotel basement and shut the door behind her. She found the router, which ran Internet traffic for the hotel. At this time of night only a few guests were logged on. She plugged her handheld computer into the box. This was a long shot, but worth a chance. If their targets were online, and broadcasting in the clear, the port mirror she was setting up would show her exactly what they were doing, bringing up their screens on hers.

Her mobile buzzed. It was Bliss.

"They're here. Room twelve thirty-one, Krung Thep wing."

"Got it."

"I hear someone talking inside. Check to see if they're on the phone or online."

Luck. The phone line was not in use, but the Internet portal showed that somebody in the room was indeed online. She jacked into the router port and sat forward. Better luck: They were having a video conversation. The man on the screen looked sleepy but intense. Looked like he'd be a good lay, too, from that confident voice and the cool intelligence in his eyes. She watched.

　　　　　　*　　*　　*

"He was a bounty hunter?" I said.

"Boyd Davies specialized in fugitive recovery. He was not and never had been a federal agent."

"A *bounty hunter*. Holy Moses." I looked up the river, trying to absorb this. "He tracked Dad and kidnapped him for the Sangers, didn't he?"

"That's my bet. And when it turned out Phil didn't have what they wanted, he thought he could get it from you."

"Do the authorities know this?"

"Yes. Based on that, plus the ransom photo of your dad, Lily Rodriguez is opening a kidnapping investigation."

"Finally." This was the first glimmer of good news I'd had since all this began. "Lily's going to come through."

"But it doesn't help you. You're being sought for murder and unlawful flight. Look, I've talked to Drew Farelli, and the feds have to drop the charge of murdering a U.S. agent. But nobody's ready to clear you."

That was no surprise. I nodded, sinking a bit.

"Nicholas Gray isn't backing off, is he?" I said.

"No, he has his claws out. He still thinks you and your dad are dirty."

He looked down, as though something were weighing on him.

"Jesse, what is it? Something else is bothering you."

"Yeah." He ran a hand over his face. "I want you to turn yourself in."

In the hot night air, I felt a chill. The shadows etching Jesse's face gave him a look of pain.

Turn myself in? "No."

"Delaney, this is the place where you hold still, calm down, and listen to me."

"No." The chill was running across my scalp. "Dad'll die." I was shaking my head. "What are you thinking?"

"I tried to tell you when you were in L.A. You have to destroy the files and stop what you're doing."

"And I tried to ask you—*why*? Do you know something I don't? What did Dad's message say to you?"

"I can't tell you."

"Can't?"

"I can only beg you to trust me. No matter what happens, know I have a good reason."

I fell silent, watching his face. Of course I trusted him. But the plea in his eyes hinted at something worse going on.

"Please, Ev, just . . ." He frowned. "What's . . . There's something moving around behind you. Is somebody with you?"

"Jax."

His eyes widened. "Fuck me, what's she doing there?"

"Helping."

His mouth went wide as well. His gaze clicked past my shoulder.

"What has she told you?" he said.

"What do you mean? What do you . . ." I was feeling increasingly uneasy, as though I were on that narrow bridge that the old monk had mentioned, and it was rocking. "Blackburn, what's going on?"

He leaned on his elbows, fingers steepled against his forehead, face unsettled and intense.

"Jesse?"

"What's she doing?"

"Unlocking the encrypted information that her computer virus loaded onto my laptop. She's going to alter it so we can give it to the Sangers without revealing certain information."

"What information?"

"Jesse, what the hell do you know that I don't?"

"Where does Jax want you to go after this?"

I hesitated. "Do you know?"

The pain on his face had deepened.

"Goddammit, Blackburn, what?"

"I tried to tell you when you called me from L.A., and

later at Wat Po, but we kept getting cut off. You have to stop. Go to the embassy and turn yourself in."

"No."

"Then . . ." He searched my face, as though memorizing the sight. "You're going to be arrested."

"Have faith. I've made it this far, and now I'm with Jax. I can do this."

"No, you can't. I told the FBI that you're in Bangkok."

20

Shiver said, "Son of a whore."

The FBI knew Delaney was here in Bangkok. This was a nightmare. And the man on the screen looked regretful, looked like he knew he'd done something damaging. She called Bliss.

"What?"

"Move. Now. Get in and get the information." Shiver yanked the cable from the router. "Leave the phone line open. I'll be listening."

She grabbed her computer and dashed out.

Upstairs on the twelfth floor, Bliss inserted an electronic master key into the door lock. It opened with a heavy click. She paused, waiting to make sure nobody inside had been alerted by the sound. After a few seconds she eased the door open. She heard a woman talking on the telephone.

"No. I don't care about protocol. Put me through to the head."

Bliss slipped noiselessly into the room. She saw the note the bellboy had slipped under the door. Pressing herself against the wall, she crept across the entryway. The black woman was pacing in the center of the suite, cell phone at her ear.

"Well, I'm not in London. I can't come in."

She was facing the window, but would be turning in a few seconds. Bliss took the injector pen from her pocket and inched into the room.

*   *   *

It felt as if a phosphorous grenade had just detonated in front of my face. I gaped at Jesse.

"You did what?"

"You need to get off the street one way or the other. And I couldn't get through to you. Evan, I'm sorry, but this is the only way to keep you safe and do what your father asked."

White flash, heat, the sense of disintegration. My life, my faith. The night, behind the phosphor shock, felt like coal slurry. Damn it, I slept with this man; I gave him my love, my loyalty, my trust. I wore his engagement ring, his pledge, his—

"Unbelievable *bastard*."

"I don't expect you to agree with this, or do anything except—"

"You treacherous shit."

"—but you have to take it calmly. This is what your dad expects me to do, and—"

"You absolute prick. Blackburn, do you— Son of a bitch. Don't you know what this means for Dad?"

"You can't give the file to the Sangers."

"Jax is—"

"It doesn't matter that Jax is with you."

"The hell it doesn't. Jesse, you don't know what you've done. Jax is going to fix this."

"No. Delaney, your dad told me, in absolutely crystal terms, that Jax is in danger too. He knew she might get involved. He does not want her to mess with the file. He thinks it will get her killed."

"Killed? I think that's a risk she's willing to take."

But why was Dad so adamant? National security? After all the garbage that had been dumped on him, was he still hanging onto his loyalty and sense of duty?

Unlike my bastard fiancé. My hand was clenched. If I could, I would have punched him through the screen and knocked him onto his ass.

"Jesse." Stupid son of a bitch, absolute shithead. "What did Dad tell you? I need to know. All of it. Now."

Abruptly, he wasn't looking at me. He was frowning past my shoulder.

"Ev, something's wrong."

"What?"

"In the room—"

A hard crack echoed right behind me. I spun and looked over my shoulder. All the air left my lungs.

Whack, again they hit the plate-glass window. I jumped to my feet. Jax and another woman were fighting. Grappling, kicking, punching. *Whack,* the attacker smashed Jax's head into the window. The glass cracked.

My skin prickled. Jax was sagging against the window, the glass bulging and crunching. The attacker grabbed her by the hair and clouted her head against the window again.

Gooseflesh ran across my skin. Every nerve in my body screamed, *Run.* It was the goblin blonde. But I couldn't bolt. From this balcony, there was only down.

Jax was in trouble. And if she fell, I would have to face the blonde alone. I tossed my computer onto a chair, picked up the table it had been sitting on, and opened the sliding glass door.

"Ev—" The words dried up in Jesse's mouth. He stared, appalled, at his computer screen.

The view was skewed, the video feed gone staticky. The camera was tilting, showing the balcony and a floor and the bottom half of the plate-glass door into the hotel room.

Jesus Christ.

Inside the room two people were tangled, battling against the window. Someone had gotten the jump on Jakarta Rivera—

"Ev, can you . . ."

The video jerked, disintegrated into stripes, came back in pieces. He saw her throw open the door and go in.

*   *   *

Shiver rushed through the lobby. "Out of my way."

The concierge glanced up, his face souring as she dashed for the lifts.

"Hold that." She jumped into the lift before the doors closed, cramming herself in among half-drunk Taiwanese businessmen and florid British tourists, and pushed twelve.

She was thrumming like a radar gun. She knew what she'd seen on her computer screen. Bliss fighting Jakarta Rivera. Bliss hadn't gotten in a clean blow, and now the American was fighting back. Damn, Bliss—second time in two days she had missed a clean jab. And the Delaney girl was going to throw her weight in as well. It was messy and was getting worse. She was going to have to finish it.

The lift rose slowly. Lights were lit for every single floor. She watched, wanting to rip the panel out, slay all these reeking people, and fly to the twelfth floor.

They were enmeshed, sliding to the floor just inside the balcony window. Blood was everywhere.

I swung the end table, bringing it down like a club onto the blonde's shoulder. She cried out. I raised the table again, but, slick as an eel, she dropped Jax and spun at me, fingernails out to gouge my eyes. Her teeth were clenched, god-awful decayed hillbilly teeth.

I turned my head and tried to get the table in front of me for protection. She wrestled it loose from my hands and swung it at me. It hit the side of my head with a sound like— *God,* that hurt. I saw stars. Pain rang off the bone.

Jax climbed to her feet, planting her legs wide as if her balance were out of reach. She crouched, staring at the blonde, cat eyes focused, winding up to strike. Blood was running from the side of her mouth and smeared across her cheek up into her scalp.

The blonde swung the table again. I put my arm up and—*ow*—it caught my forearm, and then my arm refused to follow directions. The next thing I knew, I was facedown on the floor, with the blonde on top of me.

*   *   *

Jesse gaped at his computer screen. The video was fuzzy, the sound nothing but static, but he could see it, the attacker, something frenzied and weightless. What the hell was that thing in there with Ev and Jax, a teenager on angel dust?

Evan was on the floor, flat out, the blonde dropping on her back, fingers going into her hair and slamming her face against the carpet. Then reaching to the desk, yanking a cord loose and—

The video broke into pixels again.

He raked his fingers into his hair, eyes scouring the screen, thinking, *Come on, come on . . .* and with a scritching sound, the video popped back.

The blonde had grabbed a computer cable and was wrapping it around Evan's throat like a garrotte. Fucking shit.

He had a loaded Glock nine lying in a drawer six feet away and it didn't matter. He was nine thousand useless miles away. He scanned the screen. In the room, on the coffee table, there was a bottle of wine with a note attached. If that was hotel stationery . . . He smacked the keyboard and zoomed in. Shangri-La.

He grabbed his phone and dialed, staring at the screen. He heard the phone ring, heard Drew pick up, and didn't let him talk. "Farelli. You have to call the FBI and call them *now.*"

My hands went to the cord around my neck, clawing, digging to pull it loose. It was a visceral, unnatural, *wrong* feeling, and no—my breathing was going, and I was squirming, clawing, and where the hell was Jax?

And like that, the weight was flung off my back, the cord went slack, and I yanked it loose, rolled over, and saw the blonde tossed against the nightstand. She shook her head to clear it, gave Jax a blazing glare, and bunched herself to spring.

Jax grabbed her laptop computer and smashed it down on the blonde's head, edge on.

It hit with a hideous crack. The blonde slumped to the floor, arms falling to her sides. Shoulders heaving, Jax raised the laptop and brought it down again, bashing her as if with a stone adze. The cracking sound turned wet and dull. The blonde crumpled against the nightstand, head sagging. I clutched the desk chair and climbed to my feet.

"Jax."

She took a whacking baseball-style swing and slammed the laptop across the blonde's face. She toppled over, eyes dull, arms lolling like Raggedy Ann. Blood chugged from a gash in the ugly depression on the top of her head.

I stumbled across the room. "Jax, stop."

Chest heaving, she tossed the laptop on the bed. The computer was smeared with blood and something worse. Swaying on her feet, she stared down at the blonde.

"Animal," she said.

She drew back her heavy boot and kicked her in the face. The blonde's head snapped around like a tetherball and flopped down against the carpet.

"Fucking animal."

She kicked her in the chin. The sound was sickening. A smell hit my nose as the blonde's bowels let go. I put the back of my hand to my mouth, trying not to gag. Jax drew her foot back again.

I shoved her away. "Stop it."

She pointed at her, fingers shaking. "Check her pockets."

No way, none in hell, was I going to touch her. She was dead. The smell was horrible. Jax shoved me in the shoulder, pushing me toward her.

I slapped her arm away. "No."

Blood glistened in Jax's hair. Sweat beaded brightly on her forehead. Her shoulders were shaking as though she'd just been pulled from ice water. She glared at me, angry and half-crazed, and then looked around at the floor in confusion.

"Where's the needle?" She scanned the floor. "She stuck me with something. It's . . ." She touched the back of her shoulder and held out her hands, watching them tremble.

Warily I raised my hands to her shoulders. "Sit down."

She pressed her eyes shut, put a hand to one of her ears, and worked her jaw as though trying to clear her head of an unwanted sound. "Ears ringing."

"Sit down. Come on."

Before I could catch her, she dropped like a pile of wet laundry.

The video crackled again. Jesse tossed his phone down and pressed his fingers to his forehead, trying to understand what he was seeing. The blonde was down, broken, possibly dead. In front of the bed, Jax had collapsed on the floor. Evan was bent over her, trying to lay her out flat, talking to her, positioning her head so she had a clear airway. Helplessly he smiled, almost ridiculously chilled with relief. ABC, just the way he'd taught her—airway, breathing, circulation.

And Farelli was contacting the FBI. They'd get to the Thai cops and the embassy's Bureau of Diplomatic Security.

Beneath the static and background noise he heard her voice, and a moaning sound.

"Jax, lie still. Can you hear me?"

Jax raised a hand and pawed at her arm. Her speech was slurred.

"What?" Evan leaned down closer to Jax's face, as though trying to hear better.

In the background, the light shifted. The smile fled from his face. Even blurred, he knew what he was seeing: the door to the room being opened.

Somebody was coming in. And Evan was on this side of the bed, on the floor, bent low over Jax. Even if she turned her head she wouldn't notice.

"Evan!" As he shouted, he knew it was futile. The television was blaring, the intruder was silent, and Jax was moaning. Ev couldn't hear him. She didn't know. He grabbed his phone, stabbing in the number she'd given him.

In the background a figure slid into view. He couldn't help it; he drew back from the screen as though magnetically repelled. It was a wraith, another one. And she was staring straight at Evan.

21

Leaning close to Jax's face, I struggled to keep her in our dimension, conscious and breathing. I wanted to cry; I wanted to scream; I wanted to get out of here. Jax was sweating and shaking.

"Lon . . ."

"I'm here. Lie still."

"Lon . . . on."

"London?"

"Heard." She glared at me. "She heard."

"Who?" I glanced at the blonde. She was still dead. "I don't understand."

She seemed to reach inside herself for a place to anchor her eyesight. Gritting her teeth, she grabbed my arms.

"She heard me. On the phone."

"It doesn't matter. Jax, she's dead."

"She had a cell."

I looked around, thinking that the blonde had been too busy attacking us to be bothered making a call. I heard a noise, an annoying electronic tune. Jax put a hand to her ear again, as though to quiet the ringing in her head.

Ringing. I looked toward the balcony. The annoying tune was the ring of my new cell phone.

I clambered to my feet, ran outside, and grabbed it from the chair.

"I'm okay, Jesse, but oh, God—"

"Evan, behind you. She's in the room."

I turned. The Thai was standing on the far side of the bed.

Her lips drew open to show broken teeth. Moving like light reflecting off a mirror, she veered across the suite and to the desk.

In my ear, Jesse said, "Ev, get her."

I dropped the phone and charged back inside. She was rifling the things Jax had spread out on the desk. She came up with the Singapore flash drive, spun, and ran for the door.

She got one hand on it, turned the latch, and pulled it open two inches. I crashed into her, slamming it shut again.

She turned, kicking, scratching, trying to dig her fingers into my face. Grabbing her by the hair, I flung her around, out into the room, and planted myself in front of the door. I couldn't let her out.

She backed up, looking around. Damn, for a weapon— maybe the needle Jax was talking about, Jax who couldn't help me this time. I looked around too. I grabbed one of the bottles of fine whiskey on the wet bar. Holding it by the neck, I smashed it against the wall.

I aimed the broken end at her. "Give it back."

A powerful smell of whiskey hit my nose, mixing with the fecal reek. I gagged but kept the broken bottle aimed at her. She lowered her head, glaring, long hair falling over her face. Then she turned and dashed for the balcony.

My computer. Oh, no—she was going to toss the flash drive over, maybe with the computer, and get a confederate downstairs to retrieve it. I ran into the room. She rushed onto the balcony and slammed the door shut behind her. Giving me one last look, she climbed onto the balcony railing.

"Jesus."

She stood up like a gymnast on the parallel bars. And flew out into the night.

*   *   *

Jesse threw his phone down on the table. "Holy shit."

She jumped.

Through the crazed dim video, he saw Ev at the sliding glass door. Her face was blank with astonishment.

The freak flat-out fucking jumped.

Throwing open the door, I rushed out onto the balcony. Orchestral music floated up from below. I ran to the rail, nausea halfway up my throat. Jesus, twelve floors. Through clear air it took only a few seconds to reach terminal velocity, driving straight down into palm trees and glass and concrete.

I stopped short.

At the next room over she was clinging to the railing of the balcony, legs swinging in open space. As I watched, she shimmied up and climbed over to safety.

She shot me a look over her shoulder, opened the balcony door, and disappeared.

I bolted back inside, grabbed the key, and tore out into the hall. Hearing a fire door slam shut, I took off at a run.

Down twelve flights of stairs, out into the opulent lobby, I looked around. She was nowhere. I ran to the front doors. Nothing. I hurried back through the lobby to the riverside exit. Outside, there were only waving palm trees and kids splashing in the pool. I stood under stars and reflections shimmering on the river, bereft, as the orchestra played "Shall We Dance."

When I let myself back into the room, the stench of shit and whiskey overpowered me. I forced myself not to look at the battered husk that had been the blonde. In the bathroom I heard water running, and found Jax supporting herself against the counter, cleaning the cut on the side of her head. The marble sink was pink with blood.

"Sit down," I said.

When I took the towel from her, she slumped onto the

edge of the tub. The cut looked messy but not deep. The real problem lay below the surface.

"Shiver disappeared?" she said.

"Yes. I couldn't catch her." I pressed the towel to the side of her head.

She flinched. "Bliss attacked from behind. I didn't see it coming."

"You have a concussion. Let me call somebody. Pete and Daw?"

"I'm all right."

Sure. That was what Tim said, right before he showed me the bullet hole. I kept pressure on the towel to stanch the bleeding.

"I'm all right. The juice helped." She pointed at two bottles of minibar orange juice sitting empty by the sink. "Bliss jabbed me with an injector pen. Don't know for certain, but the shaking and sweating—it might have been insulin shock. I may have been belligerent as well. That's also a symptom."

I simply stared. Belligerent? Well, yes.

"I drank to get my blood sugar up, and it worked." She glanced up. "Shiver got the flash drive, didn't she?"

"She did. Had you deleted the information from it?"

The pall in her expression said it. "No. I decrypted it and downloaded the information onto your laptop. But the flash drive didn't overwrite. The information is intact, and in the clear. Shiver has it."

"But it doesn't contain the entire Riverbend file. They only got part of it."

"Correct. But Shiver got the part of the file that tells her where the final flash drive is located. And if Rio gets that one, it's all over."

"Where is it?"

She stood up. "We're getting out. We sanitize the room and we split."

She was obviously not thinking straight. "We couldn't sanitize this suite with a blowtorch."

Her shoulders dropped. "Fine. But we can give ourselves a head start over the authorities. Wipe every surface we touched and put out the Do Not Disturb sign." She gave me a chill look. "Check your computer. The down-ticker is running."

"Oh, no. You didn't get a chance to stop it?"

"No. It reset when I jacked in the Singapore flash drive. And then . . ."

I rushed out to the balcony. On my screen I saw a California sunrise turning the sky to gold flame. Jesse had turned away from the screen.

"Blackburn," I said.

He spun back. "Ev. Thank God."

"You warned me. Jesse, thank you."

"She jumped. I saw her. Ev—"

"She didn't fall. She jumped to the next balcony and got away."

I glanced at the corner of the screen: 18:49.21 and counting down. I hit the space bar, hoping to bring up another video window. I got nothing. I didn't know what was now loaded on my machine, or where the next destination was.

I looked Jesse in the eye. "She got the flash drive. She knows where the last piece of the file is. There's no way I can turn myself in."

He was tired, fiercely focused and infinitely far away.

"I owe you for warning me. Now I'm done talking to you."

I yanked the camera hookup out of the computer.

He slammed shut the monitor on his computer. "Suck."

He looked out the window at the sun cresting the mountains. The surf was churning the beach, gulls diving and screeching.

The freak had gotten away with the flash drive that led to the final piece of the puzzle. And if she got that, everything Phil had begged him to do would come to nothing. He checked his watch and got on the phone. Evan was going to figure it out, too. He ran the distances in his head. He was closer, but still a hell of a long way away. And he couldn't jump from balcony to balcony. All he could do was beat them to the source.

A human voice broke into the Muzak. "British Airways."

"Yes. Get me on your next flight from Los Angeles to London."

22

"London?" I pulled the door shut, hung the DO NOT DIS-TURB sign, and led Jax along the hall, humping our luggage to the elevator.

She pressed the *down* button. "Call British Airways; there's a midnight flight." She handed me a page torn from the hotel's English phone book. "Number's here."

I drew in a breath. "Jesse told the FBI I'm here."

She moved just her eyes. "Why would he do that?"

"Dad told him to stop me from getting the Riverbend file. Said if Jesse didn't keep me out of this, our family would become part of the kill chain."

A weird light rose in her eyes. "Your family . . ." She stopped. After a second she cleared her throat. "Jesse's got guts to take it all the way."

"That's one way to put it."

"Want me to kill him?"

"No. I'm going to do that myself."

She watched for the elevator. "Does he know we're at this hotel?"

"I didn't tell him, but I wouldn't put it past him to figure it out. The room was visible on the Webcam."

The snake. He had refused to listen to me, just muled his way ahead. What was wrong with him?

"After you call British Airways, call Thai. Book Evan Delaney a ticket to Kuala Lumpur on their last flight out tonight. Pay with your own credit card," she said. "And we'll take separate flights to the U.K."

We rode the elevator down to the mezzanine, which overlooked the lobby from a spectacular height. When we walked to the railing, we saw no uniformed police, but a number of Thai and western men were conferring beneath one of the chandeliers.

"Them?" I said.

"Don't know. Play it safe. We'll catch a taxi outside the other wing."

Schlepping my backpack and new Louis Fauxton bag, I hurried with her down a staircase and outside past the pool and a restaurant, along the river, and into a tropical garden gushing with sweet flowers. Along a narrow path, palms and creepers arched overhead. A Western man came walking along the path toward us.

He wore a sports coat and a harried expression, and had a cell phone to his ear, talking American English. He looked straight at me. I ignored him, and he glanced away.

And looked again. His gaze sharpened.

Walk, keep moving. *Brazen,* that was the word I needed. My face felt as red as the gumball on top of a police car. Catholic guilt reaction was telling me I was busted. Shit-out-of-luck, fifteen-to-life, mandatory-sentencing busted. The crazy-devil part of my conscience shrieked, *Run.*

"What's your rush?" he said.

My vision blurred but I kept walking.

"Where you ladies off to in such a hurry?"

I strode past but heard him behind me. "It's too hot to walk so fast. Why don't you come on over to the bar and join me for a drink?"

Ten feet on, I turned. Jax had stopped. The man had his hands spread, blocking her way. On her face I saw pain, contempt, and impatience, a bad combination.

"Hey, hon," I said.

He glanced at me over his shoulder expectantly. I walked back smiling. "You're making a mistake. Say good night."

He grinned. "Wow. You guys are tough, huh?"

I shrugged, holding his gaze. Though I didn't see Jax move, a second later he gasped and buckled, grabbing his nuts.

We walked away. Outside the hotel we hopped into a cab and pulled away into the city night. Jax leaned her head back against the seat.

"You're welcome," I said.

The sweep of streetlights caught her face. Light flickering on and off, strobing over her.

"For?" she said.

"Getting him to make your favorite mistake and turn his back."

The taxi let us out at the cavernous international terminal. Jax looked around.

"If Diplomatic Security's here from the embassy, they'll stick out like an erection. If it's Bangkok plainclothes, you won't spot them."

She glanced at me again—taking in my hair, my clothing, my nervousness. She was wearing authentic Gucci and a silk scarf tied around her hair in a splashy fashion, hiding the gash on the side of her head. Lipstick covered the swelling on her mouth, but in the morning I bet she was going to have a black eye. I found a luggage cart and we headed into the fulminating light of the terminal. She held on to the cart with one hand. For balance, I sensed. But as usual she marched chin up, like a prima ballerina sweeping toward an adoring audience.

"Go through your legend," she said.

"Kathleen Rowan Larkin. Called Kit. I'm twenty-nine, born in Oklahoma, raised in Menlo Park, California. College at Berkeley. Live in San Francisco. Mom's Colleen; Dad's Louie. I have two older sisters, Sian and Kendra."

The terminal was clamorous, packed with travelers arriving for long-haul flights. We headed for the British Airways counter.

"I work for a small ad agency, but this is a pleasure trip. A sabbatical, actually. Postdivorce. My husband gained four hundred pounds and robbed a string of Krispy Kreme doughnut shops to feed his junk-food addiction. He was arrested in an orgy with Ronald McDonald and a dancing monkey. At San Quentin they had to shovel him into his cell with a forklift."

"Don't embellish. If you want me to top Jesse, just say so," she said. "Though the monkey's a nice touch."

"It scratches where he can't reach." I pushed the luggage cart through the crowd. "Don't worry; I'll remember the legend correctly."

Her hand slipped off the cart, and she wobbled. I grabbed her just before she lost her balance.

I got her out of the crowd. Off at the edge of the hall, I made her sit down atop the luggage on the cart. She held on to it, fighting to keep from toppling over.

"You're getting worse."

"I'm all right."

"You plainly aren't. Look at me."

She gazed up, and I saw something that creeped me out so hard I nearly peed myself. Her left pupil was blown. She had a serious head injury. And people were looking at us. Not just passengers, but airline personnel and security cameras. We couldn't stay here. Sooner or later somebody was going to come along and ask what was wrong. And there were cops patrolling the terminal. Armed cops.

"Can you fly?" I said.

She made to stand up again. "Got to watch—"

"Jax." I lowered my voice to a whisper and leaned right up to her face. "Tell me the truth."

She tried to shake her head, and fell back against the cart. "Got to watch out."

I took both her hands in mine. "I'm done running around in the dark. You have to tell me what's going on. It's something so bad that it made Jesse willing to have me arrested."

"I've been trying to warn you. Got to watch out for her."

"Who? Shiver? Another attack whore?" I squeezed her arm in frustration. "If you won't tell me, I have to assume that I should do what Jesse says. I'll go to the U.S. Embassy and surrender. I'll turn the Riverbend file over to the FBI and let them use it to try to rescue Dad."

Her face went gray. "No."

"I don't care if the feds get the file. My only concern is getting Dad back."

"You can't."

"Stop this." Sitting down on the luggage cart beside her, I took her shoulders tightly in my hands. "You have to trust me."

For a long, painful moment she stared at me. Then, struggling, she got her wallet and took out a snapshot. It was the photo of the little brown-eyed girl perched in the crook of a tree.

"I've been trying to warn you."

"About her?"

"Yes. Back at the hotel, I told you not to wait. To have babies, soon as possible."

My heart sank. She was losing the thread. She peered at the snapshot as though the sight of the girl's face made her head hurt.

"I was thirty-four when I had my baby." She handed me the snapshot. "My daughter. That's what this is about."

I stared at the little girl's photo, my heart stammering.

Her voice broke. "What Christian wants is his sister."

23

I clutched the snapshot. "This girl is your daughter?"

"She turned eleven last month."

"And she's in London?"

The expression on her face was defiant and defensive. Tentatively I put my hand on her arm. Confusion must have creased my face, because she said, "She and Tim and I don't live together in a ranch house on Wisteria Lane."

That wasn't what was confusing me. "She's Hank Sanger's daughter?"

She raised an eyebrow. "Goodness. It would seem you know the facts of life."

I gazed again at the photo, and my gut tightened.

Christian wanted his sister.

What the Sangers were after, beyond money, even beyond my father's death, was to punish Jax by taking her daughter and selling her into prostitution. To steal her and turn her life into a living death.

Jesus. I rubbed my fingers across my forehead. I didn't get this. Why did Jax put the information about her daughter on the flash drive?

"Who was this computer program meant for?" I said.

"It was meant to protect her. And to . . . be a last testament, if things came to that."

"Are you telling me Tim doesn't know where she is?" I said, and thought of something worse. "Doesn't Tim know you have a daughter?"

"Of course he does. But for her safety, he doesn't know the whole story. Or where she is right now."

Oh, my God. Just how dangerous *was* Tim North?

I looked at her sharply, my heart beginning to pound, remembering her rebuke on the video file. *Phil, Tim—you're the reasons I'm alive. So this hatred . . . It's wrong.*

What had really happened between Jax and Hank Sanger? How were my father and Tim North involved?

Whatever—Dad was involved now. And from the moment he was ambushed by the Sangers and their thugs, he had been trying to protect us—me, Jax, and her daughter.

She continued gazing at the photo. "If something happened to me, I wanted a way to protect her. And I wanted . . . She needs a dad. I want him to know the whole story, what really happened. Protect her, get her out."

And Jax had intended the video record to clue Tim in to protect her little girl as well. But Tim had no idea what the video contained, and so had sent me out to get it and turn it over to Rio and Christian. He had flown into action to save his wife, and ended up risking her child.

"What's her name?"

She looked at me crooked. "Haven't you figured it out?"

I shook my head, gazing at the photo. Now I saw the resemblance: the feline cast to the little girl's eyes, the warm brown tones of her skin, the self-possession with which she carried herself. Her face was full of dreams and excitement, however, that I had never seen in Jax.

"Everything that led you to the flash drives told you her name. Everything that got me the information from Pete Kongsangchai. Come on," she said. "Bring your A game."

Everything? The R & B note. *Midnight in the Garden of Good and Evil.* A map of Sherman's march through the South. Gladys Knight and the Pips lyrics.

I heard myself say, "Oh." I heard Ray Charles's voice aching across a crowded club when my father turned around at the jukebox.

"Georgia," I said.

She took the photo. This time when she looked at me, her eyes were full of want.

"I know what you're wondering. How could a mother ship her kid halfway around the world? Why do you think? I don't want her to become me." She put a hand on my arm. "And unless we keep the Sangers from finding her, that might happen. She could become my flip side. One of the Children of the Corn."

"We won't let that happen."

She smoothed her thumb over the image, as though brushing her daughter's hair. Deep within myself, deeper than the pit of my stomach, I felt that this was what my father would try to protect: the innocence of a child.

A shot of adrenaline, sick and quick, dumped into me. "Oh, God."

Jesse knew.

Of course he did. All my strength seemed to evaporate. I grabbed the handle of the luggage cart for balance.

That was what my father must have told him in that desperate phone call the night he was ambushed. And he had sworn him to secrecy, to protect us all.

I peered hard at Jax. She needed medical treatment urgently. But if I went to London alone, I didn't know how I would get her daughter out. I had no papers, no authority, I was a total stranger.

Outside the terminal, a cop was strolling along the windows, hand on his submachine gun, peering in at us.

"Come on," I said.

I nudged her into motion and took her by the elbow to the Thai Airways check-in desk. Before I turned to leave she took my wrist and turned it so she could see my watch. I felt a ghostly sense of déjà vu. Tim had done the same thing before I left him. It was ten p.m.

"The Riverbend program will ditch the next chunk of

the file to your laptop in three hours. Be sure you log on."
She let go. "I'll see you in London."

"Good. Because Kit Larkin's going to be waiting for you
at Heathrow, and if you don't show up, she'll kick your
skinny ballerina ass." I let go of her. "Get going. And don't
turn your back."

24

Jesse checked everything one final time. Ticket printout. Passport. Tire repair kit. Gloves—London could be miserable in April, and wheeling bare-handed was hellacious in the cold. He zipped his suitcase, casting a look at his desk drawer. The Glock had to stay here.

But firepower, truth be told, didn't matter. Speed did.

Jax Rivera has a little girl. These people want her, Phil had said. *That can't happen, Jesse. They're human traffickers. Do whatever it takes.*

He grabbed his backpack and keys, turned off the lights, gave a last look around, and heard a knock on the front door.

For a second he stared across the entryway. Somebody knocking at eight a.m. could only be bad news. The knock came again. He wheeled over and opened it.

He froze like a plastic toy. "P.J."

His brother grinned. "I'm ready to rock."

"What?"

"Want to start off on the right foot. Thought I'd take you out to breakfast, sort of a thank-you."

P.J. was wearing a new pair of chinos and a button-down shirt, and his hair was freshly cut. He walked in with a bounce in his step. Jesse turned, confused. P.J.'s grin slid a bit.

"My first day. Starting work at the law firm," he said. "You said yesterday was too soon. So I waited."

Don't blink, Jesse thought. Don't let your face betray you. Don't slap your forehead.

He hadn't arranged a job for his brother, hadn't even found time to speak to Lavonne about the idea. And here was P.J., practically jumping up and down like a kid at a birthday party. P.J. jammed his hands in his pockets and jingled his motorcycle keys. He glanced at the suitcase and the backpack, and at the jeans and parka Jesse was wearing. He tilted his head, perplexed.

"Going somewhere?"

"Yeah." Damn.

P.J. frowned. "Bro? What's up?"

He had to say something. He had to do something. P.J. looked so earnest. Neat and eager and humming with nerves beneath the grin.

He couldn't tell him that he'd forgotten. Couldn't tell him that he didn't have a job. And, Christ, he couldn't possibly let him go home unemployed. Disappointment, failure, empty time—that was the portal back to dope and drink and a locked cell.

"We need to change your schedule. I have an emergency," he said.

"What kind of emergency?"

"Work-related. That's all I can say."

P.J. flushed. Jesse put up his hands.

"Nothing to do with you. It's confidential. I can't even tell Evan, and believe me, that has landed me in deep shit."

"Whoa. This is for a case?" P.J. looked around and saw the passport and ticket on the kitchen counter. "Dude. You're leaving the country?"

He picked up the ticket before Jesse could stop him. "London? Are you serious?"

Jesse took the ticket. "This is privileged information. You can't tell anybody."

For a moment P.J. looked suspicious. Then his smile returned. "What's this about? Like, a high-stakes case?"

"Yeah." He grabbed his backpack and had an idea. "And I need you to drive with me to LAX."

"Really?"

"We'll take the truck. Then if you don't mind, you can drive it back here. That way I don't have to leave it in long-term parking."

And if anybody got suspicious about his whereabouts—anybody such as the U.S. Attorney or the FBI—they'd see his pickup at home in the driveway instead of parked at a major international airport.

"Why aren't you flying out of Santa Barbara?" P.J. said.

Jesse pulled his suitcase along the floor to the door. "LAX is simpler."

He shoved the suitcase out onto the front porch. It was a sunny morning, crisp and bright. His flight was leaving in four hours and it was a two-hour drive.

P.J. was quiet. Jesse glanced over his shoulder and was surprised to see him looking pensive. Without another word, P.J. grabbed the suitcase, carried it to the truck, and tossed it into the cargo bed. Jesse felt a flush of relief: His brother understood. Flying had lost the appeal it held back in his days of traveling with the U.S. swim team. And the Santa Barbara airport had no jetways—you had to board your flight via stairs. Or, in his case, by mucking around with a skinny aisle chair and getting bumped up the steps by a ground crewman like a crate of dinner trays, while the pilots and other passengers and baggage handlers all stared, silently thinking, *Poor bastard.*

"Thanks."

He locked the front door. P.J. took the backpack from him and tossed it in the backseat of the truck. When he turned around, he looked dead serious.

"Take me with you," he said.

"To London?"

"I'm serious. Let me come."

"Are you . . . ?" Don't tell him he's nuts. "No."

"I can be your assistant. Like a paralegal."

He touched his forehead, thinking, *Stay calm.* "No. Even if I needed an assistant, you don't have a ticket; you're not packed. Do you even have a passport?"

"Yeah, I found it a few weeks ago. I'd totally forgotten. So this is, like, karma." P.J. spread his hands. "Dude, come on; it would be awesome."

Awesome like *European Vacation.* He opened the driver's door. "Hop in the truck. I need to roll."

"Then how about letting me stay here and house-sit for you?"

Halfway into the truck, he nearly fell to the ground. "No."

"Don't you trust me?"

He boosted himself into the driver's seat. "Don't ask loaded questions. Come on; get in. Please." He checked his watch. "I need to haul."

"You think I want a free trip to London, that it?" P.J.'s expression was barbed. "Well, yeah, duh."

He had to laugh. "Good try."

P.J. crossed his arms. "You forgot, didn't you? About the job."

Jesse's shoulders dropped. He squeezed his eyes shut.

"That's why you want me to drive with you, isn't it?"

"I'm sorry. Things have been crazy, and it slipped my mind. I'll call Lavonne today and get it set up."

"Okay." P.J. walked toward him. "But in the meantime, look at you. You can't even get on an airplane by yourself."

"Traveling isn't a problem. It's a gigantic pain in the ass, that's all, which is why I need to get moving."

"Right." P.J. put his hands on the door to keep him from closing it. "Dude, I don't know what's going on with this emergency, but if it's got Evan pissed off at you, then you need serious backup."

"From you?"

"You know what London's like? They ride the tube. They take double-decker buses. Didn't you watch *Lock, Stock*? The sidewalks are bumpy, and there's narrow stairs in these creaky buildings—I mean everywhere. Plus it's always raining, and patience ain't your virtue, especially when you've got a bug up your ass. And if you punch some cabbie's lights out 'cause he won't let you into his taxi, you'll spend your trip banging your head against the wall in a police station instead of fixing this emergency."

Jesse felt his face heating.

"Man, you're in such a rush you can't stop looking at your watch, and I'll bet good money your hurry will only get worse once you're there. You have a total urge to move quick, and *that's* what you can't do by yourself." He held tight to the door. "You need help, and I'm it."

Jesse had almost forgotten that, clean and sober, P.J. was a pretty smart guy. For a long moment he stared at his brother, aware of the gulls shrieking and the surf foaming white in the distance.

"Can you pack in ten minutes?" he said.

One swallow, one drop of water, one touch of moisture on his tongue—that was everything. Phil lowered his lips to the minuscule puddle in the corner of the shipping container. The water soaked his cracked skin and jumped against the roof of his mouth, full of rust, thick and earthy. Like the water in the red pond where the creek had flowed into his grandfather's pasture on the Oklahoma prairie. Sharp and muddy, the heat of the day lying on his back when he and his brothers went swimming, wind ticking through the tall grass, cicadas droning from the trees with the intensity of an electrical transformer.

He rolled over and slumped against the corrugated wall of the container. His life flashing before his eyes, that was a dangerous sign.

Resting for a moment, he took stock. There was no more food. He had eaten the apple core and licked every bit of chocolate from the candy wrappers, despite the taste of mold. He had found some orange peels in an old crate and eaten them too, and scoured the salt from an empty bag of potato chips. But that was it. The water was only what dripped into the container from the hole rusted in the top. And from what he could tell, it hadn't rained in the last twenty-four hours. The insignificant puddle, now only a wet spot on the floor, was not going to be replenished.

The crack of light coming through the doors of the container was angled off to his left. Early morning, he made it. Grabbing the broomstick he had fashioned into a cane, he hitched himself over there again and pressed his ear to the metal. He'd pounded and kicked on it for hours. Yelled, too, until his voice was hoarse. Nobody came. He knew what that meant. This container was stacked among hundreds, maybe thousands of others on a massive dock, too deep in the stack for anybody to notice. It had to be Los Angeles, Long Beach or maybe Oakland.

At one point during the night, a security patrol had passed through this section. He'd heard a dog bark. But even then, kicking his foot against the door, yelling with all his strength, they hadn't come. The port worked through the night, cranes busy loading, ships' horns blaring, and they hadn't heard him.

He checked his watch, counting down. He had to stop that. He had to reset his thought process. Counting down—counting down to rescue. To the cops busting open the doors, because they'd figured out where he was. Because Rio and Christian had been arrested, broken, had talked.

He laid his head against the door. One more hour, he could hold out. And one more after that.

His family must be desperate. That was almost the worst thing. Brian and Evan, they were strong, but this would be knocking them for a loop. Angie as well. He could just hear her—*Phil, that son of a bitch. I'm going to kill him for this.* He almost laughed. Having his ex-wife kill him . . . he could hang on for that.

But it was the not knowing that bled the heat out of him.

His message—he didn't know if Jesse had gotten it in time. Or if he'd carried through. Jesse was tough and resourceful, but that might not be enough. He had to be willing to go all the way. He had lived through enough bad times to know that only the big things mattered—family, loyalty, honor. But he was hotheaded and he loved Evan, which was the problem. Love could tangle your parachute lines.

Phil had never been able to reach Jesse, not really. The man was across some wall Phil couldn't jump. He stuck to his guns, he couldn't easily be swayed, and he swung for the fences. Throw him a changeup pitch and he'd hit a line drive, straight at your head.

Moreover, even if Jesse was determined to carry through, Phil didn't know if he could. And he could hear Evan now: *Don't, Dad.* She would call his doubts cruel. She could feign blindness, could feign irrelevance, but there was only the hard truth, and a father couldn't shunt it aside. There were a lot of things Jesse couldn't do. Much as they all hated it, and Jesse fought to make the best of things, it was an insurmountable fact.

Jesse wanted to be a husband to his daughter. And Phil couldn't deny the bald truth that it looked like a fatal wish.

Phil rolled his head and looked at the line of sunlight inching its way across the floor. He pulled himself up straight, his swollen knee throbbing. The pain was good. It kept him awake, kept him focused.

There was too much pain in all of this. He remembered the time he went into Rio Sanger's club. The young people there, young women Rio had torn apart inside. He thought of Christian. Grown now, a good-looking young man but a husk. Cruel, and scoured clean of conscience, as destroyed as those other kids in the brothel. Kids he hadn't been able to help, because the op went wrong.

Christian on the road, sneering at him, putting that SIG Sauer to his head and leading him into the backseat of the car, where Rio was waiting. *Hello, old man.* Christian putting his hand on him with such strange softness and need in his touch.

Christian had something of Hank Sanger about him. Maybe it was the death in his eyes.

And Jax, so committed and daring, the girl with such flair and courage, the almost suicidal confidence in her abilities, and a need to exorcise some bottomless anger, who threw herself into a black and unredeemable world and then found herself broken and betrayed, calling him from Hank Sanger's place in Bangkok twelve years ago, calling in the clear, begging, *Get me out of here.*

That was the cruelest day of his life. Jax had looked at him afterward, torn by the not knowing, already trying to grow a scab over the emotional wound, thinking she could never heal, and had seen something in his eyes. *They're dark. I never noticed before. Like a winter sky.*

He swallowed. It might rain again. He could last. For his family, he could hold out as long as he had to.

For Jax, the girl he had sworn to protect all those years ago. For Georgia, the daughter Jax would protect even to death.

As he sat in the inky darkness, the walls of the container seemed not so much black as gray. And a sound mixed with the walls. It was sharp and deep, and somebody was trying to shut it off.

He snapped out of it. The dog—outside, the dog was back, and its master was shouting at it to quiet down. He pounded his fist against the side of the container.

"Here," he yelled. "In here."

His voice was hoarse. He pounded again, not getting enough power behind it. He turned around and began kicking his good leg against the door, hard as he could.

"Help. In here."

The dog barked.

Phil kicked with everything he had, knowing his voice might not be carrying. The dog began racketing. Phil put his fingers between his lips and whistled.

The master gave the dog a command, telling it to seek on. Phil kicked, the sound echoing in the container, his blood pounding in his ears. A drone rolled overhead, and he realized it was a stacking crane rolling along the dock among the containers, and then he heard metal clanging as the crane lowered a container into place above his.

The dog had stopped barking. The voices were fading. He kept kicking, kept shouting, even though his voice was nothing but a whisper and he was flat on the floor, his throat more parched than before, his strength gone, his head dropping back against the metal floor, the fog thickening all around him. Like a winter sky just before the sun disappears into the horizon.

In my first-class seat, I stared at the bubbles going flat in my champagne glass, and at the other passengers chatting and settling in for the twelve-hour flight. I checked my watch. I booted up my computer, plugged in my headphones, and stared at the screen, watching the ticker count down. The program loaded.

Again, no preamble. Fade in: Sanger's place, the fan lazing on the ceiling, Jax flat on the floor in the bedroom with her leg shattered by a gunshot. Her arm was out, gesturing, *Stop.*

"Don't, Hank, please. I have to tell you about Christian."

Sanger swayed above her, gun wavering in his hand. His face was bleary. "Who put you up to this?"

Sweat shone on her face. "Rio's doing something to him."

"Who put you up to this?" He put out a hand to steady himself. "What did you put in that joint?"

"You don't understand. We have to get Christian out of here. We have to get him away from Rio."

My head was thundering. I knew now why she hadn't shot him: She was pregnant. She couldn't bring herself to kill the father of her child. That was what she had turned her back on.

"She's doing something to him, dosing him with something. That's why she came to Bangkok."

The gun wavered, and Hank stared at her. "She came to see me."

"But that's not the only reason. Christian isn't healthy."

Sanger's face was suffused with blood. Half-drugged, he staggered toward Jax, gun hanging heavily from his hand. She tried to crawl out of his way but he loomed over her.

"What the hell are you talking about?" he said.

"Hank, she's grooming him."

In the background, the doorbell rang. Sanger glanced out the bedroom door at the living room, alarmed, and back down at Jax.

"Quiet. Absolutely quiet, or I put the next one . . ." He aimed the gun at her head.

The doorbell rang again, and then whoever it was began knocking. Loudly. Dimly a young voice called out, "Hank?"

His head snapped around. "Fuck."

"Hank?" The knocking stopped and there was the sound of a key turning in the lock. "Pop?"

Sanger stage-whispered at Jax, "Not a sound, not a single sound, or I kill both of you."

He lurched out, shutting the bedroom door. Through the wall came the sound of a young teen's voice.

"Pop, how come it took you so long? Hey, I—"

"Christian. What you doing here, *mijo*?"

In the bedroom Jax tried to roll over, and a creature sound slipped from her throat. She clapped her hand over her mouth, stifling it.

Falling back against the floor, she dug her hand into her back pocket and pulled out a phone. In the other room Sanger and Christian kept talking, the teenager chattering away, Sanger trying to shunt him off, get him to leave. Jax dialed and put the phone to her ear. When she spoke it was in a rushed whisper, holding back sobs.

"I'm down. It's blown," she said. "I need evac. Get me out of here, *now*."

She fell back to the floor.

The video jumped ahead: Jax had managed to roll over and crawl toward the bed. A dark slick of blood traced her path.

Out in the living room, Sanger said, "Let's go get something to eat. Come on. I'll take you out."

"Can't we stay here? I hate going out. I go out all the time. Come on, Hank."

Without warning came the sound of the front door being thrown open. Jax looked toward the wall, unable to see what was happening in the living room.

Sanger said sharply, "What are you doing here?"

"Don't move. Gun on the floor, slide it over to me."

My stomach knotted. It was my father's voice.

"What's going on?" Christian said.

"Kid, move away from him and come over here. Nobody's going to hurt you."

Sanger said, "Christian. Stay where you are."

"Hank, don't even think about it. Where is she?" Dad said.

"Fucking Judas. You're in on this?"

"Sit down and lace your hands behind your head."

"Fuck you, Delaney. You can—"

Gunfire barked. Jax threw her arms over her head. Christian began screaming. And screaming.

Dad shouted, "Down on the floor, now. You want to live, get down and put your hands on your head, Christian— *goddammit.*"

Another gunshot split the air.

The bedroom door flew open. Christian charged in, his face wild with horror. He stopped short, gaping at Jax.

She screamed, *"Phil."*

Christian threw a look back toward the living room. A cry flowed from his throat, and he careered past Jax out to the veranda. From the living room my father came charging after him, his monstrous handgun aimed at the bedroom door. Christian leaped over the veranda railing and took off across the garden.

Dad flattened himself against the wall outside the bedroom and peered around the doorjamb, gripping the gun in both hands. Crouching low, he spun through the doorway and ran to the French doors. He scanned the terrain. Christian was gone.

Pulling the shutters closed, Dad holstered the gun under his windbreaker and in two strides was at Jax's side.

She began to cry. "I blew it."

"It's okay." He began checking her wound. "I'm getting you out of here."

His voice, with its slow prairie rhythms, seemed to steady her. My eyes were stinging.

Because it wasn't okay. None of it. Behind them, through the doorway, across the house, beyond the French doors wide-open to the sunset, Hank Sanger lay splayed on the far edge of the veranda that ran outside the living room. The left half of his face was a mass of blood and pulp. A dark lake of blood shone beneath the remains of his head.

"Hang on; you're going to be all right." Dad took off his belt and cinched it around her leg as a tourniquet. She arched her back, clawing the floor, and grabbed his arm. He put a hand on her forehead.

"I couldn't pull the trigger. And then he . . ."

"Save your strength."

He knelt, preparing to gather her up like a wounded bird. She pointed at the ceiling.

"Camera. In the smoke detector."

Swiftly he climbed on a chair, pried open the smoke detector, and yanked on the wire. Though the view splintered the sound continued.

"Phil . . . Hank's—"

"Dead. Single round to the head. And we're gone."

For a second the video returned. My father was staring at the camera, almost at me, calm and unremorseful. With a single motion he ripped its guts out of the wall.

The video faded out and an address appeared.

8 Larkdown Chase
London W8

My screen went dark, but I kept staring at it. Christian's wild eyes seemed to stare back, streaming grief and fear as he ran from the man who was coming to gun him down. A man he recognized, a man he had stopped near the juke-box in his mother's club. I pressed my hands to my face but still saw Christian's hungry eyes. The eyes of the raven-haired waif in Rio's club, putting his hand on my father's chest. Christian Sanger was one of Rio's prostitutes.

Christian awoke to the sense that the house had tipped over. Something . . . What was it? He opened his eyes and the sun pierced his vision. It was in the wrong place in the sky. It was morning.

Out in the kitchen, one of the girls was screaming.

Rio was sitting on the edge of the bed, fully dressed, hands clasped, lips pressed white.

"What?" he said.

"They killed Bliss."

The pain wrenched his chest, and a sound blurted from his throat. He balled the sheets in his fists and pressed them to his mouth, but the sound kept erupting, a sound like Bliss's dog made after she disciplined it with the cane. Rio looked at him as if he were a dog himself, and he had to make the noise stop, make it stop.

"You're sure?" he said.

"Yes. Shiver saw her body."

He bunched the sheets and bit down on them, telling himself to *stop it*. He pulled his knees to his chest. Rio put a hand on his leg.

"I know she was like a sister to you, but get up."

He rolled over. Sisters, as if that were the problem. All their girls thought of him in a sisterly way. *Like doing my brother,* one of them even said after they made it. *Freaky but boring.*

"The file. What about the file?" he said.

"Shiver got part of it."

"Only part?"

Rio stood up, pulling the covers off him. "You need to get moving. The Delaney girl is going to London. Jax Rivera put her little whelp there."

He sat up. "London? We've pinpointed the location?"

"Shiver is on her way, but you can be sure Rivera is too." She urged him out of bed. "And Shiver listened to a video call that Delaney made. Talking to a man somewhere around here."

"What did he look like?"

"Fuckable, smart, and full of attitude."

"In a wheelchair?"

"She said nothing about that." She mulled it over. "It may be the man we heard that Rivera married."

"So why was Delaney talking to him?"

"That I don't know. It may not be him, but watch out. Presume he is dangerous."

She was pushing him toward the dresser, getting out briefs and socks and a clean sweater for him.

"Me? Why me?"

"I'm sending Shiver to London."

"To do what?"

God, why did she have to give him that look, like, *What did I do to deserve you?* Nobody killed Rio's girls and got away with it.

"She'll make it painful, won't she?" he said.

His mother stepped toward him. "No. You will. Do her, then *do* her, split her wide-open. Can you handle that?" She cocked an eyebrow. "Get dressed. You're going too."

25

Thursday

Standing in the vein of passengers winding toward Immigration at Heathrow, I tried to focus. My joints ached, and my ears hummed with the siren call to lie down and sleep, right here on the floor. My body clock was about to blow its springs. It was early morning, judging from the sharp sun rising in the east.

Sleep had eluded me on the endless flight in the endless night. Every time I closed my eyes I saw the horror on Christian Sanger's young face, and the gun in my father's hand.

And to think I had convinced myself that Dad cared about Jax and her daughter as much as he cared about a video that caught him committing an extrajudicial killing and attempting to kill a witness to the crime. No wonder Jesse couldn't bring himself to tell me the truth.

The line inched forward. The family ahead of me was edging from fatigue to pissiness. The kids were cranky, the parents itchy for a smoke. Their twelve-year-old daughter wore track bottoms and a hot-pink T-shirt with the word JUICY written across the bust.

Change clothes, I wanted to say.

Mom, get your daughter out of that advertisement. Girl, change into a shirt with the Powerpuff Girls or *God Save the Queen,* on it anything but clothing that draws men's eyes to your young body and announces its succulence. *Juicy* tells them to pull you apart and sink themselves into you. Pop, tell her she's not up for auction. And for chrissake, keep her away from the middle-aged European men traveling alone on my flight, looking tan and sated and disreputable.

I went to rub my eyes, and poked my fingers into the eyeglasses I was wearing. Good one, Delaney.

Larkin. Kathleen Rowan Larkin.

My head hummed louder and my vision swam, a headache building. Sexualized children, turned into prostituted teens. And Rio Sanger had turned out her own son.

Down behind my heart, fear and shame were writhing. How the hell had I managed to get in this position?

When I learned that my father had been kidnapped, I ran from the police and set out to rescue him. I set out to get the information the Sangers wanted, use it to ransom my father, and then do more. I was going to use the Riverbend file to exonerate my dad from all the smears that had been made against him. And I was going to manipulate the information to get revenge on the kidnappers, hunt them down and punish them. I thought if I got the files that Rio demanded, I would be in a strong position to do that, because I knew those files implicated Rio. I was going to copy everything, stash it someplace new and safe, and turn pertinent parts over to Tim North, the FBI, or the U.S. Attorney, and get them in on the bust.

Fool.

The whole time, I had been hunting down a little girl for Christian and Rio Sanger. The whole time, I had been unearthing the darkest secret of my father's life. He had killed a man in cold blood.

I had let desire drive me, and in response, karma had kicked my butt. Straight into a pit, which I didn't know how to get out of. Maria Auxiliadora had remained mute on this topic.

And deep in the guts of my laptop, the down-ticker was

chewing away. I had less than three hours left. I was running out of time to get the final flash drive. The headache crawled through my skull.

Finally I stepped up to the desk. The woman ran my passport, eyed me, asked the purpose of my visit.

"Pleasure."

She stamped the passport and handed it back. Outside the terminal I stepped into seeping cold. A black cab was waiting at the curb with Jax inside.

Detective Lily Rodriguez sat in the open doorway of her car, staring across the dark driveway at Jesse's house. The lights were off and his truck was gone. The surf lashed the beach. Beneath the rustling of the Monterey pines, the voice on the other end of her phone was about to drive her nuts.

"Not home, that doesn't cut it," Nicholas Gray said. "Where is he?"

"I don't know."

"Find out."

"He didn't go to work today, but the law firm's not talking," she said.

"Make them talk," Gray said.

She didn't flinch. Nicholas Gray may have been a U.S. Attorney, but he wasn't her boss. He had no authority over her. All he could do was insult her, and if she thought hard enough, she could picture him as a gerbil she was dropping into a jar. Then Gray's affronts sloughed right off.

"All we know is that Evan booked a flight out of Bangkok to Malaysia but never checked in," she said.

Gray clucked. "Blackburn gamed you, Detective."

"I disagree."

"He's in on this with her."

A skinny bald gerbil, and when she screwed the lid on the jar, he clawed helplessly at the glass. "With all due respect, that's a stretch, sir."

"She's Phil Delaney's daughter. Delaney was a black ops

type; you don't think he levered that expertise and set his kid up to slide under the radar?" Gray paused dramatically. "Find Blackburn. He's going to be with her."

"We'll check his credit card transactions. If he's traveling, it'll show up."

"And find out where his brother is. See if you can't apply some pressure there."

Lily got a sinking feeling. This was why Nicholas Gray had called her in the first place, she felt sure. It was why he wasn't hassling one of his underlings or the Santa Barbara police, but her—because she had been the investigating officer in the case against P. J. Blackburn.

"What about Boyd Davies?" she said.

"What about him?"

"His phone records. We want to find out if he's in contact with Phil Delaney's kidnappers."

"Delaney hasn't been kidnapped. Your office is wasting time opening that investigation."

"He was a bounty hunter. His job was to track people down. We're certain that he contacted these people the Sangers. We're waiting for his phone records, and for the Las Vegas police to execute a search warrant on his office."

"Tell me something new."

"What does your office know about Rio Sanger's background in prostitution?"

"Your compulsive interest in this Sanger woman is a wild-goose chase. Stick to the real case, Detective."

Lily gazed up at the moon. "Fine. Will do."

"I hope that what I hear in your voice is eagerness. Get back to me."

Dismissed, Lily gave a little smile. The gerbil had run out of hot air left in the jar.

"Find Jesse Blackburn, and you'll find Evan Delaney. Get her in shackles on a capital murder warrant, and you'll get her father to come out of hiding to help her. Got that?"

"Yeah, I got it." She slammed her car door. "Like a case of lice."

*   *   *

Horns were honking all around, a wave of noise behind and on either side, cars swerving around them. The sun was low on the horizon, blindingly bright.

"You're in neutral," Jesse said. "Put it in first gear."

P.J. shoved on the gearshift. The transmission groaned.

"Clutch," Jesse said.

This gutless rental car probably had only a couple dozen teeth on the gears, and if P.J. didn't calm down he was going to strip them all off. A dirty white van squeezed past, the driver shouting as he weaved by inches from the nose of the car.

"Wankers!"

"Hey, man." P.J. threw up his hands. "It's not my fault."

Jesse grabbed the wheel. "Easy. Don't panic."

P.J. gave him a look, eyes bulging. "Panic? It's this round-about—how does anybody get around these things?"

They were moving at three miles an hour. The air was chill and biting.

Jesse pointed ahead. "Just keep going. Don't let the car stop."

"I told you it's been three years since I drove a stick. And this car's backward. How am I supposed to shift with my left hand?"

"It would have taken them an hour to get an automatic. It was a battle we didn't have time to fight."

"You were too pissed off that they didn't have a car you could drive. You should have known, Jesse, this is . . ." He stomped on the clutch, rammed the gearshift into first, and gunned the engine.

Jesse bent over the map, tracing their route. In his head he counted to ten, then to twenty, thinking, *Stay cool.* They were going to make it into the city. Give P.J. time to adjust to the car and they would pick up speed. The engine revved and P.J. went to shift, reaching out with his right hand and flipping on the windshield wipers.

"Left hand." He saw P.J. go pale and shut off the wipers, drifting toward the Range Rover coming up on their left. "It's okay, just . . . *Shit.*"

He flinched away from the door. There was a heavy thump and the Range Rover zoomed past. Outside his window the wing mirror hung twisted, swinging back and forth by a few wires.

P.J.'s knuckles were glue white on the wheel. "Be quiet."

"Just keep going."

Getting there was all that mattered, and he reckoned they needed to get there in under an hour. He glanced at the speedometer: five mph.

A road sign inched past. CENTRAL LONDON 15 MILES.

We flew along in the black cab, heading toward central London. It was cold, and the sky, though blue, seemed thin and distant compared to Thailand. Jax looked exhausted. She had a black eye and bruises all along the side of her cheek. But she seemed to be holding it together. She seemed, in fact, more rested than I did.

"Benzedrine and ibuprofen," she explained.

The driver buzzed along, with the radio blaring. Jax ripped open a package in a thick padded envelope. She checked that the driver was watching the road and slid out a military knife. Next she took out a black ankle holster. She pulled up her trouser leg, Velcroed the holster to her calf, and shoved the knife into it.

"No gun, but it'll have to do."

"Start talking. You have a hell of a lot of explaining to do," I said.

"I ordered this cab before I left Bangkok. Also ordered the package. The driver picked it up for me on the way to Heathrow." She shot the cuffs of her wool suit. "The blade will decapitate an ox. The hilt is tungsten carbide, can break a car windshield." She smoothed her lipstick. "Always carry a knife."

"No, I mean talk about Christian. His mother didn't groom him to take over the bordello. She groomed him to be a prostitute."

"Do you really need me to comment on that? Rio started him when he was about thirteen. Working nights at the club, turning him out to her johns. Hank didn't pay attention."

"You implied that she was also doping him, doing something with drugs to delay puberty, to keep him . . . girlish. He was manipulated like Bliss and Shiver, wasn't he?"

"In the club, they called him Revel."

"Was he the third one you said to look out for?"

"Yes. Most of the customers who came to the club thought he was a girl. They didn't find out the truth until they got in a room alone with him. Then Rio caught her clients on tape messing with an underage boy. She tried to sell that to us and . . ." She paused. "Phil couldn't take it. Christian, the other teens. He said, 'No more. Shut Rio down; end the op.' That's when Hank sold me out. My mistake was in not telling him sooner. It was . . . Forget it. It was everything."

A green MINI scooted past. At home, something that size was required to be on a leash.

"Did you know about Christian all along? When you were working the operation? Did Dad?"

"No. I found out shortly before everything went balls up."

I watched the road race by. The graffiti had evolved since the last time I'd been here. What it still lacked in California style it made up for in ubiquity. Everywhere it was scrawled like spray-paint tapeworms.

"Why did you lie to me when I first met you—about what happened with Hank Sanger?"

"Did you want to know one bit of what was in that video footage?"

"No."

The other questions I held back. Did you know that you were pregnant? That my father killed Georgia's dad?

"Boyd Davies, the bounty hunter Tim shot—he was impersonating an Immigration agent," I said. "I think he helped Rio smuggle girls into the U.S. Want to bet she planned to get your daughter across the border by having him bring her in under color of authority?"

"Good guess."

"What's driving the push to get Georgia?"

"Opportunity. And her age."

"But if they really wanted to, the Sangers could have found Dad anytime. Why now? What sparked all this off?"

She looked drawn. "That's a good question."

"You said that Christian had health problems."

"Yes. I think they originated from the drugs Rio was pumping into him and the others." She glanced at me. "Rio liked to go to Bangkok for plastic surgery and rejuvenation treatments. I think she takes human growth hormone to keep herself looking young. But she tried to deprive some of her hookers of the hormone, to keep them looking childlike."

"Think that's what's wrecked their teeth?"

She considered that. "Doubt it. More likely that's from years of drug abuse. Ever hear of meth mouth?"

"Vaguely." I thought back to the sight of Christian aiming a gun at Tim's car on a Santa Barbara street. "Christian didn't look childlike to me."

"No, Rio must have abandoned the idea for him."

"Do you know what's wrong with him?"

"He seemed anemic back then. My guess is some blood-borne disease caused by the drugs."

An awful thought began coalescing. "You said he wants his sister. Could it have something to do with his health?"

She looked out the window, her jaw tight.

"Jax, if it's a blood disease, or something malignant, could he want her for more than revenge?"

The sun was sharp in our eyes, at a low angle in the sky. All along the roadside, daffodils were blooming, an extravagant gift of yellow and gold, though the trees were still bare.

She leaned her head against the window. She didn't want to answer, but when she looked at me she was thinking the same thing I was: Christian wanted to suck Georgia's blood and marrow.

"If he tries to touch her, his own blood will be the last thing he ever sees." She knocked on the driver's partition. "Faster."

The view over Hyde Park was bare. So much green grass, all those bony trees. Below on Park Lane, black cabs and Mercedes stroked around the edges of the park. Christian stood by the window, chilled. Cashmere and his greatcoat couldn't keep him warm. It was an annoyingly bright day, morning too soon; he hated morning, and he was exhausted. More so than from the anemia. Coffee wasn't doing it. He'd injected himself with EPO, knew it would bring his hematocrit up, but not immediately.

Morning was oblivion, restoration. Rio usually left him alone in the morning. The clients were gone, the cash counted. He would have showered, cleansed his skin and mouth and cock, washed off the scent of the john's breath and sweat and cum. He would have . . .

The feeling overcame him again, the disgust, the need. And his SIG was back home because he couldn't take it on the plane. Eject the magazine, check that there were nine cartridges in the clip. Strip it, clean it. Press the takedown lever, pull the slide off . . . He needed it, oh, he needed it.

He found the Swiss Army knife in his toiletry kit, took the flathead screwdriver and unscrewed the knob mechanism for the bathroom door. He sat down on the floor and disassembled it.

There was a knock on the door. When he opened it Shiver stood in the hall, hair gleaming, eyes dark and pleased. She swept past him into the suite.

"Where's your laptop?" she said.

He pointed at the desk. "You have any glass?"

"Not where you can reach it." Sitting down at the desk,

she produced a flash drive and jacked it into his computer. She saw the doorknob mechanism spread across the floor—screws and springs and levers. "Jesus, Christian. We don't have time for tinkering."

Shiver didn't care that he disliked her. She didn't care whether any man disliked her, even though she could play winsome when she wanted to, with that practiced posture of the yielding Orient. She didn't need to play nice, because scorn was a powerful aphrodisiac. Too many guys thought their cocksmanship would cure her disdain. Such a young little thing, they thought, imagining that they would teach her. Those men never bothered to look into her eyes.

Rio had finally stopped her from hooking after she blinded that Ukrainian with a corkscrew.

"Let the drive boot up. Get me the glass," he said.

"Give me a minute. Rio won't want us to wait."

"Rio isn't here." He pulled her to her feet. "I need it. I have to be sharp."

She raised her chin. "You want to get high, fine. Let me pull it out of my pussy for you."

He pursed his lips. "You couldn't be more tacky if you took a course. That's why you'll always be a whore at heart."

She shook him loose. "You too."

She slid past him to the bathroom to pull out the Baggie of crystal meth. He sat down at the desk with his Swiss Army knife and bits of the doorknob mechanism. As he fit the screws back into their slots, the flash drive downloaded to his laptop and a video began running. He heard a woman say, "I have to tell you about Christian. Rio's doing something to him."

His head jerked up. Oh, God—it was Hank's place. He watched and went still, gripping the knife.

By the time Shiver returned from the bathroom with the glass, he was pale and sweating.

They knew. Rivera. Phil Delaney. His dad. Before he died, Rivera had told him, *Rio's grooming Christian.* His dad died knowing he was heading for whoredom.

The video brought it all back. The noise, the horror, the sight of—

"God."

His father dead. The gun coming around, Delaney trying to kill *him*. Turning his whole life to trash. In the mirror on the wall behind the desk, he was so pale he had no reflection at all.

He dropped the knife, grabbed the computer, and flung it at the wall. The mirror shattered in a waterfall of glass.

"Christian, Jesus," Shiver said.

He glowered at her. Why did everybody stare at him all the time like they knew something he didn't?

"What? Don't look at me like that. Don't look at me."

Stalking over to her, he grabbed the Baggie from her hand. His weakness increased.

"This isn't glass." He threw it at her. "Pills, I don't want pills."

"Get hold of yourself. I wasn't going to take my works through Thai customs."

"I have works, you idiot. I have syringes prescribed for me, for my EPO." He sat down on the couch, raking his hands over his legs.

"What is wrong with you?" she said.

He picked up the Baggie, ripped it open, and swallowed a handful of the methamphetamine. "Let's go get the girl. One of us doesn't have long to live, and it won't be me."

26

"Kit, get ready."

Feeling a hand nudging me, I sat up, trying to shake myself awake. We were in the middle of London. I looked around: bustling streets, black cabs, and motorcycle messengers, everybody driving on the wrong side of the road, same as in Bangkok. White stucco buildings sat bright in the chill sunshine. On sidewalks, hordes of people walked fast, all wrapped in bulky coats, all talking on cell phones. My head seemed firmly on backward. Surreptitiously I wiped the drool from the edge of my mouth. My Thai clothes were brighter and thinner than what the rest of the street was wearing. We pulled into a quiet neighborhood and I pulled my jacket more tightly around me.

The cab stopped outside a Victorian building in a narrow lane. This was Kensington, home to palaces and graceful Anglican churches. The lane was lined with sleek row houses, quiet as a churchyard, and throbbing with money from empire and investment banking and pop music, virtually pouring from the sidewalks, as profuse as the wisteria that crept green above windows and doorways.

But the school looked like a nineteenth-century factory—red brick, gabled windows, wrought-iron scrollwork. It hunkered behind a grimy old wall that was rimmed at the top with barbed wire.

"Wait here," Jax told the driver.

We walked through an archway, past a row of parked bicycles, and climbed the worn stone steps to the door of St. Mary Mazzarello Salesian School.

Above the door was a CCTV camera. Inside, the hallway was chilly and faintly damp. Feeling a draft, I crossed my arms. The ceilings were high, with crown moldings and tarnished chandeliers that gave off wan light. But tacked to the walls were reams of vivid watercolors, and down the hall I heard the energetic discord of a school orchestra. On a pedestal to my right stood a plaster statue of St. John Bosco, founder of the Salesian order.

To my left was a statue of the Madonna and child, crowned in gold.

"Maria Auxiliadora," I said.

"The Salesians are devoted to honoring Our Lady as Mary, Help of Christians."

Jax headed into the school office. Behind the counter, a secretary looked up.

"Jakarta Rivera to see the headmistress. Sister's expecting me. I'm Georgia's mother."

The secretary directed us to take a seat, eyeing the bruises on Jax's face, and made a phone call. Jax lowered herself gingerly into a chair, holding her left hand in her right, rigidly upright, eyes scanning the doorways. Her pupils were still uneven, and it seemed as though her left arm might be lagging.

Outside, on a small asphalt playground, clusters of girls were squealing their way through early recess, jumping rope and playing tag and strolling in huddles near the moss-stained wall. There was no view of the playground from the street. But there were two more CCTV cameras bolted to the brickwork.

"How long has it been since you've seen her?" I said.

"Ten weeks, since her half-term break."

Across the room a door opened. "Mrs. Rivera, won't you please come in?"

She was a nun, doughty and bearish in a blue suit with a heavy cross, hair cut like a pewter bowl under a short head covering.

"Wait here," Jax said to me.

And seemingly by strength of will alone, she held herself erect and strode across the room, hand out.

"Sister Cillian."

The nun shook her hand. "My goodness, what's happened to you?"

"Car accident." She touched her cheek and followed the nun into her office. "More frightening than anything else. But I'm taking a few weeks off and wanted to reassure Georgia that I'm all right." She closed the door behind her.

I watched the children on the playground. They wore maroon skirts and jackets with white blouses and black neckties. The look was utterly English, even if the playground was cramped and urban, more hip-hop than Hogwarts.

After five minutes Sister Cillian's door opened and Jax strode out with fervor in her eyes. The nun's expression was caring but reserved, as though she trusted Jax but instinctively kept her at a distance.

"I hope you'll be fighting fit again soon." She asked the secretary to go get Georgia from the classroom, and shook Jax's hand. "You'll be in our prayers. We'll see Georgia next week."

"Thank you, Sister."

Jax walked back to me, virtually humming with energy. Like a lightbulb, right before the filament cracks and it burns out.

"The accident really shook me up. I just need some time with my daughter," she said.

Voice low, I said, "And did you explain that child traffickers might show up at the school looking for her?"

"They have a good relationship with the Metropolitan Police. Calls will be made. After we leave."

Her voice had a thick edge to it, as though she'd had novocaine. She was still cradling her left hand in her right. The hand looked limp.

From down the hallway came the sound of rushing feet.

Jax was instantly out the office door. I heard a girl's voice, spinning with joy.

"Mummy!"

Through the doorway I saw Jax spread her arms wide. Georgia flew into her embrace, burying her head against Jax's chest, shaking with excitement. Jax gripped her, kissed the top of her head, laid her cheek against her hair, eyes shut, as though holding her daughter was all she could bear; as if the sight of her would prove overwhelming. I felt myself choking up.

When Jax did open her eyes, Georgia smiled up at her. She was coltish, not yet an adolescent but pure kid. Her black hair was drawn back into a ponytail from which uncontainable curls erupted. Her skin was creamy brown, her eyes dark and restless. Her necktie was askew. Jax straightened it affectionately.

Despite my exhaustion and dread, I felt swamped with relief. Jax had her girl safe in her arms. I walked out into the hall.

She turned to me. "Come meet my sweet song. This is Georgia."

"Georgie," the girl said, raising a hand in greeting. "Hiya."

I smiled. "Hi, Georgie."

"This is Kit," Jax said. "She's my friend."

Georgie looked at me with open curiosity. Jax was jabbing at me, because in Bangkok I'd cracked that she was friendless. But it hit me that perhaps I truly was the closest thing to a friend she had. The thought was both sad and scary.

"Mum, what happened to your face?"

"My car got in a fight with a telephone pole. Don't worry, sweetness. I'm okay. It just looks disgusting."

"You sure?"

"Positive. Come on—I'll tell you all about it."

Georgie held tight to Jax's hand. "Mrs. Westerman said you're here to collect me. Are we going on holiday?"

"For a few days. Let's get your things."

"Where are we going?"

Holding on to her mom's hand, Georgie skipped down the hall toward the dormitory, a jack-in-the-box of excitement, jabbering away in an enchanting English accent. I followed a step behind, aware of Jax hanging on and somehow drawing energy from her daughter's happiness. She looked absorbed and almost, impossibly, at ease. I had never seen her seem so . . . normal. We headed outside and crossed a courtyard where the sun felt sharp and shadows lay cold against stone walls speckled green with moss. The girls who had been on the playground came streaming past, red cheeked from the cold. They stared at Georgie, inquisitive and possibly envious. She purposefully ignored them—Miss Cool, the eleven-year-old facsimile.

The dorm was unadorned and echoing. Inside the door, another statue of Maria Auxiliadora beamed at us. Upstairs on the landing, clear light streamed through a tall window. Plaster saints, brown brick, cold linoleum: not a place where I would want to grow up. Georgie's room overlooked the courtyard. The room was tidy, but barely, as though chaos roamed the corners longing to break free. Above the beds hung posters of boy bands and teen-angst TV stars. It felt comfortable, but not homey.

Georgie grabbed a backpack and shoved in a music player and a paperback and her phone. "Can I change, Mum?"

"Yes. But we have a taxi waiting, so get your booty in gear."

I walked to the window and looked down at the green grass and gray stone in the courtyard. I glanced at my watch, then at Jax. "We have ninety minutes. The flash drive?"

Jax grabbed a winter coat from the wardrobe and tossed a few items of clothing on the bed. Georgie loosened her tie and reached for a hanger. She hesitated.

"Come on, Miss Thing. Don't dawdle." Jax was packing

clothes in the rucksack. She paused and pressed her fingers to her temple as though fighting off a bout of pain.

Georgie looked around the room, perplexed. "My other uniform."

I said, "Can I help with something?"

"Where is it?" She was suddenly serious. "It was here. We have to hang them in the wardrobe. If it's lying on the floor I'll get demerited."

Down in the courtyard, movement caught my eye. I froze. "Your spare uniform is gone?"

In the shadows of the courtyard, one girl had stayed behind when the others went back inside after recess. She had waist-length black hair and nonregulation Nikes. She was walking slowly along the outside of the school building, looking in the classroom windows.

Jesus Christ. "Jax. They're here."

We rushed from the room with Jax hanging onto Georgie with her right hand and holding her rucksack in the crook of her left arm, eyes sweeping the hall.

Face fraught, Georgie said, "Mum, what's going on?"

"Where's the back way out of the school?"

Georgie gaped at her. "What's the matter?"

"Where?"

Fright seeped into her eyes. "Behind the dorm, past the sports pitch there's a path to an old gate."

We ran down the stairs. At the bottom I grabbed the miniature statue of Maria Auxiliadora. Without breaking stride I cracked it against the stairway banister, shattering off the bottom. Holding it like a broken bottle, I strode alongside Jax down a hallway to the back exit. She kept a grip on Georgie. Her head swiveled at each doorway.

"Mum, what's happening?"

"No questions, Georgia. Do exactly as I say."

I glanced behind us. With everybody in class, we were the only ones around.

"We have to warn Sister Cillian," I said.

"No time." She paused at the exit, threw open the door, and looked around. "Clear. Move."

She pulled Georgie outside. I held back. On the wall inside the door was a fire alarm. I threw my elbow against it, breaking the glass, and pulled the switch. The air filled with the shriek of the alarm.

Jax glared at me. "Move. Now."

We ran across a small playing field and found the path, overgrown with nettles. The gate was eighty yards down, bolted and rusty and veined with ivy, but unlocked. Jax handed the rucksack to Georgie and began muscling the bolt on the latch. It was stuck stiff with rust.

"Where's the flash drive?" I said.

Georgie glanced at Jax, back at me, and then her gaze lengthened, past my shoulder. Her eyes jumped. The hair on the back of my neck stood up.

I turned and saw the gremlinish figure of Shiver slide into view at the far end of the path. The school uniform looked monstrous. Her sick eyes were pinned on Georgie.

Shouting with effort, Jax slammed loose the rusted bolt and yanked the gate open.

Georgie pointed at Shiver. "Mum, who's that?"

Jax shot me a look, nothing but shards. "Take her."

I pushed Georgie through the gate. Jax came behind us, pulling it closed.

"Keep her with you," she said. "Don't let her out of your sight."

"Of course."

"What's going on?" Georgie said. "Who is that?"

"Don't let the authorities get her. None of them, ever. Take her with you; get her to the U.S." She glanced at the gate. Reaching into her pocket, she produced a key. She slapped it into my palm. "You have to get the final flash drive. That's the only way you can get her out of the U.K. and keep her with you."

"Where is it?"

"Once you get to the States you'll know who to trust."

"Where's the flash drive?"

"Georgie knows." She turned to her daughter. "Code Black. Go with Kit. I'll find you."

Georgie's face blanched. "No—Mum."

I pulled on Georgie's arm but she fought me, a little tiger, trying to break away. Jax dug her fingernails into her arm.

"Don't look. Run."

I tossed Jax the broken statue, wrapped an arm around Georgie's waist and ran. She didn't resist. I glanced back. Jax was reaching for the knife strapped to her calf.

Holding tight to Georgie, I ran out onto a street behind the school. I heard sirens in the distance.

Georgie's shoulders hunched. "My mum . . . I don't want to go . . . we have to help my mum."

I kept running. Our taxi was out in front of the school, but I didn't know if Shiver had backup watching the front entrance or whether the police were on their way. I only knew we couldn't get caught. I needed Georgie to be tough.

"That woman on the path wants to hurt you. Your mom is keeping her from doing that. And you have to do something for your mom."

"What?"

"Run like hell."

Down the block we raced, past bare trees and parked cars. A small white police car screamed past my view, blue lights flashing, headed for the front of the school. From another direction, a second siren was approaching. I vectored away from both of them, dashing along the sidewalk. Behind us, I heard the gate being thrown open.

"Faster," I said.

Georgie shifted into a higher gear, keeping pace with me.

Jax was hosed. She was fighting for Georgie, but she was already badly hurt. She would either be dead or under arrest in a matter of minutes. She wasn't going to show up on the next corner, brushing dust from her impeccable wool suit. Wasn't going to walk out of this one. That left me.

I scanned the terrain, looking for cover, for safety, for a path to freedom. And realized—"Georgie, where can we go to hide?"

She looked frantic for a moment, and pointed down the street. At the end was a brick wall with a gate leading into a park.

"Through there."

Ahead, the sidewalk was blocked by construction scaffolding. I dodged between cars and ran down the middle of the narrow street. Range Rovers and Jaguars and builders' pickups were parked bumper-to-bumper along the curb, and I felt as though I were running through a couloir, looking for a chute at the bottom.

Breathlessly Georgie said, "We're running away from the police."

"Yes."

She shot me a hot look. "This is Code Black for real, isn't it?"

"Yeah. It's for real."

Her face set. I knew I couldn't risk dishonesty with her.

"I don't know what she told you about Code Black," I said.

"Get away. Don't go to anybody unless Mum says it's okay. Not even the police." She eyed me again. "Unless Mum told me they're a friend, like you. Only go to Sister Cillian or . . ." Her chest hupped, but she fought it down. She was trying to be a big girl, to follow Code Black rules. "Get to Mum's solicitors."

"Who?"

"Goodhew Waites. Jeremy Goodhew from Goodhew Waites. She made me memorize it. I have his number in my mobile phone."

"Call him."

She grabbed for her backpack. "And fallback if I can't get to him is White City."

At the corner, a car turned into the street, heading toward us, swinging wide.

"What's at White— Jesus." I tossed her toward the parked cars. "Climb over."

She scrambled onto the hood of a car, and I made to do the same, hoping the driver would pull back to the correct side of the— Oh, crap.

He veered sharply to the right. I jumped but he was coming straight at me. Even as I heard screeching brakes I knew it was too late. I was in the air when it hit me.

The sound was awful, a deep thud that was me bouncing off the grille of the car. I hit the ground flat on my back in the middle of the road.

I saw sky. It didn't hurt. Oh, hell, was my neck broken? Then it hurt.

Bad, pounding through me. I saw car tires and bare tree branches and wisteria. Stunned, head thundering, all the breath knocked out of me. I heard sirens, and wailing, and that was Georgie.

Don't lie here. Get up, Delaney. I saw Georgie on the hood of the parked car, mouth wide, and I couldn't stay here. Move. I heard an almost physical voice saying, *Get off your ass; come on, Delaney.*

I rolled over and crawled, my head ringing, taking stock of the fact that my arms could grab, my legs could move, I could stand, could see Georgie staring at me.

"Go," I said.

"Delaney."

She looked at the car that had hit me, more confused than ever. It was idling in the street, and somebody was shouting at me. Police sirens were echoing off the old brick buildings. Slowly, blankly, I turned my head to look at the car.

What was P. J. Blackburn doing behind the wheel?

"Evan, get in."

P.J. wasn't talking, but trying to roll down his window and finally opening the door and climbing out. I put a hand to my head. Jesus, I knew he was angry at me, but to run me down with a car? In London? He raised his hands and said, "I couldn't help it; I hit the clutch instead of the brakes."

Jesse was leaning out his window. "Evan, come on."

Georgie had gone cat-cautious, eyes wary, withdrawing from me. "Kit?"

Jesse beckoned to her. "Georgia, you too. Hurry, Ev."

I stood up, and pain rang through my ribs. Georgie glared at Jesse, shoulders low, and then at me. Scrambling off the far side of the parked car, she took off into the park.

Jesse opened his door. "Get in. Evan, come on. We'll go get her."

He sounded astonished and pleading and angry. He looked past me. A police car was coming down the street. He looked overtly, too much, relieved.

He saw that I'd caught his expression. I shook my head, gave him a last look, and ran after Georgie.

27

I ran toward the park. Ahead through the gate I caught flashes of Georgie's maroon jacket and bouncing backpack. Behind me, horns honked, and I heard the sound of P.J. struggling with the clutch. What the hell were he and Jesse doing here? How did they know to show up at the Salesian school?

My stride was off, my leg killing me. I drummed through the park gate. Gnarled trees rose all around, branches grasping like arthritic fingers. Brambles crowded the view. A maze of muddy trails veered through blackberry thickets in all directions. I knew the English liked their gardens with a tousled edge, but this was too much—the evil twin of the Hundred Acre Wood.

My breath frosting the air, I ran, glancing down trails as they branched out, seeing an elderly couple sauntering arm in arm, and a mother with her toddler bundled up on a park bench. Holly trees loomed overhead, clawing archways over the path. Fifty yards down the trail, I found a map.

Holland Park. Damn, it was huge. Lawn, tennis courts, playing fields, restaurants, a freaking opera pavilion, these woods, and oh, great—a grassy knoll. Where Evil Piglet lies in wait for the presidential motorcade with his sniper rifle. My throat constricted. I couldn't lose Georgie. If I lost her everything was shattered.

And I couldn't panic and blunder around aimlessly.

Georgie knew the park and this neighborhood, and she had instructions. Code Black: Get away, call Jax's solicitor. And when I had asked her where to go, she said, *Through there*. Which meant out the park on the west side.

A dog walker ambled up the trail from that direction. I waved to him.

"Did you see a girl in a maroon school uniform running past you?"

"Yeah, down that way."

He pointed over his shoulder. I took off.

Right before the girl ran through the gate into the park, Jesse looked out the back window and saw her check over her shoulder, one glance, dread plain on her face. She must believe she was on her own, abandoned to the wolves. The thought grabbed him by the base of the throat.

He jerked his thumb over his shoulder. "Turn around. See if you can cut around the park and catch up with her."

P.J. shook his head. "You think she'll get in this car? No way. She's making tracks."

He was right. She had seen them crash into Evan. And she had seen Evan refuse to get in the car. She had no idea who they were, other than two strangers trying to hunt her down.

His brother gripped the wheel, face crimson, waiting for him to say something. Something like, *You ran over my girlfriend, you could have killed her, you could have—*

"We have to try," Jesse said.

P.J. put the car in gear and scanned the cramped street. "I can't turn around here. I have to go around the block."

"Do it."

They revved past Victorian town houses with big stone windowsills and wisteria crawling across the walls, nearly scraping the BMWs and Volvo SUVs parked at the curb. In the distance, a fire truck sped across the view, siren wailing. Ahead of them a girl rounded the corner at a dead run, sprinting for the park. He did a double take. Had Georgia made a loop?

No, it was another girl in the same school uniform. Her eyes were hot in a pale face, her black hair flying. Blood was streaked across her cheek. A chill fingered down his back.

"She's one of them."

"Who?" P.J. said.

She raced past them toward the park gate. "Christ, it's her. The freak from the hotel in Bangkok."

P.J. peered at him in open disbelief. "Bangkok? Jesse, you trippin'?"

She wore an earpiece and was clutching a handheld device, glancing from it to the street ahead and back again.

Jesse got his phone. "Find a cross street and double back around the block. Hurry."

Pummeling down a gravel path and out of the park through a wrought-iron gate, I found myself on a broad street graced with white mansions. I grabbed my side, fighting off a stitch in my ribs. I looked around and oh, thank God, there she was off to my right. Two hundred yards up the street, backpack bouncing, skinny arms pumping like a world-class sprinter, she was making for a T-intersection where this street ran into a main road.

"Georgie," I called.

She didn't hear. I ran past the angel-cake mansions decorated with chandeliers and Jeep Grand Cherokees. The cold air rasped into my lungs. Up at the distant corner, Georgie waited for a traffic light to turn green, ran across, and raced out of sight to the right, along a row of classy storefronts.

My phone rang. I dug it from my pocket. "Jax?"

"The Bangkok freak is on your tail," Jesse said.

The biting sunlight and icy air felt abruptly colder. "And Jax?"

"No."

I clenched my hands, feeling my eyes sting. I glanced over my shoulder. "I don't see her."

"She just ran into the park."

"Where are you?"

"Heading through this neighborhood, trying to double back."

"Keep P.J. away from me."

I hit the T-intersection and pulled up sharply at a red light, remembering to look right for traffic. This was Holland Park Avenue. I caught sight of Georgie running along the tree-lined sidewalk on the far side of the road.

"Georgie!" I yelled. She gave no sign of hearing me.

On the phone, Jesse said, "Ev, we're coming, but—"

"Does the FBI know I'm here? Did you call the police?"

"No."

He didn't even hesitate. I knew he was telling me the truth. The man might sell me out, but he wouldn't lie to me. The light changed and I ran across the street.

"Then don't. Jax said—" My voice caught. Jax might be dead. "Involving the police will be a disaster for Georgie."

There was no reply for a long moment. "All right."

Relief rolled across me. Sunshine streaked through the bare branches of the trees as I ran up the street.

"The freak has some kind of tracking device," Jesse said. "Watch yourself. P.J. and I will try to run interference."

"Yeah, interference, he's damned good at that."

I ran with lopsided fatigue up the street past a French bakery. Past Daunt Books, which looked like a chapel where word lovers could stop and worship. Past a boutique where the clothes were twelve shades of black. Past a charming grocery, and I didn't guess they sold squidsicles here in Holland Park. Past a butcher's shop where—holy mother, what was that in the window? What kind of animal had internal organs that slimy?

Past the Starbucks, and I saw where she was going. "She's heading for the underground station."

She ran through the entrance that yawned under the blue sign and the red underground symbol.

I said, "Georgie's heading for a law firm called Goodhew

Waites. I don't know where it is, but I figure it's down-town."

"I'll find out."

The underground station was old and not quite elegant, with glazed tiles shining on the walls. I ducked inside. Past the entrance barriers were two elevators. The door to one was just closing.

"Georgie," I called.

The door shut with no reply. Favoring my ribs, I jogged to the ticket window and put a twenty-pound note on the counter. "Do you have an all-day ticket, all stations, some-thing like that?"

"Travelcard," the woman said, and punched her key-board. She slid the ticket under the slot in the window. I pushed through the barriers and hit the call button for the elevators, thinking, *Hurry*.

I glanced back out at the street, seeing pedestrians and traffic. Forget this. I took the stairs, running down an iron spiral staircase that was clattering and cold as hell.

The phone line was still open. "I'm in the station. I haven't seen Shiver."

"Ev, I'll—"

The walls of the station cut off the call.

Jesse snapped his phone shut, looking at the map. "When we get up to Notting Hill Gate turn left."

Wrestling the car around a corner, P.J. nursed along a street where town houses were painted candy colors, sky blue and red and white. They were going in the wrong di-rection, away from the Holland Park tube station. The car accelerated, and P.J. put his left hand on the stick and shifted into second. They revved up to the corner. Cross traffic was moving fast.

A silver Aston Martin DB9 went past and pulled to the curb. A man climbed out of the car with a phone to his ear. He had hair like a magazine model, and his black greatcoat was riffling in the wind. Looking around, he stepped off the curb and glanced back and forth, waiting for a break in the traffic, wanting to cross the street.

It was the guy he had seen in the white car with the bounty hunter, outside Evan's house. Christian Sanger.

He was the one behind all of this. He was the key.

"See that guy?" he said.

P.J. looked. "Yeah."

Up the road to their right was the entrance to the Notting Hill Gate underground station. If Sanger got across the street, that was where he would head. He knew that Georgia was coming this way on the tube. He planned to grab her off the train.

Jesse pointed. "Hit him."

28

I leaped down the stairs two at a time, swinging around the spiral staircase. My hands were bone cold on the ironwork. At the bottom I ran along a tunnel and down another flight of stairs toward the tracks. A train was stopped on the east-bound side.

I ran out onto the platform as a beeper sounded, urgently. One last passenger jumped aboard and the doors slid closed. I rushed to the door of the train and pushed the *open* button. Nothing happened. I knocked on the window. A young woman in a black peacoat glanced up briefly, and returned to reading her book.

I ran along the platform looking through the train windows for Georgie. The beeping shut off and the train began to move.

Slowly at first, and I kept pace with it. I saw into the carriage ahead. Georgie was sitting at the far end of the car. She was hunched into her seat, clinging to one of the support poles as if it were the last solid thing standing in her world.

"Georgie," I shouted.

She didn't look around. The train gained speed. I called her name again. The wheels clacked and the electric whine of the motors covered the sound of my voice, even in the echoing cavern along the platform. I accelerated, trying to get her attention, reaching the carriage she was in and beating on the windows.

Georgie leaned her head against the pole and closed her eyes. The train pulled away and rattled like a snake into the black tunnel at the end of the platform.

I stopped, breathing hard. A swoosh of air blew over me and down the tunnel after the train, leaving me standing alone under curved walls plastered with gigantic car insurance ads and travel posters. VISIT THAILAND! I checked the sign above the platform; the next train was due in five minutes. Too long. She was getting farther away with every heartbeat.

Train tag would be hopeless. I needed to get back up to street level, where I could get cell phone reception and call the law firm, Goodhew Waites. I hurried back down the platform and up the stairs to the lifts. My ribs ached and my leg was throbbing.

I waited impatiently outside the heavy silver doors of the lift. The call light went out and the doors opened. I stepped in.

The lift had a second door on the opposite side for departing passengers. It was sliding closed. I stopped dead. Standing outside the other door, with her back to me, was Shiver. She was wearing the maroon jacket and skirt of the St. Mary Mazzarello school. From the back she could have been any twelve-year-old. She turned and her eyes caught mine.

Gollum eyes. Wide and withered, with a furious light. She flew at the door. Reflexively I stepped back. The door slid shut.

The lift rose. I blinked, catching my breath, knowing what had just happened. Shiver would realize that we had missed Georgie. She would be coming.

P.J.'s head swiveled. "What?"

Sanger continued checking the traffic, looking around and jittering with the energy of a human buzz saw. He jogged ten steps along the curb, stopped, and put a hand to his chest. Even from here, Jesse could see that his face was whiter than paste. Something was wrong with him. How fucking great.

"Run him over," Jesse said.

"You're joking."

"He's going to snatch Georgia. We have to stop him."

P.J.'s mouth dropped open. "Are you insane?"

"This may be our only chance." Sanger straightened up. "Go. He's going to catch his breath and get away."

"What the hell is wrong with you?"

Jesse put his hands to his head. "I can't chase him on foot. Do it."

Sanger saw a break in the traffic and crossed to the far side of the street. He strode along the sidewalk toward the tube station, talking on his cell phone.

"We're blowing it," Jesse said.

P.J. set his face, shoved the car into gear, and whipped around the corner. He swerved past a bus, a MINI, and a tow truck whose driver was changing a flat tire. He passed Sanger's Aston Martin and bundled the car to the curb. He turned off the engine.

"What are you doing?" Jesse said.

Sanger was jogging again, still making for the underground.

P.J. looked at Jesse. "I'm done."

He pulled the key from the ignition, got out, and stalked away.

Jesse sat with his mouth open, watching him go. Checking for traffic, P.J. ran across the street. Oh, no. He was chasing Sanger.

Jesse grabbed the chair frame and wheels from the back-seat, tossed them out and fit them together. P.J. ran up the sidewalk on the far side of the street toward the tube. By the time Jesse got out of the car, P.J. was a hundred yards away.

The wind cut across him. He saw Sanger jog down the stairs at the underground entrance, black greatcoat swirling. Ten seconds behind him, P.J. followed.

He found a crosswalk and reached the other side of the

road, passing a woman in a mink coat who was walking a dog the size of a piece of Kleenex. When he reached the underground station he stopped at the top of the stairs. He might be able to make it down, bumping backward hanging onto the rail, but it would be tricky.

He glanced around. Was there a way in with a ramp?

No. But there was another entrance on the other side of the street, and that was where Sanger jogged up the stairs, phone jammed to his ear. He ran back down the street toward his parked Aston Martin. Jesse's shoulders sagged. The wind caught the side of his head.

Breathing heavily, P.J. ran up the stairs beside him. "I lost him."

Christian climbed into the Aston Martin, pulled out, and made a U-turn. The Aston growled past them, heading toward central London.

P.J. watched. "Oh."

Jesse stared after it. P.J. turned to him.

"You wanted me to kill him? To hit him with the car and kill him?"

"No, I . . ." He ran a hand through his hair.

P.J.'s expression was split with shock. "Who *are* you?"

The air was freezing. Pedestrians swept around them, staring.

"You're supposed to be the good guy, the upstanding member of the family. You're in a wheelchair because somebody ran you over. And you wanted me to do the same to that guy?"

"I didn't want you to kill him. I wanted you to stop him. I still do."

"You're fucking nuts."

Joggers ran past in sleek gear. The Aston had disappeared up the road into the gleaming parade of Volvo SUVs and BMWs.

"I know where he's going. Come on," Jesse said.

P.J. shook his head, looking toward their rental car. "It's out of my hands."

Down the street where they had parked, the bus was gone. The tow truck had pulled forward and stopped next to their car. It wasn't the auto club. The driver was out of the truck, locking a bright yellow clamp on their wheel.

"What do we do?" P.J. said.

Jesse looked up at the underground symbol.

Christian raced along Notting Hill Gate in his rented Aston Martin DB9. He was pumped. The bug had worked; the phone tracker had worked; they had everything. The girl was on the underground, running to a solicitor's firm like a scared rabbit. He was going to get there first.

A few blocks over, on the narrow streets of oh-so-posh Kensington, was the girl's school. He had seen two police cars at the far end of the block as he drove past earlier. Action down in the alley, bobbies in Day-Glo yellow jackets and those silly English hats with black-and-white checkered bands around the brims, lots of radios and utility belts and not a single weapon among them besides CS spray.

He had no idea what Shiver had done to Jakarta Rivera. He couldn't creep back down the alley to see whether he could spot anything, like a body bag or blood spatter. But she must have done it good, because he had seen no sign of Rivera since they left the school. Good riddance, *puta*. He just wished he could have seen it. The bitch had set his father up for Phil Delaney to kill. He should have been the one to top her.

Ridiculous airlines, making him leave the SIG at home. The thought caused a tightness in his chest again. He rubbed his hand across his cashmere sweater, his fingers ice cold, his hands pale, nail beds as white as paper. The anemia was taking hold. The bleeding was getting more frequent, harder to stop when it happened. He needed the girl, and he needed her soon.

Up and out of the lift at Holland Park, I ran for the exit, jammed my ticket into the slot, pushed through the gates, and ran out into the cold sunshine. I needed a cab, but there was very little traffic. I took off.

Holland Park was far past posh. It exuded privilege, comfort, and understated grandeur. Imposing white houses were built on squares with private parks. Flowering trees were popcorned pink with blossoms. There was a sense of repose and privacy even along the main drag, as though noise, honking, jarring accents would be unseemly, just not done.

And screw the tourist reverie. Get me out of here. After a block, running uphill, my legs were wobbly poles. I finally flagged down a taxi. The cabbie asked me where I wanted to go.

"Goodhew Waites. It's a law firm."

"The address?"

I had my phone in my hand. "Central London. Just get going up the road. I'll get the address." I stared blankly at the phone. "How do you call Information?"

He glanced in the rearview mirror. "Just landed from the States?"

I scowled at him, catching my breath. "Floor it. There's an extra ten pounds if you get me there before somebody taking the tube."

His eyebrow went up. "You got it, love. Try one-one-eight–five hundred." He put the pedal down.

It wasn't so hard, actually. It was, in fact, scintillating.

Christian found his way to the basement of the stolid brick building in Mayfair, down to a depth where there were no CCTV cameras, but there were smoke alarms. He positioned the newspapers on the floor beneath one and tossed a lit match on the pile. The flames were so hot, their radiant heat so welcome against his chill, so *alive*.

It took Shiver's voice on the phone to break the spell. "Did you do it? Get out, quickly."

The flames blossomed, climbing and starting to dance. The sound was a bracing crackle. When the alarm rang, he ran.

By the time people poured out of the building, he was standing across the street. They held themselves against the cold and fretted with concern at their workplace, beginning to understand that it wasn't a false alarm but an actual fire—these chartered accountants and secretaries and British solicitors in their blue pinstripes and brown shoes. These people had no sense of style. They weren't like the Italians. Though in bed these weedy types were the wildest he'd ever had to deal with, and they loved their drink. It was just as well that guns were hard to come by in the U.K., because when the English let the lid off, they were animals.

He hunched into his black greatcoat, breath swirling in the air, hoping to look like a curious pedestrian. Were people staring at him? He stepped back against the building. He glanced at his watch. The fire trucks would be here soon. Shiver needed to hurry.

It took her another thirty seconds, but she came scooting along the sidewalk. She bit her lip and checked a piece of paper in her hand as though verifying the address, putting a hand over her mouth and looking forlorn. Hesitantly she approached a young woman dressed in clothes too tight and louche to be an attorney. Secretary, sisterly. Shiver fumbled for words and showed the woman the little piece of paper, keeping her face lowered, hair falling over her eyes, because with Shiver the eyes always gave it away. Her shoulders hunched with cold and worry.

Your average whore could outact a Broadway star any day.

The secretary put an arm on Shiver's elbow and called to a man who stood at the far side of the crowd. He was thin with coppery hair that flopped uselessly in the wind, a suit cut too large across the shoulders, and oh, the hopeless stiff, a lavender tie. When the secretary approached him, sheltering the frightened Catholic schoolgirl, he bent to the child, lips pursed, and with somber formality shook her hand. *Jeremy Goodhew, how do you do, my dear girl. I'm so sorry about this; we've had a bit of an emergency.* She was too spooked to look at him for long, too cowed, but when he spoke to the secretary and gestured at his smoldering office building and pointed up the street, Shiver nodded gratefully and let him lead her along the sidewalk away from the crowd and the ringing alarms. The man was undoubtedly taking her someplace quiet to talk. Someplace where she could get hot cocoa. He touched her shoulder. The gesture looked reassuring, not sexual in any way. The fool.

The secretary stood on the sidewalk, watching them walk away. Don't watch too long, Christian thought. But sirens swelled, bouncing off the brick and stone buildings, and she turned away to watch the fire engines arrive.

When Shiver tugged on Jeremy Goodhew's arm and diverted him into the alley, Christian was the only one who saw.

29

"Jesse." Finally. "I'm in a cab, heading for Mayfair. Where are you?"

"Close, but not moving fast enough. Christian Sanger's after Georgie," he said.

"Oh, God."

I bounced on the seat of the taxi. The cabbie, despite his bland-as-tapioca face, was gunning this bowling ball of a car through traffic, slewing along Bayswater Road as if he were Steve McQueen in *Bullitt*.

"Listen, I should have told you before," Jesse said. "When I saw the freak chasing Georgia. She didn't just have a tracking device; she had an earpiece."

Earpiece and tracker: That was bad. The cabbie flung us around a corner. I slid halfway across the seat before grabbing the handhold and steadying myself. This was going in my travel opus: *Cities of the World in Sixty Minutes or Less*.

"Shiver got into Georgie's room before Jax and I got to the school. She could have messed with Georgie's phone and stuck a bug in her backpack." With a sinking feeling, I realized that Shiver had most likely heard everything Georgie said to me. "She probably knows exactly where Georgie's going."

"We're a few minutes from the law firm. I'll do what I can."

"Be careful."

"I will, but . . ." His voice veered away from the phone. The crowd noise on his end was cacophonous.

"But?" I said.

"But I'm dealing with something," he said, and hung up.

The escalator was crowded. Jesse held on to the rubber handrails, leaning forward and riding it up. "He still there?"

P.J. looked back down to the bottom. "Shit, yeah."

The underground guy came into view below them. "Oy. Get off there."

"Okay," Jesse called. "As soon as I get to the top."

The man took out a walkie-talkie and thumped toward the escalator. "You can't do that. Get off."

"What do we do?" P.J. said.

Jesse smiled. "Wave to him."

They turned and waved like the royal family.

The man barreled onto the escalator. Hitting the top of the rise, Jesse held the handrails and let them pull him over the lip at the end of the escalator. They pushed through the crowd for the exit as the walkie-talkie scritched behind them. Before the tube guy could stop them they banged through the doors of the Bond Street underground station, onto a side street.

P.J. glanced back inside. "Does that make up for my driving? Are we even?"

"Getting there."

Off to the right was a major road, packed with pedestrians and traffic. They could see enormous department stores.

"That's Oxford Street." Jesse turned the map and nodded in the other direction. "The law firm's south, about three blocks."

"Catch a cab?" P.J. said.

"Too slow. Hoof it." He spun and started off.

P.J. followed. "What's next, base jumping?"

He was out of breath. Jesse thought about the steps P.J. had hauled him up, the gap between the doors of the train and the tracks, the numerous flights of stairs.

"I know it was hard work. Thank you," he said.

"You, my brother, have a major screw loose."

"It's called improvisation. And we're running out of time."

They hurried along the bumpy, canted sidewalk, cold in the sunlight. P.J. said, "People stare, don't they?"

"All the time."

The neighborhood looked Victorian, with redbrick buildings standing solid against the sharp blue sky. After a few blocks they turned a corner and saw a square ahead. Trees dotted the lawn, and magnificent Georgian buildings surrounded it on three sides. Jesse looked at the map.

"Oh, wow."

He glanced around the square. Would Sanger risk doing something here?

P.J. pointed down the road. "What's that?"

To the south, about a hundred yards beyond the square, fire trucks were parked outside an office building. A crowd milled on the sidewalk.

Jesse folded the map and put it in his pocket. "This isn't good. Come on."

Short of breath, Christian pressed the phone to his ear, inhaling the hard cold air. "Done?"

"Yes," she said.

"What—"

"Twenty units bolus, injected with an insulin pen. He didn't have time to react. He never knew what hit him."

"Is he—"

"Yeah. But you don't get to poke the body with a stick. Keep your ghoulish ass moving toward the square."

"Have you—"

"Of course I've contacted the girl. Told her I was Jeremy Goodhew's secretary and apologized that the office has been closed because of a fire in the building. Mr. Goodhew will meet her in a public place instead. She's to watch out for him. He's young and slim and has black hair and the kindest smile, and he's wearing a black overcoat. And yes, my accent was perfect fucking Estuary English, exactly like the real secretary; the girl had no clue."

Who did she think she was, speaking to him that way—his mother?

"I'm on my way to the square," he said. "Get over here."

"Five minutes. I have to clean up and change my clothes. The girl and people from the law firm saw me in the school uniform; I need to ditch it."

He rubbed his hand over his chest, feeling his heart quicken, his breath catch when he inhaled. He strode toward the square, so eager he wanted to scream.

P.J. jogged along at Jesse's side, eyes on the commotion down the block. "What are you going to do?"

What he meant was, What *can* you do? Jesse held on to his push-rims, hands cold on the metal despite his half-fingered gloves.

"One thing about that guy Sanger," P.J. said. "He acted like a speed freak."

Jesse looked at him. "Oh?"

"He was so twitchy he looked like he was about to jump out of his skin. And he kept clenching his jaw and grinding his teeth. It's what meth users do when they're tweaking a lot." He glanced at Jesse. "If he's burned out on crystal, he's probably going to be paranoid. Suspicious of everybody."

Jesse thought about it. He looked around. The pristine brick building across the street was the Marriott.

"Stay here and keep your eyes open. Maybe up there on the steps into the hotel. I'm going over to the square."

"You aren't exactly inconspicuous."

"So I'll have to use that to my advantage."

He crossed the street. The grass in the square was emerald green in the sunshine, the trees brambled.

Across the street P.J. climbed the steps to the side entrance of the Marriott. He leaned against the wall outside the door, hands tucked into his armpits for warmth.

Jesse went to the center of the square. Nearby stood the Roosevelt memorial. He gave the black statue a sharp look. The greatest president of the twentieth century, a crip who led the country through World War II, shown standing up. Image at odds with the reality. He continued scanning the perimeter. He couldn't run, couldn't hide, had no weapons. He could only improvise.

At the southeast corner of the square, a man in a sweeping black overcoat strode across the street, heading in his direction. Jesse got his phone, hit redial, and turned to greet Christian Sanger.

"Got it," I said, even as I heard the phone click off at Jesse's end. I leaned toward the cabbie. "Grosvenor Square."

He screeched around a corner into a lane the width of a sofa, squeaking past parked cars with an inch to spare. Barely pausing at an intersection, he gunned on, the heavy engine blatting like some old propeller-driven bomber. Gray stone buildings sliced up on either side of us. He keeled around another corner.

He braked so hard my butt slid off the seat.

"Bloody hell," he said.

Orange traffic cones crammed the street like dunce caps. Barricades were set up, and a British Gas truck and crew blocked the street, manhole covers off, dirt heaped around the trench they were digging. The cabbie looked out the rear window and frowned. A row of cars had backed up behind us. We were hemmed in.

He shook his head. "It's three streets away; do you want to wait for this to clear?"

"No." Grabbing my backpack, I jumped out and jammed some bills at him through the front window. "There's an extra twenty. You're a prince."

Jesse watched Sanger stride toward the center of the square. His black greatcoat flared in the wind like wings. Across the street P.J. stood in the doorway of the hotel.

Jesse checked to the west. Evan would be coming from that end. He continued panning the square and caught sight of a maroon jacket.

Georgia was walking in this direction from the far corner of the square. Her face was troubled, her thin arms hooked tightly to her chest for warmth, her bare legs mottled blue in the biting air. Eleven years old and she'd made it this far, on her own, and was going to see it through. He felt a knob of emotion in his throat.

Sanger raised a hand expansively and waved. "Georgia? I'm Jeremy Goodhew."

Georgie's gaze fastened on him, her stride quickened, and her shoulders dropped, defenses falling.

Jesse could tell her to run, but he had no doubt that of the three of them Christian was the fastest, even though he was pale, his lips liverish, veins snaking blue beneath the skin of his temples. No, run and she was lost. P.J. was too far away, and Evan wasn't here yet.

He whistled across the green. "Georgia, stop where you are." He pointed at Sanger. "That's as close as you get."

Georgie brought herself up short, about thirty meters away. Christian did a double take, hesitated, and kept walking, extending a hand to her.

His teeth flashed. "Sorry about the mess at the law firm. Just come with me, everything's okay now."

Beneath the calm smile, desire rolled around his voice. But though he was smooth and seductive, his hand was jittering. His eyes jinked at Jesse. Jesse lowered his voice.

"Yeah, you've seen me before. Outside Evan's house, when you were riding shotgun for Boyd Davies."

Christian slowed and stopped.

"That day," Jesse said, "did you plan to get out of the car and let him be the one to get blown away? Or was that dumb luck on your part?"

Georgie blinked at him, breathing hard. Christian narrowed his eyes. His smile and warmth were receding behind a carapace.

Thinly, he said, "There are laws against harassing people. Why don't you move along, friend?"

"You also saw me outside the Notting Hill Gate tube station. You missed that chance to snatch Georgie, and you're going to miss this one just as bad."

Georgie went rigid. "What?"

Christian slid his gaze her way, shaking his head. "He's lying. Ignore this man and come with me."

"Don't you want to know who I am?" Jesse said. "Why I'm following you, how I knew you'd be here?" Slowly he wheeled toward him. "You got a phone call outside the tube station. It sent you panting down the road like a dog in heat. You took off in a DB9 and came here." He glanced at Georgie. "When you phoned the law firm did you speak to Mr. Goodhew in person?"

Her face blanched. She shook her head.

"This guy doesn't have an English accent, Georgie. He's faking. His real name is Christian Sanger."

She took a step backward.

Christian's smile was patently nervous now. "This is ridiculous. Of course I'm Jeremy Goodhew. How else would I know you were coming to the law firm? Why else would I come here for you?" Puffing his chest, he walked toward her. "Let's go."

He held out his hand, but she shied back.

Jesse rolled toward him. "If you think you're safe, you're wrong. Haven't you ever heard the name Tim North?"

Christian stopped dead.

This, in the courtroom, was the fishhook moment. The instant when you caught a hostile witness on the lure, and needed to reel him into the boat. So you could hammer him senseless with a mallet and hang him up by the gills.

Jesse nodded. "Well. Maybe you're smarter than you look."

"You can't be Tim North," Christian said. "He's . . ."

And he stopped, finding himself stuck—not wanting to

blow it in front of Georgia, but scared of the person Tim North was rumored to be.

"I want to thank you," Jesse said. "You've made this convenient for me."

"What?"

Jesse pushed toward him. "Coming to Grosvenor Square."

The bravado couldn't cover Christian's ignorance. "So?"

Jesse nodded toward the west end of the plaza. "Don't you know what that building is?"

Christian glanced. "Ugly as hell."

"Granted. But that's not my point."

Christian looked at the hulking building, gilt trimmed and topped by a brass eagle. His pupils were tight as needles. His bluish lips pinched, as though trying to work it out.

"That's the U.S. Embassy," Jesse said.

Seeing Christian's face, he heard a voice in his head: *Bingo*.

"All those antennae on the roof? Half of them are trained on you. Christian, you may be an idiot, but didn't the damned flag tip you off?"

Christian's eyes jigged upward, and he gazed at the Stars and Stripes.

"We've got half a dozen agents on duty inside, and liaison with MI5 and Special Branch." He looked at Georgie. "Cover your ears."

Taken aback, she did so. Jesse's pulse was hammering.

"Not all British cops are armed, but the ones who monitor this square certainly are, and they shoot to kill. Do you know what it looks like when a high-powered rifle drills a round through the back of a man's head?"

"You're talking bullshit," Christian said, his gaze flitting around the rooftops.

"Look closely at the embassy. There's a detachment of marines standing guard inside those doors, staring out at you right now."

Christian peered at him, mouth caught someplace between

a rictus and a sneer. Seemingly without volition his hand went to his chest, fingers rubbing at the fabric of his sweater beneath the coat. Jesse gestured to Georgie, indicating that she could lower her hands from her ears.

"I want you to go over to the embassy. Evan's going to meet us there."

"No, she isn't," Christian said. "Georgia's coming back to the law firm. You can't stop me."

"Maybe I can't. But we're not alone."

Jesse looked across the square at two businessmen walking nearby. They were staring. So was the young woman sitting on the park bench farther down. And the man with the broom, sweeping up the trash. Jesse glanced over his shoulder at the Marriott. He nodded and P.J. nodded back.

Christian's shoulders seemed to shrink, as though he were withdrawing into a cracked shell.

Georgie held still. "I'm not going anywhere. Not with any of you."

Not what he wanted to hear, but he had to give her points for spine. A damned huge bunch of points.

"You're all fakers," she said.

She had begun to shudder in the cold, her knees knocking together. She backed up a step. Her hand shot out, finger pointing at Christian.

"I know you're not a lawyer; you're not English, and you're not even old enough."

She turned on Jesse, eyes going dark. God, it was a fierce look, just like Jax.

"And why do you keep calling Kit Evan?"

Hell. Jesse pushed forward. He was almost directly between them now.

"Georgia, you don't have to believe me, or him. But you can get safe by running over to the embassy right now."

She looked agitated, hot spots red on her cheeks. But Christian was cutting his eyes around, no longer at the rooftops but the street.

The freak. Where was she?

"Georgie, get going. To the guard. Go," Jesse said.

She looked torn. Why wasn't she going? Damn, Evan had said no police—had Jax told Georgie the same thing? Not to trust the cops?

"You know who's for real, right?" he said.

Voice shaking, she said, "The marines?"

"Yes. Run." Over his shoulder he shouted, "P.J."

Georgie turned tail and bolted for the embassy. Jesse spun, knowing he had fuck-all chance of stopping Christian, thinking, *Where's my brother,* seeing P.J. leap down the steps. Christian cocked a fist and burst into a run, chasing Georgie—straight toward Jesse. Thank you, stupid dick.

He grabbed Christian's belt as he ran past. They crashed to the ground in a heap.

"Give me back my wallet," Jesse yelled.

Christian thrashed beneath him, trying to pull loose and chase Georgie. "What are you—"

"Let go of me, you creep. Give it back," he shouted.

He notched his hand more firmly around Christian's belt. The woman on the bench and the man with the broom were coming this way. Christian looked confused and astonished.

"Stop," Christian said. "Fuck, motherfucker, you—"

He tried to jam a thumb in Jesse's eye. Jesse grabbed his hand, rolled, and threw his weight down on it. Christian yelled and twisted beneath him, trying to get to his feet. Jesse held on, felt Christian stop struggling, and went cold as he saw a smile come over the man's face.

Georgie was sprinting across the grass straight for the embassy. In the distance, Evan emerged from a side street, arms out, waving to her.

From the shadows a slim figure appeared, black hair swirling in the wind, aiming for Georgie like an arrow. Shiver.

Chaos. I ran out into Grosvenor Square knowing that this scene looked too much like tackle football, that Jesse had

Christian Sanger screaming on the ground, but was fighting to hold him down, that Georgie was in trouble and P.J. was too far away to help her. That Shiver was slick, fast, possibly armed, and on Georgie's tail.

The monstrosity that constituted the American Embassy was on my right, concrete and gold chintz shining in the sun. Georgie raced across the square for the front entrance. She saw Shiver.

Without a pause she bolted in another direction. Going on instinct, not giving up, but indisputably desperate.

Shouting her name, I gave chase. Heard Jesse yelling and P.J. changing directions, falling in on my tail. I gave one last look over my shoulder, fear like an ache, seeing Jesse tangle with Christian.

Georgie raced toward Oxford Street. I checked left, for once getting it correct, and followed. This neighborhood was pure beautiful London, almost like a scene from *Peter Pan,* brick Georgian buildings with dormer windows along the rooftops, from which children should fly away, first star to the right and straight on till morning.

Georgie cut down a side street and disappeared from view. I called her name but she didn't turn back. My legs felt like bricks. I had to keep her in sight, but I didn't have much fuel left in the tank.

By the time she ran into the Bond Street underground station I was a hundred yards behind her. I shot a look back down the street. Shiver had taken off the school uniform jacket and tie, and was moving with a smooth stride that put me in mind of a geisha set loose on speed rails. I charged through double doors into the underground station.

Shoot. This wasn't like Holland Park. This was a shopping center. People all around, hands crammed with shopping bags, phones pressed to their ears, everywhere bright lights, and at least heat, thank God. I hurried along a hallway, spotted the underground sign, and jumped on the escalator. Jeebus. This place wasn't like any normal mall, but a loud futuristic vision, like a Disney World of Tomorrow ride, circa 1969. And I thought London was just West End musicals and soccer riots.

Off the escalator at the bottom, I ran for the barriers. And gagged—two lines ran through this station. Central Line. Jubilee Line. And I had lost sight of Georgie.

I pushed through the barriers, looking for her, trying to think. Was she running blindly?

No. She had said something to me earlier: Code Black had a fallback location if things went wrong with Goodhew Waites. I found a map of the underground. It looked like the vascular system, veins and arteries snaking out in all directions in multiple colors. Come on, what was it?

White City. Central Line.

I dashed for it, jumping onto a packed escalator headed down into the bowels of the station. I tried to run past people, but with their heavy coats and bulging shopping bags they took the width of the stairs. What was with all the black clothing? This town was Cassock Central. Above me came the sound of a commotion. A woman squealed, "Hey!" and some teenagery voice, "Stupid cow—"

One look back: Shiver was shoving people aside, gaining on me. I looked around. Between the up and down escalators was an aluminum divider about four feet wide. It looked like a particularly long, nasty playground slide. It was studded with red emergency stop buttons.

"Look out." I squeezed between a pair of sixteen-year-olds who were necking like the apocalypse was upon us. I climbed over the rubber handrail onto the aluminum divider and pushed off.

I sailed down. The first thing I hit was a NO SMOKING sign. My butt took it and I kept going, tilting sideways like a pinball and gaining speed. Five feet ahead was a *stop* button. I kicked it. And kept going, spinning around.

The shouts came fast and loud. The escalator stopped. The packed crowd bumbled to a halt, but momentum pushed them forward, bumping into one another and grabbing for the handrails. Shiver was trapped near the top. She shoved her way through but was falling behind.

I flew off the bottom of the slide, landed on all fours, and clambered to my feet. People shouted at me. An alarm rang, and a station employee in an orange reflective vest jogged toward us.

I pointed up the escalator. "That nasty American girl hit the *stop* button."

Before he could stop me, I ran past. Hitching up my backpack, I coursed through a tunnel and down a flight of stairs to the Central Line. The eastbound platform was crowded. I cut through to the westbound side.

"Georgia. Oh, God."

She stood on the deserted platform, watching desperately for a train. When I ran toward her, arms out, her breath caught and her eyes widened. I stuck my arm around her shoulder and pulled her farther down the platform.

"We can't wait on this side. We can blend with the crowd on the other platform," I said.

"That train's not going the right way."

I cut through to the other track. "We can switch at the next stop."

She looked up with increasing relief, and increasing fright, if that was possible. "I thought you were hurt; I saw that car run into you." Red splotches marked her cheeks. "And I got lost trying to find Goodhew Waites, and then that man wasn't Mr. Goodhew, and . . ."

"I know. Hang tight." I pulled us into the center of the crowd. "What's at White City?"

"The BBC."

"You're kidding."

"Mum says it has lots of cameras everywhere, and a thousand journalists. 'Stand outside and don't stop screaming.' "

Above the platform the sign flashed: TRAIN APPROACHING. Sound clattered from the tunnel, and headlights reflected off the curved tunnel walls. With a rush of air the train rattled into the station. As soon as the doors slid open we jumped on.

I pulled her along the crowded carriage. Businessmen wore iPods and bent their heads to newspapers. Teenage boys with earrings held crumpled Burger King bags, talking what seemed a language as foreign as Thai. Stout tourists from Chicago clutched tube maps, wearing Reeboks, jeans as big as sails, and red-white-and-blue sweatshirts.

I headed for the front of the train. People continued crowding aboard. The doors began beeping.

"Are we going to get away?" Georgie said.

Or die trying. "Yes. Hang onto me."

The doors slid closed. The train pulled out, throwing me off balance. I grabbed the handrail above my head, steadied myself, and kept going. The train lurched and swayed. The electric roar of the wheels rose as we accelerated. The movie and travel posters outside strobed by, the station blurred past, and we rolled into the abrupt darkness of the tunnel. I knew only that we were ahead of Shiver and had to keep it that way.

Georgie tugged on my arm. "Kit, look."

She pointed back down the train. The windows at the ends of the carriage gave a clear view of the cars behind. The tunnel created an optical illusion, the sense that this carriage was holding still and the ones behind were rocking maniacally, swinging wildly to the side when we turned, like kids in a game of Crack the Whip. We straightened and I saw through the next carriage to the one behind that.

"Shit."

I didn't mean to say it out loud, but Shiver was weaving between passengers, coming like a tendril of smoke, pale and heated, eyes locked on Georgie.

The train braked, sharply, and I held hard to the handrail as Georgie swung against me. We pulled into the next station. The doors opened. Passengers streamed off, but Shiver continued working toward us.

Georgie tugged on my arm. "We have to get out. We can change trains and lose her."

Damn, she was brave. "Yes, but not here. Come on. We're going to trick her."

I pulled her along the carriage. Passengers flowed out the doors as if through a bleeding wound, and the crowd aboard the train momentarily thinned. Reaching the door at the end of the carriage, we hurried through to the car ahead.

"We need to get off," Georgie said.

"We will."

We rushed along the carriage. A new crowd gushed aboard from the platform, jostling us. The doors began beeping.

"Now. They're going to close," she said.

I glanced back. Shiver threw open the door at the end of the carriage and pushed toward us through the mass of people, twenty feet back. A final rush of passengers jumped on board, jumbling into me. They knocked me sideways, bumping my backpack off my right shoulder and throwing me off balance. I wrangled past them toward the doors.

"Kit, we need to get off."

Behind us, a clot of black coats had blocked Shiver between the two rows of seats.

"Now," I said.

I swung Georgie out the doors ahead of me just as they slid shut.

She landed on the platform. The doors closed on my backpack. I felt myself caught, and twisted, pulling, thinking, *No, not now, not this*—I couldn't lose my laptop. And my feet were a and a half ahead of my shoulders and planted awkwardly on that big sign that read MIND THE GAP.

"Kit!"

Georgie clasped my hand and tried to grab my backpack. Shiver bled free of the crowd and rushed forward.

Georgie tugged. "You're stuck, Kit; the train's going to go. She's coming, oh, Kit."

It was hopeless. I twisted out of my pack and broke free, staggering for balance. The doors opened and I saw it lying on the floor of the train. People stared but nobody touched it. Georgie bunched as though to grab it. Shiver worked her way down the aisle toward the door.

"No, Georgie. Run." I shoved her toward the stairs.

The doors shut tight and the beeping stopped. I stared through the window. Inside the carriage Shiver stared straight back at me, surrounded by oblivious passengers, helpless and trapped. I took a step back.

She raised her arm. In her right hand she held Jax's specialist knife. She leaped at the window and rammed the hilt against the safety glass. It shattered white.

Inside the carriage, people leaped to their feet and scattered away from the window, shouting and shoving clear of Shiver. I stood frozen on the platform, hair on end.

Georgie cried from the stairs, "Kit, come on."

The window of the train had crazed white. I saw Shiver leap and grab the handrail above her head. She swung her feet like a gymnast and kicked at the glass. Once, twice, three times, and the window sagged and fell out.

"Kit."

An alarm sounded. People scattered off the platform. We joined them, ran up a flight of stairs and around a corner into a high-ceilinged hall. My shoulders fell. There was another long escalator. I could barely breathe, and my legs were practically shaking with fatigue. Behind us we heard shouts.

"Up," I said.

I pushed Georgie ahead of me, struggling to run. Passengers coming down watched with confusion, and some began to turn around and march up the down escalator. Georgie jogged ahead of me, ponytail and backpack bouncing. I gripped the rail, pulling myself up step by step.

Two flights, three flights, and finally we hit the top and ran into the station, still belowground. It was packed with people, jammed with tiny newsstands and cheap sandwich kiosks and photo booths. We pushed through the barriers and out, saw a staircase where sunlight poured down the steps, beckoning to us. I held tight to Georgie's hand and we stumbled up to the street.

The street was heaving with people, a manic intersection where traffic roared past in all directions. The sun was glaring off the granite walls of the buildings, the sky searing blue.

"Where are we?" I said.

"Oxford Circus."

I pulled her toward a crosswalk. The traffic light was yellow. I read the sign on the road saying LOOK RIGHT, checked, and yanked her halfway across the road to an island in the center. The light turned red. We stopped and I looked back. Traffic dinned into action and taxis, trucks, and motorcycles sliced past behind and in front of us. With a rush of air, a bus swept by two feet from my face, a thunderous wall of red.

Behind it there was a break in the traffic. Looking left, I yanked Georgie with me across the second half of the road. A Ferrari laid on its horn. I threw Georgie toward the sidewalk and jumped out of its way. It whined past, followed by a long roll of black cabs. The crowd bustled around us. We looked back.

Shiver was on the far side of the street, waiting for the light. Cars and trucks and buses streamed between us in both directions along Oxford Street, obscuring her, revealing her, like another optical illusion, streaks giving me only enough of a glimpse to think that she still had the knife in her hand. She checked left and ran halfway across the street to the island. Every nerve in my body went cold.

I grabbed Georgie by the shoulders and pulled her against my chest. Hold still for five seconds. Georgie tried to look back, but I put a hand on her head, held her tight, and pressed her face into my shoulder.

"Don't watch," I said.

Shiver checked right and saw the clear street, turned to stare straight at me, and ran into the road. The double-decker bus hit her going full speed.

30

Dazed, hanging tight to Georgie, I walked down Regent Street, just putting one foot in front of the other. She had cinched her arm around my waist and was clutching my sweater beneath her fingers. Above the stone walls of the stores along the street, the sky was acrylic blue. Behind us sirens echoed. Police officers ran toward Oxford Circus, shouting into their shoulder-mounted radios, their flak jackets and heavy equipment belts humping up and down. Georgie was no longer trying to look back at Oxford Street. She had seen the face of the bus driver, warped and glazed through his cracked windshield. She had seen the furrow in the front end of the bus. I had rushed her away from the scene before she could see the broken bundle up the street, black hair fanned across the road.

I couldn't let go of her. What else did she have to hold on to? She couldn't go back to school, not as long as Christian was on the loose, not as long as Rio Sanger knew that she was enrolled.

She couldn't go to her mother. We had heard nothing from Jax.

And I was in trouble so deep, I would never climb out. I had lost my laptop.

I felt it like a fist to my ribs. All this way, all this effort, my life tossed overboard to rescue Dad, and I had lost my laptop on the tube. I couldn't possibly retrieve it now, not from the floor of the underground car where Shiver had smashed out the window.

Other passengers had undoubtedly left belongings behind in their panic to escape, but the police would have shut the platform, cordoned off the train, would be collecting everybody's things to see what could be tied to the manic attacker or the people she was chasing.

CCTV. Oh, God. Cameras were everywhere. They would get the footage and match it to me and Georgie in a heartbeat. They'd see me get stuck in the doors and drop the pack in my rush to get away. There would be no question that Shiver smashed the window so she could chase us.

They wouldn't find any identification in my backpack, because both my passports were in my pocket. But they would find the dossiers and my computer.

I pressed my fist to my mouth, fighting back despair.

Everything was on my computer. Not only the files I needed to rescue Dad, but information I needed to get Georgie out of the country. There was one flash drive left and half an hour remaining to find it—and Jax had told me that the only way to get Georgie safely to the U.S. was to obtain it. But without the rest of the Riverbend program, that single flash drive would be useless.

The street, the bustling crowd, the gleaming storefront windows, and the crystalline sky all swam before my vision. I was going to have to turn myself in. I would have to go to the embassy and see if the FBI liaison would allow me to surrender myself into their custody.

Georgie tugged on my sleeve. She seemed thinner than I had reckoned, so vulnerable, and trembling with the cold. I hitched my arm tighter around her shoulder.

"Where are we going?" she said.

"To find a quiet place where I can make a phone call."

It sounded lame even to me. She gazed up. Her look was slow and hard, a showdown look, edgy and familiar—American despite her Englishness.

"Why did that man call you Evan?"

There was nothing for it. If I was certain of anything at this stage, it was that lying to this girl would be a fatal mistake.

"It's my middle name. It's what I usually go by."

"So you're not Kit at all."

Young girls can dispense acid with such incredible purity. "Kit's a nickname from when I was a kid. My first name's Kathleen, and it's what . . ." I had to breathe against the catch in my throat. "It's what my dad calls me." I looked at her again. "He's a friend of your mom's too."

Tears rose in her eyes, shining under the sun. I wiped them away with my thumb.

"We're going to go someplace where I can make some calls and figure out where your mom is, all right?"

She nodded. Her bottom lip juddered and her shoulders dropped. God, what things she didn't know. That her life was wrought in violence and her family sworn to lies. Jax had tried to shield her from it behind convent walls, but she had been thrown into the heat storm anyway. She softened and bent to me, letting me hold her up. Around us people walked and chatted and pushed past, sweeping us along like leaves caught in a current, flowing helplessly toward the sea.

Christian walked down the street, holding his arm to his chest. He was crashing. The speed was back at the hotel room. He didn't want to think about what was behind him in Grosvenor Square.

That hadn't really happened, had it? God, he had to lie down. Lie down and sleep. What was Rio thinking, sending him to fucking London to do this thing?

He broke into a lope, running down the block past these fabulous mansions, looking for his rented Aston Martin. Sirens moaned on the wind. The sun hurt his eyes. He was hungry. He was bleeding.

Weak, he needed blood. Needed the glass, and his works,

but most of all needed blood. He needed his baby sister, and she had gotten away. He started to rub his hand over his cashmere sweater, but his hand wasn't working right.

Tim North. That wasn't actually him, was it? He glanced back toward the square. All those people watching him, eyes on him, staring.

A police car turned onto the road and sped toward him. He slowed to a walk and cut around a corner, heading off in another direction. Where had he parked? Someplace past a bunch of scaffolding and construction materials. Not this street.

He stumbled on. He saw his torn knuckles, pulled his hand out from beneath his coat, and looked at the odd way it hung from the wrist, that funny bump and the weird swellings. Rio would kill him. He had let a cripple break his thumb.

He couldn't see the guy anymore and wasn't going back. All those people staring at him, watching from the edges of the square, from the park benches—he wasn't going back. He would leave the guy. He would leave him where he was.

Spotting a café down a side street, I took Georgie inside and settled her at a table in a corner.

"Give me your phone."

When she handed it over, I turned it off and removed the battery.

"What are you doing?"

"I think the woman who chased us was tracking your location with the phone."

"Oh." Her jaw went tight.

"Let me see your backpack."

I took everything out and searched it. My spirits sank even further. Deep in a pocket, beneath chewing gum and nubby pencils, I found a bug the size of a shirt button. I put it on the hardwood floor, set the leg of my chair on top of it, and crushed it.

Georgie was so wide-eyed and tense that I attempted a

smile and wiped the salt and coffee stains off the tabletop, simply for something menial and ordinary to do. Light from the big windows along the front of the café caught one side of her face.

"How about some hot chocolate?" I said.

She nodded. Caught between sunlight and shadow, her face looked older, hinting at the woman she would become. When she outgrew the coltishness, she was going to be striking. And something about her seemed bound for the sky. I saw Jax in her rich brown skin and the feline focus of her eyes. They were the deepest brown I had ever seen, and they were dry.

The door to the café burst open. In the entryway, breathless and flushed with cold, stood P.J.

"Evan. I ran after you from Grosvenor Square and—"

"Oh, my God." I leaped to my feet.

"I got to the tube station and I saw the whole thing. I got on the train behind you." He rushed toward me. "That woman smashed the window; I saw all of it."

I flung my arms around him. I felt my legs weaken, was aware that he didn't know where to put his hands.

"Thank you," I said.

He had my backpack. I took it from him, clasping it to my chest.

"How did you get it?"

"I was in the car behind you on the train. When everybody stampeded off, it got kicked out the door." His hands were freckled red with nicks and cuts. "I found it on the tracks between the train and the platform."

He began brushing dust and bits of glass from his shirt. He looked up, his blue eyes dismayed. "I didn't hit you with the rental car on purpose."

"I know." I clasped his arm. "Thank you. You have no idea how important this is." I pulled him over to the table. "This is Georgie. Georgie, P. J. Blackburn."

She eyed him. "You were in Grosvenor Square."

He lifted his chin in greeting. "You've got wheels, girl. I couldn't keep up."

"Where's Jesse?" I said.

"I was hoping he'd be here with you."

He must not have liked the expression on my face. He reddened, and an old look came over him, cagey and defensive.

"He told me to go after Georgie, so I did," he said.

My nerves drew tight. I hiked my backpack onto my shoulders and beckoned to Georgie. "Come on; we need to get somewhere. Fast."

By the time we hit the sidewalk, the phone was pressed to my ear. Jesse didn't answer.

I hustled toward Regent Street. "We only have twenty-five minutes. We need a cab."

"No luck getting Jesse?" P.J. said.

"No."

His eyes, which looked so much like his brother's, took on a hard sheen in the sunlight. "I'll go back to Grosvenor Square."

"No." My stomach was knotting all over again. I gave him a desperate look. "I need you to help watch out for Georgie."

Her voice piped in. "You don't have to."

"Yes. I want him with us."

She pointed. "I mean you don't need to go back to Grosvenor Square. Isn't that him?"

P.J. and I turned. Stopped in traffic on Regent Street was a silver Aston Martin DB9, the most beautiful car I had ever seen. In the passenger seat, a young man with an earring and a baseball cap was leaning out the window trying to see what was jamming up the traffic. Behind the wheel, so was Jesse.

P.J.'s eyes narrowed. "How does he do shit like that?"

I put two fingers to my teeth and whistled. He saw me. When the light changed, he pulled to the curb.

The man in the passenger seat got out and held the door for me. He wore a soccer team shirt and paint-stained Adidas sweatpants. "Would you be Evan?"

"You bet."

"Is your man always so bloody-minded?" He smiled, leaned back inside the car, and shook Jesse's hand. "Be safe. You wouldn't exactly pass a road safety check."

"You want me to ship any of this gear back when I'm done?" Jesse said.

The young man laughed and shook his head. They were talking about the sawed-off dowels bound to the pedals with duct tape.

"Mind, don't go smashing through the front of any shops. I find out you used a DB9 as a ram raider, I'll be cheesed off."

"Not this car," Jesse said. "Thanks, man."

"Pleasure, mate."

The young man straightened, looking at me. "I was working at the building site up the road from the embassy and couldn't let that bastard get away with pounding on a fellow who's, you know . . ." He glanced at the car. "But turns out Jesse put paid to him. I just rode along till he was sure he had the driving sussed."

"Thank you," I said.

"Cheers."

He smiled, stuck his hands in his pockets, and strolled away. We jumped in the car, P.J. and Georgie piling into the tiny backseat. I shook my head at Jesse. His lip was busted and he had a scrape on his forehead. He stared back, eyes cool.

"Where we heading?" he said.

"Georgie?" I said. "Your mom told me you know the address."

"Wakefield House, Berkeley Walk," she said. "Like the place she went to university."

I got the map. "And this car would belong to whom, exactly? The Avengers?"

"Christian Sanger. Check the glove compartment; the car rental agreement has his contact information." He cut his eyes at me. "And a medical certificate from his doctor at home that he was using like a disabled sticker."

"How . . ." I began, and put up a hand. "Never mind."

"Keys," he said. "I got them from his pocket. The key chain had the make and license number on it. I found this parked near the building that was on fire."

Georgie leaned between the seats. "Are we going to Mum's solicitors?"

"No." His tone told me that something had gone very wrong at Goodhew Waites. "The solicitors won't be able to help."

"Oh." She glanced back and forth between us. "Then you will, right?"

"You got it." He shoved the car into gear. "Ev, how long do you have?"

"Floor it," I said.

31

We cut around the corner onto Berkeley Walk with the Aston's engine growling. Jesse braked with typical alacrity. The duct-tape method of London driving was pretty raw, but no wilder than the rest of the traffic, and unlike P.J. he hadn't hit anybody. Something told me he was keeping score on that track. He pulled to the curb in front of Wakefield House.

"I don't believe it," I said. "It's a bank."

P.J. looked out the window. "What does a double yellow line mean?"

Jesse opened his door. "Valet parking. Come on."

Wakefield House was a solid piggy bank of a building, with Ionic columns and enough marble on the facade to rebuild the Acropolis. For all I knew, the facade actually was the Acropolis. Inside the austere lobby I gestured P.J. and Georgie to a couple of leather chairs, and nodded at Jesse.

"You come with me."

The sylph behind the desk wore a tight, fetching black cassock and radiated the scent of Chanel and cigarettes. Her manner was smoother than glass.

"Your name, madam?"

"Kit Larkin."

I handed her my passport and the key Jax had given to me. I kept hold of the Aston's car-hire agreement and Christian's medical certificate.

She glanced at the passport, typed on a tablet computer, and made a phone call.

"A bank officer will meet you downstairs," she said.

We headed to the lift. When the door closed, Jesse gave me a cool appraisal.

"Brunette looks good on you." His gaze slid down my body. "Didn't know you could wear clothes like that. Jax dress you?"

I watched the floor numbers above the door, going down. "Did you tell the FBI that I changed my appearance? Before you took up boosting cars, I mean."

"No. I haven't told anybody you're here, aside from P.J."

What was that, an admission that he'd been wrong? My heart felt as though it were working overtime pumping whatever substance ran through my veins: ice, acid, sand. I stared hard at the numbers.

"Did Dad send you on this quest?" I said.

"I thought you knew that."

Now I looked at him. "To keep the truth hidden? To keep me and everybody else from knowing about his guilt?"

"That's harsh."

"Don't." I shook my head. "I know you came in part to help Georgie. That means an incredible amount. And I know Dad swore you to confidentiality because he didn't want any of this to come to light. But if he was trying to protect his family, it was a sham." I glanced at him. "Did you know the truth?"

His gaze was both opaque and incisive. "Yes."

Whatever else he knew, he was holding back. I wanted to drop him to the floor and throttle him. Or rip his shirt off and jump him. I looked away but still felt his gaze on me.

"What?" I said.

"Kit Larkin?"

"Jax's idea. You hate it?"

"I think Kit Larkin is hot."

I scrunched my mouth and shook my head.

"Too bad for me she's engaged." The lift decelerated to a stop. "At least, I think she is. She's wearing a ring."

The door opened. We walked out into a subbasement that had cool marble walls and thick carpet. Standing directly ahead, chubby hands clasped, was the bank officer. Her ankles, luckily, were sturdy enough to support the swathes of red tartan that comprised her suit.

"Please follow me," she said.

She led us down a long hall to the vault. I gave her the key. She retrieved the box and showed us to a private room.

When she opened the door, recognition clicked. I saw the polished desk, the mahogany paneling, the sconces on the walls. This was where Jax had recorded her videos.

"Thank you," I said.

Closing the door behind us, I began searching the room. I scanned the ceiling. I ran my hands over the sconces on the walls, under the table, and along the seams of the polished wood.

"What are you doing?" Jesse said.

I checked the potted ficus in the corner and looked under the desk chair.

"This fiasco has been made possible by the fact that everybody involved recorded what they did, usually on hidden cameras." I glanced around one more time. "Wish I had a bug detector, but this'll have to do."

He eyed me as though I were odd. I sat down and opened the box.

Wow. Whatever I was expecting to find, it wasn't a stack of fifty-pound notes four inches thick. And next to that, a stack of hundred-dollar bills.

"Jax. Thank you." This meant escape for Georgie, no questions asked. It possibly meant college for Georgie, paid in cash.

Underneath the money was a manila envelope, and beneath that the flash drive. I grabbed it, pulled out my computer, and jacked it in. The down-ticker appeared: 00:07.04.

Sweet Jesus. Jesse reached for the manila envelope, asking permission to open it. I nodded.

He split the seal and poured the contents on the table: a passport, several credit cards, legal documents.

"Guardianship papers, medical authorization, power of attorney," he said.

On-screen Jax appeared, at this desk, eyes fierce with what I now understood to be a mother's protectiveness and despair at the losses in her life.

"If you've made it this far, you know," she said. "I want you to get Georgia. Take her with you, take her far away, and guard her with your life.

"All her papers are here. Birth certificate, guardianship, custody. And credit cards in her name. They're clean; you can travel on them without any bells going off. And I've put your name on the passport as her father."

Exhausted and angry and frayed though I was, all at once I felt like an interloper. I was voyeur to a plea that crossed primal lines, a plea that Tim North, who ended lives for money, would act against predator instinct and protect another man's child.

"The security services and the government mustn't know of her existence. If they ever connected her to me she'd become a pawn. They'd send her into foster care as a cover for keeping her under surveillance, to draw me out. That's the last we'd see of her unless I gave myself up. So don't let her get anywhere near the Met, Special Branch, any of them."

She paused, gazing off to the side as though gathering her thoughts.

"And I've left an insurance policy for her. You'll see the document there, signed, sealed, delivered. If you have to, that's it."

Jesse found another envelope. He opened it and began reading.

Still she hesitated. "Don't hate me. I want you to under-stand why I did what I did, why it took me so long to tell

you about Georgia. I thought you couldn't handle it. But
it's time to let go of the blame and forgive the people who
helped me." She looked as though she were trying to hold
back her emotions. "You were my everything. You and
Georgie. Make her your own. Don't let me down."

She typed for a few seconds on her computer keyboard.

"I obtained the NSA satellite feed." She looked back at
the camera. "You were right; they kept it archived. Somebody wanted it under wraps. They were happy with the way
things turned out and didn't want competing narratives
getting into circulation." More typing. "But I can be very
persuasive."

She hit one more key. "Video only, but you know the tune."

For a second I felt disoriented, unsure what we were seeing. Then my throat knotted.

It was an overhead view from an NSA satellite. The res-
olution was incredible. It showed Hank Sanger's house:
rooftop, veranda, tropical garden; an alley beyond, more
houses, and an apartment building beyond that, air-
conditioning units on its roof casting blocky shadows.

I gazed at Jesse, distraught. Watching Hank Sanger's
murder was bad enough the first time. I didn't want to see
these events again from a new angle, and I didn't want him
to see this footage at all.

On the veranda Christian and Sanger appeared, small
figures seen from overhead, shadows twice as long as their
bodies. Christian was bopping around, animated, happy to
be with his father. In the alley, a dog sniffed at a trash can.
A flock of birds flew across the view, startlingly clear considering they were being filmed from outer space.

Shadows stretched from trees and buildings as the sun
angled toward the evening. Jesse leaned his elbows on the
desk, staring at the screen.

In the alley behind Sanger's house a motor scooter
darted past. The dog knocked over the trash can and began
pawing through the garbage.

Sanger was pulling on Christian's arm, trying to get him to leave. *Let's go get something to eat,* he was saying. *Come on.*

Christian spread his arms. *Can't we stay here?* He hated going out; he went out all the time.

And God, now I knew why he hated it. Out all the time with men from his mother's club. I studied the screen, trying to understand what we were waiting for.

Jesse pointed. "Look."

Across the alley from Sanger's house, on top of the apartment building, a door opened and a figure crept across the roof. Black hair gleaming in the evening sunlight. Rucksack on her back.

"That's . . ." I said.

She crouched down next to the edge, unzipped her rucksack, and took out a big stubby gun, more than a pistol and less than an Uzi. Hunching below the rooftop ledge, she got her phone and made a call.

I put a hand on my head. "Oh, my God."

She peeked across the street at Hank Sanger and his son. She hacked her hand through the air, seemingly arguing with the person she was calling. Made a gesture for two. One big, one small. Shook her head. Gestured again that a small one was across the street. She looked again across the alley, past the dog chewing the garbage, over the fence and garden, at Sanger and Christian talking in the sunset. She spoke into the phone, shaking her head.

"It's Shiver," Jesse said.

I didn't speak, just stared at the screen. Shiver held still, and finally nodded. She was going to work. And I knew who she worked for.

Putting the phone in her pocket, she tucked the stock of the gun into the crook of her arm and turned to set the barrel on the railing.

On the veranda Hank turned sharply, no longer talking to Christian but looking inside. Christian froze.

I felt piano wire running through my nerves. Dad was there.

He edged into sight, gun aimed carefully at Sanger, looking around for danger, one hand out to Christian, trying to convince him to move away from his father.

Sanger gave up his gun and pointed at Dad. *Fucking Judas.*

Dad pointed back. *Sit down and lace your hands behind your head.*

Shiver fired.

We saw the muzzle flash. Hank Sanger's head snapped sideways and he keeled to the veranda. Christian began screaming.

Dad tackled him to the ground. Christian went wild, punching and clawing his way loose and scrabbling away from his father's dead body.

Dad tried to pull him back. Shouting. *Down on the floor. You want to live, get down and put your hands on your head.* Trying to keep him out of the line of fire while his eyes swept the garden and rooftops.

Across the street Shiver cast a final glance at Sanger's body and spun away from the railing. As she did, the barrel of her gun caught the dying sun.

Dad swung his own gun toward the source of the light, gripped it with both hands, and fired. Christian clapped his hands to his ears, clawed to his feet, and ran screaming into the house. Shiver crouched low and skittered across the roof to the stairs.

Christian burst out onto the bedroom veranda, clambered over the railing, and dropped to the lawn. He shot a glance back at the house, terrified that Dad was shooting at him, trying to kill the only witness to his slaughter. He raced across the grass, shadow flailing behind him. At the wall he leaped over and took off down the alley.

I gazed, horrified, at the screen. *You can't believe everything you hear. Remember that, if everything else fails.*

I felt myself sinking, my vision tingling. Gradually I became aware that Jesse had pulled me against him, that his arms were tight around me, and that I was crying.

I buried my head against his shoulder. "You knew none of this, did you?"

"No. It's . . ." His voice dropped. "Brutal. I'm sorry you had to see it."

I looked up at him. "Why did you come to London?"

"Georgie."

"Dad knows she's here?"

"No. He knows that Jax enrolled her daughter in a boarding school run by the Salesian sisters. He didn't know where. But when you were in Bangkok I overheard Jax mention London to you, and I put two and two together."

On my computer screen, the NSA satellite imagery ended. Jax reappeared.

"As I said, I'm very persuasive." A smile creased her mouth. "Petch Kongsangchai has never been able to turn me down, and he never will, no matter how much he claims to love selling dinosaur bones instead of playing spook. And Colonel Chittiburong is not one to forget things that are owed. What goes around comes around; that's karma in a nutshell. He may be a monk now, but Niram knows who buttered his bread."

"My God," I said.

"Those names mean something to you?"

I nodded.

Jax looked tired and emotional. "I can't be certain why Rio had Hank killed. It may be pure spite, for his relationship with me. Or it may have tied into the blackmail business. You never know who Rio will ally herself with, or for how long. But one thing you can be sure of—she nurtured Christian's belief that Phil Delaney murdered his father and attempted to murder him as well, all to protect that slimy *puta* Jakarta Rivera. Christian has had a dozen years to feed that belief. His hatred will be awesome."

I glanced at Jesse. "There's something else. Christian wants Georgie because she's his half sister."

"Sister?" His eyebrows rose. Confusion crossed his face. "That's what this is about?"

He picked up the medical certificate I had found in the Aston. As a parking scam, it was cack. But it explained a whole lot.

Myelodysplastic syndrome. A hematological condition characterized by severe anemia and frequent bleeding. Mr. Sanger should be considered to have a medical disability.

Carefully Jesse said, "He's not going to get her. He can't."

On-screen, Jax had a weariness that seemed deeper than physical fatigue, as if she knew that whoever was watching this would have come to the end of the line, the end of the story, and that it wouldn't be happy.

"I've blown a lot of things in my life. Not just the River-bend op. Was it worth it? Using Hank Sanger and Rio's hookers to turn people to our advantage?" She let out a non laugh. "Why do you think I left the agency? I know you never forgave me, but sometimes a girl needs clarity. Simplicity is good. Getting things *done* is good. Even if it's without congressional oversight."

I pinched the bridge of my nose, wanting to clear my eyes.

"You didn't approve; I know that. You objected to a lot of things over the past decade. As to why I didn't tell you about Georgia for so long . . . did I truly need to destroy my marriage? I blew so many things in my life. I didn't need that."

She looked as though she were trying to keep her composure. The slinky detachment was long gone.

"It's too late now; it was too late for us back then. We never would have made it. That's why I didn't tell you.

"You'd only been divorced, what, a few months? You weren't ready for that—for a child, a new family, with a woman like me." Briefly she cocked her head self-mockingly. "Clarity, remember? That's my gift. I'm a badass, and don't you forget it. I made my choices, and we have to live with them. I left you and married Tim."

Her eyes broke from the screen.

"Oklahoma man and Texas girl, it would have been a disaster. But I want you to know that you're the one." She looked back. "Tim gave me a chance at a stable life, much as you object to him and his line of work. But you were the one. You always were, Phil."

I closed my eyes. When I opened them she was still there, gazing with longing and regret across a distance she couldn't span, speaking words to a man who couldn't hear them.

Jesse touched my arm and held out the passport that had been in the manila envelope. I saw Georgie's photo, and the name.

Georgia Delaney.

Jax raised a hand as if in benediction. "Good-bye."

The screen went gray.

For a long minute I sat silent. Jesse's hand rested on my arm. I felt as though I'd been given a weight I didn't know how to carry. A chain I needed to reel in, to rescue Georgia and then to haul even further and find my father.

"Jax wants to get Georgie to the U.S.," I said.

"Evan?"

"Let me think." I glanced at my watch. It was ten a.m. I tried to put that in terms of Pacific time and couldn't manage it. "What time is it at home?"

"Two in the morning. Ev, are you okay?"

I squeezed my eyes shut, counting. "I think it's been fifty-six hours since Rio called and demanded the videos. That leaves sixteen to get to Dad."

An hour to get to Heathrow, check in, eleven in flight to Los Angeles, delivering the Riverbend file to Rio, then getting to Dad before time ran out. It left no time for sitting around.

"I think we can do it. Christian doesn't know that Rio was involved in his father's death. We can use that."

I rubbed a hand over my face. "I'll wait to call the London police and give them a statement about what happened on the tube until I'm back in California." I felt a pang. "I know it's all a mess. I have to turn myself in sooner or later."

I might lose my law license. I might go to jail.

Sixteen hours: Hold those thoughts for sixteen hours. Get Dad, and let the chips fall where they may. I could cope with it all, if I could just get my father home safely. I picked up the passport Jax had placed in the envelope.

"If I fly under my own passport, nobody will question Georgie flying with me. Same last name, it will be fine."

Jesse took the passport from me, set it on the desk, and wrapped his hands tightly around mine. I felt my resistance, the denials, fall from my shoulders. My head dropped low.

"My sister," I said.

Of course. The shadow of the girl I saw her growing into—restless, longing to soar, and fast: She reminded me of everybody else in my family. I saw my brother, Brian, and his drive to raise the roof off the sky. I saw Dad's searching looks and ice-cool confidence.

A girl bred from warriors and spies, from people who were dangerous and fierce. And loyal and courageous and cool, sometimes crazy with love and longing, difficult and infuriating and everything to me.

For years I had wondered why Jakarta Rivera crept around the corners of my life like some malign guardian angel. And I had wondered why my father never remarried after he and my mother divorced. He never even seemed to talk about other women in his life.

I didn't even begin to know how to handle this. How to tell Georgie. How to face my dad.

I looked at Jesse. "You knew? Dad told you?"

He kept his face neutral. Right. Lawyer-client confidentiality.

"What am I going to do?" I said.

"Get home with Georgie. And get your dad back."

"I don't think I should tell her yet."

"Yeah. Let one of her parents do that."

I leaned my forehead against his fists, grateful for that expression of belief. Sixteen hours left. I could do it. Then I could let go and face whatever came afterward. Releasing his hands, I stood up, yanked out the flash drive, and shut off my computer.

"I'm going to get him," I said.

When he didn't reply, I gave him a look.

"You doubt me?" I said.

"Not for one moment. I'm just trying to figure out how to do that."

"You have something in mind?"

He had that look in his eye, the one I loved, the predatory look. He handed me the document Jax had called an insurance policy. I read for a minute and glanced up sharply.

"Come on. Let's go," he said.

When we stepped out of the elevator into the lobby, P.J. and Georgie were slouched low on the leather sofa. They each wore one earphone from Georgie's music player, heads bent together, fiddling with the controls.

I tried smiling at Georgie. "We're out of here."

P.J. sat up straight. "Coolness. Where to?"

"The airport." I extended a hand to Georgie, wanting to hold tight when I told her I was wrenching her away from her world. "We're going to California."

Her eyes widened. "No kidding?"

"No kidding."

P.J.'s mouth dropped open. "We've been here three hours."

I nodded to Jesse. "You guys go on. We'll be right behind you."

He went ahead of us and opened the door. "Oh, look, they left a take-out menu under the wipers."

P.J. followed him out into the cold sunshine. "Three hours. This is ludicrous." He gestured toward the Aston. "How come I get wheel clamped but you only get a ticket?"

Under my grasp Georgie's hand felt thin, small, and strong. She looked both thrilled and apprehensive.

"What about Mum?"

"I'm going to check on that right now."

We stepped outside the door and I dialed Jax's number. I got voice mail. I left a vague message, on the chance that Jax might not have possession of the phone.

"We're fine. Call when you get a chance."

Georgie looked fraught. I got her phone, replaced the battery, and turned it on. It immediately began beeping with voice and text messages. Lots of them. I gazed, astonished, as she bent over it, thumbing the controls like mad.

"Anything from your mom?"

She shook her head. As gently as I could, I took the phone from her again.

"No contact with anybody else for now." I was already shaking my head, seeing her disbelief. "Code Black."

She sagged with disappointment, but nodded. She plainly trusted me, even through her fear. I worked to keep from breaking down. Georgia, my sister.

She was looking at me for assurance. "Is my mum okay?"

"I hope so. She can take care of herself."

"Then where is she? Why hasn't she called?"

My heart went out to her. No mom. No school. I was blocking her from talking to her friends. She must feel as though everything had been ripped out from under her.

"We're going to find out where she is. But first we do what she wants, which is to get you out of here."

"I don't want to go without her."

"I know, honey."

Her chin began quivering. Putting a hand around her shoulder, I led her toward the car. Her voice went small.

"My mum doesn't really work for an NGO, does she?"

Oh, Jax. Bitches without Borders. "No."

"She's a spy, isn't she?"

"Why do you think that?"

"It's one of those things. Your parents tell you stuff that doesn't make sense, and then you figure it out later. Like why they hide so much from you."

"I hear you, kid," I said. "I hear you."

We left the DB9 parked in the passenger-loading zone outside the terminal. P.J. humped their bags, which we had retrieved from their dented, clamped rental car, onto a luggage cart and pushed it toward the building.

"Not even fish and chips," he said. "I can't believe this."

The airline didn't bat an eye at our ragtag group. They were happy to take Jesse's corporate credit card and charge our tickets to Sanchez Marks. We would soon enough reimburse the firm, but this way nothing would flash on an AmEx screen about somebody named Blackburn or Delaney purchasing transatlantic airline tickets. The check-in agent didn't blink twice at either my passport or Georgie's. Jesse kept her distracted arranging wheelchair access to the plane.

In the glitzy shopping mall of a terminal, I bought Georgie some new clothes to augment the few items she had in her backpack. Jesse took my computer to a mobile hot spot where he could log on. I let Georgie browse in a music store with P.J. He was exhausted and pissy, but he had the solid instincts to stick close to a kid who was feeling lost and uncertain.

When they were out of range, I sat down and called Sister Cillian.

"Is everything all right at the school?" I said.

"Fine, except that a false alarm brought out the fire brigade and police. Would you know anything about that?"

"Keep an eye out for strangers."

"I always do."

I didn't know how to ask about Jax. "Anything else?"

"The back gate was open. Is there a reason you and Mrs. Rivera left via that route instead of taking your taxi?"

You and Mrs. Rivera. So Jax wasn't there. Nor her body.

The nun's voice was arid. "I do hope Mrs. Rivera recovers fully from her car accident, and that she and Georgia have a pleasant holiday."

"Yes, Sister." I hung up, realizing my hand was trembling.

Above me a television was turned to a news channel. I saw a view of Oxford Circus, the double-decker bus and a red banner headline: SECURITY INCIDENT. The reporter described the scene with clipped precision. If this had been a Los Angeles channel, a news chopper would be hovering overhead, speculating that this involved a busload of porn stars or escaped convicts or even both, hopefully wearing cheerleader uniforms. But this reporter said *Central Line train* and *two sugars in my tea* and *my goodness, I've set my trousers alight,* all in the same dry tone.

Stiff upper lip. Fourteen hours, I could do it.

We boarded the plane first. Georgie and P.J. watched intently when Jesse transferred onto the airline's skinny wheelchair, more like a freight dolly, that fit between the aisles of the airliner. The Heathrow staffer held out his hand and got the word *help* halfway out of his mouth before Jesse said, "I got it, thanks." Georgie retreated behind P.J., staring from behind his back, as though she didn't want anyone to see her as part of this event.

On board, Jesse hiked himself into his seat. When I sat down beside him he handed me a sheet of notes he had written down.

"Got this online back in the terminal."

> *Myelodysplastic syndrome. Bone marrow disorder,*
> *can transform into acute myelogenous leukemia.*
> *Symptoms—anemia, fatigue, chest pain, chills, infec-*
> *tion, bleeding. Sixty percent mortality from bleeding*
> *or infection. Supportive therapy—antibiotics, growth*
> *factors (EPO to stimulate red blood cell production).*
> *No known drugs can cure the disease, only bone mar-*
> *row transplant.*

Georgie was sitting across the aisle next to P.J. I lowered my voice.

"The Sangers think she can provide the transplant." With my extreme fatigue, jitters, and a headache knocking at the back of my head, the thought made me feel that I was going to retch. I didn't even know whether a half sibling would make a likely donor. But the Sangers were desperate.

"I don't suppose they'd believe us if we told them they're out of luck," I said.

No. They wanted her. And when they learned she was not Christian's half sister, they would still want her. The blood feud would get carried out one way or another.

Jesse got out his phone. "You sure you want me to do this?"

"Yes."

He dialed. The sun wasn't even up yet in California, but that couldn't be helped. While I listened to him, I got the papers Christian Sanger had left in his rented Jaguar. He was a good little customer, giving his credit card number and name and address, making sure he would get extra air miles for renting a premium vehicle.

He had also given work and cell phone numbers, both in Los Angeles.

I called the work number. Around me, other passengers were boarding, pouring down the aisles with carry-on baggage, bumping seat backs along the way. Across the aisle,

P.J. and Georgie were going over the movie listings for the flight.

The phone rang. A woman answered, sounding peeved but wide awake. "Yes?"

"Give me Rio Sanger."

A moment later a new voice came on the line. "Rio."

Slutty, slaggy, thick, warm, smoky, the voice seemed like a dirty river sliding through throbbing greenery, full of authority and the power to drown.

"I have the Riverbend file. Christian and Shiver didn't get it."

There was a long pause, and when she spoke her voice was metallic. "Good for you. But I did not say you needed to get it. I said you had seventy-two hours to get it to me. You are nowhere close to that."

"Shiver is dead. Christian's injured. You've been double-crossing me from the get-go, trying to steal the information from me. How's that working?"

Quiet again.

"You get nothing from me until you tell me where my father is."

"That is not going to—"

"That's exactly what's going to happen." I lowered my voice. "You don't want to answer me now? I'll give you some time to think it over."

"You? You? Who do you think you are talking to?"

"I'll get back to you."

I hung up. My heart was pounding. Jesse took my hand.

"You did good," he said.

I turned off the phone. "I need a shower. I may need a new skin."

He squeezed my hand. I let my head fall back against the headrest.

After a moment he said, "Something's bothering me. Rio's not a native-born American. How'd she get naturalized?"

"Hank Sanger? She married him?" No, I realized. Jax had said they were common law. "But she's operating in Southern California with impunity. Nobody hassles her." I looked at him.

"What do you know about her relationship with the U.S. government?"

"What Tim and Jax told me. She sold information to U.S. intelligence agencies. And she has the dirt on plenty of people."

"So she has both contacts and dirt on people in positions of power. Don't you think?"

"Hell. She has protection."

I closed my eyes and ran my fingers over my forehead. There wasn't much I could do about that right now.

He held on to my hand. "What do you need me to do?"

Pray. Beam my father to safety. Get me the beverage cart and line 'em up for the next eleven hours.

But I didn't say anything. I didn't move. I felt his hand on mine.

Ever since Dad had disappeared, and for a long time before that, since the awful events that caused me to lose the baby, I had felt that my world was tearing apart. And it was—as if a scythe had cut the supports out from under it. But I was not going to fall.

Jesse had been there all along to catch me.

I turned to him. In his blue eyes I saw his concern, his resolve, his determination to pull all of us through this if he had to fight or crawl or bleed to do it. What did I need him to do?

"Let me be your wife," I said.

He gave me a look. "That was my plan when I bought the ring."

"This weekend."

His eyes widened, and he saw that I was serious. "Better or worse. Till death. This Saturday."

"Yeah."

He held my gaze, as though expecting me to explode, or the pod person to erupt out of my head.

"Phil's going to walk you down the aisle," he said.

"Fuck, yeah."

He smiled. "Forget 'I do.' You just wrote our vows."

For a second he looked wry. Then he sobered. "I'm signing up for the clinical trial."

I gripped his hand. He looked worn and torn far beyond the jet lag. I felt a pain in my chest. I knew the risk he was taking, daring to put his hope in something that might only lead to crushing disappointment.

"You're not saying anything," he noted.

"I don't need you to do this. You know that, right? Don't do it for me, because it doesn't matter."

"I'm not. I want it, bad as all hell."

Don't cry. I was done crying, no matter how difficult the situation was. I squeezed his hand.

"It may not help," he said. "But even if it doesn't, it's worth trying for a chance to run up a hill with our kids."

Oh, you did not just say that. I shook my head.

"What?" he said.

I put a hand over my eyes. "I hate it when you do this."

"Do what?"

"Say something brave and worthy."

He glanced across the aisle at his brother. "You weren't with me earlier, when P.J. declared that I was Lucifer."

People continued crowding past us. The plane was filling up, flight attendants squeezing around them. He looked perplexed.

"Ev, I thought this would make you happy. Never say die. As long as you're breathing, you have to look for another chance, another way to solve the problem. You taught me that."

And he had taught me about loss. How close it was, and how quickly things can change—how tragedy is always there, an inch and a breath away from grabbing you. It made him pragmatic and cynical. And it made him build

meaning out of the chaos: Grab hold of those you love.
Don't waste time. Do what counts.

"If it doesn't work out . . ." I said.

"That's life."

Except that it isn't always. Sometimes it's death.

32

The sun hit me in the eyes. Clouds streamed by overhead, pink in a California sky that was clearing to blue after a rainstorm. A vast parade of American cars and trucks rolled past, headlights shining on the wet roadway in the afternoon light. The softness in the air, the faint brown tinge and slightest taste of smog, the very fact that traffic was driving on the right side of the road, felt surprising and foreign and familiar all at once. Not quite three days since I'd lifted off this shore, and now I was back with a sister at my side, an arrest warrant hanging over my head and a few sands left in the hourglass.

When we stepped off the elevator into the foyer of Crescendo Ltd., the church lady behind the receptionist's desk glanced up in surprise. She was wearing a wild green head wrap and a cross bigger than Sister Cillian's. The sound system was playing "Start Me Up."

She frowned, looking over my hair, the contacts and glasses, my fashionable filthy trousers, which had a big black stain on them, thirty yards of grime I'd picked up sliding down the escalator in the Bond Street tube station. Her forehead wrinkled, as though we were in the wrong place for our audition. London kid, felon, wheelchair punk, and me, Chrissie Hynde.

"We're the Pretenders," I said. "Kani Tanaka is expecting us."

She got on the phone. A minute later, Manga Barbie

came through the frosted-glass door looking nervous. I smiled at her.

"We need your expertise, and we need it in the next fifteen minutes," I said.

She led us back into the archive. Georgie gazed out the windows at the Santa Monica Mountains, acting as though she had just stepped onto the surface of Jupiter.

"Can we see the Hollywood sign?" she said.

Kani did a double take, perhaps at hearing the English accent coming from a biracial kid. Most Americans don't expect black girls to sound like Narnia characters. She got Georgie a soda and let her watch a movie on one of their cinema display screens.

I got out my laptop. "When I was here last time, you explained that you handle the remastering of rare recordings."

"Right." She chewed on a fingernail. "What's this about?"

"Preserving evidence of a crime," Jesse said. "And about how you snitched on Ms. Delaney when she visited the archive earlier."

I said, "After I left the vault, you called somebody. They caught up with me ten thousand miles later and kicked the crap out of me."

She went rigid. "I didn't know...." She glanced at Jesse's face, the split lip and scrape on his forehead.

He smiled at her. "Wasn't me. I'm just Ms. Delaney's lawyer."

She went even more rigid.

My laptop booted up. "We need you to duplicate a file and pull it onto a disk. And it's partially encrypted."

She said that even if the file had been encrypted originally, once it was loaded onto my machine she should be able to find a way to duplicate it. She would run it through a virus filter, but simply transferring it to another storage medium shouldn't be a problem. Even if it was, the part of the file we planned to give to Rio had been decrypted by Jax.

Jesse gave her his business card and the billing information for the firm. It took fifteen minutes. When she finished, she handed me two flash drives. I gave Jesse my laptop, put one drive on the chain around my neck, and handed Kani the key to the safe-deposit box.

"I need to access the box."

I put the second new flash drive in the vault and checked my watch. We were down to an hour and forty-five minutes.

"You sure you're ready for this?" Jesse said.

"Yes." I called to Georgie. When she came over, I said, "I have to go somewhere for a while. I want you to stay with P.J. Okay?"

Her face seemed to say that this wasn't part of the bargain. This didn't fit with Code Black rules. Once more it hit me, even harder: What was I going to do about her? I couldn't keep her by my side day and night until Jax turned up. I couldn't leave her on her own or send her back to London. And yet I didn't want to let her out of my sight, and felt as though I were about to break a promise to her.

But the bottom line was this: If I didn't stop the Sangers, she would never be safe. The only way to protect her was to choke off their lust to have her. And the only way I could do that was by walking outside into the turmoil of Los Angeles and rolling the dice.

"I know it's hard. But trust me, Georgie."

Her lips pressed together. For a second she looked as though she were going to throw a tantrum. Then she softened.

"You'll be back, right?" she said.

"Absolutely." To P.J., I said, "Starbucks. Wait with her there. No place else."

He nodded. "Got it."

I gave Georgie a hug. She was warm and yielding in my arms. "See you soon."

She pressed her head against me. "Hurry."

Jesse and I rode down in the elevator together. He took

two more aspirin, passed me his water bottle, and I downed another No-Doz.

"I wish it didn't have to come to this," he said.

"It was always going to come to this. There's no way around it unless I want to flee to Tahiti and live under a false identity, leave Dad and Georgie and you behind, abandon everybody." Once again I checked my watch. "Synchronize?"

A smile darkened his face. "I leave you with Jax for two days and you come back with tradecraft."

"Let's hope it works."

We walked out into the echoing lobby. My Thai phone didn't work in the U.S., so Jesse handed me his. I found the sheet of paper with Christian Sanger's phone numbers on it. Sunlight was pouring across the lobby, fracturing gold on the plate-glass windows, burnishing the marble floor. Giving Jesse a last look, seeing his faith in my steadiness, I dialed.

"Elysium Concierge," a woman said.

"Evan Delaney calling for Rio Sanger. Get her."

People flowed around us, talk and laughter echoing up to the ceiling. I could feel the No-Doz kicking in, the jitters ramping up my nervous system.

Rio's voice came on, slow and suspicious, like a thick tongue sliding over me. "I gave you a message phone number. Use that, not this line."

"I have the file. I'll exchange it for my father. We do it now."

"You are very impolite."

"However, there's a problem with the file."

"So she does not like what she learned about Daddy. Such a shame."

Jesse watched me. I nodded at him. This was as I had suspected: Rio didn't know about the NSA satellite footage. She knew only about the hidden camera in Hank's house. This was good. This might work.

"I've busted my ass going around the world to collect

the Riverbend file. I got everything I possibly could, but there's one piece missing and I can't obtain it."

"That wasn't our deal."

"Let's not talk about our deal. You screwed our deal. The first chance you had, you double-crossed me. We're going to talk about a new deal."

"We will not. You will do what I say."

"You're not listening to me. There's a piece I can't get, because you hold the key to it," I said. "I will give you the videos of Hank's death. But if you want the money, you have to tell me where my father is."

There was a restive quiet on her end. This was the crux of it. I listened, hoping to hear her sound disconcerted.

"Didn't Christian tell you about that part? Oh, wait—he couldn't. He was too busy trying to capture a little girl. Well, child snatching was a nice diversion, but I know what you're after. I'd like to split it with you, but I can't. Because I don't know where Dad is. Only you do."

"Stop talking in riddles."

"The last piece of the Riverbend file is encrypted. And that's the piece that provides the location of the bearer bonds. If you want to get the money, you need the decryption key."

Now, I hoped, I was talking a language she understood.

"The money," I said. "Jax Rivera's private blackmail stash."

Jesse watched, rubbing his palm over his leg as though it ached. I was flying by the seat of my pants. His expression said, *Sail on, girl.*

"Rio, I know you never planned to tell me where Dad is. You wanted to get the Riverbend file from me and leave him to die. But I'm telling you that if he dies, you're screwed."

"I think you do not understand. I hold the cards here."

"Then deal. The final piece of the puzzle is a type one crypto key. And the reason I can't give it to you is that Dad has it."

"What?"

"The crypto key consists of two numbers—an algorithm and a time stamp. Dad has the first number engraved on the inside of his Naval Academy ring. The second he memorized," I said. "Which means you need to get those numbers from him. Now. While he's still alive."

There was a long silence that slowly seemed to congeal to anger. "You're lying."

"No."

"Prove this."

"We don't have time for this game. Rio." I let out a breath in exasperation. "You know I have the file. Hank shooting Jax. Dad shooting Hank. The daughter Hank had with Jax, sent to boarding school in England. Jax encrypted all the information so nobody could access it unless she wanted them to. Dad's the only other person with the decryption key, because he was involved in the Riverbend operation."

She remained silent. Assessing, I hoped. Without effort I put desperation into my voice.

"I'll give you the file. Tell me where to bring it to you. Look at the videos yourself. You can see Dad wearing the ring. He never takes it off. He threw away his wedding ring when he divorced my mom, but the academy ring he'll take to his grave."

I walked slowly toward the exit. My heart was drumming out a staccato cadence. She had to buy this. I had no other option and no more time.

"I'll meet you," I said.

"You will not. You will drop the file off where I tell you."

Jesse paced me, saying nothing, watching my face.

"I need some guarantee that if I drop off the file, you'll release Dad."

"You get nothing. You do what I say."

We rounded the corner to the marble foyer leading out to the street. The automatic doors slid open to cool sunshine and the whir of traffic. Jesse's truck was parked at the curb in front of the building.

A black-and-white police car was parked behind it. Lily Rodriguez was leaning against the fender. She straightened when she saw us and walked grimly across the plaza, accompanied by two uniformed LAPD officers.

I froze in place. "Oh, God."

Rio's voice sharpened. "What now?"

I stepped back. "Jesse . . ."

"Don't run." He put a hand on my arm. "Don't even think about it."

Lily approached, shaking her head at my brunette hair and slick-but-dirty clothes. She flashed her sheriff's star.

"Rio," I said. "The file is at Crescendo Limited in Century City. Box three five seven." I dropped the phone into Jesse's hand.

Lily pulled out a set of handcuffs. "Kathleen Evan Delaney? You're under arrest."

33

Lily put her hand on my hair and loaded me into her un-marked sheriff's department car, making sure I didn't bump my head as she shoved me into the backseat. I sat down, aware that eyes were everywhere staring at me, passersby on the street and several thousand office workers in the surrounding skyscrapers. She shackled me to a ring in the floor, slammed the door, and turned to shake hands with the LAPD officers.

"Appreciate the courtesy of letting me make the arrest. And the backup." Tossing Jesse a glance, she said, "You know where you can find her."

I stared at him, my mouth dry. He wasn't saying anything. Arguing with Lily wasn't on the cards. Nor was bail. Or a jailbreak.

She got behind the wheel and pulled out. I felt my nerves frying.

She glanced at me in the rearview mirror, pixie haircut flickering. "You make a hell of a desperado. *Extreme Makeover, Fugitive Edition.*"

She turned at Olympic Boulevard, drove around the block, and parked on a side street that had a view back to the Crescendo building. Shutting off the engine, she turned and unshackled my cuffs from the ring in the floor.

"If this doesn't work, it's my butt on the line," she said.

"It's Dad's life on the line." I held out my hands to her. "Please?"

She took a moment, as if considering. "Well, seeing as how you called all the way from London and got me out of bed and agreed to surrender yourself to me, and you're co-operating with our investigation into his kidnapping . . ." She unlocked the cuffs. "Don't make me regret this."

I climbed into the front seat. "If this works, Rio will show up across the street like her clothes are on fire."

Lily poured me a cup of coffee from a thermos. I drank it in four seconds.

"Caffeine bender?" she said.

My ears were humming, my bones were humming, my hair was humming. I needed another cup. I needed her to hook me up to an electrical socket.

"I can't condone what you've done, you know," she said.

"I can hope for some understanding."

"*Chica,* you're doing this for your pop; you think I don't feel for you? But prosecution is out of my hands. The DA will make that decision. And you know there's a federal warrant, too. Unlawful flight."

"Yeah."

That was bad enough. I didn't mention that Jax had provided me with a fake passport. We watched the traffic flow past on the boulevard. I could no longer see Jesse's truck. He had driven farther down Century Park East to wait.

"What else has your investigation come up with?" I said. "The bounty hunter—have you traced his phone calls?"

"We're making progress. Speaking of which . . ."

She got out her phone and called the department to ask whether there was an update. The sun slid between two skyscrapers and threw a streak of light onto the street. I glanced at my watch again.

She hung up. "They'll get back to me within the hour. And staring at your watch won't make things happen any quicker."

"Dad doesn't have much time." I held out my coffee cup. "*Uno más.* Fast."

As she poured, I glanced across the street at the

crowded Starbucks in the lobby of the Jenkins & Strachan building. P.J. and Georgie were at a table inside. I didn't have time to get them to a major international news studio, so they were sitting surrounded by one of the biggest law firms in Los Angeles. Let somebody try something. "I'll sue" beats "It's a scoop" any day.

Fifteen minutes later by my watch, the black Mercedes rolled down the street and stopped outside the Crescendo building. A woman climbed out. She strode toward the entrance, looking up at the skyscraper.

Lily straightened. "Is that her?"

Her black hair was winched into a chignon. She wore a sable-trimmed coat that swept out behind her like a blade, and snake-print jeans slicked to her body like saliva. Her boots had heels sharp enough to give somebody a tracheotomy. She swept through the doors into the building.

"It's her," I said.

She got on the phone. "Blackburn, she's here." She listened. "Got it." Hung up. "How long you think?"

"Ten minutes, fifteen max," I said.

It took her twelve. Rio dashed out of the building and jumped in the Mercedes. She roared away from the curb and out of sight.

Lily started her engine and called Jesse. "Heading your way." She listened and hung up. "He's got her."

We turned onto Century Park East. Down the block I saw the Mercedes, and the truck pulling into traffic fifty yards behind it.

A brown station wagon zoomed past us. The driver honked and gestured for us to pull over. I gaped at him. He accelerated past us, raced down the block toward the pickup, swerved into Jesse's lane, and braked, forcing him to stop.

"Oh, my God," I said.

It was Drew Farelli. Lily kept cruising down the avenue. Drew hopped out of his car and ran to the window of the truck. His cannoli cheeks were bright red. Jesse leaned out the window, hands in the air. We drove past.

"What the hell is he doing here?" I said.

"He's late." Lily tossed me her phone. "Tell Jesse to calm down."

"What are you talking about?" I turned on her. "You called Farelli?"

"Yes. I was liaising with the U.S. Attorney's office."

I felt my hopes drying to dust. "Lily, what if he calls the FBI and gets them to take me into custody?"

"Get a grip. This is a question of timing, not betrayal. Everybody's going to know you're here real soon. You're not going into Witness Protection. Besides, what do you think, Farelli's going to get the FBI to steal you from me? I got you first. You're my prisoner."

I looked out the back window. Farelli stood next to the truck, arguing with Jesse.

Lily's voice turned hot. "Besides, Farelli and Nicholas Gray have been busting my chops. Claiming the kidnapping is a crock, but trying to squeeze information out of me. This is our chance to prove we're right," she said. "Gray got so high and mighty when he thought a federal agent had been killed. Let me rub it in that Davies turned out to be a skanky bounty hunter."

"Lily, you should have told me."

"I can't do everything by myself. L.A.'s Farelli's jurisdiction. If we need him to, he can grease the wheels, keep Gray and the FBI off your back for the next few hours at least." She looked at me, annoyed. "You want Farelli to believe your dad's been kidnapped? He's about to." She shook her head. "You've been running too hard. This isn't a one-man rescue."

"Fine."

I slumped in my seat. The Mercedes slid through traffic half a block ahead.

Within ten minutes we hit the 405, heading south. Lily's car had a sonorous engine, and she drove with rabid rock music barking from the stereo. The Mercedes cruised along the freeway two hundred yards in front of us. Clouds and sunlight strobed over me, and the sun arced across the sky like a shooting star.

I heard Lily talking on the phone, and jerked upright.

She glanced at me, hanging up. "You alive? That was the department. The Santa Barbara call that bounty hunter received on Sunday came from a pay phone outside Windcatchers restaurant. Not much help."

I rubbed my hands over my face. "Turn up the stereo. I need to bang my head. Hard." I looked around and came wider awake. "Oh, no."

Up the road, a suspension bridge soared into the afternoon, a sweeping green dragon that curved over the water ahead. We were in San Pedro, headed for the harbor.

"She has him locked up down on the docks," I said.

"Looks that way." Her voice was terse. "No other point in going to Terminal Island."

I blinked myself into focus. Rain clouds scudded across the sky, purple and orange against the sinking sun. We swept up the approach to the bridge and I saw the black Mercedes, still a couple of hundred yards ahead.

"Where's Jesse?" I said.

"Behind. Call him."

I got on her phone. "You see it?"

"I know," he said.

San Pedro was home to the Port of Los Angeles. These were the busiest docks in the country.

The bridge rose steeply, its pea green towers soaring skyward. Suspension cables streaked by on my right. Big rigs crowded the roadway. Far below I saw glittering water, and a colossal container ship steaming under the bridge.

The port was massive. It was a metropolis of cargo containers, trucks, railroad sidings, and ships—cruise ships, container vessels, a naval frigate. Gantry cranes lined the docks, metal beasts that reared higher than the deck of the bridge. Beyond them I saw the immense expanse of the freight terminals: a savanna of cargo containers, each the size of a railroad boxcar, stacked two, three, five high, spreading out literally for miles. There was only one reason Rio could be coming here, and it gave me emotional vertigo.

"Don't lose her, Lily. If she gets away from us in there, we'll never find him in time."

"We're tailing her with two vehicles. And don't worry; I can contact the port authorities and get them to examine outgoing containers."

All of them? I gazed over miles of blue and red and green boxes. Tens, maybe hundreds of thousands.

"No chance," I said.

"The fact that she's hauling buns down here means he's still around."

"Right." I rubbed my hands over my legs. "But if we lose her and she gets to him before we can find her . . . if she finds out we scammed her, she could kill him."

We rolled down the far side of the bridge. The pickup swept into view. Jesse glanced at us; Lily nodded him ahead and he accelerated to take the tail. Drew Farelli put his phone to his ear and gestured for me to do likewise.

He sounded chastened. "I take it back, Evan. Looks like this is for real."

"When we get there we can't lose Rio."

"Not planning on it. Has Detective Rodriguez alerted the port police?"

I turned to Lily. "The port police?"

In my ear, Farelli said, "Let me handle it. I'm not a cop, but this is my jurisdiction, not hers."

I passed that along, and Lily said, "Give us a bit of time. If they show up too soon it might spook Rio off."

"Get that, Drew?"

"Got it."

The pickup sped down the bridge and curved away after Rio's Mercedes. Compulsively, like a sick reflex, I checked my watch again. Whatever was supposed to happen after seventy-two hours, we were down to fifty-six minutes and counting.

Past the bridge we soon reached an entrance to the port, where freight trains clacked along toward container terminals and big rigs came and went. At the exit, an eighteen-wheeler slowed to pass between bright yellow bollards. Lily saw me eyeing it.

"Radiation sensors," she said.

The road veered toward the lowering clouds, and the vista opened to a colossal asphalt expanse. My throat went tight. Containers were stacked seven high in places and packed side by side like bricks. Cranes, trucks, trains, ships, and forklifts created a serious racket. Even if Dad had been hollering his lungs out night and day, nobody would have heard him.

Ahead, the pickup was stopped outside a gate in a chain-link fence, beside a security guard's wooden hut with a sign that read, PACIFIC GATEWAY FREIGHT COMPANY. Farelli hopped out and jogged inside to speak to the guard. We pulled up.

Jesse pointed through the fence at a block of containers stacked about two hundred yards ahead. "Rio stopped here and talked to the guard, then laid rubber toward that stack. There's a corridor between the rows. She drove in."

"What's Drew doing?"

"Telling the guard where to send the port police."

Lily put the car in gear. "We're on it."

She accelerated through the gate and across the tarmac. The sun reflected orange from puddles on the ground. Seagulls wheeled overhead. Through the open window I smelled salt water and diesel exhaust.

The stack was about four hundred yards wide and half a mile long, rising fifty feet over our heads. Unmanned cranes rolled along tracks that cut through it. Though the containers were forty feet long and probably weighed twenty tons, the cranes dropped their hooks, grabbed hold, and hoisted them sixty feet in the air as if they were snacks. It looked as if they were grazing on trailer homes. They carried the containers over the top of the stack and across a wide stretch of empty asphalt to a loading area where they set them down. Immense forklifts then carried them across a final width of tarmac to the dockside.

"Rio has to have a tracking number for the container," I said.

"Yeah. I bet she uses Pacific Gateway as her regular shipping company."

"Want to bet she stashed Dad in a container she uses for bringing trafficked women to the U.S.?"

"And she pays somebody off to keep them from taking an interest in the cargo she imports."

We found the corridor Jesse had mentioned. Lily drove into it a hundred yards, stopped, and turned off the engine. I took my backpack, opened the door, and she put a hand on my arm.

"Farelli's calling for backup," she said. "We wait."

"We don't have time. Dad could be dehydrated or injured and if Rio—" My voice caught. I pulled free. "You're armed, right? Come on."

I jumped out and ran along the corridor. Behind me Lily muttered and hurried to catch up. We were alone, as if in a dim back alley in the center of a bustling city. As I reached a corner, she grabbed my arm and put a finger to her lips. Her jacket was unzipped. She had hooked her badge to her belt and popped the snap on her holster. She glanced back toward her car. There was no sign of Jesse's truck or the port police.

"Farelli's not coming," I said. "What are you waiting for?"

"I'm out of my jurisdiction. I don't have arrest authority outside of Santa Barbara County."

"You arrested me."

"I mean arrest without a warrant and the locals' okay."

"Getting a warrant on Rio won't work, unless you can get a judge on the phone in the next four seconds."

"Don't mention my mother." She pressed her lips together. "You're a pain in the ass."

" 'Cause we're shit out of time." I ran a hand through my hair. "Extenuating circumstances. Come on, Rodriguez. Hot pursuit. Dangerous felon. Something, or give me your damned Smith and Wesson and deputize me to do this myself."

She glowered. "You're still my prisoner, you know."

"Kidnapping, false imprisonment, if you stand here dithering Rio will escape."

For a second longer she glared. "Fine. I have probable cause to believe a public offense has been committed in my presence and there's immediate danger to a citizen's life."

"Good. Totally legal. Come on."

She drew her weapon. "Stay behind me."

Gripping the gun with both hands, aimed at the ground, she edged toward the corner. She pressed her back flat against the side of a container, leaned around, and pulled back.

"Mercedes is about fifty yards down that aisle, driver's door open. No sign of Rio."

I moved and she put a hand against my chest.

"This stack is a maze. Rio obviously knows where she's going, but we don't. We could get lost or trapped down a dead end."

She glanced back one last time past her own car. Still no sign of the port police. Her face tightened. She could look so young and at the same time so worn with care and duty and the burden of witness.

"I know this is your pop," she said, "but watch yourself. Stay safe. I don't want you getting into worse trouble."

"As if that's possible."

Giving me a black look, she nodded *one, two, three*. She spun around the corner and ran down the alley. I ran behind her, heart in my mouth. The driver's door to the Mercedes was open. On the stereo, opera was playing.

Lily ran to the door and swung her weapon at the interior. Her eyes looked diamond bright. The car was boiling with music, a soprano flinging her voice through the roof in a fit of emotion. Lily swung forward, walked past the car, and stalked toward the next container. Again she peered around the corner and ducked into the maze. I followed. The containers were packed end to end, but some had already been grabbed and taken away, leaving neat rectangular spaces in their absence. The farther we went, the lower the stack became and the more gaps we saw. The cranes were loading from this end. Dad was almost out of time.

We reached another corner. Lily stopped and put a finger to her lips. We heard the sound of shoes clattering against metal.

She peered around the corner and pulled back, whispering, "She's climbing on top of a container."

We heard sounds of effort, then heels jumping onto a metal surface and running into the distance. We dashed around the corner.

The container was about eight feet high by eight wide, and had plenty of handholds—locks, latches, and rods that bolted the doors. It was quick work to boost Lily up. She grabbed the top, peeped over, and climbed up. I grabbed a locking rod, stepped on a latch, and hoisted myself up after her, trying to ignore the stiffness and aches in my ribs and leg.

Lily pointed. "She climbed down again two containers ahead."

Gingerly we ran, stepping softly on the metal. The racket of machines was constant, but we took no chances. We hopped to the next container and kept going. From this vantage we could see that the stack was sparse ahead, only one or two containers high in most spots. A crane clacked past us overhead, its latching mechanism swinging on massive cables. It stopped, grabbed a blue container from ground level, and swung it into the sky.

We approached the end of the container and laid ourselves flat. Inching forward, we heard the sound of a key turning in a heavy lock below us. Lily crept to the edge, looked down, and pulled back.

"Ground level, five yards to the right. She's unlocking the doors."

I nodded.

"When she goes in, I'll climb down. There's enough of an angle that once she steps inside, she won't be able to see me. You wait here." She raised a finger. "I mean it."

"Fine."

I kept my head low, listening. The key rattled, and with a sharp creak the container doors hinged open. Boots stepped onto metal.

Rio said, "Oh, my."

34

Quicker than a cat Lily scrambled over the edge of the container and slid down the locking bar to the ground. I crawled forward and looked down.

To my right, across an alley about ten feet wide, the door to a rusting red container stood open. I couldn't see the interior. Keeping herself out of Rio's sight, Lily drew her gun and crept forward. She rounded the door, turned, and raised her weapon.

"Sheriff's department. Don't move."

Noise erupted inside the container. Lily held still, gun rigid in both hands, eyes pinned on the interior.

"Do not move. Facedown. Hands out flat."

I didn't breathe, didn't blink, wanted to scream. Weapon poised, face grim, Lily inched forward into the container. The quiet stretched.

"Evan," she said.

I swung myself over the edge, kicked out, and dropped to the tarmac. I ran to the container door. In the murky depths inside, Lily knelt with one knee planted in Rio's back, cuffing her. Rio had a leather belt twisted tight around her neck. My father held the ends wrapped around his forearms and was strangling her for all he was worth. Rio's face was bloodred. He was two inches from lynching her.

Lily slammed the handcuffs and stood up. "Done."

He let go of the belt and Rio's head dropped to the floor. She screeched in a breath.

"Dad." I ran into the container, tears lashing my voice.

He struggled to stand, pressing one hand against the corrugated metal wall and grimacing to his feet. "Kit."

His voice sounded like sand. I grabbed hold of him. His arms went around me, solid and trembling, and I felt his chest rise, felt the heat of my own tears as they soaked into his shirt. I couldn't speak.

He swayed, working to stay standing. I held him tighter. His face was bruised and haggard, lips scabbed, eyes sunken. He breathed deep, despite the smell of rust and urine. He was blinking as though the sunlight pained him after so long in the dark. But through the pain I saw fire in his eyes, and amazement, pride, and gratitude.

"You shouldn't be here," he said.

"You shouldn't either."

Joy and astonishment spun in circles within my chest. My heart pounded in my ears. Behind it I heard Rio spitting at Lily, "Hands off, filthy pig." And Lily reciting the deputy's litany, "You have the right to remain silent." Dad shifted his weight, wincing.

"What's wrong?" I said.

"Bum knee."

He reached for a thick broomstick that was leaning against the wall. Using it as a cane, he let me get under his shoulder and take part of his weight.

"Same damn injury I got rushing the defensive line in high school," he said.

"Let's get out of here."

"You betcha." He took a faltering step, then had to stop. "Sorry, Kit. I'm slam wore out."

He looked down at Rio. She was gleamingly groomed, as though buffed with a floor waxer. Everything was too big, too much: the manicured nails, the raven hair, the makeup. She had red ligature marks around her neck.

Lily turned to him. "How'd you do that with the belt?"

"Kenpo move," he said.

Shaking her head in admiration, she frisked Rio from boots to chignon. Rio twisted on the floor.

"I want my lawyer," she said.

"Fine," Lily said.

"Sit me up. You cannot treat me this way."

"Stay put."

"This is offensive. I am a businesswoman. This is harassment. How dare you?" Rio arched her back to get a good look at me. "Bitch. Hole."

Her face was overpolished, and the makeup gave her a road-worn look, but her skin was remarkably youthful, smooth and supple all the way down into her cleavage.

"What did you do to Christian?" I said. "Hormones? Drugs? Was that what's made him so sick, or was it the needles?"

"Do not speak of my son. Dirty slut." She looked at Lily. "I will sue the sheriff's department into the ground. You cannot hold me, you Mexican trash."

Lily made a sour face. "Shut up, old bag." Grabbing a crate from the corner of the container, she walked out the doorway into the alley. "Something stinks in there. Come on."

I wedged myself under Dad's arm and helped him out into the alley. He slumped down onto the crate. Lily glanced around, perhaps looking for the port police, and went back inside. Taking Dad's belt, she cinched it around Rio's ankles. Then she got out her phone and dialed 911.

"Officer needs assistance. Det. Lilia Rodriguez, Santa Barbara County Sheriff's Department." She gave the dispatcher her badge number and requested backup from the nearest available officers. "I've made a felony arrest and need support."

I took off my backpack and pulled out the bottled water, rehydration kit, and an armload of candy bars I had bought at the airport. Dad was going to need intravenous rehydration, but for now this would have to do.

"You came prepared," he said.

"From the first-aid kit Jesse keeps in his truck. Once with county rescue, always with."

Lily listened to the dispatcher. "I'll meet the officers and lead them to the scene." She hung up. "I'll be back."

Sticking her phone in her back pocket, she scrambled up the side of a container and took off across the top, running back toward her car.

I shook the rehydration mixture and handed it to Dad. He got it halfway to his mouth and returned his hand to his lap. I took the bottle and tipped it to his lips. He struggled, swallowing with a mixture of agony and deliverance.

Rio squirmed on the floor of the container. "Phil Delaney. Get AIDS and die."

I didn't want to look at her anymore, and didn't want to hear the verbal acid she was disgorging. Handing Dad the bottle, I shut one door of the container and stretched to close the second one.

She rolled on her side. "I have everything I want. It does not matter that your dyke pig put me under arrest. You are going to let me go."

"Fat chance." I shut the second door and flipped the latch.

She shouted, "We have the video showing Phil shooting Hank. Let me go or I give it to the U.S. Attorney. Then Phil gets sent to Thailand to stand trial for murder."

"You have it wrong," I said.

"If you think you will leave me in here, you are a more stupid hole than I thought. Look at your father. After three days in this container he needs the paramedics. Imagine how he will look after five years in a Thai prison."

Dad shook his head, willing me to step away from the container. The sun lit his face to stark angles. He looked so bad I wanted to faint. I didn't intentionally lower my voice, but my words came out as whispers anyway.

"I know you didn't kill Hank Sanger."

He squinted, feigning light in his eyes. "Appreciate the vote of confidence."

The stinging in my own eyes was full of shame, because my confidence arose from evidence rather than from trust in him. "I got the proof in London."

"London?"

"Jax obtained NSA satellite imagery of the shooting."

His eyes widened, but he slumped. "Didn't know there was satellite imagery."

"Your friend Colonel Chittiburong helped obtain it."

"Niram? Lord alive."

I glanced at the container, continuing to speak quietly, so that Rio wouldn't hear. "Rio ordered the killing."

His gaze lengthened. After a pensive moment he drank the rest of the water and ate the candy bar I handed him, and then another. He chewed with a pleasure that looked close to anguish.

Finally he wiped his mouth. "You know why Hank died?"

"I think so. Dad, listen. Jax left an insurance policy. It was a memo from the Senate Select Committee on Intelligence, authorizing Riverbend."

"My Lord. Then, doesn't matter why Hank was killed. That memo's what counts."

"It was signed," I said. "U.S. senators put their names on the document, authorizing everything."

"Everybody blames the CIA and the president for this kind of operation, but those senators gave it the okay." He shook his head. "The kill chain. That's where it ended. That's what Rio wants, those names."

He finished the candy bar, and this time when I handed him the water bottle he was able to hold it himself. However, my own throat was dry. I knew that the Senate memo wasn't what Rio wanted. Dad simply didn't realize that yet.

A shadow swept over the ground as a stacking crane approached. Whirring and clattering, its cables extended and the latching gear neatly grabbed the container next to Rio's, setting down on top of it like a lid. Its hooks slid home into the corner fittings, and with barely a groan it lifted the thing straight up and carried it away.

Dad watched. "If it comes for Rio, let it take her."

I saw no trace of humor on his face. Though exhausted and weak, he nevertheless had his cavalry scout glare: Out there, it's nothing but Apaches. Watch your back and strike first if you have to.

Was this what had connected him to Jax—this pitiless belief that justice called for an instant reckoning? Was this how Jax justified her actions—as a refiner's fire, sword of death, all nuance ablated to tactics and craft, while her life became a knife?

Now buried deep into my own life. I stared at my father, but in my mind I saw Jax's face in that final video footage from the London bank, her longing and remorse, knowing he was gone from her for good. I glanced away at the shining tarmac, not ready to bring up the subject. Let him get some more water, some more strength.

Footsteps clunked in the distance as somebody came thudding along the tops of the containers. Above us Drew Farelli appeared. He waved, clambered awkwardly down, and ran up looking windblown and shocked as hell.

"Mr. Delaney?" He shook Dad's hand, his face fighting disbelief and horror. "Are you all right?"

Dad nodded.

"Where's Lily?" I said.

"At her car, waiting for the port police. She told me how to find you."

"Did she call the paramedics?"

He kept staring at Dad, his cheeks growing ever redder. "Don't know; I didn't stick around to hear the conversation."

"Where's Jesse?"

Dad put his hands on his knees. "My question exactly."

"With Lily." Drew looked puzzled, sensing an undertone of displeasure, and glanced around. "Rio Sanger?"

Dad and I pointed at the container.

Drew stared at it as though wanting to peer in but afraid that snakes would burst out if he touched the doors. I gave

Dad another bottle of the rehydration mixture, anxious to get more H_2O and electrolytes into his system. He took it but could still barely clench his hand around the bottle.

"Drew, give me your phone," I said. "I want to double-check that they're sending the paramedics."

He hesitated a moment, still looking at the container doors, and handed it over. I dialed Lily's phone. Busy.

Drew turned to Dad. "You were held prisoner in this container?"

Dad nodded and peered up at me. His expression was severe. "I told Jesse to keep you out of this."

"And he's ruthless at carrying out your wishes," I said. "It's just that I'm even more ruthless at evading them."

I tried Lily again. Still busy. Dialed Jesse. Unavailable. I bet his phone was dead.

Drew's face was crimson, as though comprehension had finally dawned. "What happened to you?"

Getting out a few words at a time, Dad told him the bare bones. *Believe him, doofus,* I wanted to say. *Hear what he's saying and pay attention. This man is not your enemy. Not a criminal. He's a goddamned hero.*

I felt tears coming on again. Fumbling with the phone through shimmering vision, I scrolled past Jesse's number and hit the call button.

I heard it ring. Finally. I waited for Lily to pick up.

"What?"

I didn't respond. It was a man's voice.

"Who is this?" he said. "Farelli?"

My skin went cold. I checked the display: It was a Los Angeles number. I hadn't called Lily or Jesse, but the last number Drew Farelli had dialed.

It was Christian Sanger.

35

I stood frozen. Sunlight glared from wet pavement. A gust of wind ruffled my hair.

"Farelli, what do you want?" Christian said.

I glanced more carefully at the number on the display. It was the same cell phone number Christian had written on his Aston Martin car-hire agreement. We were screwed.

Quietly I hung up and immediately dialed Lily again. It was still busy, or perhaps just out of order. Tried Jesse. Still no service.

Farelli continued talking to Dad, so concerned, so embarrassed and excited. Or maybe just jumpy.

Drew had not called the port police or LAPD SWAT. He had called Christian. We were in unbelievable trouble, but I couldn't give the game away. Setting the phone to *vibrate* so Farelli wouldn't hear it if Christian called back, I panned the scene for weapons. A stick, a bolt, a sharp object.

Dad was my best weapon.

Farelli stood with his arms crossed, feet wide, a courtroom stance, nodding pensively as Dad eked out a few simple words at a time. I tucked the phone in my pocket and crouched down at Dad's side.

I handed him a candy bar. "We need that Kenpo thing again."

He glanced at me.

"Think I could do it?" I said.

He locked eyes with me. He didn't even look at Farelli, had stopped looking at him completely.

"The knee's the worst thing," he said. "Hit it sideways and *bam,* school's out. Was a woman did it, too, smaller than you, Kit." He nodded at the broom handle he was using as a cane. "If I hadn't found that, I'd have been up the creek."

"Really?"

"Clip him."

Behind me Farelli said, "Evan, my phone?"

I saw his shadow and his figure distorted in the reflection from the puddles.

"Sure."

I half stood, as though reaching into my pocket. I picked up the broom handle. It had some heft but not a huge amount. I told myself, *Hard.*

I spun, arm extended, and with everything I had I slammed the handle against the side of Farelli's knee.

I heard a crack. Farelli shouted and dropped to the ground. He crumpled in a puddle and lay writhing and shrieking, grabbing his leg. I stared in surprise at how it had worked.

"Kit, again."

Breaking out of the spell, I swung the handle and hammered his other knee. The blow rang up my arm. Farelli tried to ball up and couldn't. I rammed the handle down on his kneecap like a pile driver. He screamed, arched his back, and gave me a crazed look.

"What the fuck was that for?"

Dad dived on him. He punched him in the head. He punched him in the jaw and in the mouth. Blood streamed from Farelli's lips and nose. Dad lay on top of him and pressed his forearm across his windpipe.

"Don't talk to my daughter that way."

Drew clawed at Dad's arm but made no headway. Weak though Dad was, all he had to do was continue leaning on Drew's neck and the pressure would suffocate him.

I dropped down on all fours next to them like a wrestling referee and leaned close to Farelli's ear.

"Where's Christian?" I said.

Farelli dug his fingernails into Dad's forearm like a rat clawing to escape a trap. His face was beet red, his eyes bloodshot and leaking tears.

"Where's Christian? Tell me and I'll get Dad to stop this."

Farelli's eyes jumped to me and he mouthed, *Don't know.*

"Not good enough." I nodded to Dad. "Finish him."

They both looked at me. Farelli was hysterical, Dad alarmed.

Farelli choked, "I'll find out."

I watched him suffuse and his pain turn to terror, and in my head I counted to five. "Fine."

Dad rolled off him. Farelli gasped for breath, palms going to his throat, tears rolling down his face.

I took off my belt. "Hands."

He held them out. I bound him and frisked him, pulling pens from his pockets, running my hands down his legs, and forcing myself not to flinch as he barked like an injured dog when I touched his knees. Finding no weapons, I stood up and planted a foot on his stomach. His breathing turned to sobs. His legs were trembling in pain, one knee skewed at an odd angle. Dad sat up and stared at me, eyes remote.

"How did they get to you?" I said. "Money?"

"What?" His nose was running, bloody saliva slobbering from his lips.

"You called Christian Sanger. What did he bribe you with, sex? Girls? Boys?"

"What are you talking about?"

"You phoned Dad's kidnappers. Why?" I straddled him and knelt down on his chest, pinning his arms to his sides. "Want me to scoot back two more feet and bounce on your knees?"

He shook his head. "Christian isn't a kidnapper; he's an informant in our investigation of your father."

Incredulous couldn't begin to cover my expression. Or Dad's.

Farelli huffed, eyes bright, arrogance reasserting itself. "I'm not the bad guy here. You're wanted for murder. Your father committed treason. Sanger and his mother have been helping us gather the evidence we need to indict."

"Are you really that stupid?"

I stared at him, and a link snapped into place in my brain. Boyd Davies had received a call on Sunday morning from a pay phone in Santa Barbara.

I glanced at Dad. "Sunday you met with Lavonne and Jesse to go over strategy, and Nicholas Gray interrupted you. Where?"

"Restaurant at that conference center on Cabrillo. Windcatchers."

I grabbed Farelli's shirt. "You called Boyd Davies from that restaurant."

"I didn't."

Dad shook his head. "No. Gray was by himself."

"Oh, hell."

Nicholas Gray had been feeding the Sangers information about Dad. I felt everything crumbling.

"How does Gray know the Sangers?" I said.

Farelli hesitated. I twisted his shirt in my fists and scooted back an inch, as though preparing to stomp on his knees. His eyes bugged.

"Before he joined the U.S. Attorney's office, he was counsel for a Senate subcommittee. That's where he heard of Mrs. Sanger," he said.

"Select Committee on Intelligence?"

He nodded.

Gray knew about Riverbend. Ambitious, Machiavellian, scalp-taking Nicholas Gray. I recalled Jesse asking why Rio seemed to operate with impunity—because she had contacts, and dirt on people in positions of power. Gray thought Rio had the dirt on Dad, proof of Dad's misdeeds in covert ops.

"Gray contacted Rio, didn't he?" I said. "He told her he needed her help. Which she provided, because she's been getting government protection—what, immunity from prosecution because of the help she gave U.S. intelligence over the years?"

My nerves were ringing. "Gray hasn't been able to make a legitimate case against Dad. He thought Rio could dig out some muck."

I looked at Dad, distraught. Heat was climbing up my arms, spreading across my chest. "But Rio demanded a price for getting hold of the Riverbend file, and that was for Gray to set you up. I'd bet my life." I had to breathe. "Gray called Boyd Davies and told him you were headed up the coast."

I tightened my grip on Farelli's shirt. "Where's Lily?"

He went still, eyes pinging off to the right. All my doubts disappeared.

"Oh, you bastard. What did you do to her?"

He stared down the alley, at the container blocking the end. "She's in this with you—don't you think I know that? Don't get huffy."

"Did you hurt her?" I went hot all over. "Where's Jesse?"

Dad grabbed Farelli's ankle and pressed a foot against the outside of his knee. Drew keened, voice rising, and shouted, "I didn't kill her, all right, stop it, stop, Jesus, that hurts!"

Dad kept up the pressure. "Jesse."

"I sent him off to another part of the port—sweet Jesus, it hurts, it hurts."

Rio. Oh, God, Rio had said it didn't matter. We were going to let her go because she had what she wanted. Not the Riverbend file—that was a footnote to her plan. She didn't care about it in the long run.

I shook Farelli. "Why did you call Christian earlier? Did you tell him Lily and I were here?"

"No. I just passed along some information."

"Passed it along from where?"

"The FBI. But it was legit. It was on orders."

"You mean from Nicholas Gray?"

"Yes."

"What information?"

"A number, that's all." He blinked. "Just a number. Nine thirty-five."

All the heat fled from my body. I held him, shirt in my fists, staring at his frightened, stupid eyes. From the inside of the container came a sound that made my skin slink. It was Rio, laughing.

Nine thirty-five was the final payoff for the information that Rio was going to give Gray. It was the number of our flight from London to Los Angeles.

"Kit?" Dad said.

I dropped Farelli. "He gave them Georgie."

36

The water spraying him in the face was cold. Icy, and spewing hard. P.J. blinked and shut his eyes again, moaning. He put a hand to his head and it came away bloody.

"Fuck." He glanced around as the room came into focus. Bright overhead lights, big mirrors, sinks, wet tile. He put out his hand to brace himself against something as he climbed to his feet. He found the toilet. He was on the floor in a public bathroom.

"Oh, my God."

Somebody was pounding on the door outside. He pushed himself to his knees and tried to stand. He crashed face-first into the stall.

"Open up," the somebody called.

P.J. felt a deep and fearful nausea. Georgie. He'd been having coffee with Georgie and came in here to use the head. He tried again to stand. Made it, staggered out of the stall, saw a sink broken and the faucet spewing water. The porcelain was bloody. He caught sight of himself in the mirror and had a bad feeling that his head was what had broken it. He staggered to the door, pulled, found it locked.

He pounded on it with the heel of his hand. "Get the key."

Georgie. A black pain descended on him, pounding through his head. He was supposed to be watching out for her.

Keys rattled into the lock and the door swung open. He lurched out into the hallway past a startled waitress.

"Omigod," she said.

Pressing his hands against the wall for balance, he swerved down the hall and out into the Starbucks.

A sound, like getting hit in the gut, fell from his lips. Georgie was gone.

"Sir, are you all right?" the waitress said.

"The girl, where did she go?"

The waitress looked at the empty table. "With the police officer."

"What?"

"A woman came in from the police department and said there was news about her mother. Little gal in uniform. The girl went out with her." She pointed out the window. "I saw a police car and everything."

Everybody was staring. His head was splitting. He was going to throw up in a minute.

"I need a phone," he said.

Christian drove the Viper with one hand on the wheel, the SIG in his lap and his eyes on the prize. The girl was beautiful, smooth, dark-skinned and fresh. Her eyes were enormous and watchful. She was cringing away from him in the passenger seat. He reached out and stroked her cheek.

She jerked away from him so sharply that her head hit the window. He felt his stomach go hot. Resisting him—that would soon end. She was not going to reject him. He touched his palm to her cheek and ran his hand into her soft hair. She whimpered.

"Just relax," he said. "I'm sorry about back at Starbucks. Tricking you wasn't the nicest thing to do. But you don't need to be so tense."

"Let me out."

Eden had played a policewoman very convincingly. What a wonderful little whore, in her surplus Culver City cop's uniform. She got Georgia all the way out onto the sidewalk to talk to her mom on the police radio. He smiled. This was it. Victory.

His left thumb still looked wrong, swollen and blue, but with the meth, the Vicodin, and his joy, it felt fine. He pushed the pedal down, loving the power of the engine and the warm feel of the girl's skin.

"This is the way it's supposed to be. Those other people, they weren't your family."

"I want my mum."

"Ssh." He stroked his thumb over her ear, around the curve of her chin, across her throat. She sat bolt still, looking like she might retch or pee herself. He knew exactly how she felt.

"Everything's fine, Georgia. You're home." His heart was racing. Her skin was soft, supple, healthy. He felt her pulse beating in her neck, good and strong. "In London I told you I was a lawyer because I didn't want to shock you. But it's okay; now I can tell you the truth. I'm your brother, Christian."

She didn't move, but her eyes slid his way.

He tilted his head and smiled. "Didn't your mom tell you? Didn't Evan tell you who I was?"

"You're not my brother. I don't have a brother."

"Well, technically your half brother. I'm sorry your mother never told you about me. But she likes to keep secrets, doesn't she?"

She held as still as glass, but her eyes ran over him. Admiring him—she would have to be. Now, at the very last minute, everything was coming together. They were in a hurry—Rio wanted him to come immediately—but not even her rough urgency could upset him this afternoon. He had Georgia. He smoothed his hand along the nape of her neck.

"I know this is all a shock. But you're home now. And we're going to be close. Very close."

They were here. He squealed to a stop, grinning.

* * *

The port was buzzing toward the evening. The sun had sunk from gold to orange, hanging fire off the bottom of the rain clouds and glaring from puddles on the ground. Jesse stared through the windshield. In the distance, a gigantic forklift carried a twenty-foot container toward the dock like an offering. Half a mile away across the enormous tarmac, a container ship was tied up. Lights illuminated the gantry cranes that were loading cargo into the hold. Farther on, cruise ships were lit up like party favors. But here it was dead.

He checked his watch. He had been here ten minutes. No sign of Rio. No sign of the police. He scanned the view one more time, wanting to put his finger on what was wrong.

Everything.

He put his hand on the ignition just as the phone rang. He barely had a signal. He grabbed it, seeing an unfamiliar number. The voice on the other end was barely coherent.

"They got her; Jesse, they have her. Jesus Christ."

"P.J.?" He felt the cold going through him like an ice pick. "How?"

"From the Starbucks. I went to the head and they punched my lights out. A woman claimed she was a cop with information about Georgie's mom. You have to find her."

"How long ago?"

"I don't know. You have to get her."

"Did you have time to drink your coffee?"

"What? I don't . . . Two cups are here on the table. Georgie's hot chocolate, it's, like, full."

Right after they got there, then. Maybe forty-five minutes ago. Too long.

P.J. broke into tears. "Jess, bro, oh, God."

"I'm on it."

He hung up, fired up the truck, and floored it. The back end slid on the wet tarmac. He straightened out and accelerated back toward the entrance to Pacific Gateway

Freight. He called Lily. Busy. Tried Drew Farelli: same. He hit 911. The dispatcher answered smoothly.

"What is the nature of your emergency?"

"I need the L.A. port police. There's an assault in progress at the harbor, and a law enforcement officer may be down."

There was a pause. "Sir, is this in relation to an earlier call?"

"Andrew Farelli of the U.S. Attorney's Office called the port police. Detective Lilia Rodriguez of the Santa Barbara County Sheriff's Department may also have called in."

"One moment, sir."

The truck bore across the tarmac. A new voice came on the line.

"Sir, we received the call from someone identifying herself as a Santa Barbara County sheriff's detective, but then got a call from the shipping company at that location telling us that the call was a hoax."

"You canceled the dispatch?" he said.

"We confirmed with the security guard at the shipping company that the call was a hoax. You're abusing the nine-one-one system. Get off the line or you'll be prosecuted."

"It was no hoax. Assault, kidnapping, a little girl's missing. Get everybody within five miles of the Pacific Gateway Freight terminal over here, now."

He gunned the pickup toward the guard hut and chain-link rolling gate. The guard had told the dispatcher not to send the cops. That meant Rio had paid him off. Jesse knew what was going to happen next: 911 would call the guard again and he would tell them, again, that it was all a hoax. At this stage the cops would probably send an officer to investigate, but maybe not fast enough. And in the meantime, the guard would shut the gate so he couldn't get in.

He heard the broken desperation in his brother's voice. Georgie. Flat out, he drove toward the gate.

*   *   *

Inside the container, Rio continued laughing. "Evan Delaney. Did you really think you could beat me?"

Dad wore a heart-rending look. An airless dread took hold of me.

I dropped Farelli and stood up. He swiped his hands at my ankle.

"You can't leave me lying here," he said. "Get me an ambulance."

I opened the doors of the container. Rio had worked herself into an awkward sitting position against the wall, like a fur-clad slug. Behind her I saw dirty blankets bunched in the corner, and scratch marks on the walls. A girl's shoe. Notches. Graffiti. Days, weeks spent in here, desperation, prayers clawed into the paint. Rio was smiling. She looked imperious and carnal.

I stepped through the doorway. "I know Christian has myelodysplastic syndrome."

The smile faded.

Dad turned to her. "Fatal, isn't it?"

I nodded. "Yes. Sixty-five percent mortality within five years of diagnosis."

She swallowed. "Don't you dare speak about this. It is a horrible thing. Watching my son slip away more every month. Stop that look."

"But you think you've found a cure." Taking Farelli's phone from my pocket, I dialed Christian's number. "You think you've found a bone marrow donor."

I put the phone to my ear. It rang and Christian's breathless, annoyed voice came on the line.

"Farelli, what's going on down there? It's cold as hell, and I gotta take care of something. Who's doing all that crying and whining?"

Oh, my God. He was here.

I forced myself not to look around for him. *Think.* I had to use this to my advantage. Christ, was he armed? Getting himself into a position where he had a clear shot at us? I pushed the doors to the container wide-open and stared at Rio.

"Nicholas Gray knew you from his days as counsel to the Senate Committee on Intelligence, right?" I said.

"He understands how things work," she said.

"He wanted information about Dad, showing him in a bad light?"

"How hard was that? It was like a gift from heaven."

"How did you know that the Riverbend file contained video of Hank's murder?"

"The camera was ripped out of the wall at Hank's place. Only two people could have taken it." She looked at Dad. "You or Jakarta Rivera."

"And you planned to turn it over to Gray if he told you where to find Dad?"

From the ground behind me came a groan. Drew said, "Oh, my God."

So, he was a sucker. I turned away from him.

"Two problems, Rio. One, the Riverbend file doesn't show Dad killing Hank."

"And your father has a crypto key in his ring. Stop this lying. You are bad at it."

"The camera in Hank's house wasn't the only one recording the event. There's satellite footage." I turned to Dad. "Why do you think that was?"

"NSA must have had a satellite in position over Thailand, probably observing a military exercise. Lucky timing."

"The satellite feed shows Shiver on a roof across the street, pulling the trigger. You ordered her to go ahead with the hit, even though she called and told you that Christian was there."

She opened her mouth, but maybe for once in her life didn't have anything to latch onto.

"That footage proves Dad's innocence, and your guilt. You had Christian's father killed."

Drew knocked his head back against the ground. The guy really was an asshat.

Rio wriggled and her fur slipped from her shoulders.

"You know, I like this attitude. The nerve you show when you cannot possibly escape. I think you would make a decent whore."

"You haven't heard the worst part yet. You sent your freaks to snatch Georgie, because you wanted a blood relative who could give Christian a bone marrow transplant. But Georgie isn't Christian's sister."

She laughed.

In my backpack I had Georgie's birth certificate and passport. I took them out and set them on her lap.

"Hank Sanger wasn't Georgie's father." I backed out of the container. "Phil Delaney is."

Silence cracked the space around us. Rio stared at the documents. Dad let out a breath. I didn't look at him and he didn't speak to me.

Rio shook her head. "This is . . ."

"Georgie was born eleven years ago. I haven't verified the time stamp on the NSA satellite imagery, but Hank died twelve years ago. Correct?"

Still she looked at the papers, no longer in disbelief but distress. I retrieved them and returned them to my backpack.

"Georgie was conceived months after Hank was murdered. He couldn't have been her father."

"You cannot . . ."

She gulped a breath and cried out, doubling over so hard that for a second I thought something had burst inside her gut.

"No," she said. "No."

"Christian has no sister. He has no other blood relatives besides you. And I'm guessing you're not a tissue match."

"This . . . It can't be. You are lying."

"No. I'm a bad liar. You said so yourself."

She pressed her forehead to the floor of the container, breathing hard.

"It's because of the drugs you gave him when he was a teenager, isn't it? What, chemotherapy to shut off his endocrine system at a critical stage of puberty, so he could pass as a girl? Radiation therapy, something that disrupted his cell structure?"

Dad picked up the broom handle and levered himself to his feet. "She got her clients to ask for the beautiful black-haired girl, then caught them on camera messing with an underage boy. Even in the world's worst diplomatic back alleys, that's a career killer. It means you put a bullet through the roof of your mouth." He limped up next to me. "Christian was her unbeatable blackmail tool."

"You caused this illness, Rio. And now he's going to die, because there's nobody to save him."

She looked at us and lifted her chin, defiant. "Fuck you."

She burst into tears. For a second I watched her sob, head thrown back, teeth bared. I put Farelli's phone to my ear.

"Christian, did you get that?" I said.

He didn't say anything. That was a yes, then.

"Here's the deal. I'll trade Georgie for your mother," I said.

Dad and Rio both glared at me.

"You want your mother, don't you? Badly. Do it now, before the police come."

His voice was raspy. "I hate you."

I hung up. He would understand my offer. It wasn't about altruism. It was about blood.

37

Jesse drove toward the security hut. The guard stepped outside and watched him approach. The 911 dispatcher was still scolding him.

"This is no joking matter, sir. If you do not get off the line—"

"Send someone to the harbor." He steered straight ahead. "There's a smashup at the guard hut at Pacific Gateway."

The dispatcher's nagging turned to alarm. "When did this happen?"

"Right now."

He dropped the phone. The guard glanced at the gate and ran back inside the hut. That could only mean he was going to push the button to shut it.

Jesse leaned on the horn. It was just a wooden hut with a chair and a couple of TVs inside. The guard looked up. Sixty yards, fifty, and he hit the brakes hard, spun the wheel, and pulled the emergency brake. The tail of the truck whipped around, and he slid sideways toward the hut, rubber smoking off the tires.

Run, man.

The guard gaped at him for a second. Then he hauled butt out of the way.

The tail of the truck swung 180 degrees. With a hard *whump* the tailgate smashed into the hut. His head snapped back against the headrest.

The guard waved his arms. "Asshole! Fuck you doing?"

Getting the cops to come. Jesse caught his breath, cleared his head, and put the truck in drive. The guard waddled toward the gate, planning to close it by hand. Jesse floored it through.

The sun was an orange glare on the horizon. He ripped across the tarmac to the spot where he had let Farelli out, at the entrance to the corridor between the stacks. He skidded into it. Ahead he saw Lily's car.

He screeched to a stop beside it. The driver's door was open.

"Lily. Shit, Lily."

She was unconscious inside the car, slumped on her side across the front seat. He turned the truck around, backed up, and approached her, driver's door to driver's door. He hucked himself out, holding onto the frame of the truck, and grabbed her door so he could stand up and not lose his balance.

"Lily."

She didn't respond. Her right hand was cuffed to the steering wheel. He reached down, trying to get hold of her left hand and check for a pulse, and felt himself going over. Dammit.

He hung onto the car door, but it swung with him and he found himself on his butt on the wet ground. He gritted his teeth. He didn't have time for this.

"Lily."

He hauled himself to the door, grabbed her arm, and pulled. It was bad procedure, but he had no time to observe rescue protocol. She came upright, a rag doll, and kept coming, toppling toward him out the door. He caught her and put his fingers against her neck.

Pulse, good and strong. And she was breathing. Her eyelids fluttered.

"Lily, it's Jesse. Can you hear me?" She didn't respond. He snapped his index finger against her cheek, hard. "Wake up, Rodriguez."

He snapped her again. She winced and opened her eyes—lazily, without focus—and then she saw him. Looked up at his face, realized she was in his arms and the car all at once.

"What am I doing like this?"

"What happened to you?"

It took a moment. "Drew."

"Farelli?"

"Choked me."

He felt colder than the wind. "What?"

"Got his hands around my neck and . . . I blacked out. He must have— Oh, God, my head kills. He punched me in the head."

She sounded scared. Deeply scared, and embarrassed, and out of control. Her hands moved. He felt her try to sit up and saw her move her legs. Good.

"How am I doing?" she said.

"Better than I am."

Her voice chipped around the edges. "My gun." She felt under her jacket and relaxed. It was in her holster.

"Can you sit up?"

She tried and failed. "No." She was fighting back tears.

"Don't worry."

He saw the bruises on her neck, and a rage fell over him. Drew had sent him on a wild-goose chase and beaten Lily up. He lifted her up straight and leaned her back in the seat. She slumped against the headrest, drifting out of focus again.

Her eyes closed. "Can't. Sorry."

"I have it covered."

When he slipped her gun out of the holster, she didn't notice. He hitched himself back up into the truck, swung it around, and hauled down the corridor. He squeezed around another corner in the metal maze and saw Rio's black Mercedes. Behind it was parked a low-slung red Viper. Pulling up next to it, he saw a narrow path heading off to the side, back into the stacks. And then a dead end, nothing but containers. Hell.

Maybe there was another way in. He gunned the truck down the lane and out of the stack onto an empty patch of tarmac. At the water's edge, lights blazed from the gantry cranes. Two forklifts were lugging their way toward the dock, bullish monster trucks with wheels the height of a man. A third was idling about fifty yards away.

He drove toward it. The driver was drinking a cup of coffee in the cab while he watched the stacking crane wheel its load this way across the top of the container stack. The tines on the front of the forklift were massive, prongs like I beams extending nine or ten feet. He honked. The driver looked up, startled, and put down the window in his cab.

He looked florid and suspicious. "Who are you?"

"I need help. Some people are trapped in the center of the stack. The cops are on the way, but there's no time. One officer's down, back the other way."

"You yanking my chain?"

"No way."

"Why you driving around out here?"

Jesse jerked his thumb toward the cargo bed, where the wheelchair was lashed down. "I'm no good at climbing over containers. I need some lifting capacity."

The guy stared at him, trying to figure out if this was for real, and probably how much grief he would get for messing with the loading sequence, and whether the union would back him up.

"Come on," the driver said.

The wind whorled down the metal gully where I stood, dense with salt air and diesel exhaust. Dad stood beside me, leaning on the broomstick. We looked up.

On the top of a container stacked two high, Christian appeared. His pale face was tinted red with the sun, hair swirling in the wind, black coat flying.

"Lord Almighty." Dad took a step. "Georgia—"

Christian had her, clasped tight to his side. One hand was clawed into her hair, holding her by her ponytail. The other held a gun to her throat. She looked terrified—frozen, as if her mind were shutting down in the face of overload. My heart broke. Don't fold, girl. Hang on.

I called up. "You're running out of time, Christian. The police will be here in a minute. Let Georgie go."

Inside the container, Rio squirmed herself closer to the door. She let out a noise of disgust. "You brought her? What the hell were you thinking?"

He looked down at her. "Is what they're saying true?"

"No, they're full of lies."

"Stop it, Mom. Am I hosed?"

She sighed and shut her eyes. "Trade the girl, Christian. Let's get out of here."

Motionless, he stared at her. Gulls circled in the sky. The stacking crane lumbered along its tracks and stopped above him.

"Untie my mother," he said.

I stepped into the container, knelt at Rio's side, and removed Dad's belt from her ankles. "I don't have the key to the handcuffs. This'll have to do."

Rio slid her hands under her butt so they were in front of her. "Frigid hole."

I stepped back outside. "Let Georgie go."

Christian untangled his fingers from her ponytail and pushed her away. She took an unsteady step and looked at him, as if questioning her freedom.

"Georgie, climb down," I called.

"Come on, hon," Dad said.

She took another uncertain step, but a racket of metal and cables distracted her. She glanced up as the crane lowered its latching mechanism. For a second she seemed to think it was coming down to grab her. Instead it settled over the container next to the one she and Christian were standing on. The mechanism's hooks slid home.

Christian nudged the gun against her head. "Get on."

She looked at him, horrified. "What?"

"Get on the crane."

Dad and I both moved at the same time. "No!"

Christian pushed her onto the latching mechanism, now hooked solidly to the container like a giant hand. She sat down, grabbed hold of a metal strut, and started crying. With the whir of motors, the rigging cables retracted and the whole thing lifted into the air, carrying her into the sky on top of the container.

Christian watched the container swing fifty feet into the air. The crane rolled into action, crawling past us toward the dock, carrying the container and Georgie overhead. She was crying loudly.

"Kit!" she yelled.

My breathing faltered. God, don't fall off. If she held on, the crane would bear her over the top of the stack, across the tarmac, and set her down in the loading area. Then if she moved quickly, she could climb down before the latching mechanism retracted on its rigging cables.

Rio's lips parted. She stared at her son. "Why did you do that?"

Christian stepped to the edge of the container and jumped down a level onto the one below. His feet rang on the metal. He walked to the edge, eight feet above the alley, and surveyed us.

Rio stood up. Her face was livid. "Christian, we need her. What the fuck is wrong with you?"

His coat swirled in the wind. "What did you say to me?"

"What is fucking wrong with you? Go get her back."

"Excuse me? What is wrong with me?"

He jumped from the top of the container to the ground. He hit hard and straightened.

At the end of the alley, beyond the spot where it dead-ended at a rusting blue container, we heard an engine. Metal squealed along metal, and at the bottom of the container two tines appeared. The container rose off the ground, a backup horn beeped and a forklift reversed down the alley, carrying the container away. Yellow lights spun off the asphalt.

Christian walked toward us. "What is wrong with me?"

Rio flicked her shackled wrists at him. "Stop it. Settle down and go get the girl."

He kept coming. "Wrong?"

He lifted his gun, pointed it at Rio's head, and squeezed the trigger.

There was a hard *snap*. Rio jumped, eyes popping.

The gun had misfired. Her face went ashen as she realized what Christian had just done.

He stepped back, eyes on the pistol. "No."

He pulled on the slide, trying to rack it, but his left thumb was grotesquely swollen. He looked sweaty, and so pale that the red sun seemed to sink through his skin to illuminate his veins.

Dad stepped toward him. Christian straight-armed the gun at him.

"I'll do it, it's loaded, fuck off, old man, fuck off."

His eyes were burning. Dad stopped dead.

Rio bolted. Hands manacled, she sprinted for freedom down the alley. Christian spun.

"No. *No.*"

He lit out after her, fumbling with the pistol. She cut between containers and ducked out of sight, heading in the direction of the dock. He followed, yelling, *"Stop."*

The forklift carried the container out of the stack and angled out of sight. On the tarmac I saw Jesse's pickup.

Dad said, "About damned time."

I ran toward the truck. Faintly I heard sirens. More faintly I heard a child's sobbing. I couldn't bear it. Waving at Jesse, I pointed and yelled, "Georgie!" His head swiveled and his face went stark. The crane was rolling through the stack. He put the truck in gear, spun the wheel, and took off in the direction it was headed.

I heard a man's voice, rough and shocked. "Jesus, how'd she get up there?"

It was the forklift driver. He had set down the rusty blue

container and stood in the open door of the cab, staring in dismay.

I ran out of the alley onto the tarmac. "Can you shut off that crane?"

"Yeah." He looked at it. "Take a minute, but I'll get it done."

The crane rolled out of the stack and headed toward the loading zone a hundred yards away. I cut toward it.

The driver shouted, "Holy shit. Don't."

I spun. Christian was climbing on the forklift, gun aimed at the driver. He barked, "Out."

The driver scrambled from the cab. Christian got in, slammed the door, and put the forklift in gear.

He was going after Rio.

Jesse saw it too clearly. Georgie clung like a limpet to the crane's hoisting gear as it carried the container through the evening sky to the loading zone, where containers that had been removed from the stack sat on the ground. She was hanging on for her life.

At the edge of his vision he saw Rio run out of the stack, hands cuffed, black hair tumbling from her bun, fur coat flapping. For the weight of the fur and the strictures of the handcuffs, she was making tracks. She looked back over her shoulder, face panic-stricken.

Christian was coming after her with the forklift. The thing couldn't go fast, but it could definitely overtake a woman running in spike-heeled boots. Christian poured on the gas. Smoke roared from the exhaust pipe.

Jesse stared. Fucking hell.

Rio aimed for the loading zone. The containers there were lined up about four feet apart, which meant she would have enough room to cut between them, but the forklift wouldn't.

The crane carrying Georgie reached the loading zone, stopped, and lowered the container to the ground. Rio headed straight for it. So did the forklift. The crane's hoist-

ing gear unclamped. Georgie stood up and picked her way
toward the edge.

She had to get off. If she didn't, eventually she was
bound to fall or get caught in the rigging. It was a death
trap. He had to do something, but he couldn't possibly get
her down. His throat closed up. He kept driving.

He passed Rio, running like the world champion whore
sprinter, and barreled toward the container. Georgie scampered to the edge of the hoisting gear. With a huge breath
and an amazing reservoir of courage, she jumped.

Running toward the loading zone, I gasped, seeing Georgie
leap. She hit the ground hard and smacked down onto all
fours.

Rio made a beeline for her, planning either to grab her,
throw her in Christian's path, or use her as a human shield.
Jesse was driving toward her from an angle, trying to get
between her and the forklift. Christian was aiming to run
Rio down or gore her with one of those giant tines, and he
didn't care that Georgie was in his way. All Jesse could
hope to do was block him, and perhaps get Georgie in the
truck in time to escape. I ran as hard as I could, but with in-
adequate speed, no breath, and the sound of screaming inside my head.

They were almost a hundred yards away from me, and
Georgie was still on all fours. She had hurt herself in the
fall.

Behind me, Dad shouted, "Kit."

He ran toward me, limping heavily, face torn. I slowed
and he caught up.

"We have to do something," I said.

Jesse saw Georgie struggle to stand up. Rio and the forklift
were coming full steam from the right. Georgie was ahead
on his left. He hit the brakes.

He slammed forward against his seat belt, the ABS
shook the wheel, and the truck shrieked to a stop. Georgie

was on the ground directly to his left, shielded. Rio was sprinting from the right.

"Get in," he shouted.

She pushed to her feet, took a step, and stumbled, eyes jerking wide with pain. She stammer-stepped toward the truck and opened the back door.

"Come on," he said.

She climbed in, pulled the door shut, and yelled, "Jesse!"

He looked. Rio was heading for him. The forklift was right behind her.

"No. Oh, God," I said.

Rio ran toward the pickup. It looked as if she were planning to jump in the cargo bed and ride to freedom as Jesse hauled Georgie clear. She turned and looked back over her shoulder.

"Holy living Christ," Dad said.

Christian rammed her.

The force of the blow threw her backward. She flew against the side of the pickup. The forklift plowed forward and, with the sound of tearing metal, the tines impaled Jesse's truck.

Christian bashed the truck into a container, and the whole package stopped in a heap. Dad and I ran toward it. Sirens were audible behind us. A higher-pitched sound poured out ahead. Rio, screaming.

She was pinned against the cargo bed of the truck. Christian put the forklift into reverse, backed up, and simultaneously raised the lift. The truck rose in the air. Rio dangled, legs kicking. Christian put the forklift in gear, swung it clear of the containers, and rumbled across the tarmac toward the dock.

Jesse felt the truck lift into the air. The frame groaned as Christian swung around the containers and accelerated across the tarmac, carrying them along ten feet off the ground. Getting smashed against the container had bent the frame of the truck, meaning it was impaled at an angle, one tine six feet through the cargo bed, the other four feet through the back door. It had come halfway across the cab and nearly gored Georgie. She was scrunched in a ball on the backseat, staring at it.

"Are you okay?" he said.

"I think so." Her voice was tiny.

He looked through the back window. Rio was plastered against the side of the truck, hair snaking in the wind, ribs smashed, fighting with her bare hands to rip free from the forklift.

In the cab Christian's eyes were dry, as though everything inside him had been consumed to dust and the only thing holding him together was his frenzy at the woman writhing in front of him.

Rio threw back her head and screamed. Georgie's chest heaved.

"Don't look," Jesse said. "Climb up here."

She scrambled into the front seat. Her face was pale, her eyes eerily big. He held out his arms and she fell into them, shaking.

He couldn't hide the urgency of their situation. If Christian couldn't crush his mother to death, he'd drive off the dock and drown her. They had to get out before he pitched them straight into Los Angeles harbor. But if they tried to go out the front doors they'd die under the wheels of the forklift.

"We have to get through the back window and jump off the tailgate," he said.

"How are you going to do that? Do you need help?"

Oh, God bless this child. He hugged her tight.

"Go," he said.

"He's going to drive off the dock," I said.

Dad was breathing as if he'd run a marathon. He was dry as a bone, face gray, eyes pinned on the awful spectacle a hundred yards ahead. With every step he took, he grimaced.

"Evan," he said, his voice rasping, "I didn't mean to keep Georgia's existence from you. I didn't know about her until last year."

"It doesn't matter now."

I seemed to watch this as if in a dream, where I tried to run but my legs fought through waist-high sand. Behind me came the wail of a police siren. I glanced back. At the container stack, the forklift driver was waving down a squad car. Ahead of us, there were two hundred yards of open ground between Christian and the edge of the dock, where gantry cranes were loading a cargo ship. He was pulling away from us. Dad and I weren't going to make it.

Georgie climbed into the backseat, fighting the increasing tilt as Christian raised the truck higher on the lift. The pickup bounced, squealing like a stuck pig. She squeezed around the steel tine that had pierced the back door.

"That's it, you got it, now slide the window open," Jesse said.

Rio was flailing, hair flying, screeching like nothing he'd ever heard. Georgie bit her lip and pulled on the window.

"It's stuck," she said.

"Keep trying."

She hauled on it, small hands digging into the latch. He saw that with the frame of the truck bent by the impact against the container, the window frame was out of true.

"Hang on."

He hauled himself between the seats and tumbled into the back. He reached down to the floor, trying to grab the tire iron, and couldn't stretch far enough.

"Georgie, under the seat there's a tire iron. Get it. I have to break the window."

She squirreled her arm under the seat and came up with it. They were a hundred yards from the edge of the dock.

"Turn away and cover your face," he said.

She curled up, hands over her eyes, and he began hacking at the window. It was thick automotive safety glass, tougher than hell. He hammered, two blows, three, and only chipped a hole in it. The dock was fifty yards away. Dockworkers shouted at Christian and dashed out of their way. The massive cargo ship loomed off to one side. Beyond it, the water pinged with sunlight. He hacked harder, saw the hole enlarge, kept whacking. Looked again, and his hopes crashed.

They were at the dock.

38

I felt it as if I had vomited up all my nightmares. Rio
screamed. Dockworkers scattered. Going full steam, bearing the truck in the air like a grotesque sacrifice, the forklift hit the heavy wooden bumper at the edge of the dock.
It bucked upward, its front wheels leaped over the bumper,
and with an enormous crash it slammed down again.

Stopped dead.

The back end sat on the dock, tires hard against the
wood. The front end hung over the water, wheels spinning
madly. The engine screamed. Dad and I ran toward it.

"What happened?" I said.

"Front wheel drive," Dad said. "And the forklift's so
damn heavy that all the weight's in the back end, even with
the truck . . ."

I nearly peed my pants. Even with the truck sagging over
the water on the tines. The force of the sudden stop had
twisted it so that the front tine was through the door only
by a few inches now.

Sirens blared behind me, lights a red pinwheel across the
wet ground. Out on the water, a police boat cut a white
wake across the harbor. In the backseat of the truck, Jesse
was hacking at the window with what looked like the tire
iron.

I ran, heedless, toward the forklift. Fifty yards from it
Dad yanked me to a stop.

"Christian's armed," he said.

"With a jammed gun and a bum hand." I tried to shake loose.

He held me back. "No, Evan. Don't count on him getting it wrong again."

"We can't just stand here."

Trapped near the rear tine against the cargo bed of the truck, tangled in the machinery of the forklift, Rio had stopped screaming. She was clawing at her own body, as if hoping to tear out enough chunks to give herself room to breathe. Blood coated her chin and soaked her chest.

Above on the deck of the ship men rushed along the railing, pointing and shouting. Christian gunned the engine, overrevving it, and kept working the lift. A couple of longshoremen ran down the dock in his direction.

Dad put up a hand. "He has a gun."

The men stopped. They looked across the tarmac at the police cars and backed away, one calling, "What can we do?" The other ran back up the dock, shouting at other workers who were hustling this way. "Get a hoist. And chains—we gotta tie down the back end of the forklift."

Dad stared at the truck. "We don't have time."

"What?"

He pointed. "The truck's not stable."

As if to confirm that, the pickup creaked on the tines. Christian worked the lift, lowering the truck and then jerking it up, fifteen feet off the ground, trying to pitch it into the murky water far below. The truck moaned and tilted farther in the front. Georgie squealed.

Jesse dropped the tire iron and began trying to shoulder the window loose from the frame. Finally he slammed it so hard the whole thing fell out, crunching into the cargo bed.

Rio moaned and kicked, head lolling. "Help me."

Christian threw open the door of the cab. "Why won't you fall?"

He jumped down and ran to the front of the forklift. Seeing the gun in his hand, Jesse pushed Georgie down out of sight.

Christian waved his arms. "What is *wrong* with me? You won't die; that's what's *wrong*."

Rio stopped kicking and hung limp, staring at him. He jammed the gun in his belt, climbed on the front of the forklift, and jumped into the bed of the truck. The pickup groaned at his weight.

"Oh, Christ," Dad said.

Christian bent over Rio, snaked his hands into her hair, and pulled her head back, forcing her to stare up at him. "I'm dead. That's what's wrong with me."

Feebly she raised her hands, perhaps to fend him off, perhaps in supplication. He bent over her, teeth clenched, gripping her hair. Though he moved his lips to speak again, all that emerged was a moan and a long thread of drool.

I stepped toward him. Dad grabbed my arm, but this time I shook him off.

"Christian," I said, "they're coming for you. You only have two choices."

He looked at me, his face stricken, and then at the police cars driving across the tarmac and at the longshoremen lining up at a safe distance. He shook his head. And he heard a sound in the cab of the truck. It was the click of a gun being cocked.

Slowly Christian turned. Jesse held Lily Rodriguez's revolver aimed at his head.

"I won't miss," he said.

Christian gazed at him, and then he looked down at his mother. She mouthed, *Please.*

He shook his head. "You killed me."

He took the pistol from his belt, put it to his temple, and squeezed the trigger. This time he got it right.

The gunshot blew Christian sideways. He hit the tailgate and pinwheeled out of sight. The pickup vibrated from the blow. We stood motionless with the sound of the shot ringing in our ears. After long, long seconds we heard a splash.

Rio let out a single helpless sob.

The truck creaked again. The longshoremen shouted for equipment, but we had no time to wait for cranes or launches or the police.

I grabbed Dad's arm. "There's a rope in the cargo bed."

He climbed onto the front of the forklift, groaning as he bent his knee, and into the bed of the truck. I followed. Scrambling over the wall of the cargo bed, I balanced on the tine that had slammed through it, trying to stay close enough to help without adding any more weight to the equation. Rio hung bloody below me. Dad unlashed the rope from the hooks and inched up to the back window. Fast as the old sailor he was, he let out a length and passed it through to Jesse.

"Can you tie a bowline?" he said.

"Yeah."

Jesse pulled Georgie upright. Thank God she hadn't seen Christian shoot himself. He ran the rope around her waist and tied the knot.

"I'm scared," she said.

"It's okay. Phil's going to take you."

Dad crouched low and held out his hand. "Come here, honey."

Face fraught, Georgie nudged up to the window. Dad checked that the knot was secure and threw me the rope.

"Tie it off on the dock, Kit."

The truck shifted. Metal screeched, the front end of the pickup keeled, and the cab dropped two feet. Georgie screamed. I grabbed the tailgate for balance.

I glanced at the cab. Jesse was holding Georgie still, hoping to keep the truck from shifting any further. We looked at each other. He might as well have been twelve thousand miles away.

With a sound like piano strings bursting, the pickup twisted. The door tore loose from the front tine.

Screaming, Rio fell free and plunged toward the water. I clawed to hold on to the tailgate. Suddenly stuck on only one tine, the truck swung down like a broken arm and hung above the harbor with all of us aboard.

I dangled from the tailgate. The truck rocked back and forth, metal shrieking against metal.

Gripping the rope, I wedged my foot against a hook on the inside of the cargo bed, got a secure foothold, and pushed myself up. I got my elbows over the edge of the tailgate, boosted myself onto it, and lay flat, feeling the wind, the height, the swaying. Scared shitless, I looked down.

"Oh, my God."

They were all inside the cab. Dad had fallen through the empty window frame and landed against the back of the passenger's seat. He had knocked Jesse down between the seats. He was bundled on top of the steering wheel.

Below them Georgie lay on the windshield. Seventy feet above the water, swinging back and forth with nothing between her and death but fifty millimeters of safety glass, she held as still as ice, whimpering.

Metal creaked. The hole the tine had punched through the truck had stretched into a rip, curled at the edges. We were unzipping.

"Kit," Dad said quietly, "get off. There's too much weight."

"I'm going." Flat on my belly, I inched forward.

"Hurry. It won't hold."

I clawed my fingers against the metal. From the cab came the sound of rubber stretching, and Georgie whimpered harder. Christ—the truck's chassis was bent, and the seal on the frame of the windshield had popped open at one corner. Jesse eased his hand toward her.

"Careful, don't move, let me pull you up," he said.

On the dock, a police car screeched to a halt and an officer jumped out, radio to his face. I heard a megaphone from the police boat circling on the water below. They had dive teams, but if this rig plunged into the harbor they would be doing body recovery. With everybody trapped in the cab, if the fall didn't kill them, they'd drown.

A longshoreman cupped his hands to his mouth. "Throw me the rope."

If I missed we were screwed, and I didn't trust my arm. "Get on the forklift; I'll hand it to you."

He looked as if he'd rather shoot out his eyes with a nail gun. I crawled forward, grabbed the machinery of the forklift, and climbed onto it, pulling myself off the tailgate.

With the squeal of aluminum and the clatter of junk and hardware and people, the tine sliced another six inches. Georgie shrieked. Dad lost his grip, fell between the seats, and landed next to her. The impact tore loose more of the seal around the windshield. Slowly it began coming unglued. An inch, two inches, a foot.

Jesse held out his arm. "Phil."

Dad grabbed his wrist. The break in the seal accelerated and began running around the edge of the frame like a lit fuse. Jesse tried to pull Dad up but the rip tore around in a circle, the seal came completely unstuck, and the windshield popped out. Dad and Georgie plunged through.

I was too horrified to think anything beyond *Hold on.* I slung the rope around my waist, locked an arm around a spar on the forklift, and braced myself. And abruptly everything stopped.

Hanging in midair, bound by the slim strength of the knot Jesse had tied, Georgie spun in open space below the truck. Above her, feet dangling, Dad hung onto Jesse's wrists. Jesse was wedged against the steering column with his arms and head hanging out.

Dockworkers shouted, climbed onto the forklift, and edged toward me. There shouldn't have been slack in my end of the rope. I reeled it in and felt it catch.

"The rope's caught on something in the cab," I said.

Jesse looked. "Gearshift. Shit."

Georgie cried, "Don't let me fall; please don't let me fall."

Dad called down to her, "Grab my leg. Climb."

She spun in a circle and hooked her hands around his ankles like a monkey, feet wheeling. He looked up at Jesse. "Hold on. Don't let go for anything."

"I won't."

Jesse's voice was harsh with exertion, his hands white from the strain of holding Georgie's extra weight. Christ, he wasn't going to be able to hold on much longer, and he couldn't pull with his legs. I whipped the rope and yanked on it, but it wouldn't budge. With another groan from the truck, Georgie slipped down past Dad's feet again, squealing.

"Jesse, you have to free the rope," Dad said.

He let go of Jesse's right wrist and grabbed his left arm with both hands. Jesse reached back inside the cab and tugged on the rope. I heard him fighting for breath, desperate with the effort.

"I need two hands to free it. Phil, you have to grab hold of something."

Hell, this wasn't going to work. "I'm coming. I'll get it."

"Don't do that," Jesse said.

"No," Dad shouted. "Any more weight and it'll collapse."

Throat dry, I stayed put and looked around for a pole, a chain, some other tool we could use to reach them.

A longshoreman climbed on the forklift. "Give me the end of the rope, I'll tie it off. You stay here and belay."

I reeled it out to him. "Get another forklift to brace the truck."

I heard Jesse. "Phil, grab the frame of the windshield."

"I can't," Dad said.

Jesse's voice rose. "Hang on, you son of a bitch. You have to walk Evan down the aisle on Saturday."

"Don't think Saturday's gonna work," Dad said.

Whatever reserves of horror I still retained now emptied. "Hang on, Dad. Don't give up."

He looked at me, and his eyes filled with resolve. I hooked my arm tightly around the spars of the forklift and pulled on the rope, getting ready to take the weight when

Jesse freed it. The creak of the truck shifted up to an alarming pitch. Glancing at the dock, I watched the longshoreman run toward a cleat where he planned to tie down the rope.

Dad said, "Jesse, there's only one way to do this."

Jesse shouted, "No. Grab hold."

"Come on," Dad said.

Jesse's voice went hollow with effort. "Phil, I can't."

But he was the only one who could—he had the strongest grip; he could lift two hundred pounds with one hand. I yelled, "Blackburn, damn it, you can do it."

"Jesse, you can," Dad said calmly. "Let go of me."

My head whipped around. Dad had deliberately released his grip from Jesse's wrist. The only thing holding him up was Jesse's refusal to let go.

"The truck won't hold with my weight. If you hang onto me, we all go down."

All the blood fled from my head, from my heart, from my soul. "Dad, no. Jesse, hang onto him."

Jesse's voice was almost gone with the strain. "Phil, you wouldn't survive. If the fall didn't kill you, the truck coming down on you would."

Dad said, "If the truck goes with the rope caught, it'll pull Evan over. It's me or it's all of us."

My pulse thundered in my ears. "Dad, *no.* I can hang on. They're tying down the rope. We'll find a way to stabilize the pickup. Jesus Christ, Jesse, hold him."

"Phil, I won't do it," Jesse said.

"Hang onto me and they'll die," Dad said. "Let go. Free the rope and pull Georgie up."

"Don't!" I yelled.

"I know what I'm asking," Dad said. "Forgive me."

Jesse choked, "Damn it, Phil."

"Jesse, *no,*" I shouted.

"Do it for my daughters. Now, for the love of Christ."

His gaze was hard and bright, brimming with a certainty beyond anything I had ever seen. The sky seemed to still.

And with the slightest motion, the single action that will haunt me for the rest of my life, Jesse let go.

Dad hung in the air, eyes pinned to Jesse's, and he fell.

I know the incoherent screams I heard were my own. I know that Jesse swung the rope free from the gearshift, that two longshoremen grabbed the rope from me, that they pulled in unison and Georgie came up through the window with Jesse hanging on beside her. That as they did, the tine ripped through wall of the cargo bed. It shattered the taillights, caught for a moment on the tailgate, and then the truck's three thousand pounds broke loose and hammered down on my father in the cold black water of the harbor.

They had to drag me kicking and screaming off the forklift. Georgie sobbed and clung to Jesse as they hauled them to shore. The police swarmed over us. I fought loose from the longshoremen, crawled to the edge of the dock, and stared down. The police boat circled, shining a spotlight on the water. The surface was already smoothed over. I watched, waiting, begging, and all around me lights flashed, noise abounded, the stars sank invisible beyond the searchlights and vaulting empty heaven. Eventually somebody, maybe even Lily, pulled me back from the edge. Georgie was crumpled against Jesse's chest. Spent and shattered, they held each other. Jesse stared at the undulating water for an agonizing endless time, until finally, when there was no doubt, he dared to look at me.

Maybe he prayed. Maybe he spoke. I couldn't feel, couldn't see straight, could only know. I climbed to my feet. Somehow I walked toward him, and managed to put out my hand.

"Georgie," I said.

She grabbed my hand, clawed up into my arms, and sobbed against my chest. I held her tight and walked away.

39

Might have been will make you insane. I knew that. But I didn't know that it would make my ears ring and my throat lock. That it would turn the light in the sky too bright, anesthetize my fingers and heart and even time itself, somehow permitting the world to flow forward while I hung suspended, caught on emotional barbed wire.

The day I was arraigned on charges of unlawful flight to avoid prosecution, Lavonne Marks stood beside me in federal court. When the judge asked, "How do you plead?" my voice didn't shake. "Not guilty," I said. Lily Rodriguez sat in the visitors' gallery, and afterward promised that if the case went to trial, she would testify on my behalf. I appreciated that. I didn't care about the rest.

Nicholas Gray wasn't in attendance, nor Drew Farelli. They had been suspended from the U.S. Attorney's office. Gray faced indictment for solicitation to kidnapping, Farelli for conspiracy and assault on a law enforcement officer. Disgrace was only a start on what they deserved.

The warrant seeking my arrest for the murder of Boyd Davies had been dropped. Somebody had convinced the Santa Barbara district attorney to declare me a hostage in the shootout. The men in the shadows were working to bury this debacle. Charges were not going to be brought over the Bangkok death of the ex-hooker named Bliss. Drew Farelli had never called the FBI about the attack—he and Gray had cared only about obtaining the evidence they thought would put my father in prison, and so had let me face Rio's hit team. However, the Bangkok police closed the case. Shiver's fingerprints were found in the hotel room, and she took the fall for killing her partner. The people behind Riverbend were slowly ensuring that everything connected with the operation would sink out of sight.

Given that, Lavonne felt confident that I could bargain my way down to a misdemeanor plea. I wouldn't go to jail. My law license was going to be suspended, but so what? What mattered anymore?

The gold blaze of anger, the ceaseless roll of anguish, the finality of death. The way the world went on behind a screen, a dazzling, oblivious swirl of lives and cares and laughter, paying no attention. Things should stop. The planet should have come to a halt in silent observance. My brother, Brian, understood that. My mother, Angie, seemed to understand that, if only on my behalf. They would bring me into their embrace, and sometimes I would fall, would let go.

And then I would remember the consequences of letting go.

What mattered? That with Nicholas Gray exposed and the government eager to smooth things over, Dad's whistle-blowing was set aside. And so he got a sendoff with full military honors.

On a spring afternoon in Shawnee, beneath an endless prairie sky, with the wind soft against my face and a sea of bluebonnets spilling down the hillside, I stood with my family and heard the priest's words. Ashes to ashes. Alpha and omega. Brian looked as dry as iron in his dress blues. My nephew, Luke, squirmed against me, sad and tired in his jacket and tie. Georgie was silent and drawn. My mother seemed faraway and angry, as though she had expected this all along, all her life, and wasn't about to forgive Dad for it.

In the flag that draped the coffin, I saw Dad's life. For a

moment that vision forced away the rest, the sight of him
pulled from the harbor, the irrevocable stillness of his hand
when I took it, the sound of my own sobs, the comprehension that I had failed and was forever powerless to undo
this. My breathing snagged. Two sailors removed the flag
and folded it. Because Mom was his ex-wife, they gave it to
me. I pressed it to my chest and bent my head low.

Brian put an arm around my shoulder. As he drew me
close, I heard the thunder of jet engines. The sound sank
into my bones, and from out of the sun a formation of F/A-
18s raked the sky above us. Dad had been NAVAIR, and
Brian's squadron was giving him this honor. When they
swept near, a single fighter curved skyward. The other jets
roared overhead in the missing-man formation, but I
watched the lone fighter arc upward.

I wondered where Dad was, out beyond never. I wondered about his choices. About his call to action, and how
it had split my world in two. About the price he exacted
from the man I had loved so fiercely.

The jet soared higher, the sun flashing off its wings, until
the light forced me to shut my eyes. When I looked again,
it was gone.

What mattered? Georgie.

Her father was deceased. Her mother was missing. As
much as I tried, I could uncover no information about
what happened to Jax on that London street after she told
me to take her girl and run. Perhaps she was dead. Perhaps she was in custody. I simply didn't know. In the
meantime, Brian and I were Georgie's closest known relatives, and she was staying with me while Lavonne
arranged for me to assume guardianship. She spent her
days wary and blank behind a wall of confusion, watching
Nickelodeon and attending the school up the street, trying
to feel her way into this exploded world. It was more than
I could manage myself.

As I sat on my porch in the spring twilight one evening,

two stars hung on the western horizon, white fire against the cobalt sky. Circling, entwined, hundreds of million miles apart and destined never to come together, except in the well of eternity, which eats us all. Georgie came out and dropped down at my side. I put an arm around her shoulder and watched the night come on.

It was a thundery May morning, strange weather, when a burst of rain brought me out of bed to grab the morning paper from the front porch. When I opened the door I saw the envelope sitting on top of the *News-Press*. My hands went cold.

I stood vacantly on the porch, getting soaked. After a minute I brought the envelope in, set it on my kitchen table, and stared at it.

I knew the handwriting. It was the hand of the man who had slipped a diamond ring on my finger, who had held me and pledged himself to me and ended my father's life. I ran my fingers over the ink, smeared with rain. I wondered how long it had been sitting there. Wondered if he was waiting outside for me. Wondered if he was asking me to write, to call, to talk to him. To tell him I hate him. I love him. I can't love him. To take a step, any step. Forward, backward, into a chasm, into the future. I wondered what the hell he could possibly say. How could he attempt to unravel the chaos, when my own heart was so tangled? My hand closed around the envelope. My eyes were stinging. I crumpled it and grabbed it with both hands, ready to tear it in half.

I stopped and tilted my head back.

Life is like a narrow bridge. The important thing is not to be afraid.

When I looked again at my name, the ink was smeared with tears as well as rain. I pressed the envelope to my chest and slowly smoothed it out.

If only will scour your soul, because *if* is never. But it's also possibility. And it's all I had.

Fucking Fact of Life.

Read on for an exciting preview
of Meg Gardiner's brand-new thriller,

THE DIRTY SECRETS CLUB

Available wherever books
are sold or at penguin.com

Fire alarms sang through the skyscraper, piercing and relentless. Under the din people poured across the marble lobby toward the doors, dodging fallen ceiling plaster and broken glass. Outside, Montgomery Street crackled with the lights of emergency vehicles. A police officer fought upstream to get inside. The blonde was ten feet behind, struggling through the crowd.

The man in the corner paced, head down, needing her to hurry.

People rushed by him, jumpy. "Everything crashed off the bookshelves. I thought for sure it was the Big One."

The man turned, shoulders shifting. The Big One? Hardly. This earthquake had just been San Francisco's regular kick in the butt. But it was bad enough. On the street, steam geysered from manholes. And he could smell gas. Pipes had ruptured under the building. The quake was Hell saying, *Don't forget I'm down here—you fall, I'm waiting for you.*

He checked his watch. Come on, girl, faster. They had ten minutes before this building shut down.

A fire captain glanced at him. He was tall and young and moved like the athlete he was, but nothing clicked in the fire captain's eyes, no suspicion, no *Is that who I think it is?* Out of uniform he looked ordinary, a plain vanilla all-American.

The blonde neared the doors. She stood out from the

crowd, platinum sleek, hair cinched into a tight French twist, body cinched into a tighter black suit. A cop stuck out an arm like he was going to clothesline her. She flashed an ID and slid around him.

He smiled. Right under their noses.

She pushed through the doors and walked up, giving him a hard blue stare. "Here? Now?"

"It's the ultimate test. Secrets are hardest to keep in broad daylight."

"I smell gas, and that steam pipe sounds like a volcano erupting. If a valve blows and causes a spark—"

"You dared me. Do it in public, and get proof." He wiped his palms on his jeans. "This is as public as it gets. You'll supply my proof."

Her hands clenched, but her eyes shone. "Where?"

His heart beat faster. "Top floor. My lawyer's office."

Upstairs, they strode out of the express elevator to find the law firm abandoned. The fire alarm was shrieking. At the receptionist's desk, a computer was streaming a television news feed.

" . . . minor damage, but we're getting reports of a ruptured gas line in the financial district . . ."

The blonde looked around. "Security cameras?"

"Only in the stairwells. It's bad business for a law firm to videotape its clients."

She nodded at a wall of windows. The October sunset was fading to dusk, but downtown was ablaze with light. "You plan to do this stunt against the glass?"

He crossed the lobby. "This way. The building's going to shut down in"—he looked at a red digital clock on the wall—"six minutes."

"What?"

"Emergency procedure. If there's a gas leak the building evacuates; they shut down the elevators and seal the fire doors. We have to be out by then."

"You're joking."

The wall clock counted down to 5:59. He started a timer on his watch.

"Yeah. I was meeting with my lawyers when the quake hit. It limits damage from any gas explosion." He pulled her toward a hallway. "I can't believe you're scared of getting caught with me. Not Hardgirl."

"What part of 'secret' do you not understand?"

"If we're caught, they'll ask what we're doing here, not what we're hiding in our pasts."

"Fair point." She hurried alongside him, eyes bright. "Were you waiting for an earthquake before you did this?"

Good guess—this was the third minor quake in the last month. "I got lucky. I've been looking for the perfect opportunity for weeks. Chaos, downtown—it was karma. I figured seize the day."

He rounded a corner. A glass-fronted display case along the wall had cracked, spilling sports memorabilia onto the floor.

She rushed past. "Is that a Joe Montana jersey?"

His stopwatch beeped. "Five minutes."

He opened a mahogany door. Across a conference room the red embers of sunset caught them in the eyes. The hills of San Francisco rose in front of them, electric with light and packed to the rafters like a stadium.

He shrugged off his coat, took a camera from the pocket and handed it to her. "When I tell you, point and click."

He crossed the room and opened the doors to a rooftop terrace. Kicking off his shoes, he strode outside.

"You complained I was using the club as a confessional. You told me I was seeking expiation for my sins, but said you couldn't give me absolution," he said.

Deep below them, the building groaned. She walked outside, breathing hard.

"Damn, Scott, this is dangerous—"

"Your dare was—and I quote—for me 'to offer a public display of penitence, and for chrissake, get proof.' "

He pulled his polo shirt over his head. Her gaze seared its way down his chest.

Now, he thought. Before his courage and exhilaration evaporated. He unzipped and dropped his jeans.

She gaped.

He backed toward the waist-high brick railing at the edge of the terrace. "Turn on the camera."

"You came commando-style to a meeting with your lawyers?"

Naked, he climbed onto the brick ledge and stood up, facing her. Her lips parted. Thrilled to his fingertips, he turned to face Montgomery Street.

A salt breeze licked his bare skin. Two hundred feet below, fire and police lights flickered through steam boiling from the ruptured pipe, turning the scene an eerie red.

He spread his arms. "Shoot."

"You have got to be kidding me."

"Take the photo. Hurry."

"That's not penitent."

He glanced over his shoulder. She was shaking her head.

"*Bad?* You tattooed *Bad* on your tailbone?"

His watch beeped. "Four minutes. Do it."

"You're a badass?" She put her fists on her hips. "You get all torn up about a nasty thing you did in college, and want to unload it on us—fine. But you can't tattoo some preening jock statement on your butt and call it repentance. That's not remorse. Hell, it's not even close to being dirty."

Frowning, she stormed inside.

He turned around. "Hey!"

Was she leaving? No, everything depended on her getting the photo. . . .

She ran back out, holding a piece of sports memorabilia from the display case. It was a jockey's riding crop. He swallowed.

She whipped it against a potted plant with a wicked crack. "Somebody needs to take you down a notch."

He nearly whimpered. She wanted points, too. This was even better.

Snapping the crop against her thigh, she crossed the terrace. Evaluating the ledge, she unzipped her ass-hugging skirt, wriggled it down, and stepped out of it.

"It's time to make your act of contrition," she said.

In the tight-fitting black jacket, she looked martial. The stilettos could have put out his eyes. The black stockings ran all the way to the tops of her thighs. All the way to—

"What's that garter belt made from?"

"Iguana hide."

"Jesus, help me."

"I have a drawerful. I got them in the divorce." She held out her hand. "Don't let me fall."

"I won't. I have perfect balance." He felt crazed and desperate and *God,* he needed to get her up here, now. "I get paid four million dollars a year to catch things and never let them drop."

A wisp of her blond hair had escaped the perfect do. It softened her. He wanted her to put it back in place. He wanted her to put on leather gloves and maybe an eye patch. He pulled her up on the ledge beside him.

She gripped his hand. Her smooth stocking brushed his leg.

He could barely speak. "This is penance?"

"Pain is just one step from paradise."

She looked down. Her voice dropped. "Christ. This is asking for a heart attack."

"Don't joke."

She looked up. "No—I didn't mean it as a crack about David."

But if David hadn't dropped facedown with a coronary, they wouldn't be here. The doctor's death had created an opening, and Scott wanted to fill it. This was his chance to prove himself and gain admission to the top level of the club.

The breeze kicked up. In the lighted windows of the skyscraper across the street, people gazed down at the fire trucks. Nobody was looking at them.

"Right under their noses," he said. "Bonus points for both of us."

"Not yet." She handed him the camera. "Set it so we're both in the frame."

He set the autotimer to take a five-shot series and set the camera on the ledge. His stopwatch beeped. Three minutes.

She planted her feet wide for balance. "What happens to guilty people?"

Blinking, he turned around and carefully knelt down on all fours. "I've been bad. Spank me."

She slapped the crop against her palm. "What's the magic word?"

Relief and desire rushed through him. "Hard."

The camera flashed. She brought the crop down.

The pain was a stripe of fire along his backside. He gasped and grabbed the ledge.

"Harder," he said.

She whipped the crop down. The camera flashed.

He clawed the bricks. "*Mea culpa.* I've been very, very bad. *More.*"

She didn't hit him. He looked up. Her chest was heaving, her hair spilling from the French twist.

"My God, you actually want to be punished, don't you?" she said.

"Do it."

She swung the crop. It slashed him so hard, he shouted in pain. She wanted to dish out punishment, all right, but not to him. She would use this to send a message to somebody else. The watch beeped.

"Christ, two minutes," she said. "Let's get the hell out of here."

His eyes were watering. "Not yet. Nobody's looking."

"*Looking*? You're nuts. If there's an aftershock I'll lose my balance. We—"

A thumping sound echoed off skyscraper walls. A helicopter swooped over the top of the building above them.

It turned and hovered above Montgomery Street, rotors blaring. Everything on the terrace blew about in the air. Dust, leaves, their clothes. The camera tipped over. Scott grabbed for it but it fell off the ledge.

She yelled, "No, the evidence—"

The camera dropped, hit the building and sprang apart. He let out a cry. His penance, his memories—

The terrace lit with a blinding white searchlight.

"Oh, no—it's a news chopper," she said.

She leapt from the ledge to the terrace. Landed like a gazelle on her stilettos. He scrambled after her, buttocks stinging. They grabbed their clothes and ran for the door. The chopper rotated in the air, searchlight sweeping after them.

She looked back, her eyes brimming with joy and fury. The searchlight lit her hair like a halo.

"Turn around," he shouted. "You want them to get a close-up?"

"The city knows your face, not mine."

"But it's about to know your glorious ass."

He ran into the conference room, stopped and wriggled his left leg into his jeans. The spotlight caught them. He bumbled for the door.

Fumbling her way into her skirt, she sprinted into the hallway. "It's chasing us like those things from the damned *War of the Worlds.*"

He urged her forward. "Take the service elevator. The lobby downstairs is full of cops."

She ran beside him, agile in the heels. His watch beeped.

"Oh, crap. No time."

In the lobby, the fire alarm wailed a high-pitched tone. The digital clock flashed red: :58, :57. The TV news was showing pictures from the chopper's camera.

"Two people are trapped on the roof," shouted the reporter. "A woman was signaling for help. If we swing around . . ."

The alarm rose in pitch.

"How long to get down?" she said.

They ran to the service elevator and she pounded on the button. The searchlight panned along the windows. Like a white flare, it caught them in the eyes.

"I see them. They're attempting to escape from this deadly tower...."

She whacked the elevator button with the riding crop. *"Open."*

With a *ping*, the elevator arrived. They lunged inside.

On the ground floor they burst out a back exit into an alley. The asphalt was wet and steaming. Scott clicked his stopwatch.

"Seven seconds. Time to spare."

"Maniac," she said.

They dashed through puddles toward the end of the alley. On the street a police car blew past, lights flashing. The helicopter thumped overhead, searchlight pinned on the roof.

Scott nodded at it. "They got it on tape. You have evidence."

"You're reckless. I think you actually want to get caught."

"I carried out the dare. Did I make the cut?"

She fought with her zipper. "We'll put it to a vote. No promises."

They rushed out of the alley. The street, lined with banks and swanky stores, was being cleared by the police. They slowed to a walk, trying to look normal. He buttoned his jacket. She smoothed down her hair.

Elation flooded him.

"Admit it—that was awesome."

"It was outrageous." She pointed at him. "And do not tell me it ended with a flourish."

"Really?" He reached into his coat pocket and withdrew a baseball.

"What's that?"

He tossed it to her. She caught it.

"A Willie Mays autographed ball?" She looked up, surprised. "From the law firm's memorabilia collection? You stole it?"

"On our way out. And it's not just any baseball. It's *the* ball—from the 1954 World Series. The greatest catch of all time."

She gawked. "It's got to be worth—"

"Hundred thousand." He smiled broadly. "Right under *your* nose."

Anger flashed across her face. She shoved the ball back into his hands. "Okay, bonus points for chutzpah."

He laughed and tossed the baseball into his other hand. "Fear not—it'll be returned. That's the next challenge."

"How? The building's locked down. And your fingerprints are all over it."

"So? I'm a star client. My lawyer let me hold it. It doesn't matter that my fingerprints are on it." He glanced at the police car down the block, then back at her. "How will you explain that yours are?"

She stopped dead on the sidewalk.

He held up the ball. "Return it without getting prosecuted. I dare you."

He turned, faced the jewelry store they were passing and hurled the ball straight through its front window. Glass crashed. An alarm shrieked. He spun back around.

"Have fun, Hardgirl."

He took off running down the street.

"THE NEXT SUSPENSE SUPERSTAR"—STEPHEN KING

MEET MEG GARDINER'S NEWEST HEROINE, JO BECKETT, IN . . .

The city of San Francisco is being rattled—by a series of earthquakes and high-profile murder-suicides. People with seemingly perfect lives who choose to throw it all away. And when star prosecutor Callie Harding intentionally hurls her car off a highway overpass, killing herself and three others, it is up to forensic psychologist Jo Beckett to figure out the motivation behind her death. Before long, she is steeped in an investigation that leads to a shadowy organization called THE DIRTY SECRETS CLUB, a group of local A-listers with nothing but money and plenty to hide.

NOW AVAILABLE
WHEREVER BOOKS ARE SOLD

DUTTON   a member of Penguin Group (USA)

"THE FINEST CRIME SUSPENSE SERIES I'VE COME ACROSS IN THE LAST TWENTY YEARS."
—Stephen King

FROM

MEG GARDINER
The Evan Delaney Novels

Available for the first time in the U.S.

China Lake
Mission Canyon
Jericho Point
Crosscut
Kill Chain

**Available wherever books are sold,
or at penguin.com**

GET CLUED IN

Ever wonder how to find out about all the latest Berkley Prime Crime and Obsidian mysteries?

berkleyobsidianmysteries.com

- See what's new
- Find author appearances
- Win fantastic prizes
- Get reading recommendations
- Sign up for the mystery newsletter
- Chat with authors and other fans
- Read interviews with authors you love

Mystery Solved.